CAUGHT
UP

AN INTO DARKNESS NOVEL

CAUGHT UP

NAVESSA ALLEN

SLOWBURN

A **zando** IMPRINT

NEW YORK

zando

Copyright © 2025 by Navessa Allen

zandoprojects.com

First Zando Edition: June 2025

Design by Neuwirth & Associates, Inc.
Cover design by Christopher Brian King

The publisher does not have control over and is not responsible for author or other third-party websites (or their content).

Library of Congress Control Number: 2025932239

978-1-63893-225-3 (TR)
978-1-63893-300-7 (BN)
978-1-63893-346-5 (BAM)
978-1-63893-360-1 (TGT)
978-1-63893-226-0 (EBK)

10 9 8 7 6 5 4 3 2 1

Manufactured in the United States of America

TRIGGER WARNINGS

Caught Up is a dark, stalker romcom with heavy themes.
Reader discretion is advised as this book contains:

Camwork

Sex work

Mafia and organized crime

Blackmail

Coercion

Religion

Blood

Violence

Gore (brief)

Graphic sex (including
multi-partner)

Breath play

Primal play

Fear play

Voyeurism

Exhibitionism

Bondage

Light BDSM

Stalking

Child abuse

Domestic abuse
(remembered)

Bullying (remembered)

Slut-shaming

Alcohol

Gambling

Smoking

Mention of serial killers
and their crimes

Cannibalism
(off-page, alluded to)

For everyone ready to play.

CAUGHT
UP

1

JUNIOR

THE BLOOD WAS EVERYWHERE. SOAKED into my shirt, sprayed onto my pants, and buried beneath my blunted nail bits. This was why I always wore head-to-toe black. With any other color, the blood would be too obvious, but with black, the wet spots were easier to explain: Someone threw a drink at me, or a passing car hit a puddle, and I got splashed. I'd had to come up with countless excuses over the years.

Thankfully, I wouldn't need any of them tonight because it was pissing down rain. Lightning arced overhead, painting the distant high-rises in silver and white. Thunder chased after it, rattling the windows of nearby buildings. The city looked like Gotham on nights like this. Gritty, dangerous.

I pulled my gaze from the storm. Three figures stood beside me on the river's edge, all dressed in black because they'd learned the same lesson I had about bloodstains. They were motionless, eyes dead as they stared straight ahead, jackets flapping around them like errant wings. Another bolt of lightning tore through the sky, bathing us in silver. We looked more like a flock of vultures ready to descend on a corpse than a group of brothers who were supposed to be out celebrating.

Four days. It had been raining for four fucking days, and the river was so bloated with runoff that the car we'd just pushed into it was being sucked beneath the surface with alarming ease. Maybe we'd get lucky, and the cops would think its owner had gotten caught in a flash flood and drowned instead of what we'd *really* done to him.

A spark of red flared to life in my periphery. I turned to see my youngest brother, Greg, lift a cigarette to his lips.

"Those things will kill you," I said.

He blew smoke into the wind. "Not before something else does."

With that, he turned and strode away, Stefan trailing in his wake.

Alec, the brother closest to me in age, met my eyes across the gap they'd left between us. "We done here?"

I nodded. Yeah, we were done. Tommy Marchetti had been dealt with. Just like Dad ordered.

Alec pulled up the collar of his jacket to keep the rain off his neck as he followed after our younger brothers, leaving me alone to watch the tail end of Tommy's Beamer disappear into the night-black water. The old bastard was finally gone, finally out of the way, and I couldn't have asked for a better birthday present.

I waited just long enough to make sure the car wasn't going to inconveniently bob back to the surface, before striding into the warehouse crouched at the river's edge. The floor was poured concrete, and the clapboard walls were old enough that the wind whistled through the cracks between them with every gust, but at least I wasn't getting rained on anymore.

My brothers stood beneath the glow of a fluorescent light, their eyes trained on a large red smear at their feet.

Alec pointed at it. "What do you want us to do about this?"

"Bleach," I said.

He headed toward a back closet.

I eyed Greg. "He bled a lot."

Greg's dark eyes rose to mine as he took another pull from his cigarette. "Fresh corpses tend to do that."

I might have been "Junior," but out of all of us, Greg resembled Dad the most, especially now that the humor had started to fade from his eyes and the same jaded look the rest of us wore was creeping into his expression.

Alec rejoined us, and we moved back as he upended an entire bottle of bleach over the stain. When he was finished, he tossed the empty bottle toward some other trash gathered in a corner. This place used to belong to a fishmonger before the local industry collapsed. Now it was owned by one of my father's associates, a man who turned a blind eye to our occasional use of it.

Alec shifted to face me. "You still wanna go out?"

I leveled my gaze at him. "What do you think?"

He shrugged. "I'm down if you are."

Stefan gave Alec an *Are you fucking serious?* look he didn't see. Beside Stefan, Greg watched me, waiting for my decision. As the oldest, I was the de facto leader. The one Dad trusted the most, the one my brothers turned to for guidance. Just once, I wished someone else would make a goddamn decision so I didn't have to think so fucking much all the time.

I refocused my gaze on Alec. "No, I don't want to go out. I'm drenched and I'm tired, and by the time we all shower and change, it'll be two o'clock in the morning and everything will be closing."

"So you're gonna spend your last birthday in your twenties sad and alone?" Alec asked. "Sounds pretty fucking depressing."

I shook my head, starting to get annoyed. "I didn't spend it alone. We had family dinner, and then the four of us got to come on this fun little field trip." He opened his mouth to argue but I cut him off. "We're done here. I don't care what the fuck the three of you do for the rest of the night, but I'm going to my apartment. Tell Mom and Dad I won't be back for a few days."

Without waiting for a response, I left. Maybe it was depressing, but I wanted to be alone. I wanted quiet and the solitude of my own space, and there was no way I'd get that if I went back to our parents' house with my asshole brothers.

My apartment wasn't far from the docks, maybe ten minutes on foot, and I was already soaked, so I didn't give a fuck about getting rained on. It almost felt good to be a little cold. The deep heat of summer was descending on the city, and with all the water around us, the air had turned cloying and fetid. The storm was blowing some of it away, but I knew it was only temporary. We'd be lucky if we got a day or two of cooler temps before the mercury crept back toward ninety.

People rushed past me on the sidewalk. Most were hunched over like that somehow protected them from the downpour, but I strode through it upright, hoping the rain would wash away the evidence of my sins. Fuck, I was tired. And not because of what I'd just done. This was a bone-deep exhaustion that gnawed at me like a rabid wolf.

I wondered if my father ever felt like this. If our "work" weighed on him in the same way. Unlike me, Dad hadn't been born into the mob. He'd carved out a space among their foot soldiers and slowly fought his way up the ranks. Now he was the guy the big shots turned to when they needed their messes cleaned up, but since he thought too much of himself to get his hands dirty anymore, he delegated.

A humorless grin tugged at my lips. Of course our work didn't weigh on Dad. He wasn't the one doing it. *I* was. Well, me and my brothers. We bore the brunt of everything. The risk of getting caught. The risk of getting hurt. The risk of never being able to sleep again because every time we closed our eyes, images of the things we'd done swelled to the surface and threatened to drown us in the depths of our own memories.

Or maybe that was just me. Maybe I was being a morose motherfucker, because instead of spending my birthday out on the town, like I'd planned, I'd spent it down at the docks creating more nightmares for myself.

I shook my head and focused on my surroundings. This part of the city was old, and not in a nice way; old in a forgotten way that had so far escaped the gentrification taking over other neighborhoods. The brick-and-mortar buildings crowded close to the street were only a few stories high. Puddles gathered on the sidewalk, reflecting the neon glow of nearby shop signs. Small groups of people huddled beneath awnings, smoking cigarettes or talking with friends while they waited for the rain to end. This neighborhood was working class, immigrants mostly, and the streets were teeming with the evidence of it. It was a good place to get lost, to go unnoticed, and that's why I rented an apartment here.

Most of the time, Dad liked to keep us close because he was a paranoid old man. My brothers and I, despite being in our twenties, still spent a lot of time sleeping in our childhood bedrooms. I stayed away on nights like tonight, when I needed to disappear, clear my head for a while before I was fit to be around other people again. The sights and sounds of the city reminded me that the world kept turning. That people were out here living their lives, blissfully unaware of the darkness that seethed just beneath the surface. It gave me hope, reminded me that there was more to life than death and destruction and the constant threat of spending the rest of my days behind bars.

By the time I reached the unobtrusive door tucked between a jeweler and a bakery, I was more than ready to be out of the rain. Up a narrow flight of stairs, my small studio apartment sat dark and stagnant, with a moldy note in the air that spoke of neglect. When was the last time I'd been here? A month ago? Two? This spring had passed in a blur, kicked off by an accidental homicide that my idiot cousin, Aly, and her boyfriend committed. Their victim had been a serial killer, but he'd also been the spawn of a billion-dollar family, and it had taken all of *my* family's time and resources to trick the Feds into thinking Bradley Bluhm was still alive and on the run. During that time, Dad's paranoia reached new heights, and he'd barely let any of his children out of his sight. I'd probably catch hell for staying away, tonight of all nights, but I needed some time to myself.

I flipped the light switch next to the door and was relieved when a nearby lamp flickered to life. At least I'd remembered to keep up with the utility bills. The glow from the light illuminated a compact space that could best be described as utilitarian. Bed to the right, sofa to the left, kitchen straight ahead, with a door beside the fridge that led to the bathroom.

I grabbed a change of clothes and went to shower, turning the water up until it was scalding. Trails of pink ran down the drain as I scoured the last of the blood from my skin. In my mind, I replayed the memory of Tommy's car disappearing beneath the black surface of the water, and I grinned. I was glad he was gone, because it freed up one of the last hurdles standing between me and his daughter.

Lauren Marchetti.

The girl I'd grown up with back in the "old neighborhood," as we called Little Italy, before my parents moved us out of the city and into a swanky suburb. She'd been a grade below me, and at the end of my senior year, a situation involving the two of us had spun out of control, getting so bad that she'd ended up transferring out of the district.

I closed my eyes, thinking back, my smile slipping as I remembered the feeling of Tommy's knuckles hammering into the side of my face, hearing his enraged voice tell me that if I ever so much as looked at his daughter again, he would kill me. I'd gone home afterward, making a beeline toward my room, wanting to hide the shame of getting my ass kicked by an old man, but my father had caught me, taken one look at my face, and demanded to know what happened.

I shook my head as the water rushed over me, thinking back to what a naïve kid I'd been, even at eighteen, even after all the shit I'd already seen and done. Dad had forced the story out of me, and I'd been terrified he'd make everything worse by going on the warpath against Tommy. Mafia men weren't exactly known for letting slights against their family go unanswered. But instead of promising retribution, Dad only offered more threats.

Well, Tommy was no longer around to follow through on his, and I didn't fear my old man as much as I used to. I was done fucking around. I was done waiting. I'd spent nearly a decade keeping my distance from Lauren, and god help anyone who tried to get between us this time.

Once I was out of the shower, I bagged up my dirty clothes and carried them down to a dumpster around the corner. Dumpsters were great for disposing evidence. By the time the cops got suspicious, the trash was already in the landfill, and good luck sorting through it. Even if they eventually found my clothes, being left out in the elements and surrounded by rotting refuse would contaminate them enough that any samples would be useless in court.

I kicked my shoes off by the front door afterward and collapsed onto the threadbare couch. And then I did what I did every night without fail: I pulled my phone from my pocket, opened my favorite social media app, and went straight to Lauren's profile. Her page was filled with barely clad photos of herself, all artfully posed and perfectly lit.

Interspersed among these shots were small slices of life: what she'd had for lunch; a snap of her hugging her monstrous dog; her holding a sign at a rally. Today's picture featured her wearing a fitted black pantsuit, shaking hands with an older white woman in an office. I smiled to see it. Marion Blackwell had been a hard nut to crack. Lauren had been trying to meet the councilwoman for months, hoping to secure her vote on a new city ordinance aimed at making sex work safer. The more conservative-leaning Blackwell had been avoiding Lauren, but a little digging revealed her son's "white powder" problem, and all it took was the threat of leaking photos of him snorting lines in the back of a strip club for Blackwell to change her mind and take the meeting.

I would have done much worse to see this picture of Lauren looking so triumphant. She'd come a long way from the quiet, bespectacled honor roll student with an arm full of textbooks I remembered. This curvaceous goddess barely resembled her anymore, but the evidence was irrefutable: large brown eyes, a button nose, that slight gap between her two front teeth, and most damning of all, a beauty mark right beneath her left eye.

Scrolling back to the top of her profile, I clicked on the link in her bio, and up popped my Me4U app. Lauren was so determined to secure rights for sex workers because she was one herself.

And I was her number one fan.

Just beneath her creator profile was a small button that allowed you to request a custom video from her. I tapped it and then sent my latest request, along with a message.

Good job with Blackwell today. I'm proud of you. Now show me how proud you are of yourself, Lauren.

2

LAUREN

I STOOD OVER MY ROOMMATE'S shoulder, watching their computer screen while a video of me finger-fucking myself played in slow motion. It was dark as a cave in Ryan's room, the blackout curtains doing their job to block the bright light of late afternoon. Onscreen, I looked stunning. Nude. Lost in the throes of passion. A veritable goddess of sex. Right up until I suddenly let out a silent shriek (Ryan's volume was muted) and fell sideways off the bed.

Ryan snapped back a few frames and hit pause. "Here," they said, pointing at the editing software beneath the video. "If we cut it here and then transition to the side, it'll make it seem like it was one continuous filming session, and you switched the camera position to be artsy."

I arched a brow. "And not like I had to stop in the middle of recording because someone set the fire alarm off? *Again?*"

Ryan tucked a strand of long blond hair behind their ear, turning the spectacular shade of red that only the very pale can achieve. "I didn't want to turn the stove fan on too high in case your mic picked it up."

"Uh huh," I said. "I'm sure that was it."

Ryan turned even redder. Tormenting them was as easy as it was enjoyable.

I opened my mouth to see if I could make them flush all the way to their toes, but their door burst open behind us, and we turned, blinking against the sudden brightness as our third roommate, Taylor, swept into the room. At first, all I saw was her outline, but as my eyes adjusted, I noted her lavender hair swaying around her shoulders and the floral silk robe tied loosely around her curves. She wore a full face of makeup, her skin highlighted and bronzed, her almond eyes framed with false lashes, telling me she was either getting ready to film, or had just finished.

She stopped a few feet away and hefted a small box in each hand, looking from me to Ryan and back again. "A sub just sent me a video request for a close-up of my asshole." Her grin turned taunting. "Who wants to help me bleach and wax it?"

I swiveled to Ryan, who already held their finger to their nose in a *not it* gesture.

"I'm out," they said. "I'll have to stare at it the whole time I'm filming and editing. I shouldn't have to prep it, too."

My shoulders slumped in exaggerated defeat as I turned back to Taylor. "Fine. I'll do it."

She shimmied her shoulders, looking pleased. Her subscriber must have offered her a ton of money for the shot. She and I might have made a living filming spicy videos for our subs, but we both felt that close-ups were much more intimate and required a level of vulnerability that we weren't usually comfortable with.

Her gaze slid past me to Ryan's computer screen. "Is that the shot Ryan ruined when they burned dinner last night?"

Ryan swiveled back toward their monitor, cheeks still pink. "I didn't ruin it. Lauren was able to finish filming."

Taylor and I shared a smirking glance. As part of chore rotation, we took turns cooking. Some nights that meant mac 'n' cheese with hot dogs cut up in it (Taylor), traditional Italian fare (me), and increasingly elaborate dishes from across the globe that were either incredible or ended up splattered all over our kitchen (Ryan). In Ryan's defense, at least they were trying to expand their culinary skills. And they *had* gotten better recently. It was only when they attempted some complicated new recipe, like last night, that our house filled with smoke.

"You owe me a new saucepan," I said. "I think tandoori paste is burned into the metal of the one you used last night."

Ryan bristled. "Keep making fun of me, and I'll show Taylor the video I cut together of you falling and unfalling over and over again."

I sucked in a horrified gasp. "You didn't."

With a click, Ryan pulled up another tab in their editing software, and there I went, tumbling off the bed in slo-mo. And then back onto it. Off again. On. These were deeply unflattering angles for my boobs, which seemed to be trying to flee from each other in opposite directions. My hair looked electrified, and the horror on my face made it clear I thought I was about to be serial murdered.

"I might never recover from seeing myself like this," I said.

Ryan cackled. Beside me, Taylor was laughing so hard that she'd stopped making noise. My revenge for this betrayal would make headline news.

It took five solid minutes and increasingly violent threats of bodily harm for Ryan to close out the tab and promise to delete it.

Another several passed before Taylor was able to speak. "Who's the video even for?"

"My favorite sub," I told her.

She glanced my way, wiping tears from her eyes. "NT95?"

I nodded. Even though I'd been doing this for years, I still got nervous filming certain video requests, especially ones with large price tags attached to them. I wanted them to be perfect. Wanted my subs desperate for more. And NT95 was a day-one subscriber, my very first, in fact, signing up almost as soon as I announced my Me4U page on social media. We'd spent countless hours sexting. I knew about his horrible father and the constant pressure he was under at work. He sent me congratulatory notes every time I won a new politician over, asked me to please be safe when I attended public rallies. He wasn't just some faceless sub anymore. He was important to me. Hence me hovering over Ryan's shoulder instead of leaving them alone to work in peace.

"What did he request?" Taylor asked.

"A striptease followed by solo work," I told her. "Creator's choice."

She shot me a sly glance. "Think he'd like Ryan's special edit?"

"I will murder you for putting that idea into their head."

Ryan snorted but remained suspiciously quiet as they finished cutting the scene together. I would have to watch them closely in the coming days. Once that was finished, they started color correcting the raw footage. The three of us had the perfect setup. Taylor and I were the on-screen talent, and Ryan was our background magician, editing our videos and even stepping in to help film complicated shots like the one I'd agreed to prep Taylor for.

"God," she said. "The lighting in your room is so nice during sunset."

I was about to respond when a snuffling noise caught my attention. Taylor and I turned toward the door just in time to watch Walter, our massive Shiloh shepherd, wiggle his way into the room looking pleased with himself, his ears back, eyes slitted in doggy bliss. He carried what I first thought was a chew toy in his mouth but on closer inspection looked a lot like—

"My favorite whip!" I yelled, launching myself at him. Shit, he was going to ruin it.

He woofed and danced away, head down, ready to play.

I pulled up short and tried to sound stern. "That is not a toy, Walter. Drop it."

"Technically . . ." Ryan began.

I pointed a finger in their general direction, unwilling to look away from Walter in case he noticed my distraction and booked it. "You're already on my shit list. Don't make it worse by siding with the dog."

Behind me, Taylor began to laugh.

Walter, taking that as his sign that this was definitely play time, gave the whip handle a chew and started prancing toward me, shaking his head side to side in typical *I have a toy and you can't get it* fashion. Unfortunately, that sent the five leather straps attached to it flying through the air. At us.

"Fuck!" Taylor yelped, dodging sideways.

Ryan leapt from their seat, barely avoiding a strike to the arm.

Walter woofed around the handle and plowed toward us with what could only be described as maniacal glee. We scrambled out of the room and went barreling downstairs, tripping over one another in our haste to escape.

I broke right at the bottom. Ryan swerved left.

Taylor vaulted the living room couch.

"Go get Ryan!" I ordered Walter. "Avenge me!"

"Hey!" Ryan shrieked, sprinting for their life, our deranged canine hot on their heels.

Thankfully, our place was a three-story brownstone, so there were no neighbors below us to complain about the sudden chaos. We'd chosen it for its superior insulation because it helped with soundproofing—our line of work came with a lot of very visceral noises. The hidden bonus was that the occasional outburst of barking, yelling, and fleeing from a whip-baring canine went *mostly* unnoticed.

Since the toy was mine, it was probably my responsibility to fall on the metaphorical sword, despite how much fun I was having watching Walter torment my roommates. There was one thing we could count on to get him to behave, so while Taylor and Ryan kept him occupied (see, ran from him in terror), I headed toward the biscuit jar we kept on the kitchen counter. The second I popped it open, I heard nails clattering on hardwood and knew Walter was headed my way.

He rounded the island and tried to slow down, but he was moving so fast that he went into a full slide. The thing about being five feet tall and on the slimmer side is that when your dog is half your height and almost your full weight, you don't stand a chance against them. Walter seemed to realize we were on the cusp of catastrophe the same time I did but there was nothing we could do to prevent it.

Our eyes caught, and we shared an *Oh, fuck* look that transcended species before he took me out at the knees. I went down with a strangled yelp, landing hard on the tile floor and taking the brunt of the fall on my elbow and shoulder to keep from crushing my idiot dog.

"Oh my god," Taylor wheezed. "Are you okay?"

I looked up to see my roommates standing over me, Ryan with their hand covering their mouth to smother their laughter, Taylor bent over at the waist, openly cackling.

I rolled onto my back. "I think so?"

Wetness coated my left hand. I glanced sideways to see Walter gently take the biscuit from my fingers and then slink away like he hoped no one would notice him.

At least he'd dropped the whip.

■　■　■

An hour later, the apartment was cleaned up, Taylor's asshole was camera ready, and she and Ryan were shut in her room.

Tonight was my turn to cook, and while my roommates filmed, I got to work in the kitchen with my laptop open on the island so I could watch the progress bar while my weekly video uploaded to my Me4U page—this one of me doing pole work in our spare bedroom turned kink palace.

I hoped my subs liked it. My pole work had greatly improved since I'd first started posting, thanks to the weekly classes I attended, but I was by no means an expert. I just did it because it was fun, made for great content, and was a surprisingly good workout—multitasking at its finest.

Every Me4U creator was different and had varying levels of activity, but since this was my full-time job, I posted a spicy picture to my page at least once a day, and a long-form video every Wednesday like clock-work to my main page for all my paid subscribers. Usually, I had my posts scheduled ahead of time, but this past week had been especially hectic. I was down to the wire and didn't like it. This wasn't just a job to me. My subscribers weren't just random people; they were my community.

I'd received countless messages over the years from subs thanking me for one post or another because they'd had a terrible day or were going through a hard time. My videos made them feel good, helped them briefly forget about all the ugly shit. Many had come to depend on me and my strict schedule. It gave them something to look forward to, and the thought of disappointing any of them by being late weighed heavily on my mind.

A hissing sound had me jerking my gaze up just in time to see the pot of water on the stove start to bubble over. If I ruined dinner right after giving Ryan a hard time for doing the same, I'd never live it down.

I stepped over Walter, who was inconveniently sprawled in the middle of the kitchen floor (plotting his next attack, I was sure), and turned the burner to a simmer before slowly adding pasta to the pot. Once it was stirred in, I set a timer and started working on the sauce—butter and shallots and garlic and white wine with a small tin of clams mixed in at the very end.

The wine was just starting to cook off when my phone chimed with a notification. I scooped it up to see a message through the Me4U app from NT95.

Excited to see what you have in store for us tonight, it read.

I grinned and wrote back, *I have a feeling you'll like this one*. I sent him a screenshot from the video, in which I was topless and biting my lip while looking into the camera. Ryan always saved several shots from each video that Taylor and I filmed so we could use them to tease our subs while they waited for posts to go live.

Another notification popped up. NT95 had tipped me fifty bucks.

Just wait until you see YOUR video, I said, followed by several kissy-face emojis.

Can't wait, he wrote back. *Hope you have a good night, Lauren, and congrats again on yesterday's big win.*

Thank you!!!

I was still riding high from swaying Councilwoman Blackwell over to our side. With her vote secured, the legislation had a good chance of passing, and soon the sex workers of this city would be able to report any assaults that were committed against them while working without facing solicitation charges. It would be a huge win, one we'd been fighting for years to achieve, and even though it had been a long, exhausting slog, we were getting there. It made me hopeful that with enough hard work, we could eventually drag this blue-collar city into the modern age.

NT95 liked my last message, and I set my phone down, smiling. It was funny, thinking back over our shared history and how much had changed since he'd first subscribed. Now, I had a "menu" on my Me4U page that subs could order from. When I started, I'd calculated custom prices for every request, but as my account grew, I couldn't keep up, so I switched to charging a flat rate of twenty-five dollars per minute of camera time, with a three-minute minimum. There were added rates for toy and kink work, and for name or specific phrase usage. NT95 had requested a $700 video a few days ago, and I'd wasted no time filming it.

My smile widened as I checked on the pasta. I'd pulled in fifteen grand this week. There was so much good I could do with that kind of money that it left me feeling giddy. It took me two solid years of posting to get to this point, but now I was making so much that I'd only *need* to work for a few more before I was able to comfortably live out the rest of my days doing whatever the fuck I wanted.

The thing was, this work *was* what I wanted to do. I loved what I did, and the fact that I got paid so much for it still felt surreal. Journalists and therapists and politicians and keyboard warriors bent over backward analyzing sex work and why people did it, and while they had good right to because it was a large and very complex issue with so many problematic and dangerous elements, to me, personally, it wasn't that complicated.

I found camwork both liberating and healing. I'd been raised Catholic in an incredibly patriarchal Italian neighborhood where shame was a large part of the culture, where any woman who lived outside of the strict, unwritten code of norms was ostracized. As a teenager, I'd felt the lash of judgment fall upon me over and over again, the blows strong enough that I nearly broke beneath the force of them. It had taken me years to heal those invisible wounds, but now, I *liked* sex. I *liked* filming myself naked. I *liked* getting others off.

It was as simple as that.

Over the past decade, I'd reclaimed my agency, my power, and I lived my life out in the open for all to see, embracing my sexuality, encouraging others to do the same, fighting for those who were still shamed, still pushed to the edges of society because so many people refused to see that sex work was valid work and should come with the same protections as any other career.

My win with Councilwoman Blackwell was a huge step in the right direction, but there were still many other politicians to convince. Not just in our city, but in the rest of the state and country. Camwork was what I loved, but advocacy work was my passion in life. Even if all my Me4U subs disappeared tomorrow, I would spend the rest of my time here on earth making sex work safer for everyone who came after me.

A door swung open upstairs, pulling me from my thoughts.

"How'd it go?" I called out.

"Good," Ryan yelled, the shutting of another door telling me they'd gone into their bedroom.

Taylor flounced down the stairs a minute later, tying her floral robe back in place as she joined me in the kitchen. Her nose led her straight to the bubbling saucepan. "This smells amazing."

"Thanks," I said, pointing my wooden spoon at the fridge. "The wine that goes with it is chilling."

Taking the hint, she spun away to pour us glasses. We clinked ours together and each took a sip before she left to deliver the third one to Ryan in their editing cave. While she was gone, my video finished uploading, and I quickly posted it before the alarm I'd set for the pasta went off.

Taylor rejoined me just in time to help plate everything up.

"Come down and eat with us, you antisocial bitch!" I called to Ryan.

They descended the stairs looking only slightly disgruntled and settled in their usual seat at the dining table. Taylor and I sat on either side of them, and together, the three of us tucked into dinner, with Walter asleep underfoot while we ate and laughed and drank until our plates were empty and our bellies full. It was a perfect evening. I was blissfully happy, endlessly grateful for this life I'd created for myself.

And then my phone rang.

3

JUNIOR

IT WAS THREE O'CLOCK IN the morning on Friday by the time I got back to my dingy apartment. This time, half the blood wetting my shirt was mine.

I peeled the fabric off in the bathroom, wincing when I caught sight of my stomach in the mirror. There was a three-inch gash on my left side from a knife I hadn't been fast enough to dodge. Goddamn turf war bullshit. Why the fuck had we even been involved? That wasn't what we usually did for the higher-ups. My old man must have owed someone a favor or something.

Fucking Christ, I thought, reliving the night in my head. If I'd been any slower dodging the blade, it would have punctured my lung.

My eyes dropped to the scars riddling the rest of my torso. They stood as a stark reminder of how many close calls I'd had over the years, how a split second of distraction could have ended with me in the hospital, or worse.

I bent down, wincing, and grabbed the first aid kit from beneath the bathroom sink. After showering off, I went about dressing the wound. I'd gotten good at stitching myself up, though luckily, tonight, no actual stitches were required since the gash was pretty shallow.

Only after it was dressed did I allow myself to pull up Lauren's latest video as a reward. With a tap, it started playing, her familiar bedroom

19

flashing to life before my eyes. Golden light streamed into the room, bathing her four-poster bed in dappled shafts of amber. She kneeled in the middle of the comforter, wearing a matching set of cream-colored shorts and a tank top.

Her fingers toyed with the hem of the shirt as she gave the camera a sultry smile. I hit pause just as she started to pull it over her head and went back to the beginning again. Tugging my phone close, I zoomed in on her face, focusing on her eyes, studying her expression. Several days had passed since my brothers and I sank her father's car in the river—plenty of time for Tommy to get reported missing—but I saw no grief in Lauren's eyes. No worry.

Had she not heard? Or did she know and not care? Not that I would blame her if she didn't, but *not* knowing if the news had broken about Tommy was starting to get on my nerves, and I decided it was time to bite the bullet.

I pulled up my dad's contact, my thumb hovering over the call button. He and I hadn't exactly been seeing eye to eye lately, and a large part of why I was holed up in the city was to avoid him. It felt like every interaction turned into an argument, and living under his thumb during the whole Bradley Bluhm debacle had pushed us to a breaking point. I needed this time away from him, but my need for information about Lauren was even stronger, so, with a deep breath, I called him.

He answered on the first ring. "Where the fuck have you been?"

I almost hung up. The man made nothing easy. Every fucking conversation had to be contentious from the start. "Busy."

"Fucking busy?" Dad barked. "It's been *days*, Junior."

"And I got all the shit done that you asked me to," I fired back. "It's not like I'm out here fucking around. It's not like I took a blade to the ribs tonight because I was sitting in my apartment twiddling my thumbs."

He sucked in a breath. "Are you okay?"

"I'm fine," I bit out, refusing to let the concern in his tone soften me. He wasn't worried about my safety, not really; knowing Dad, he was more concerned with how my death would impact *his* life. "Can I ask you something, or do you want to nag me some more?"

Dad shut his mouth so fast, I heard his teeth click over the line. I didn't have to see him to know he was clenching his jaw hard enough to crack a molar. A small, ugly thrill of triumph zipped through me, knowing I'd gotten to him.

We always brought out the worst in each other.

"Ask," he growled.

"Has the news broken about Tommy yet?"

Dad was quiet for so long that I didn't think he'd answer me. "Why do you want to know?"

Fuck, I should have asked someone else. I thought enough time had passed and I'd done a good enough job covering my tracks that Dad would have forgotten all about Lauren by now, but I could tell from the suspicion in his tone that I was wrong.

"I just do," I said.

"This isn't about his whore daughter, is it?"

Rage boiled up from the pit of my stomach. Men like my father were why patricide was a thing.

I took a deep breath and pushed my anger back down, forcing an unaffected calm into my tone that had taken me years to perfect. "No. Has Tommy been reported missing yet or not?"

"Yesterday. When are you coming home? Your mom's been worried."

Ah, the guilt trip. Of course he would turn to that when badgering hadn't worked.

"A few days. I've got some shit to look into in the city."

He hung up on me.

I set my phone down, hands shaking. One day, this goddamn temper of mine was going to bubble up and explode all over everyone around me. Years of unresolved resentment sat heavy between me and my father, most of it so ugly I repressed the shit out of it. My fallout with Lauren occupied the top spot on the list. I'd never forget what he said to me the night Tommy kicked my ass: *Better it happen now, like this, than for Lauren to get* really *hurt.*

Taken at face value, it might sound like he'd been looking out for her, but his ominous tone had turned it into a threat, like if I didn't stay away from Lauren, *he'd* be the one to hurt her next.

Yeah, Tommy was out of the picture, but my old man was still a problem. One I would have to deal with, and soon. A fight had been brewing between us for years, and not just your run-of-the-mill yelling match, but the big one. The one where I told him I didn't want to do this anymore, that I didn't want to end up like him, which was where I was going if I continued down my current path.

Needing a distraction from my troubled thoughts, I swiped my thumb across my phone and brought up Lauren's video, still paused, still zoomed in on her face. Fuck, she was beautiful. I hit play and let the video keep rolling, and up went Lauren's shirt, over her head before getting tossed out of frame. My cock swelled at the sight of her dusky nipples, already pebbled from the air rushing over them. Her waist was flat and narrow, flaring at the hips. She'd filled out some in the last decade, and the curves looked good on her.

I watched while she stroked her hands up her stomach and cupped her tits. *Perfect tits.* Her head fell back as she played with her nipples. She didn't look like she was acting. She looked like she was enjoying herself, and that's why it was so goddamn addicting to watch her, why I'd watched nearly every video on her Me4U page over the years. The woman came to life on screen. She was completely unselfconscious, gave herself entirely over to pleasure. But my favorite thing was when her personality peeked through whenever she laughed or made that low, frustrated moan that hinted she was close, but needed something more to push herself over the edge.

I'd learned *all* her sounds, studied the way she made herself climax. It might have seemed obsessive, but it wasn't; it was strategic. One day, I would use everything I'd learned against her, make her come faster than anyone else had, convince her that my hands and my tongue and my dick were made to get her off. I wanted her to crave me, *need me*.

Was it manipulative? All kinds of messed up? Absolutely.

I didn't give a single, solitary fuck.

On-screen, Lauren opened her large dark eyes and stared directly into the camera. "This is what I'd have you do to me." She gently pinched her nipples, and I decided the extra hundred bucks I'd paid for dirty talk this time was more than worth it. "I'd make you stay right here, first with your hands, and then your mouth, until I was absolutely soaked."

I unbuttoned my jeans and reached inside my boxers to grip my dick. "What else?" I demanded, my voice low with need.

She slid a hand over her stomach and plunged it inside her shorts. "And then I'd have you touch me here. Not my clit or my cunt," she said, and my dick went rock hard to hear such filthy words coming out of what was once such a sweet mouth. "I'd have you tease me, close, but not where I need you most."

My eyes tracked the movement of her hand beneath the whisper-thin fabric of her shorts. She was doing exactly what she'd said, teasing herself, running her fingertips ever closer to her center.

"Do you want to see?" she asked.

"Yes. Show me," I ground out, stroking my hand up my cock. This was why Lauren had so many subs. She was good at her job, made it feel more like we were doing this together and I wasn't jerking it to a prerecorded video.

Her smile turned coy as she pulled her hand from her shorts and slid her fingers along the waistband. "Say please."

I shook my head. I'd never begged for it in my fucking life, and I wasn't about to make an exception, not even for her. "Drop them, Lauren. I want to see how wet you are for me."

She smiled wider, like my answer pleased her, and slowly began shimmying them off. A small triangle of hair, neatly trimmed, came into sight, and then her shorts went the way of her shirt and she was completely naked.

Her hands returned to her tits, cupping, kneading, stroking. My gaze roamed over her. With so much skin on display, I didn't know where to look. I wanted to memorize the sight of her, and not just the way she teased herself, but the smaller tells that showed me how much she liked

The way her stomach tensed. The way her breath shuddered
~~~e gently pinched herself.

~~~~ her eyes, her lids fluttering, and I knew she was ready for
more. And yet she stayed right where she was, pushing herself higher,
harder, until she was forced to sit back on her heels because her thighs
started to shake. All through it she spoke, telling me what she liked not
just with her body but with her words.

"Here. Right here."

"Just like that."

"Soft, and then hard."

I wondered if she knew how much she was giving away, how much
ammunition I'd stockpiled over the years. She wouldn't stand a chance
against me when I finally got her within my grasp. Instead of drawing
it out like this, I'd go straight in for the kill.

"Stop teasing us both," I growled, my hand starting to move faster
over my cock. I wasn't used to waiting for the things I wanted. I'd been
teasing myself right along with her, and my impatience was starting to
get the better of me.

As if she heard my command, she dragged a pillow between her
thighs and trailed the fingers of a hand down, down, before slipping
them between herself and the pillow.

"I'm soaked," she said, the words more of a moan than anything
articulate.

"I bet you are," I told her. "You took your damn time getting us
here, Lo."

She cracked her eyes open, a mischievous smile splitting her face.
"So grumpy."

My hand froze on the head of my dick, and I hit the pause button to
double-check that this was, in fact, a prerecorded video, and I hadn't
accidentally accepted an invite to a live session or something. On
screen, Lauren froze, and a rueful grin tugged at my lips. She'd probably clocked my impatient streak from past sexting sessions and was
now using it against me.

I'd have to find some way to pay her back later, once she was mine.

With a tap, I hit play, my pulse thundering in my ears as Lauren started to move. I started moving again, too, my hand stroking up and down my cock as I watched her. I'd seen too many videos of this woman to count, but these custom ones were always my favorite. Because they were just for me.

The camera angle shifted slightly, showing me more of a sideview, and I had just enough time to wonder if there was someone in the room with her, helping her film, before the first moan slipped through her lips and nothing else but Lauren mattered anymore.

Her position and the pillow hid most of what was happening from sight, but I knew the moment she slid her finger—fingers?—inside herself, because her lips popped open on an even louder gasp, and she turned her head to stare straight into the camera.

"God, you feel so good," she said, her eyes fluttering shut again as if she were imagining me there in the room with her.

I stepped into the fantasy with her, kneeling behind her on the bed and shoving her hand out of the way so I could replace it with mine. She teased one of her breasts herself, while I went to work on the other, pinching and stroking her nipple even as I sank my fingers into her slick, tight heat.

"Do you like how wet I got for you?" she asked.

"Yes," I ground out. "But I want you wetter."

She shifted her hips forward, grinding her clit against my palm, fucking herself onto my fingers with total abandon. She was glorious. Wild. Perfect.

"I want to feel you come," I ordered.

"I'm going to come," she said, as if she'd heard me. "You're going to make me come so hard."

"I'm right there with you," I told her, my balls starting to tighten.

A heartbeat later, we came together, both of us shuddering, both of us breathing hard. Spots danced across my eyes. Fuck, that was amazing. *She* was amazing.

I watched her slump sideways onto the bed, laughing in a way that made my chest hurt. She sounded so free, so *happy*. I would have killed, literally, to feel that alive for once; I couldn't even remember the last time I'd laughed.

Her gaze met mine through the camera. "Holy shit, that was good. Was it good for you, too?"

I grabbed a wad of paper towels and started mopping myself up. "I think I got some on the ceiling, so, yeah, I'd say it was."

Again, that infectious laugh. "I'm going to sleep so well tonight." She stretched on the bed, languorously, her arms high overhead and her toes pointed.

I wanted to crawl on top of her and make her come again. And again. Until she was so exhausted she could barely keep her eyes open. Only then would I let her sleep, and only for a few hours before I woke her for more.

"Hey," she said, drawing my gaze back up her body. Her expression was open, intimate, her eyes soft with the afterglow of pleasure. "Thank you for doing this with me."

"Don't thank me, Lo," I told her. "Don't ever thank me."

I locked my phone and finished cleaning myself off, and as the haze of pleasure dissipated, my mind began to spin. No, I hadn't figured out how to get free from my father yet, but I needed to find some way to do it. And fast. Because it was time for a new chapter of my life to start.

I was done fucking around on the internet like some weirdo; I needed to see Lauren in person.

4

JUNIOR

I SHOULDN'T BE HERE.

That thought hit me like a thunderbolt the second I stepped inside the church. I hadn't been to Mass in years, and I half expected someone to point at me as I crossed the threshold and declare that my kind wasn't welcome here.

A glance down revealed that my long sleeves, which were completely inappropriate in this godforsaken heat, hid most of the tattoos on my arms and hands. Likewise, my shirt was buttoned all the way up, covering the ink on my neck. With my dark hair slicked back and my face shaved, I looked respectable enough, but from the way the church greeter's eyes widened at the sight of me, I wasn't fooling anyone.

She was a plump grandmother type with short gray hair and a hooked nose. Instead of saying hello, she jerked her head to the right, looking nervous. "Your mom and brother are already inside."

I gave her a nod and moved past her, my gaze shifting toward the nave as I wondered which of my siblings had tagged along with Mom. This was the largest Catholic church in the city, a huge, ornately decorated gothic monstrosity that would have been more at home in Eastern Europe than middle America. You'd think Saturday Mass would be less crowded than Sunday, but a sea of people was packed into the nave.

Turning left, I headed toward the far aisle, my gaze scanning the crowd. Today wasn't about being a good little Catholic; it was recon. This was my family's church, Lauren's family's church. I knew for a fact that her Nonna Bianchi still attended Saturday Mass, because Mom was in the event-planning group with her and mentioned her during a recent family dinner. And if Lauren getting all dolled up and heading to her nonna's apartment early this morning was any indication, they would both be in attendance today.

I swiveled my head, looking for them.

"Junior? Is that you?" came a lilting Irish voice.

Fucksake. Mom had already spotted me. My luck was the goddamn worst. So much for scoping out the crowd.

I paused mid-step and turned, plastering on a smile. Mom extracted herself from a group of other women and headed my way. She wore her church mouse best: a demure floral dress, comfortable heels, and a nondescript purse. Her light brown hair was loose to her shoulders, and she'd framed her green eyes with mascara. Looking at her, you'd never know that she'd spent her youth helping her father make bombs in their basement.

"Hi, Mom," I said, leaning down to hug her. At five ten, I was average height, but I still dwarfed her tiny form.

"It's so nice of you to come to Mass," she said, tacking on "for once" because she couldn't help herself. To her, being neck-deep in death and destruction was acceptable. Skipping church as often as I did? Unforgivable. But being raised in the IRA during the height of the Troubles could do that to a person, so I tried not to let her comment get to me.

I pulled back, keeping my smile firmly in place. "I wanted to surprise you."

"Consider me surprised," she said, looping her arm through mine. Her voice dropped into something a little softer, a little sadder, as she leaned into my side. "You've stayed away awhile this time."

Guilt washed over me. Fuck. How could I get away from Dad without risking my relationship with her? "I know," I said. "I'm sorry."

She squeezed my arm. "I understand, but please be better about texting me. I worry."

"I will," I told her.

Mom tugged me forward, and I reluctantly let her drag me to the front of the church, where people were starting to file into the pews. There weren't exactly assigned seats, but the congregants knew not to sit in the first several rows unless they belonged to certain families. They were a place of privilege, prestige. Every single person around us had a surname ending in a vowel.

I was surprised to see Alec already in his seat when we approached, turned away from us as he spoke to an older man I vaguely recognized. Out of all my brothers, I least expected him to be here. If I was a lapsed Catholic, he was a full-blown atheist.

"Look who decided to join us," Mom said.

Alec turned, and we locked eyes, both of us wearing equally suspicious looks.

What the fuck are you doing here? I wondered, and I could tell Alec was thinking the same thing. Neither of us did anything without reason. I was here for Lauren; I had no idea why he'd come. Maybe he needed to get on Mom's good side for some reason, or he was trying to make a deal with the retired don beside him.

I made a mental note to interrogate Alec about it later as he rose from his seat and offered his hand. We shook, squeezing each other harder than necessary.

"Nice of you to finally show your ugly face," he said.

I grinned. "Not as ugly as yours. Is that a new mole?"

He looked me over, unperturbed. "Your eyes are set too close together. That's what it is."

"I think the mole is growing hair," I told him. Other families might show their affection for each other the normal way, open and easy, but in the Trocci household, our love language was antagonism. This exchange was my and Alec's fucked-up way of saying we'd missed each other.

He opened his mouth to fire something back at me, but a woman's voice cut him off.

"Is that little Nicky?"

Shit.

Alec's eyes lit with unadulterated glee. I hated that old nickname, and he knew it.

"It sure is," he said, banding an arm around my shoulders and jerking us in the direction of the speaker.

The wound at my side pulled, painfully, and I stomped on Alec's toes to get him to release me. He let out a low curse, his arm falling away.

"Behave," Mom hissed.

We assumed innocent expressions.

"Mrs. Mancini," I said, facing the woman in the pew ahead of us. She had to be pushing ninety, but her fingers were firm when she reached out to shake my hand.

"Oh, you grew up so handsome," she said. "Even better looking than your brother."

I shot Alec a shit-eating grin and dropped my voice. "She must have noticed the mole."

He shook his head, but I could tell from the way his lips twitched that I'd almost made him laugh with that one.

Mrs. Mancini's gaze shifted to Mom as she released me. "Why don't you bring them to Mass more and show them off? Some of us have single granddaughters."

"Unfortunately, I'm taken," I lied through my teeth. "But Alec isn't." Putting my hands on his shoulders, I shoved him forward like a sacrificial lamb.

His glare promised vengeance. My answering smile felt diabolical. Mom looked heavenward, as if praying for patience.

More people continued to filter in, offering a welcome distraction from the attempted matchmaking. The next several reintroductions went about the same way, though. Alec and I got the standard hellos and how have you beens followed by a nice strong shot of Catholic guilt about me and my wayward brothers, directed at Mom.

By the time we finally took our seats, she was over it. "Jesus Christ," she muttered between me and Alec, crossing herself even as she blasphemed. "You'd think it's all my fault you're not here every weekend."

"Isn't it?" I asked, deadpan.

She glared, knowing my dry sense of humor well enough to pick up on the troll. "One more word, and I'll volunteer you to be an usher next week."

I lifted my hands in surrender. Mom didn't make idle threats.

Slowly, the seats around us filled while this week's volunteers moved about the sanctuary as they prepared for Mass. Where the fuck were Lauren and Mrs. Bianchi? They should have been in the pew right across from ours, but the spot was conspicuously empty. I turned, scanning the back of the crowd. The whole reason I'd come here was for the chance of seeing Lauren in the flesh, and if I had to sit/kneel/stand through an hour of bullshit for nothing, I'd be *pissed*.

I was just starting to turn back around when a flash of color caught my eye. Entering the nave were two women, one as old as the rest, leaning on the arm of someone much younger. Someone wearing a pastel pink sundress that contrasted beautifully with her tan skin. It was them. They'd made it.

My gaze zeroed in on Lauren. Need and possessiveness roared through me at the sight of her, and I briefly entertained the idea of striding down the center aisle, throwing Lauren over my shoulder, and walking out to the sweet sound of her startled shriek. Instead, I turned back around to keep from drawing attention to myself. I couldn't help my self-satisfied grin, though. Earlier, I'd watched Lauren just long enough to guess that she was escorting her grandmother here, and it felt good to be right, especially because it would put me within touching distance of her.

I kept my gaze on the altar, eyes unfocused while my full attention went to my periphery. Any second now, she would walk into sight, and I wanted to be looking at her when she noticed me. I wanted to see her up close and personal, study that split second of recognition and gut reaction before her brain caught up to her eyes and she schooled her face or tried to hide her feelings. That tiny moment of time was where the truth lived.

Suddenly, pink bloomed in my periphery as Lauren pulled even with our pew.

I turned my head, but instead of looking my way, she had her back to me as she helped her grandmother to her seat. Not that I was complaining. It gave me a moment to study her, my gaze trailing up her shapely legs to her spankable ass. The echoes of her moans filled my ears as the memory of her riding her own hand floated to the forefront of my mind. Just last night, this woman had made me come so hard I'd seen stars, and she didn't even know it.

Once her grandmother was settled, Lauren took her seat, her face downturned as she flipped through today's church program. Since her hair was tucked behind her ears, I had a clear view of her profile. She didn't look upset or worried, and she had to have heard the news about her dad by now.

Maybe she didn't think there was a reason to worry. Tommy Marchetti had never been the most reliable person, and even when he *was* around, he wasn't exactly winning any father of the year awards. The first time I'd ever met the guy was when he'd kicked my ass, and she and I had practically grown up together. He'd never been at our school plays, or her soccer games. He hadn't even come to Lauren's confirmation, a huge event for young Catholics. Who knew, maybe this wasn't even the first time he'd disappeared from her life?

Movement behind her drew my gaze, and I glanced over to see people nearby casting looks her way. One or two even leaned in to whisper something to those seated next to them. I thought they were talking about Tommy at first—news traveled fast in the old neighborhood—but then I caught sight of their censuring glances and realized this wasn't idle church gossip; this had teeth. It brought to mind Dad's insult. *Whore.*

Were these motherfuckers talking shit about Lauren? *My* Lauren?

From the unbothered way she lifted her head and scanned the people around her, she either didn't notice the way they stared and whispered, or she didn't care. Which meant there was no need for *me* to be bothered by it. But try as I might to talk myself down from the ledge, my temper clawed its ugly way out of the abyss and sank its teeth into me.

What pissed me off more than anything was the hypocrisy. Half these assholes had family members in the mob, men who'd committed innumerable crimes, done unspeakable things to other humans. I was one of them, and they were fine talking to me, but take your top off for money and you were shunned.

My expression flattened, and I locked eyes with several of the gossipers, one after another, who wisely decided to go back to minding their own fucking business.

"Hey, Lauren!" Alec called.

She turned toward the sound of her name, spotting him. The beginning of a smile tugged at her mouth, but her gaze tripped sideways, landing on me, and I finally got to watch that split second of recognition wash over her.

Hello, beautiful.

Her eyes flashed wide as her full lips, painted a muted pink to match her dress, popped open in surprise. Our gazes caught and held. Despite the crowd of onlookers, something sparked between us right there in the middle of church. Something dark, hungry. Ravenous because it had barely gotten a taste ten years ago and had been starving ever since.

"Junior," she said, sounding out of breath.

I flashed her a knowing grin. "You look good, Lo. It's nice to see you."

She blushed prettily and glanced away.

"Yeah, nice to see you," Alec muttered, but I could tell from his tone that he was amused. The bastard knew about my history with Lauren better than anyone else, and I was sure he'd called her name hoping to stir up some drama.

I should probably look away from her—people were starting to notice my staring—but for the life of me, I couldn't tear my gaze free. Lauren's sundress was fitted through the bodice, tight enough that it was obvious she was still breathing fast. From desire? Or fear, too? No one outside of the inner mob circle and immediate family knew exactly what my dad, brothers, and I did, only that we'd climbed high enough in the ranks that we had the ear of Lorenzo, the head of the organization, so Lauren shouldn't have had any knowledge of my involvement in her dad's disappearance. Especially since the only ties she seemed to have to the old neighborhood were her sister and grandmother.

I was tempted to say something more, get her to look my way again so I could get a better read on her, but the altar servers were marching out of a side door with their lit taper candles, indicating that Mass was about to start.

Reluctantly, I faced forward, biding my time until this spectacle was over and I got a chance to speak with Lauren one-on-one. Out of the corner of my eye, I saw her sneak a quick glance my way, and I grinned to myself as the priest took his place behind the altar. She might have been surprised by my presence, but there was no denying that she'd felt it, too, the pull between us that couldn't be denied.

Good thing I had such an iron control over my body, or standing when the priest ordered us up would have been *real* awkward. The memory of Lauren's latest video was seared into my mind, and I couldn't stop replaying it. What I wouldn't give to see her come in person, to *make* her come, using my tongue to drive her over the edge. Yeah, that's what I'd do first, drop her onto whatever flat surface was closest and shove her knees wide before burying my face in her cu—

Mom elbowed me, and I realized everyone around us was speaking. Right, the time for congregation participation had begun. Though it had been years since I'd attended church, the right words fell from my lips almost without thought. They'd been drilled into my head during my youth, and I guess they'd stuck.

I looked left to see Lauren speaking the same words, though the sight of her lips moving turned my thoughts more blasphemous than holy. As if she could feel me staring, she glanced my way again, just long enough to meet my eyes, her brows lifting almost in question, like she wondered why I'd suddenly shown up here after nearly a decade of absence.

I couldn't help it; I winked at her. *You're why, sweetheart.*

Her frown turned into a glare, and she jerked her gaze back to the front of the church.

Oh, so she *wasn't* afraid; she was pissed. It was good to know what I was working with. I'd rather have her angry at me than afraid. Coming back from fear was difficult. But rage? Rage could turn into desire if you knew what you were doing, and I liked my odds.

Behind the altar, the priest continued to drone. Down we went to our knees for prayer. Back up to our seats. We stood. Then kneeled again. I snuck glances at Lauren, because I couldn't help myself, but her gaze stayed steadfastly fixed ahead after our last exchange.

A small eternity seemed to pass before the priest gave us his final blessing. I got to my feet afterward and forced myself to do the right thing, to wait with my family while Mom said her goodbyes to those who wouldn't be joining in on coffee hour.

"What the fuck are you doing?" Alec demanded as we trailed Mom up the aisle a few minutes later.

I schooled my face. "What do you mean?"

He dropped his voice. "With Lauren, you asshole."

"Nothing," I said. *Yet.*

"Don't be an idiot."

The comment put my back up. "Since when am I ever an idiot?"

Being stupid wasn't a luxury I was allowed to enjoy. I always had to be "on," always had to be ready in case the shit hit the fan. It was why I never drank, never did drugs. I was on call twenty-four seven, and I'd learned from a young age how much trouble you could get in if you were careless.

Alec glanced ahead of us, toward where Lauren was passing through a side door into the back of the church. "Haven't you done enough to that woman?"

My anger sparked. Probably because there was a thread of truth in his words I didn't want to hear. "Relax. I'm just making sure she's okay after everything." *With her dad*, I didn't have to add.

"She seems perfectly fine to me," Alec said. "Job done. You can leave now."

I studied him before responding. "You seem awfully eager to get me out of here. Is that why you came today? You want to finally shoot your shot with her?" Alec's history with Lauren was even longer than mine. They'd been in the same class from kindergarten until she'd transferred out of the district right before their senior year.

Alec scoffed. "No. Fuck off. I just don't want to see an old friend get hurt."

"You haven't talked to her since she left school, so don't try to pull the protective friend bullshit with me. Why are you really trying to push me out of here so fast? What are *you* up to?"

He clamped his mouth shut as we entered the rear event hall, and I knew I had him on the ropes.

"Yeah, that's what I thought," I said. "Look, don't get in between me and Lauren, and I won't interfere with whatever business you're trying to get into with these old bastards."

"Fine," he muttered.

I spotted my quarry heading toward the restrooms in the rear of the hall and elbowed my brother. "Do me one more favor? Run interference?"

I didn't give him a chance to respond before stalking after Lauren, trusting that Alec was so used to following orders that he would do what I said.

5

LAUREN

I DEATH-GRIPPED THE BATHROOM SINK as I tried to calm my racing heart. My eyes were wide in the mirror, cheeks pink from more than just the blush I'd spread over them.

Oh, this wasn't good. I hadn't seen Nico "Junior" Trocci in ten years, yet all it had taken was one shared glance across the aisle to set my blood on fire. In a *church*, of all places, surrounded by enough elderly people to fill a nursing home. Thank god for the setting, because if I was that turned on under those circumstances, who knew what would have happened if I'd run into him in the wild somewhere.

But, really, who could blame me? Junior looked *good*. Like the third deadly sin had sat down in the middle of Mass just to challenge my willpower. His dark hair had been slicked back from his face, exposing the angular features I'd once obsessed over: high cheekbones, arched brows, the green eyes he'd unfairly inherited from his mother. Junior had always been more striking than traditionally handsome, but it only made him more attractive, because his was a face you didn't want to look away from. The longer you studied it, the more you wanted to learn all its secrets. What did those full lips look like when he smiled? Did those impossible eyes do anything but smolder?

A shiver slipped down my spine. I thought I'd had it bad back when he was a gangly teen with shoulders a touch too wide for his body, but now that he'd grown into said shoulders, I was in real trouble. One look. One *goddamn* look, and I'd spent all of Mass trying not to squirm in my seat like a . . . well, like a jezebel in a church. What was it that caused this kind of instant response between people? Was it just mutual attraction? Or was there something more to it, something the subconscious part of our brain sensed like pheromones or genetic compatibility or mutual assured destruction?

Whatever the case, it was a problem. One I wanted to avoid because I didn't know what to do about it. Maybe I could hide out in the bathroom for the rest of coffee hour.

I sighed. No, I couldn't be a coward, not with my grandmother out there waiting for me. She'd been the one to call me the other night during dinner with the news that my father had disappeared for what felt like the eighth time in my life, and before we'd gotten off the phone, she'd coerced me into coming here with her. I couldn't abandon her now, not before she had a chance to show off her "wildly *sex*cessful" (her words) granddaughter to all the "prissy old bitches" (again, her words) she was forced to endure Mass with.

I took a deep breath and opened the door. I was getting ahead of myself; there was no reason to panic. Junior had never been one to participate in anything growing up, and it was a minor miracle that his mother, Moira, had wrangled both him and Alec here in the first place. I couldn't for the life of me picture them sitting down at a table full of old people and politely carrying on conversations for the next hour. It would be like two wolves taking a nap with a herd of sheep.

Feeling bolstered, I smoothed my hands over my dress and left the bathroom. Everything would be fine. The Trocci brothers were long gone by now.

I pulled up short just after rounding a bend in the hall. There, leaning against the wall with one knee bent and his foot propped behind him, was Junior. His hands were in his pockets, head tilted back, looking like the epitome of calm. Meanwhile, at the mere sight of him, my heart was trying to break free from my chest and throw itself at his feet like a teenager at a K-pop concert. Embarrassing, but that was still better than what my *vagina* was doing.

Ignoring the dampness in my underwear, I started walking again. Junior heard me coming and rolled his head sideways, pinning me with a gaze that made me think our meeting like this was no accident and he'd been waiting for me.

"Hey, Lo," he said in that rough, accented voice of his. You could take the man out of the neighborhood, but you couldn't take the neighborhood out of the man.

I narrowed my eyes at him. Lo was short for Lauren Olivia. I hadn't heard that nickname in years. Not since I was forced to switch schools. Memories of what Junior had done back then swam to the surface. Or more like what he *hadn't* done. The way he'd left me all alone to deal with the fallout by myself. The way he'd blocked my number, stopped coming to church, pretended I never existed at all. This sonofabitch was the main reason I now had a one-strike policy with romantic partners.

The memories put some steel back into my spine, had me lifting my chin, meeting his bold look with one of my own. "Junior," I said, my tone as neutral as I could make it.

I planned to stride right past him and go back to forgetting he even existed, but in a fluid motion, he hooked his fingers around my arm. The hallway blurred, and before I knew what was happening, my back was to the wall and one of his hands was pinning my wrists overhead. His other hand slid around my hip, his thumb stroking over my stomach in a way that spoke of possessiveness, familiarity, like we did this all the time.

I sucked in a breath to either scream or moan (my body was very confused right now), and ended up dragging in a nose full of his cologne, something dark and far too sinful for church. How the hell had I gone from walking past him one second to getting pinned against a wall the next?

Panicking that someone would notice us, I glanced right only to see the back of Alec filling up the door to the hall like a bouncer at a club. Sonofabitch. Junior had definitely planned this little run-in.

I lifted my eyes to his, ready to tell him off and then run like my life depended on it. Because it felt like it did. Junior was dangerous, and not just because he scrambled my brain, but because he worked for his father. Doing what, exactly, I had no idea, but I knew it involved the mob, and I'd seen enough shit growing up in Little Italy to know that smart people stayed as far away from the Mafia as possible. But when my eyes landed on Junior, I froze. He was looking at me like he used to all those years ago, in stolen moments when no one was watching.

His gaze roamed over my face, intense, *electric*, before settling on my lips. That damn thumb was still tracing tantalizing circles over my stomach, and the hand holding mine to the wall gripped so hard it felt inescapable. I couldn't think with him this close, couldn't remember all the reasons he was a bad idea.

He licked his lips, a hungry look entering his eyes that went straight to my traitorous vagina. Damn it, I'd spent too much time fucking myself lately, and not enough time fucking other people.

"Did you miss me?" he asked, his voice low and intimate, for my ears only.

"No," I forced myself to say. "I've barely thought of you at all. After what happened, you became nothing to me, no one."

My tone made the words sharp enough to cut, but Junior only smiled, one arched brow climbing as he finally lifted his eyes to mine. This close, I realized they weren't just green; they had flecks of amber in them, too, explaining why they always looked like they were lit by some inner flame.

"This is how you respond to no one?" he asked, gripping me harder, his gaze running over my body.

I glanced down, horrified to see that I was arching into him against my will. It must have been some horny church ghost possessing me. Some nun who'd lived an entire life of celibacy and now that she was dead, all she wanted before she passed into the afterlife was one rough fuck.

"The power of Christ compels you," I muttered, desperate to expel her from my body.

Junior's lips twitched. "You trying to exorcise me, Lo?"

"I heard that's what you're supposed to do when the ghost of an ex shows up."

He glanced down again, to where I was *still* arching into him. "Doesn't look like it's working."

"Don't let it get to your head," I told him. "It's just because you come in a pretty package. Too bad it's empty inside."

Look, was it my best insult? No, but I was a bit distracted trying to banish Sister Mary Francis from my body before she made me do something *truly* stupid.

"Awww," Junior said, his grin widening. "You think I'm pretty."

Damn it. I'd forgotten what a smart-ass he was.

"Let me go, *Nico*," I said, using his full name, his father's name, in an effort to put some much-needed distance between us. "I don't know what you think you're doing, but I don't want any part of it."

"Funny," he said, ignoring my request and leaning in instead. His chest bumped against mine. Lips ghosted over the shell of my ear. The scent of him filled my nose, and despite myself, I dragged in a deep breath just to get another hit of it. If hell had orgies, his cologne was what they smelled like: dark, smoky, with a seductive hint of spiced musk and the subtle tang of sadism. "From what I remember," he whispered into my ear, "you would have begged me to put my hands on you like this in high school."

Mother. Fucker.

The lust cleared from my head, and with a jerk, I tried to knee him in the balls, but he must have anticipated it, because he shifted sideways enough that I hit him in the thigh instead. He still grunted in what might have been pain or surprise, his fingers loosening enough that I was able to slip free. My hand went into my purse as I strode away as fast as my heels would allow.

I didn't hear any footsteps chasing me, but I glanced over my shoulder just to make sure. Junior stood in the middle of the hall, legs spread, hands back in his pockets as he watched me leave. Something about his stance felt like a power move. He was indolent, smug. Like a cat who'd just knocked a glass off a counter and wanted to know what the fuck you planned to do about it.

I whipped back around and picked up my pace.

Alec turned at the sound of my approach, his charming smile a twin for his older brother's. I wasn't about to fall for it a second time.

"Where do you think you're going?" he asked.

I lifted my hand from my purse and pointed my taser at his face. "Away from you two assholes. Don't think I won't drop you in front of everyone if you get in my way." These people already thought the worst of me; it wasn't like tasing a man in a church would make much of a difference. If anything, it'd probably be the highlight of their morning and give them something to gossip about for the next week.

Behind me, a low chuckle echoed through the corridor. Of course Junior would find the idea of me face-tasing his brother hilarious.

Alec lifted his hands and stepped wisely out of the way. His smile seemed genuine. "Atta girl. Glad to see you've grown a spine since high school."

"Unlike you," I shot back. "Still your brother's little crony, I see."

He gripped his chest and pulled a pained expression. "Shots fired."

I rolled my eyes and kept walking, stowing my taser back in my bag as I reemerged into the safety of the event room.

My Nonna Bianchi, sharp as a tack even at eighty-eight, noticed something was off as soon as I sat down. "What happened?" she asked, her gaze going to the corner of the room, where Junior and Alec stood together at the mouth of the hall, watching me. "Did those boys give you any trouble?"

I shook my head and forced my gaze away from them. "I'm fine."

Her eyes narrowed, and she gripped the table like she was getting ready to stand. "That doesn't answer my question."

I grabbed her arm, hoping to keep her in place. Knowing her, she'd hidden a wooden spoon (the analog version of my taser) somewhere in her purse and was about to go hit the Trocci brothers about the head with it. "Nonna, I'm fine. Junior was just being . . . Junior." There was no other PG way to describe what just happened, and I doubted she'd believe me about Sister Mary Francis.

She shot the men one last glare before turning back to me. "I didn't know they would be here. Usually, it's just Moira and sometimes Nico in their pew."

I gave her arm a squeeze before releasing her. "It's not your fault. And nothing happened that I couldn't handle."

"Are you sure?" she pressed. "I'm certain Moira would give them a good whooping if I told her they needed one."

The thought made me grin. "I'm sure, but I'll let you know if I change my mind."

She nodded, her gaze going past me. "In that case, I want you to meet my friend Barb." One bony arm rose, and she waved it overhead. "Barb! Over here!" Nonna let out a huff and pushed back from the table. "One second. The woman is blind as a bat." She stood, grabbed her cane, and started tottering away. "Let me go get her before she walks into another wall."

■   ■   ■

An hour and a half later, I strode through my apartment door, feeling drained. Junior had left shortly after our run-in, and Alec not long after. My relief at their absence had only been momentary, though, because Nonna's friends were *a lot*.

We'd spent a good chunk of coffee hour talking about my father. Nonna and I tried to change the subject away from him and downplay his alleged disappearance, but the other ladies were full of theories. Several thought he must have pissed someone off and had to flee to Florida. A few others were convinced he'd been picked up by the Feds. Three more thought he was dead.

Nonna downplayed every one of them. Tommy—he hadn't earned the right to be called Dad—came and went as he pleased, and I'd hardly spoken to him in years. He could have disappeared months ago, and

I wouldn't have noticed. Or cared. To me, he was just the man who'd contributed half my DNA. My real father—and mother, while we were at it—was Nonna Bianchi, who'd raised me and my older sister, Kristen, since I was still in diapers.

"Incoming!" Ryan called, all the warning I had before Walter came flying straight at me.

I managed to turn sideways just in time to keep from getting taken out again as he wiggle-butted his way around me in excitement, his tail slapping the shit out of my legs, a happy whine climbing out of his throat. He had his favorite toy—a battered elephant with half the stuffing pulled out—clutched in his mouth, which meant that he and my roommates had probably been in their usual Saturday morning spot before I walked in: crowded together on the couch watching reruns of *Love Island*—we all agreed the first five UK seasons were the best.

I slipped my heels off by the door and followed Walter into the living room.

Ryan and Taylor swiveled their heads over the back of the couch to look at me.

"How was church?" Ryan asked.

In answer, I flopped face-first onto the chaise longue beside them and let out a loud groan.

"That bad, huh?" Taylor guessed.

"Junior was there," I said, but it was so muffled by the cushion that I had to raise my head and repeat myself.

Ryan winced when they heard the name.

Taylor looked between us, confused. "Who's Junior?"

Ryan and I met over a decade ago, during my senior year at my new school, when I was still a mess after everything that happened, so they knew all the sordid details. We'd met Taylor five years later, after I'd banished thoughts of Junior from my mind. This was the first time I'd ever even spoken his name around her.

Ryan unfolded their tall frame from beside Taylor and strode toward the kitchen. "We're going to need mimosas for this story."

Taylor's eyes widened as she looked from them to me. "Oh, really?"

I nodded. Walter chose that moment to round the chaise and shove his toy in my face. The stench of drool hit my nose, and I recoiled. "Let me go change, and I'll tell you the whole story."

I was halfway up the stairs when my phone rang. "Nonna" flashed across the caller ID, and I answered, thinking she had one last bit of gossip to fill me in on.

"Are you okay?" she asked, sounding out of breath.

I frowned. "Yeah, why? What's going on?"

"Someone slashed a bunch of tires in the church parking lot," she said. "I was worried that you'd been picked up by street youths."

"I'm fine, Nonna," I assured her.

"Oh, thank god," she said. "The neighborhood is going to shit, I tell you."

6

LAUREN

"So, what happened?" Taylor asked.

Love Island was paused, and she, Ryan, and I sat facing each other on the couch, mimosas in hand.

"Well," I hedged, "do you want the longer version involving my AO3 addiction in high school, or the abridged version?"

Taylor made a face at me. "The long version, *obviously*."

I dragged in a steadying breath. "There was a boy a year ahead of me in school that I was obsessed with."

"The aforementioned Junior?" Taylor asked.

I nodded. "He was your standard bad boy type. Tattoos. Family had mob ties. Was once suspected of putting the principal's car on the cafeteria roof."

Ryan snorted. "How?"

I shrugged. "Crane? Helicopter? There are many theories. None have ever been proved."

Taylor crossed her legs and leaned closer. "Say no more. I'm invested."

"We went to the same church," I told her, "so we kind of grew up together, but we were never close. Junior was so *cool*, and I was this shy, quiet bookworm. Back then, I could hardly bring myself to speak in his presence. Then, one weekend close to the end of my junior year, our church had its annual fundraiser. It's this big fair with booths and face painting and donkey rides for kids, all to raise money for the diocese. I looked forward to it every spring."

I dropped my gaze to Walter, splayed out beside me, as my mind went back in time. "I was a volunteer that year. My friend Kelly and I ran the ring toss booth. Across from us, Junior and his brothers were in charge of the bean bag toss, but they did so much goofing around that I don't think they even remembered to take people's tickets. Kelly and I got dragged into their shenanigans at one point, and it was the first time I remember Junior looking at me. *Really* looking at me. We flirted a little during the day, nothing wild, just some light teasing that still sent my pulse into the stratosphere because *oh my god, Junior Trocci actually talked to me.*"

Ryan shuddered and drained the rest of their mimosa. "Teenage hormones were hell."

Taylor nodded. "The absolute worst."

"Refills?" Ryan asked.

Taylor and I slugged back our drinks and handed over our empty glasses.

"There were fireworks that night," I continued while Ryan padded toward the kitchen. They'd already heard this story; I was telling it mostly for Taylor. "I was sitting on a blanket, watching them with Kelly, when I saw Junior hanging out near the back of the church. He motioned me over, and I made some excuse and got up and went to him. I don't know what I was expecting, but it wasn't for him to drag me into the shadows and kiss me."

Taylor's eyes widened. "Hot."

"Understatement," I said. "I still can't smell cotton candy without getting turned on."

"Then what happened?" she asked.

"Junior spun me around, slipped his hand into my shorts, and got me off while the fireworks exploded overhead. Anyone could have seen us if they'd looked in the right spot, but they were all too busy watching the display."

Ryan returned with our drinks, their grin wicked as they handed mine over. "And you've liked it kinky ever since."

I clinked my glass against theirs. "Guilty."

Taylor frowned. "But that sounds awesome?"

My smile faltered. "It was. And so were the next few weeks. We fooled around every chance we got. I used to slip him notes of where to meet and what I wanted to do with him, and this is where my fanfic obsession comes into play."

Taylor cringed. "Tell me a parent or grandparent or teacher didn't find one."

"They didn't," Ryan said.

Relief swept over Taylor's face.

I crushed it with a single sentence. "My friend Kelly did."

"Okay, and?" Taylor asked, looking wary.

"Well, she was obsessed with Junior, too," I explained. "I didn't tell her about hooking up with him because I knew she'd be upset—we'd always had this weirdly competitive edge to our friendship, and she would have seen it as losing to me, which she couldn't stand. One night during a sleepover, I think she got bored or something while I was showering and started snooping through my room. She found my diary, read the entries about everything I'd done with Junior, and confronted me about it. I apologized for not telling her, but she wouldn't hear it. She actually refused to believe it was real. Said I was lying and it was all some freaky fan fiction I'd written about him like a total stalker. She stormed out of my house afterward, and I didn't realize until she was gone that she'd taken the diary with her."

Taylor gasped. "No."

I nodded. "She took pictures of all the entries and posted them to Instagram, and they took off like wildfire from there because no one could believe that shy little Lauren Marchetti was secretly such a slut."

Taylor covered her mouth, her eyes wide. "Oh my god."

"Yup," I said, taking a swig of my drink.

Her hand fell. "That's like something out of a nightmare."

"Oh, it was," I told her. "I think Kelly must have regretted it pretty quickly, because she took the posts down, but it was too late. People were already sending screenshots to their friends. It was all over school by the time Monday rolled around."

"What did you do?" Taylor asked.

"Pretended to be sick so I didn't have to go," I said.

"Nonna Bianchi must have known something was up," Ryan said, having met my grandmother enough times to get a good read on her.

"I've never asked," I said. "But she let me stay home all that week, and that wasn't like her at all. If my sister wasn't the one to tell her, one of the neighborhood moms must have." I turned back to Taylor. "I tried going in the following Monday, but someone had printed copies of the posts and stuck them up all over school."

Taylor looked like she might puke. "Did the principal do anything to shut it down?"

"No," I told her. "In our neighborhood, everyone grew up knowing that snitches get stitches, so no one ever ratted anyone else out. Plus, our principal was one of those hands-off administrators who let way more shit go than he should have."

"Bastard," Taylor muttered.

"Yeah, well, karma's a bitch," I said. "He got in a car accident not long after and wound up in the hospital with more broken bones than you could count."

Taylor frowned. "So how does Junior come back into play?"

I sighed. "He denied that we ever hooked up."

Rage swept over her face. "Are you fucking serious?"

I nodded. "As a heart attack. I looked like the stalker Kelly had accused me of being, and she was quick to blab all over school about how she had seen it coming because I secretly wrote fan fiction under a pen name—because apparently my humiliation wasn't complete enough before."

And that was why it was so hard for me to trust people. The bonfire of my social and school life only exacerbated my unresolved feelings about being abandoned by my parents. It was the darkest time in my life. Nowadays, I lived by that Maya Angelou quote: "When someone shows you who they are, believe them the first time." It had become my mantra because I had learned the hard way that if you give people second chances, they'll only use them to hurt you more.

I dropped my gaze back to Walter, scratching him between the ears. "People thought I was crazy. The bullying got so bad that my nonna pulled me from the last few weeks of the year, and I did all my homework and testing from home. I spent that summer so isolated and depressed that she even let me change schools in the fall."

Ryan pulled me into a one-armed side hug. "Where she met me and began her healing journey."

I smiled up at them. They might have been teasing, but it was the truth. I would be forever grateful for Ryan's empathy, because they'd taken one look at broken seventeen-year-old me and known that I needed someone by my side. They'd also sensed that I was skittish, so being the introverted genius that they were, they didn't try too hard to befriend me or get me to open up. Instead, Ryan was just . . . there. Quietly beside me at the lunch table, loitering near my locker in between classes. Eventually, I started coming out of my shell, started talking more, and our tentative friendship was born. A decade later, Ryan was no longer my friend; they were family.

"So what happened with Kelly?" Taylor asked. "Did she ever apologize?"

I shook my head.

Taylor set her drink aside and started to stand. "We ride at dawn."

Ryan yanked her back to her seat. "Calm down, weirdo. Karma got her, too."

"How?" Taylor asked. "I'll need details to determine whether it was enough punishment."

I grinned and shook my head. God, I loved her. Even in the middle of recanting the worst story of my life, she found a way to make me smile.

"Kelly got busted for having drugs at school," I said. "She was actually top of our class, headed like five extracurricular groups, and had already been pre-accepted to her college of choice. Then she got caught with, like, half a pound of pot in her locker, and it all went to shit."

I frowned, thinking back. "It was so weird. She seemed as straitlaced as they came. Kelly swore the drugs weren't hers, but when the cops searched her bedroom at home, they found more, so there wasn't really a way to keep claiming innocence after that. In the end, I think she had to take a plea deal to avoid going to juvie."

Taylor shrugged. "Just goes to show that sometimes you don't know people as well as you think."

"Maybe," I said. "But even now, after everything, it's still hard to believe she hid a drug operation that large from me. Everyone else was shocked, too."

"So what happened today?" Taylor asked. "Did you get an apology from Junior?"

I huffed a humorless snort. "Hardly."

She started to stand again. "At dawn."

It was my turn to tug her back down, laughing. "He's not worth it."

Ryan didn't share my amusement, instead, studying my face. "He did something to you, didn't he?"

"Um . . ." I broke eye contact and tucked my hair behind my ears, a nervous tell I was sure they picked up on. "He might have cornered me in a back hall, and—" God, how did I even explain what happened between us?

"And what?" Ryan said.

I grimaced, knowing there was no way to get around this. "Let's just say that one look at him turned me back into teenage Lauren."

Ryan choked.

Taylor let out a whoop.

Walter barked, and maybe it was because I had regrets about earlier, but it sounded judgy.

"Details. Now," Taylor demanded.

"There's not much to tell," I said. "I came out of the bathroom to find him waiting for me in the hall. He had his brother Alec standing guard to keep anyone from bothering us, and I ended up pinned to a wall."

"Okay," Taylor said. "That's kind of fucking hot, though." She turned to look at Ryan for confirmation.

Ryan stared at her like she'd grown a second head. "Did you not just hear that whole story about how he betrayed her? We hate him."

"Oh, obviously we hate him," Taylor said with an eye roll. "But it doesn't make it any *less* hot. If anything . . ." Her gaze slipped to me, and she had the audacity to start fanning herself.

I grabbed a nearby pillow and chucked it at her head. Goddamn it. I needed her to help Ryan talk me down from my momentary stupidity, not enable it.

Taylor ducked the pillow, unperturbed. Walter let out an excited yip and went barreling after it.

"How'd you react?" Ryan asked.

"I froze," I said.

Taylor waggled her brows. "Froze, or went boneless like the submissive little slut you are?"

Walter returned carrying the pillow. I politely thanked him and then lobbed it at Taylor again. My aim was better this time, and she nearly fell off the couch trying to avoid it.

"I *froze*," I repeated. "He grabbed me and was just . . . there, and I was so caught off guard that I—" I could tell from my roommates' unimpressed expressions that they weren't buying a single fucking word. Time to speak my truth. "It wasn't my fault; I was the victim of a possession."

Taylor grinned. "By a randy priest?"

"Sexually frustrated nun."

She nodded along like she was fully onboard with my bullshit.

Ryan, however . . .

"Fine," I huffed. "I went boneless like the submissive slut I am, but in my defense, I haven't seen Junior in a decade, and he's grown into his man body. Those *fucking green eyes* of his stared straight into my horny little soul. I couldn't help it."

Taylor fell against the couch cushions, pumping her fists into the air while chanting, "Hate sex, hate sex, hate sex."

Walter returned with the pillow again, and I lobbed it at her a final time. "Stop that. I'm not sleeping with the man."

Ryan eyed me. "Did he say anything to you, or was it just the manhandling?"

I sobered, recalling the exchange. "There was an attempted flirtation." I couldn't bring myself to confess that Junior's charm had almost worked on me, instead giving them a rundown of our mini altercation and my quick escape to Nonna Bianchi and her friends.

Ryan's grin was rueful. "The wooden spoon brigade to the rescue."

"Those old biddies don't mess around," I agreed. "Both brothers left right after, so nothing else happened, thankfully. With any luck, another decade will pass before I run into Junior again."

Taylor sat back up. "But don't you feel like there's unfinished business between you?"

"What do you mean?"

"Clearly, the man needs to apologize," she said.

I shrugged. "I don't need an apology from him. Not anymore. I've moved on."

Taylor's perfectly arched brows climbed up her forehead. "What if he apologized . . . with his body?" She started pumping her arms like she was about to break into chant again.

This time it was Ryan's turn to throw a pillow. Since they were seated right next to her, it bounced off the side of her head and went spinning toward the kitchen, much to Walter's delight.

"No hate sex," I said. "Although . . ." I closed my eyes, and it was like I was back in the hallway with Junior pressed close, his hand gripping my hip, his breath warm against the skin of my neck. I swore I could still smell a lingering hint of his cologne. Still felt his thumb drawing circles on my side. If we'd been anywhere else besides a church . . .

A not-so-subtle cough brought me back to myself, and I blinked my eyes open to find my friends staring at me like they knew exactly where my thoughts had gone.

Taylor grinned. "Hate sex, ha—"

I reached past Ryan and clamped a hand over her mouth. We'd run out of pillows. "That's a bad idea for nine million reasons."

Taylor licked my palm.

I wiped it off on her pajama pants.

"Hey!" she whined.

I sat back, out of her reach and whatever retaliation she was plotting. "Junior hurt me once, badly. And while I might have been temporarily lobotomized by lust, I will never, *ever* give that man a chance to do it again. I'm sure the only reason I was so caught up by him was because it's been too long since I've fooled around with someone."

Ryan set their drink aside and stood. "Okay. We're going to the club tonight to fix that."

Taylor let out an excited shriek. "Yes!" She looked to me. "Right? Yes?"

"Yes," I agreed, pushing up from the couch. "I'll take Walter out now if someone else takes him right before we leave."

"I can," Ryan said.

In less than a minute, I had Walter in his walking harness and out the door.

The sun was starting its slow descent toward the horizon, painting the brick and stone buildings around me in gold. It had been hot earlier, but a slight breeze had picked up since I'd gotten home, blowing some of the heat away, and I tried to soak it all in while I could, knowing that winter would eventually come back around to ruin the vibes.

Motion across the street caught my eye. I looked up just in time to see a man kick his leg over the back of an expensive-looking motorcycle. He dropped into the seat, helmet already in place, leather jacket more suited to a DC villain than a biker. With a flick of his hand, the engine rumbled to life, low and throaty. This wasn't the first time I'd caught sight of him, and I figured he must live nearby. Unfortunately, I'd never seen him without his helmet on. Or maybe fortunately, for me. Something about a man on a bike scrambled my brain to the point that if I ever tried to speak to him, I'd probably blurt something stupid like, "Hi. Hot. Fuck?"

He must have clocked me staring, because he gave a jerk of his head like he was saying *What's up*. I smiled, waved, and quickly looked away, my mouth dry, my nether regions . . . not. What was it about a guy kitted out in motorcycle gear that was such a turn-on? Was it the badass stereotype? The fact that so many bikers had been depicted as rebels without a cause in film and TV? Or was it the anonymity of the helmet? Anyone could be underneath that thing, and I'd always had a bit of a mask kink.

Whatever it was, one thing was for certain: It had definitely been too long since I'd gotten laid.

Here's hoping that all changed tonight.

7

JUNIOR

THE ENGINE RUMBLED BETWEEN MY thighs as Lauren shot me a look before continuing up the sidewalk, her bear-sized shepherd mix leading the way. She'd changed into linen shorts and a tank top since church and had switched out her heels for a pair of flip-flops. Her hair looked different, too, like she'd run her fingers through it. Or at least I hoped it was her who'd done it and not some, as of yet undiscovered, significant other who I would obviously have to kill, *violently*, so there would be nothing left between us, and I could—

Another not-so-sneaky peek over her shoulder at me.

I grinned, my murderous thoughts forgotten. Nah, she was single. I'd bet money on it. Or if she was seeing someone, it wasn't serious enough to warrant bloodshed. A person in a happy, committed relationship wouldn't be shooting looks at me like this. And they definitely wouldn't have responded to me like she had in the church hallway. That spark between us was still there, burning even hotter now than it had when we were teens. I'd felt it the second I got close to her, knew she did, too, from her reaction alone: dilated eyes, slightly parted lips, the way she'd arched into me on instinct and then immediately tried to banish me to hell when she realized what she'd been doing.

I shook my head, glad that some of the old Lauren was still in there. Yeah, she'd been shy and studious, but she'd also been a little weird, and that was one of the things I'd liked about her most.

Earlier, she'd been so distracted trying to pretend she didn't still want me that slipping a discreet tracker into her handbag had been child's play. I knew she hadn't discovered it afterward because she'd led me straight to her house. I mean, I'd already *known* where she lived because I'd made it my business to learn everything about her over the years. The tracker was just so I could keep up with her when I wasn't free to watch her in person.

She disappeared behind the cars lining the street between us, and reluctantly, I pulled my gaze away and inspected my surroundings. This side of the city was nice. The cars were mostly luxury European models, the brownstones were in good repair, and enough plant life was crowded together that this neighborhood felt like a small oasis of green in a concrete desert.

I might have barely graduated from high school, but math was never my issue. If I'd been born into a different life, a different family, I could have made a career out of it. Hell, if things had gone better between me and Lauren, I might have. She was the only person who ever told me I could be *more*, that I didn't have to follow in my father's footsteps. No wonder Dad was hell-bent on keeping me away from her.

If my memory was correct, Lauren charged a monthly forty-dollar flat-rate fee for her Me4U page. With that, you got her entire back-log, four new videos a month, and endless photos of her. It might seem pricey, but over sixteen hundred people had subscribed, which meant she was pulling in over three quarters of a million dollars in revenue a year, *not* including all the tips she received and paid requests from subs like me who wanted her all to themselves for a few minutes. That kind of money was harder to predict, but based on her rates, I was guessing it added several thousand to her monthly income.

Lauren could more than afford to live in this part of town, and something inside me always loosened at the sight of her so at ease. She looked content, happy. Like she belonged. Every time I'd seen her here had been the same.

Lauren was okay. What happened back in high school hadn't ruined her life. She'd found her footing and made something of herself, grown into someone who didn't take shit from anyone. Her attempting to knee me in the balls and then threatening to face-tase my brother proved that.

My phone buzzed in my pocket. I dug it out to see a text from my father.

Now, was all it said.

I sighed. That was our code for an emergency, the sign to drop whatever you were doing and get home immediately. The temptation to ignore the order for once was strong, but Dad wasn't one to cry wolf. Shit was going down.

Reluctantly, I guided my bike out of the parking spot. It'd be faster to go south down the street, but Lauren was headed north, and I couldn't resist one last look at her. Revving the engine higher than necessary, I pulled into the lane, my head turned just enough to see her watch me pass.

Don't worry, Lo. I'll be back soon.

■ ■ ■

"I'm telling you," Alec said, "it's the perfect size for a head."

I stabbed my shovel into the ground and turned to face him in the lantern light. It was ten o'clock at night, and we were playing the age-old game of Guess What's in the Box.

"Why would he have us bury a head?" I asked.

My brother shrugged. "I don't know? Future blackmail on whoever killed the guy?"

"It's something else," I argued. Dad was too smart to hold on to body parts.

"Fine," Alec said, spearing his shovel into our halfway-dug hole and hefting out another load of claggy soil. "It's a priceless chalice."

"Gold bars," I countered. "It's heavy enough for it."

"Maybe," Alec said.

I let him dig on his own while I stretched my shoulders. My muscles were starting to tighten up, and I was worried the knife wound had bled through its bandages because there was a stickiness dripping down my side that felt too thick to be sweat. We'd been out here for an hour already, fighting through layers of clay, but Dad told us to dig the hole deeper than normal, so that's what we were doing.

My phone dinged with a familiar notification. Alec seemed like he was fine on his own for a few more minutes, so I pulled it out of my pocket to see a photo message from Lauren on Me4U. She was in a well-appointed bathroom with bright marble floors, dark patterned wallpaper, and antique brass fixtures. Her outfit was ridiculous. Not because it was ostentatious, but because all it would take was one brush of my fingers to have that loose-fitting white silk minidress sliding down her curves.

Want to see more? the message read. Below was an option to tip her twenty dollars. Lauren did this at least once a week, so I knew that if I hit the tip button, I'd get another, spicier photo as a reward. This was where she must make bank. The message went out on blast to all her subscribers, and I was sure the vast majority of us were more than willing to shell out twenty bucks to see her tits or ass or—*please, god*—her completely nude body, bent over the bathroom sink, waiting to be taken from behind.

I glanced up at Alec, but he was still sweating away digging the hole, so I tipped Lauren. A few seconds later, the second photo hit my inbox. She stood in the same position, but with her arms braced on the counter behind her and her head tilted back. Her dress was pooled at her hips, tits on full display in the golden light.

Goddamn. What I wouldn't give to step into the picture and suck one pert nipple into my mouth aft—

"Or it's so heavy because it's lead-lined," Alec said, jarring me back to reality.

I locked the phone and stashed it away. Now wasn't the time to day-dream. Hefting my shovel, I started digging again, and even though I knew I would probably regret it, I took Alec's bait. "Why would the box be lead-lined?"

"Plutonium."

He had obviously started using drugs. "Fucking plutonium?"

Alec grinned, looking unhinged because of the harsh angle of the lantern. "Why not? Dad's gotten awfully cozy with that Bratva guy."

"Boris? He's not Bratva. He's a butcher."

"Suuure he is," Alec said, his tone exaggerated.

I shook my head. "You and your conspiracy theories. It's obviously some kind of test."

He lifted out another load of soil, and I stabbed my shovel down as soon as his was clear, both of us working in tandem, as we had countless times before. The amount of random shit buried in this part of the forest would one day confuse the fuck out of a future archaeologist.

"What do you mean, it's a test?" Alec said.

"I bet there's a tracker in here or something, and he wants to see how deep it needs to be buried for the soil to dampen the emission."

"Now who's the conspiracy theorist?"

I shrugged. "Or maybe he ordered us to do this because he knew that not knowing would drive us crazy."

Alec threw his shovel aside and dropped to his knees. "What's in the box?" he yelled, doing his best Brad Pitt impersonation.

I shoved his shoulder. "Would you shut the fuck up? There could be campers out here."

He wisely shut up, and we got back to shoveling, our game forgotten. It felt like an hour had passed while we worked, enough time for me to get annoyed by how long this was taking. I'd planned to go back to Lauren's tonight but it looked like that wouldn't be happening.

"Why does he always order us to bury shit for him right after it rains?" I asked.

"Because he's a bastard," Alec said. "Hey, can I ask you something?"

"Might as well. We're going to be here all night."

"What'd you say to Lauren earlier that made her threaten to tase me?"

"Told her to look at your mole," I said. "She was probably offering to remove it for you."

He threw a handful of dirt at me. "I'm being serious."

I sighed, wishing I was out here with Stefan instead. Blessedly silent Stefan. "No idea," I told Alec.

"Quit lying." He shot me an annoyed look as he stabbed his shovel back in. "You must have really pissed her off. I've never seen Lauren so mad."

"You see her a lot?" I asked, eyeing him in the lamplight.

"Just every now and then when I go to church with Mom."

"And why *exactly* have you turned into such a choirboy all of a sudden?"

He shook his head. "Uh-uh. You're not turning this around on me. What'd you say to Lauren?"

"I don't know," I lied. I knew exactly what I'd fucking said. "Something about how much she wanted me back in high school?"

Alec groaned. "No, you didn't."

I went back to shoveling and ignored him.

"Please tell me you didn't," he repeated.

I shrugged, feigning ignorance. My relationship with Lauren, past, present, and hopefully future, was none of his goddamn business. I knew he was probably judging the shit out of me, but I'd said what I said to see how she responded to being provoked, and even though it might have pissed her off, I was pleased with the results. Because it gave me the answers I'd been looking for.

"God, you're fucking thick sometimes," Alec said.

"What do you mean?" I asked, playing into the conversation for his sake.

"You ruined her fucking life."

I stopped digging. "No, I didn't. I thought so, too, at first, but she's fine now. Lives in some fancy neighborhood and pulls in nearly as much cash as we do."

He frowned. "And how do you know that?"

Careful . . . "I checked up on her."

"Checked up on her how, exactly? You get Josh to do some side work for you?"

"Yeah," I said, because Alec thinking I'd asked our cousin's boyfriend for help was preferable to him finding out what I'd really been up to.

My brother eyed me. I kept my expression stone-cold. He was almost as good at sniffing out bullshit as I was, and nearly a minute passed in silence while he waited for me to say more. I knew better than that.

Finally, his attention returned to the hole between us. Down went his shovel. I picked mine up, and we got back to work.

"It doesn't matter how well she's doing now," Alec said. "You still destroyed her back then. Telling people you never touched her was fucking low, even for you."

"I did it to protect her."

"How could that have possibly protected her?" he demanded.

"Better people think she was living in a fantasy world than that we actually hooked up."

"I call bullshit," he said. "You threw her to the fucking wolves because you didn't want to be part of the drama."

Now I was getting pissed. I threw her to the fucking wolves because they were better than the lion waiting behind a nearby tree. If only Alec knew how far our father had been willing to go back then, how far *her* father had been ready to go right along with him. They'd been gearing up for some *Romeo and Juliet*–style shit, and I'd done what I had to do to stop them.

I'd kept it all to myself back then, not just to protect Lauren, but to protect my brothers from the reality that our father was an even bigger monster than they realized. And I wasn't ready to come clean now, because I was still grappling with how to break free from Dad and had no idea how to tell my brothers they were about to be on their own with him. Instead, I settled for a half-truth to get Alec off my back.

"That's not what happened," I said, forcing myself to stay calm. "You've seen all the shit Mom's been through because of Dad. Because of us. Everyone at school freaking out about Lauren proved that any woman I ended up with would be put through the same hell. I cared about her too much to do that to her."

I cared about her so much that I'd broken both our hearts to keep her safe.

Alec's expression shifted into reluctant understanding. "Fine, but you still could have come clean after everything died down and she transferred schools, just to clear her name."

I nearly groaned. "Jesus, I get it. You think I still owe her an apology."

"Yeah, you do," he said. "You owe that woman the fucking world. You owe that woman the favor of all favors. If you want a second chance with her, you better be willing to do whatever it takes to gain her forgiveness."

Getting lectured by my younger brother. What had my life come to? "Look, whatever does or doesn't happen between me and Lo is none of your goddamn business."

I expected Alec to snap back, or at least make some snarky comment, but his expression was sober in the lamplight. "Hey, why don't you get out of here? The hole is deep enough. Just help me lower the box down, and I can fill the rest in myself."

I eyed him. Where was this coming from? The sudden topic change was suspicious as hell, and it made me wonder if he was serious about his conspiracy theory bullshit. "You're not going to try and open it as soon as I'm out of sight, are you?"

He shuddered. "Fuck, no. We learned that lesson five years ago."

A memory tried to float to the surface, but I squashed it down, back into the black pit of ugly things in the bottom of my psyche that I worked real hard to suppress. "Then why?"

Alec broke our gaze and set his shovel aside. "You still call her Lo."

I shook my head. "Don't read into it. This isn't some love story. This is about scratching a ten-year-old itch."

He ambled over to the box. "Whatever you say."

"I'm serious," I told him, following in his wake. "I *just* explained why that romantic shit isn't in the cards for me."

He leaned down and grabbed his side of the box. I followed suit, and together, we hefted it aloft. The fucking thing was well over a hundred pounds, an outrageous amount considering it was barely larger than the box my motorcycle helmet came in. The sounds of our grunts and cursing drowned out the nearby crickets as slowly, carefully, we lowered it in. I pulled half the muscles in my back by the time it was finally in place, and I could tell from the way my shirt clung to me that I was freely bleeding. At this rate, I would never heal.

Alec straightened with a groan, his hands on his hips. At least I wasn't the only one in pain. He turned to me with a grimace. "Why don't you think you're worthy of love, Nic?"

"Fucking hell," I ground out, spinning away.

"Because you should know that you are," he continued, and I could *hear* the grin in his words. "Worthy of love."

Only the threat of being overheard by a nosy camper kept me from hitting him with my shovel. I'd have to find some way to pay him back for this later, but for now, I was taking him up on his offer and leaving him out here to finish the job on his own. Dad kept saying I needed to trust Alec with more responsibility, and here was his first test.

"Don't get eaten by a bear before you're done," I told him.

"But afterward is fine?" he asked in mock outrage.

"After is perfect," I called over my shoulder. "And if you say anything to Dad about Lauren, I'll tell him about that mistake you made last year."

"You wouldn't," he hissed.

I threw him the middle finger and kept on walking.

8

JUNIOR

THE TRACKER I'D SLIPPED INTO Lauren's purse was still working, pinging out her location somewhere on the West Side, far from her upscale neighborhood. I didn't like the idea of her being over there. I knew who controlled each block of this city, who ran the drugs, who ran the girls, and where you were most likely to get mugged on a night out. Lauren was in prime mugging territory. She better have that fucking taser on her still. If not, our next discussion would probably end with *her* almost getting kneed in the crotch.

I revved my bike and switched lanes. It looked like half the city was out on the sidewalks, scantily clad women sashaying together in small groups, puffed up men peacocking as they tried to get their attention. Traffic was just as heavy, moving at a crawl through the intersections as drivers swerved to avoid the drunken pedestrians.

Brake lights painted the night red. My pulse thundered with impatience. *Move. MOVE*, it demanded. I hadn't raced home to shower and change at record speed just to be bogged down by idiots.

Fuck it.

I revved the bike again and threaded the needle, slipping between idling cars as my wheels traced the dotted white lines. This was stupid, dangerous, but I had so much adrenaline pumping through my veins at the thought of seeing Lauren again that I felt invincible.

A cab cut left in front of me, and I swerved around it at the last second, a smile splitting my face at the close call. My parents complained about my motorcycle, but I'd never give it up. I spent so much time having to be meticulously careful to keep from getting caught or accidentally starting a turf war or revealing too much to my family's enemies. Every word was guarded, I never let my expression belie my true emotions, and I kept my cool even under the worst circumstances—though lately that had become more difficult thanks to my temper. This bike was my rebellion, a way to burn off stress. I felt reckless on it, careless. Like I could do anything. Like my whole family wasn't dependent on me in some way or another. Like I was free.

A horn blared to life behind me. Someone shouted a curse out their open window when I zipped past. I ignored it all and kept riding. Two more blocks to go before I could see Lauren. Two more blocks before I found out if she was as bold in person as she was online.

Neon lights flashed in my periphery. The wind ripped at my leather jacket, and I grinned, feeling borderline unhinged. Since dealing with Tommy, my interest in Lauren had shifted from a manageable obsession to something much darker. Something closer to a feeling of possession. Like I already *owned her*, body and soul, and all that was left to do was claim my prize.

I blamed the past decade. I'd spent too much of that time watching and not touching, and now, all the feelings I'd suppressed were roaring to the surface.

Those two weeks I'd spent fooling around with Lauren were some of my favorite memories. They were moments I'd stolen for myself— the last real thing I'd let myself *have*. My interest in her hadn't suddenly sprung to life watching her work the carnival booth across from mine. I'd been aware of her for years: since I was twelve and first realized girls weren't as annoying as I'd once thought. But even back then, I'd understood she was off-limits. Lauren was a good girl. Nonna Bianchi expected her to go off to college, get a degree and a fancy job. She was too respectable to be slumming it with the son of a mobster.

I'd kept my distance as long as I could, but that day at the fair had been my undoing. Going against my better judgment and finally letting myself kiss her, touch her, after denying myself for so long had been better than I could have imagined.

Maybe that was why I was so obsessed. Being with Lauren was the last time I'd let myself feel anything other than dead inside, and part of me wanted to remember what it was like to be alive.

A light turned yellow up ahead. I dropped low over my bike and revved the engine again, putting on one last burst of speed. My phone was mounted to my bike's inner right handlebar, the tracker pulled up, guiding me to Lauren. Following it, I took a left down a side street.

I slowed as I approached the green dot radiating on the screen, indicating her location. The device I'd slipped into her handbag might have been small, but it was a powerful, military-grade tracker that wasn't widely available for civilian use. It came with pinpoint accuracy, including elevation data. Lauren was somewhere on the second floor of the building directly across from me.

Not wanting to draw attention to myself, I continued past and parked a block away. I stuck to the sidewalk on the far side of the street as I reapproached, my gaze glued to the building's façade. It was four stories and built out of brick like everything else on the block.

I'd done enough surveillance work over the years that I knew how to keep a low profile, so I slowed my steps and dug around in my jacket pocket until I found the cigarettes and lighter I'd stashed there. I didn't smoke, not really, but I kept a pack on me at all times because it made a great excuse to stop for a minute or two to take in my surroundings.

I lit the cigarette and took a fake drag, holding the smoke in my mouth while I eyed the building. It didn't have any signage out front, and I was starting to think Lauren was over at a friend's place until a quick Google search set me straight. It wasn't apartments; it was a club of some kind. *Velvet. Where fantasy becomes reality*, read the tagline.

The club's website was annoyingly unhelpful. It didn't even have a navigation menu, just an address and a phone number listed beneath the words *Call for inquiries.*

Back to Google I went, which led me to an eighteen-and-up Reddit forum about underground sex clubs. I scanned the comment section until I found the name Velvet and then read the words: *"Great atmosphere. Phenomenal security. We felt very welcome and safe. Definitely recommend the private viewing rooms, which have a rotating cast of performers. Last Friday, we spent a lovely night watching a man get pegged onstage by a woman with the biggest tits I've ever seen. Great bouncing on both their parts. 10/10."*

I sucked in a surprised breath and immediately started choking on smoke.

Jesus Christ, I wasn't ready to read that.

The cigarette fell from my lips as I looked at the building with new eyes. A kink club. Lauren was currently inside a kink club. Where Reddit told me she could fulfill any sexual need she might have.

With someone else.

Oh, hell fuck, no.

I pulled up the club's website and clicked on the listed phone number without hesitation. My SIM card was a burner, so I wasn't worried about the number getting logged or traced; I'd have a new one this time next week, anyway.

"This is Velvet," a woman said after the third ring, her tone low and smoky. "How may I help you?"

I smoothed the rough edge off my accent in an attempt to disguise my voice. "I'll be in the city next week and would like to visit your club."

"We'd be happy to have you," the woman said. "You should know that we're members only, and you'll have to set up an account before gaining entry."

I hung up on her. A membership meant giving out my personal information and undergoing some kind of background check, which meant I needed to make another call.

This time, a man picked up. "Yo, Junior. What can I do for you?"

It was Mack, my dad's tech guy. I'd thought he was a top-notch hacker until I'd watched my cousin's boyfriend, Josh, at work. Now I wasn't so sure.

"That fake ID you gave me," I said, "does it have legs, or is it just plastic?"

"It has legs," he assured me.

"How long are they? I might need to run it through a background check."

"Long enough. There's an address, a social security number, and medical records attached to it," he said, a note of pride in his tone.

"You're sure it'll check out?" I asked.

"Absolutely," he said.

I thanked him and hung up. He'd better fucking hope he was right.

■   ■   ■

Half an hour later, I walked into the main room of Velvet wearing a courtesy mask provided by the hostess. It was plain, black, made of plastic, and covered me from my forehead to the top of my mouth. I felt like a fucking idiot in it, but the alternative was walking around a kink club—sorry, *play club*, as I'd been informed—with my whole-ass face on display for anyone to see, and that wasn't happening.

My newly printed membership card was burning a hole in my pocket, ready to be used at any of the private rooms I wanted to pop into. I'd say one thing for this place: It was well-run. While a doughty older woman took my fake ID and ran a background check, the much more pleasant host staff led me to a well-appointed office and gone through the surprisingly extensive list of rules. There were commonsense ones like respecting people's boundaries and keeping your hands to yourself unless explicit consent was given, along with some more *interesting* ones like stopping if someone's lips started to turn blue while you were choking them.

I'd cracked a joke about them not having to worry about me. I strangled people for a living; didn't want it encroaching on my me time. Alec would have found it hilarious, but the staff just blinked at me, and I had to quickly backtrack and spew some bullshit about how I meant it *financially*. Afterward, I kept my mouth shut. This was why mobsters and normal people didn't mix well.

Now, as I walked through the first-floor lounge, I had to agree with the anonymous Reddit post I'd read outside. This place took not only their rules but their security seriously. There were large men guarding the entrance. I spotted several cameras high in the corners, barely visible because their matte black coating blended in with the wallpaper. All the play room doors had scanners on them, and you had to swipe your member card to gain entry. I was betting each card stroke was recorded, so if anything went awry, whoever monitored them would know every single person who'd been inside when the incident occurred.

It was impressive. And so was the décor: dark, moody, tactile. Instead of bright overhead lights like I saw in a lot of clubs, this one was lit with floor and table lamps that cast the occupants in a soft, forgiving light. The furniture was clad in tweed and velvet and leather. Along the far wall, an antique mahogany bar gleamed with a fresh coat of polish. It smelled like citrus and old books, but beneath that were the undeniable hints of sex and latex.

I scanned the people around me. This lounge seemed to be the main hub of the club, a place where members gathered while they waited to enter other rooms, meet friends, or take a breather between . . . sessions? Scenes? I didn't know the lingo. All I knew was that it was crowded, and the soft light made it hard to pick out faces, which I'm sure was intentional.

I wasn't the only anonymous person in attendance. A few others wore what looked like custom masks, everything from a standard balaclava to a horror-movie-inspired face covering. The sight weirded me out, but more than a few women were crowded around the Jason wannabee, so maybe it was some kind of fetish?

I felt eyes on me as I moved through the room. These people seemed much more at ease than I was, like they'd been here often enough that they knew most others in attendance, understood the rules, both written and unspoken. I was the fresh blood, so of course I drew notice.

A woman broke away from the wall and approached me. She was a few inches shorter than I was, curvy, attractive, with blond hair and blue eyes. Eyes that were downturned as she stopped right in front of me. I glanced around us, but the people nearest were only watching with mild interest, no cutting amusement in their eyes to tell me I was being punked or something. My confusion only deepened as the blond *bowed* to me, lifting her hands in offering, some sort of leather accessory—a collar?—resting on her palms.

The fuck was I supposed to do with that?

I waited for her to explain herself, but she just stood there, silent.

"Uh . . ." Not wanting to appear rude, I reached out and patted the top of her head. "No thank you."

She bowed deeper and stepped away, so I assumed I'd at least avoided some kind of faux pas. I moved past her, on the verge of sweating. Jesus Christ, this was uncomfortable. If I'd paused for a second before storming in here, I probably would have talked myself out of it, but the thought of Lauren with someone else sent me barreling inside without a single thought besides getting to her. Had she been coming here all these years? How many of these assholes knew what she felt like? Tasted like? How many tongues would I have to cut out of people's—

Nope. Stop that, I told myself. *You're trying to be a better human being, and homicidal thoughts like that aren't helping you find her.*

Glancing at my phone, I saw that Lauren was still on the second floor, so I headed toward the stairs. They spat me out in a dimly lit hallway. The sounds were more overt up here, and every closed door I passed seemed to hold something new. Laughter, moans, the sharp snap of leather connecting with flesh.

The doors had placards on them, but the labels were as frustratingly vague as Velvet's website, at least to someone like me who wasn't in the know. *Learn, Hunt, Warm, Secure.* My phone told me Lauren was in

Watch (because of course she was), and, taking a deep breath, I scanned my membership card and carefully pushed the door open, not knowing what the fuck I was about to walk in on.

I found the room surprisingly full, most people already sitting, the rest loitering at the back while they sipped their drinks and talked quietly amongst themselves. The lighting was even dimmer than in the hallway, with just a single overhead fixture shining down on the far side, where a platform stood, looking more like a dais than a stage. A bed sat front and center on it, piled with dark silk sheets.

The sound of a soft, *familiar* laugh drew my gaze. Lauren sat in the front row. She was still wearing that enticingly flimsy silk dress, talking to the person next to her with enough animation that when she gestured with a hand, the motion sent one of the whisper-thin straps sliding down her shoulder. It was only with monumental effort that I stayed where I was while she casually slipped it back into place.

My gaze snagged on the person beside her. It was a man. A man who was looking at her with far too much hunger in his eyes for my liking. Nope. Not happening. I hadn't waited all these years just to let some fucking rando move in on her in front of me.

I slipped through the crowd and rounded several rows of chairs, approaching Lauren, my gaze trained on the man beside her. In a split second, I had to decide how to play this: by force or coercion. Force would be the obvious choice for some, a way to flex their dominance, show the competition who they were dealing with. I discarded it out of turn. As tempting as it was, this was a tight space, and I didn't know the guy or how he'd react to direct confrontation. My goal was to get close to Lauren and *stay* close to her, not get kicked out of this club right after gaining entry.

Plus, coercion was much more fun. And yes, I was aware of how fucked-up that made me sound, but I felt like it showed real growth that I'd so quickly moved past the temptation of tongue removal.

I stopped in front of my target, giving him an affable smile. "Hey, there." My voice was friendlier than normal, borderline unrecognizable to anyone who knew me. "I'm so sorry, but you're in my seat."

He looked up at me, his light brown hair artfully tussled, the black-framed glasses perched on his nose reflecting the overhead light. I wasn't usually one to judge, but he looked like a pretentious fuck. Like he belonged in a lecture hall, making inappropriate advances on his students. "I'm sorry?"

"No problem," I said, intentionally misinterpreting his apology.

I clapped him on the shoulder in an affable way, prompting him to stand, and he frowned, even as he started to rise, like he was confused about what was happening but was too polite to make a fuss. Just as I'd hoped. People could be talked into doing all sorts of shit they didn't want to if the right amount of pressure was exerted. Lucky for me, the professor seemed more vulnerable to coercion than most of the assholes I was used to dealing with.

"I appreciate you moving," I said.

His frown deepened. "Um . . . you're welcome?"

"Thanks." I patted him on the shoulder one last time before taking the seat he'd just vacated.

Lauren sat there looking stunned, allowing me a moment to take her in. She was just as beautiful in person as she was in the bathroom selfies she'd posted, makeup more dramatic than this morning, hair curled into loose waves. The gloss she wore made me want to lean in and bite her lower lip, but after her violent outburst in the back of the church, it probably wouldn't end with us making out, so I held myself in check.

Slowly, her focus shifted from the retreating man to my masked face. And then her eyes caught mine and narrowed before dropping to my hands and the words "La Famiglia" tattooed across my knuckles.

"I see my exorcism didn't work," she said.

I grinned. "You should try holy water next time."

She turned fully toward me and leaned in, her voice low. "What are you doing here?"

I leaned in, too, glad for the excuse to get close to her. "Filing my taxes, you?"

"Filing a restraining order," she shot back.

"Against who? The nerdy professor?" I half rose from my seat, pretending to look for him. "No need for paperwork. I can take care of that for you."

She yanked me back down. "I'm serious, Junior. Why are you here?"

"I came to talk to you."

"Well, you can't be here," she said, glancing around like she was afraid to be seen with me.

I tried not to be offended. "Why not?"

Her gaze returned to mine, the fire I'd glimpsed earlier in the day returning. "Because this is *my* place."

"And you don't let people like me in?" I shifted an inch closer, unable to help myself. "Discrimination is illegal, Lo."

"I didn't mean it like that," she said. "I meant that this place is just for me, and I don't want someone from my past coming in here and bringing up bad memories and ruining my night."

Goddamn it. Alec was right. I needed to apologize to her if the sight of me alone was enough to spoil her evening.

"I'm sorry," I said.

She blinked and sat back.

"For what I said to you earlier," I clarified, "but mostly for what happened between us all those years ago. I was already getting dragged into my dad's shit, and I figured it was better people thought you were just another obsessed moll than someone important to me."

Her brows creased, large eyes lambent in the soft light. "Wait, are you saying I was in danger?"

I held her gaze and nodded.

Those glossy lips parted, but her response was cut off by a low chime from the overhead speakers. Instead, she said, "The show is about to start. You need to leave."

"Are you leaving with me?" I asked, reaching out to wrap my fingers behind the backs of her knees and pull her closer. Fuck, her skin was soft.

Her nose nearly brushed mine, pupils wide in the dim light. "Are you out of your mind? No, I'm—"

A side door opened, and a man and a woman walked through it, holding hands. The man was tall, broad, with pale skin and dark blond hair. His companion was over a foot shorter, Latine, her voluptuous curves barely contained by her red dress. Though the room was packed with people, they seemed unaware of us, their gazes drinking each other in as they slowly made their way forward.

"Junior," Lauren whispered, drawing my gaze back to her, "you have to go."

I shook my head, our eyes locking, my thumbs stroking the outside of her knees. "If you're staying, I'm staying." No fucking way was I letting her out of my sight now.

She opened her mouth to protest, but the person behind me shushed her.

I grinned and put a finger to my lips, facing forward in my seat, one hand still holding on to her because she was close enough to touch, and, miracle of miracles, was actually letting me touch her.

My triumph only lasted a second before she brushed me away and crossed her legs as if trying to put some distance between us. I schooled my face, fighting my amusement, loving that Lauren knew her worth and was going to make me work for it. I'd always preferred the thrill of the chase over the easy kill, metaphorically speaking.

Mostly.

Movement drew my gaze back to the stage. I don't know what I'd expected. Visions of whips and chains had popped into my head, the stereotypical shit most tourists like me associated with play clubs. I figured they'd make a big show of it, be over the top and cringe. Part of me was waiting for an MC to follow the couple through the side door and make some big announcement.

None of that happened. Instead, the man led the woman to a chair beside the bed. She took a seat, and he dropped to a knee in front of her.

"Give me your feet," he said, his voice low and intimate, like there weren't thirty fucking people watching him.

The woman smiled mischievously and planted her high heel directly onto his chest hard enough to rock him back a few inches. He chuckled, the low sound rolling through the room, and kissed her shin before slowly starting to undo the strap around her ankle.

Soft, feminine sighs swept through the crowd at my back. Someone whispered to their neighbor close enough for me to catch the words, "That level of devotion or I don't want him."

I suddenly felt even more uncomfortable than I had downstairs. This was a private moment between two people who obviously cared about each other. I shouldn't be sitting here watching it like a creep.

And yet . . .

I couldn't take my eyes off them.

9

LAUREN

JUNIOR WAS AT VELVET. SITTING in the voyeur room. Right next to me. After he'd just given me a ten-year-late apology like it was no big deal.

My brain couldn't process what was happening. How had he found me? Had he followed me all day after church? Or had I somehow summoned him with my unholy thoughts? After this morning's possession, I couldn't rule out the paranormal.

I turned my head just enough to side-eye him. Black boots. Black pants. Black button-down. Paired with the black half mask and tattoos, he looked like exactly what he was: an obvious sex demon come to claim my horny soul.

I craned my neck even farther, catching Taylor's gaze two rows back. *IS THAT HIM?* she scream-mouthed at me, pointing at Junior's back. She must have seen him walk in (matching his description to the one I'd given her earlier) and then talk to me and made a lucky guess.

I nodded, and that traitor swooned sideways into her boyfriend and started fanning herself. Jackson, a nearly seven-foot-tall redhead who was just as unserious as his girlfriend, caught sight of me and waved emphatically, a huge grin splitting his face.

No help there.

I turned the other way and tried to find Ryan in the crowd but couldn't spot them. Panic swirled in my belly. Junior had to leave. Now. Before things *really* got started. Maybe I could find some way to force him out, threaten to call the cops or something. I didn't want him here, in my safe space. This was for me, my friends, and like-minded people, and Junior wasn't among them. He was a ghost from my old life who ran in backward, misogynistic circles. I doubted he'd understand, let alone approve of what was about to take place.

Shit, what if he ruined this? Made some gross joke or said something offensive in the middle of the scene? Or worse, kink-shamed everyone in here?

My face started burning with anticipatory embarrassment. I had to get rid of him.

Uncrossing my legs, I leaned over just enough to whisper, "Leave, or I'll call in a bomb threat and blame it on you."

He cocked a brow. "That feels like an overreaction."

"Don't test me. I have Homeland Security on speed dial."

The bastard lifted his hand and brushed my hair over my shoulder, exposing my ear so he could whisper back, "Call them. I dare you."

And then he kissed my neck.

My entire body clenched up, and not with the rage or fear or disgust I *should* be feeling.

Oh, this was bad. All the years I'd spent exploring kinks with past partners were coming back to bite me in the ass. Because the fear play, rough sex, and danger were just pretend, and I'd been protected by safe words. Junior was the real deal, might pose an actual threat to me, and instead of being freaked out like I should have been, I was turned on.

This time, I didn't even have a raunchy nun to blame it on. This was all me.

Belatedly, I wrenched myself away from him. Shit, shit, *shit*.

Onstage, Morgan finished untying Stephanie's second heel and slowly set it on the ground. Then he lifted her leg and planted a kiss on her toes. She made a low hum of approval, and he began kneading the ball of her foot in a way I knew must feel like heaven.

Soft music filtered down from the speakers, low, melodic, sensual but not in an overt way. The song was more of a suggestion, a promise of pleasure to come. I was starting to get desperate.

"Please," I whispered, turning back to Junior.

He dragged his gaze to mine—he'd been focused on the couple onstage. "Don't worry. I'm not going to embarrass you."

I blinked. How had he known where my thoughts had gone?

He shifted sideways, bumping his shoulder against mine. "Because I know you, Lo."

I glared at him. The actual nerve of this man. Ten years had passed since the last time we'd seen each other, and a lot had changed in that time. He didn't know the first thing about me, and I resented the insinuation that he did.

I shot him one last warning look, trying not to get sucked into the vortex of his green eyes, and then faced forward in my seat. Lord help him if he didn't keep his word or his chill through what was about to play out in front of us, because I wouldn't be so forgiving.

I hadn't been lying when I said this was *my* place. Velvet was a shared-ownership club, with my friend Sylvia holding the largest stake. Ryan, Taylor, myself, and several other acquaintances and performers held smaller portions, having bought in when times were tough to give the club a much-needed boost and keep it afloat. We all believed in Velvet. We were invested, not just financially, but with our whole hearts, willing to do whatever it took to keep this safe space open and thriving.

Onstage, Morgan's fingers continued to work their way up his wife's leg, moving from her foot to her ankle.

"That feels amazing," she told him.

Normally, at this part of the scene, I'd be feeling the beginning stages of arousal, but instead of a welcome rush of soft desire, my body was at war with itself. What I felt was closer to aggression. Electric, charged. Uncomfortable. Far from what I'd come to expect at Velvet. And it was all because of the man at my side. I might not have thought of him much over the past decade, but now I couldn't stop the flood of memories from breaching the dam. Him fingering me beneath the fireworks. Me jerking him off in a stairwell at school. The night he'd snuck into my bedroom and I lost my virginity to him. Three days later, he'd denied ever knowing me.

I tried to look at it logically. Core memories were especially a *thing* when it came to a person's first sexual encounters. We all had our own examples. Taylor couldn't smell cigarettes mixed with cheap cologne without getting turned on. Likewise, Ryan experienced their first public boner after an especially handsome waiter served them mediocre pizza at a well-known chain restaurant, and now they couldn't walk into one without having to quickly sit down.

My reaction to Junior was a natural response, but it didn't have to mean anything more than that. Fighting it would only make it worse. Instead, I chose to accept that this was how he made me feel, physically, so I could move past it and focus on the more important matter: how he made me feel emotionally.

Which was confused. Very confused.

As much as I hated to admit it, our back-and-forth exchanges were kind of . . . fun. And he'd apologized so *quickly* after realizing he'd fucked up at church. Was that why he'd tracked me down? Just to say sorry? If that were the case, today's stalking suddenly seemed a lot less concerning and a lot more, I don't know, determined, maybe? I wasn't used to men owning up to their mistakes like this, mostly because I wasn't in the habit of giving them the chance to, and I didn't know how to feel about it. I also hadn't missed Junior's last comment: *I figured it was better people thought you were just another obsessed moll than someone important to me.*

I'd been important to him back then? That was surprising. Before the fair, he'd never even looked at me, and he'd dropped me so fast afterward that I figured our hookups meant nothing to him.

No. He must have been lying when he said that, trying to get into my pants. It'd been so easy back then and he thought it'd be just as easy now. Well, it wouldn't be. He was a huge part of why I had so many trust issues, and I wasn't about to let him charm me into forgetting that.

I sent him a sideways glance, but he seemed too distracted by the couple onstage to notice. His gaze was fixed on them, spine straight, body almost completely still, only the steady rise and fall of his chest to indicate his mood. I'd seen other people who'd jumped into the deep end at Velvet before they were ready, and they'd looked nothing like Junior. They'd been twitchy, obviously nervous, unable to watch what was happening in front of them, looking everywhere but at the stage. Junior was a man transfixed. Like he was caught in the spell that Morgan and Stephanie were casting over the audience.

Huh. Maybe I didn't have to worry about him embarrassing me after all.

I faced the stage, still battling my inner turmoil. And to think, before Junior showed up, I'd been having a nice moment with . . . what was his name again? Oh, right, Kevin. Or was it Carl? Shit. Faces, I never forgot, but names were my nemesis. Either way, there had been some chemistry there. Kevin-or-maybe-Carl had been soft spoken, affable, and obviously interested: The perfect person to share a bit of fun with because the stakes were so low. Maybe once the show was done, I could find him again. Send Junior packing and go back to having a good night.

A soft moan echoed through the room, and I let my thoughts of Junior slip away as I turned my whole focus back to the scene. Morgan had kissed his way up Stephanie's leg, all the way to her inner thighs. The red dress she wore was hitched around her hips, and she'd arched forward, arms straining as she gripped the seat of the chair behind her. As I watched, Morgan shifted closer, opening her legs wide enough that the audience could see when he hooked a finger into her underwear and gently tugged it aside, revealing her to us.

Her pussy was waxed bare, the folds of her lips already shiny with the evidence of her arousal. The frenetic energy of my own desire shifted at the sight into a calmer, more welcome heat. Morgan and Steph were my favorite couple to watch. Not only were they both hot as hell, but their love for each other was palpable. And their lust? Good lord. It set the room on fire.

They also came from a theater background, so they had fantastic stage presence and understood how to pose themselves so the audience got the best view of every touch, stroke, and lick. I'd been hoping to find a willing partner in the crowd—audience participation was more than welcome at Velvet—but this might be even better, getting turned on to the point of discomfort before finally finding release on the fingers or tongue or cock of someone else. If Kevin/Carl was no longer an option, I'd seen Moriah downstairs earlier, a gorgeous femme who bore a striking resemblance to Zoe Saldana. We'd hooked up here several times before, and she'd recently split from her girlfriend. Was two weeks post-breakup too soon to make my move?

Up front, Morgan made a low sound of masculine approval that rumbled through the room. I shivered. His voice was trained for the stage, deep, resonant, one of those voices that could probably talk you into an orgasm under the right conditions, no touching required.

He glanced up at his wife. "You're soaked, Steph."

She drew him closer, her smile turning seductive. "What are you going to do about it?"

With a low groan, he leaned in. If they were alone, he probably would have gotten straight to work, but a little teasing went a long way, both for the audience, and your partner, and Morgan understood that better than most. One big hand went to her knee, spreading her wider, showing us just how much she wanted him.

"Here?" he asked, kissing her thigh.

She shook her head and exhaled a breathy "no."

He shifted to the other leg. "Here?"

"Almost," she told him.

He lifted a finger and stroked it down the crease of her inner thigh, and I was close enough to see the full-body shiver roll through her. Morgan repeated the motion on the other side, taking his sweet time, moving his finger a little so that he nearly brushed her folds on the way past. The tease.

Behind me, people started to shift in their seats, and I grinned. Their impatience was palpable. I could almost hear them begging, *Just touch her already!* But Morgan was immune to peer pressure. Instead, he leaned in and breathed over Stephanie's heated flesh, making her toes curl and her arms strain from gripping the chair so tightly.

Just when I thought he might finally taste her, he started to pull away. Someone let out a disbelieving whimper in the crowd, and we all laughed, glad that the tension had been broken. There was almost always a moment like this in a scene, usually early on, that helped both the performers and the crowd settle in.

"Let's get you out of these," Morgan said, his melodic voice tinged with amusement as he gripped the sides of Stephanie's underwear.

She lifted just enough to let him slip them over her hips. And then he was dragging them down her legs, taking his time to drop kisses on her skin. Once her underwear were past her feet, he pulled them to his face, breathing deeply.

"I love the smell of you," he said, low, guttural.

Junior shifted beside me, dragging me out of the moment. My gaze snapped to him, expecting the worst, even though he'd promised to behave, but he was only readjusting himself.

Don't look, don't look, don't look, I begged myself, but down went my eyes, just in time to catch the outline of his obvious arousal beneath his dark pants.

Goddamn it.

I wrenched my gaze away, trying to calm my pulse. Junior was as turned on as I was by what we were watching, and I didn't know what to do with that information.

How about this? my brain helpfully supplied, flashing an image of him fucking me from behind, one hand dug into my hair, the other gripping my hip, his expression ruthless, thrusts brutal. I nearly swore, wondering what I'd ever done to my brain for it to suddenly turn against me like this.

Onstage, Morgan balled his wife's underwear up and slipped them into his pocket, and I lost all control of my heartrate. Something about that was so innately sexy to me. Like he'd put them there for safekeeping, or to pull them back out and sniff them later, whenever he needed another hit of his wife. It spoke of possession, obsession, and there was nothing hotter to me than someone who was so unselfconsciously infatuated with their partner.

Morgan leaned back in, his wide shoulders making room between Steph's knees. She arched her back, scooting closer to him, and he wrapped his arms under her thighs and gripped her hips, holding her in place.

A low moan echoed from the far corner of the room. The sound of shifting fabric filled my ears. We'd reached the point of audience participation, and I knew that if I turned around, I'd find people making out or surreptitiously touching their partners in the darkness. Some nights, I sat in the front row because I wanted all my focus on the show. Others, I chose the way back, so I could watch not only the stage, but everyone around me. I was still undecided as to which was hotter. As a voyeur, it was hard to choose.

Morgan finally put us out of our misery, leaning in without hesitation, his fingers dimpling his wife's hips as he fit his mouth to her pussy. The moan she let out was low and ragged, a sound that raised goose bumps along my skin. Morgan angled his head slightly, and whatever he'd done made Steph shudder, her lips popping open to form a perfect O of surprise.

"Again," she said, releasing the chair to palm her own breasts.

Morgan repeated the movement. With another moan, Steph exposed her chest and bumped her fingers over her nipples. The sight made me want to squirm in my seat. God, these two were fucking hot.

"Touch yourself," Steph panted.

Morgan didn't have to be told twice. He dropped a hand to the waistband of his pants and made quick work of the button and zipper. His cock sprang free, and then one big hand was wrapped around it, his arm bobbing as he worked himself.

My curiosity got the better of me, and I glanced sideways again, wondering what Junior thought of all this. The mob was notorious for its misogyny and machismo. Watching another man jerk off was probably against *all* their unwritten rules and could get you labeled as whatever their current favorite homophobic slur was. But Junior didn't look like he was ready to bolt. He was tilted just slightly forward in his seat, watching the stage with rapt attention, his gaze shifting from where Morgan's head was buried in his wife's pussy, up to where Steph played with herself and back again like he couldn't decide where he'd rather look.

Was he . . . *into this?*

A glance at his lap revealed that he was now rock hard. I could see the entire outline of his large dick shoved down a pant leg. That couldn't be comfortable. It must have been hot and tight, cutting off blood flow, and . . . oh no. Now wasn't the time to imagine him pulling it out to readjust himself. But there went my goddamn mind anyway, reminding me of how smooth it was, the way he'd liked it when I'd licked my way around the underside of his head. Saliva pooled in my mouth at the memory of trying to fit something that big down my throat.

He shifted, like he felt me watching him, and started to turn my way.

I snapped my gaze back to the stage before getting caught. Real nice, Lauren. Vow to never think of the man again only to imagine gagging down his dick five seconds later.

An image of Taylor chanting *Hate sex, hate sex, hate sex* popped into my mind unbidden.

No. I couldn't. That would be too much. Hook up with the man who'd stood by and watched my world burn to the ground? Absolutely not. I had too much self-respect for that. As soon as this scene was over, I'd go grab Moriah and the biggest strap-on I could find and fuck her in one of the upstairs bedrooms like the well-adjusted adult I was.

Stephanie let out a desperate moan, her hands falling from her breasts to her husband's head. She dug her nails into his hair and gripped him tight, her hips shifting as she rode his face. Softer moans echoed hers throughout the crowd, and I heard hot, wet noises from a few rows back. I wouldn't be surprised if Steph wasn't the only one getting great head right now.

Instead of working himself faster, Morgan released his dick to put both hands on his wife's hips, helping her thrust into him as he

87

tongue-fucked her. I had to bite my lip to keep from whimpering at the sight, especially when Steph's eyes fluttered shut and her head fell back.

"Babe, I'm close," she said, moving at a frenetic pace.

Morgan, knowing what she needed, stayed right where he was, pulling her into him as she started to lose the rhythm. She came a heartbeat later, shuddering and moaning, a blush stealing into her cheeks as she called out her husband's name. It was stunning, beyond sexy. All it would take at this moment was the brush of someone's fingers against my clit and I would come, too.

Junior let out an audible exhale beside me. I saw his right hand white-knuckling his knee out of the corner of my eye. He turned my way, and, knowing it was probably a mistake, I lifted my eyes to his.

"Lo," he said, his voice deliciously rough. His pupils were blown wide, a wild look in them that made me worry he was about to drag me to the floor and fuck me right here in front of everyone.

God help me, in my current state, I might let him.

This was the real reason I'd been so desperate for him to leave. I'd told myself that it was because I was afraid he would embarrass me, but the truth was, I was more worried I'd embarrass myself. Ryan and Taylor were in the crowd, and I'd *just* spilled my guts to them about how much Junior had hurt me. How pathetic would it look if I hooked up with him right after?

Movement onstage drew my gaze forward again. Morgan had scooped Steph off the chair, her legs wrapped around his waist as he carried her to the bed.

The real show was about to begin.

10

JUNIOR

I'D NEVER BEEN SO AROUSED in my goddamn life, not just physically, but emotionally, too. It bordered on stimulation overload. Until this moment, I hadn't realized how numb I'd become to everything, how much my work had stolen from me. I was completely desensitized from the nonstop pain and death, because that's what I *had* to be to keep from turning into a full-blown psychopath. Now I was firing on all synapses for the first time in years, and I didn't want the feeling to end.

Lauren's eyes were on the stage again, but I couldn't pull my gaze from her. She sat upright in her seat, hands death-gripping each other like she didn't trust what she would do with them if they were allowed to roam free. Pink stained her cheeks and upper chest, and every now and then her lips parted on a shaky exhale.

At least I wasn't the only one about to implode, but knowing she was just as turned on as I was didn't help my current situation. I wanted to grab her, drag her onto my lap, shred that flimsy excuse for a dress with my bare hands, and fucking *ruin* her with my cock.

For the first time in my life, I kept my desires in check. I felt dangerous, out of control in a way that made me distrust myself. The last thing I wanted was to hurt her any more than I already had.

What the fuck was happening to me right now? Sure, I liked sex as much as the next guy, and I'd watched plenty of porn, but watching live sex in a room full of other people was never something I'd fantasized about.

A groan hit my ears, and I turned my head even more, glancing past Lauren into the dimly lit crowd. It was a mistake. Because the performers weren't the only ones enjoying their evening. I clocked a woman on her knees, her head bobbing as she blew a man. Two guys jerked each other off right next to them, and behind that pair, a petite Asian woman with lavender hair rode a giant redheaded man, reverse cowgirl style so they could both watch the show. I swiveled in my seat before we could make eye contact, but facing forward was just as bad; the couple onstage had moved to the bed.

"I need it, Steph," the man said, his voice dropping into a growl.

"Take it, Morgan," she told him. "Take this pussy."

Oh, fuck.

Morgan flipped her onto her stomach and wrenched her hips up. He positioned his dick against her entrance, gripped her hips, and thrust deep. Steph let out a startled gasp that was quickly followed by a moan. And then they were moving, him shunting his hips forward, her using her hands to push backward. This close, I could see every vein on his cock, heard his balls slapping against her pussy. I even smelled it, that indistinguishable musky scent of sex.

This was going to ruin porn for me. Because how the fuck was I expected to jerk off to a video after seeing the real thing live and in person?

"You squeeze me so good, Steph," Morgan groaned.

"You fill me so good," she told him.

"I want another one," he demanded, slipping a hand around her hip to stimulate her clit while he continued to fuck her. "Let me feel you come around your husband's dick."

My eyebrows rose at that. They were married? For some reason, I'd assumed they were just two people paid to fuck in front of a crowd. I'd never imagined that a couple in a committed relationship would want to do something like this. Not that I was judging; I'd just literally never thought about anything like this before. All of the relationships in my life were the hetero-normative kind. The mob wasn't exactly known for its inclusivity, and in a way, I'd grown up pretty fucking sheltered because of it.

"I'm gonna come," Steph said, her hands digging into the comforter, her spine bowing as she rocked backward.

Morgan picked up the pace, his wife's moans gaining a keening edge. Other voices hit my ears, whispered supplications and devotions as the rest of the crowd followed Morgan and Steph into the abyss. My dick was so hard it felt like it might rip through the fabric of my pants. I was half tempted to adjust it but held back on the fear that the second I touched it, I'd end up jizzing all over myself.

"Yes, Steph," Morgan said, slamming into her as she came. "Good. Fucking. Girl."

Lauren whimpered beside me, and it was all I could do not to turn and look at her, not to betray the fact that I'd filed her response to praise away like I had all the other facts I'd collected over the past ten years.

"Where do you want it?" Morgan asked.

"On my tits," his wife answered.

He pulled out of her, and she turned to face him, yanking the bodice of her dress down to her waist. Morgan stroked himself once, twice, and then he was coming, spurting semen all over his wife's pretty breasts. The sounds of other people coming with him filled the room, and my arousal ratcheted up to an uncomfortable degree. I needed to get off, soon, or else this was going to turn into the worst case of blue balls I'd ever had in my life.

Onstage, Morgan let out one last groan and grinned down at his wife. She smiled back up at him, looking like the happiest woman on the planet, white streaking between the valley of her breasts. Hopefully she had a change of clothes backstage. And hopefully there was one hell of a janitor to clean up after this, because whatever was still happening behind me sounded *messy*.

Someone let out a catcall, and then everyone was cheering and clapping—everyone but those who were still moaning. Finally, as if just now realizing we were here, Morgan and Steph turned toward the crowd. I dropped my gaze but clapped along with everyone else. Watching them fuck was one thing. Making eye contact right after? That made me want to crawl out of my skin.

"Thank you," Morgan said.

His wife echoed him, and the side door opened again. I turned my head to see a woman carrying a small stack of hand towels enter the room. It was in that split second of distraction that Lauren slipped from her seat and attempted to sneak away.

Oh, Lo, I thought. *You should know better than this.*

I stood from my chair and stalked after her.

The hallway outside was just as dimly lit, but her white dress popped in the darkness, calling out to me like a beacon as I pursued her. She glanced over her shoulder and picked up speed when she saw me. I gave chase, wondering what she was thinking. She certainly wasn't behaving like a frightened woman. No screams, no calls for help, and I hadn't missed the fact that instead of fleeing back downstairs toward the safety of the crowded foyer, she was headed toward the end of the hall and a door with an illuminated "Exit" sign above it.

"Run, Lauren," I said, unable to stop myself. "Make it good for both of us."

She let out a noise torn between lust and panic and broke into as much of a run as she could manage in those sky-high heels.

I let her get a good head start, let her close in on the door, let her think she had a chance to get away before sprinting after her.

She hit the handle with both palms, shoving it open and darting past. Before she could slam it behind her, I got my boot inside the frame, the steel tip protecting my foot when the door bounced off it.

"Shit," she said, turning toward the stairs.

I grabbed her arm.

She finally opened her mouth to yell.

I clamped a hand over it and spun her, pinning her against the wall, stomach first, my body pressed against hers to keep her there. The door closed behind us, sounding like a coffin slamming shut. This close, Lauren smelled delicious, like sex and sugar, and I leaned down to nuzzle my nose against her neck, where the scent of her perfume was strongest.

"If you wanted to get me alone, all you had to do was ask," I told her.

She muttered something into my palm that sounded highly sarcastic.

I grinned and ground my arousal into her lower back, and she squirmed against it in a way that told me my instincts were right, and she was into this, at least a little bit. No fighting. No cries for help. No further attempts to banish me back to hell.

I wanted her to be *more* than a little into it, though. I wanted a willing participant, and it was time to swallow my lingering pride and do what it took to get her there.

"I'm sorry, Lo," I said. "For everything."

My palm muffled her response.

"Are you going to scream?" I asked.

She shook her head.

I pulled my hand away, but I kept the rest of myself shoved tight, not wanting her to bolt again if she suddenly turned skittish.

"Sorry isn't good enough," she said, her voice low and angry, her body betraying her as she pushed back into my arousal. "I lost all my friends. People thought I was crazy. I had to change schools, Junior."

I wrapped an arm around the top of her chest and pulled her into me. Fuck, she felt good. Warm, welcoming. Small enough to tuck her head beneath my chin. "I remember," I said. "I thought I was doing the right thing at the time."

She twisted in my arms and tried to shove me away, but I only held on tighter. "You ruined my life!" The words were punctuated with a fist to my chest.

"I know," I said as another punch glanced off my shoulder, this one weaker than the first, like her heart wasn't in it. "I wish I could go back, but I can't. Tell me what I can do to make it up to you. Beat Principal Michaels up again? Plant more drugs on Kelly?"

She went so still it felt like she'd stopped breathing. "What?"

I shifted, rubbing the side of my face against her temple. "Come on, Lo. You never wondered how Kelly wound up facing drug charges? Or why the man who refused to punish the worst of the bullies spent that summer in the hospital?"

"I thought it was a car accident," she breathed.

My lips skimmed the shell of her ear. "It wasn't."

She pushed back to stare up at me. "You did that?"

I'd done a hell of a lot more over the years, but what she didn't know wouldn't hurt her. "I did. It was the least they deserved. Just say the word, and I'll do worse."

"No, I . . . I don't want that," she said, sounding like she was trying to convince herself. "I don't want anyone hurt on my account."

"Are you sure?" I asked, smirking.

A slap to my shoulder. "Yes, psycho."

Unable to help myself, I ground closer to her, pushing her back against the wall, knowing she could feel how hard I was. "Then tell me what to do, Lo. Tell me how I can make you feel better. You want me to confess everything online? Tell the world how much I wanted you? I'll do it." Another lie, but I prayed she wouldn't call my bluff. Dad couldn't know about this. Not yet. From his tone the other night, he was just as against Lauren and I being together now as he was when we were kids.

She shook her head. "I don't want that either. I don't care what anyone thinks of me, especially not the assholes from the old neighborhood."

"Then tell me what you *do* want."

She was quiet for a beat, but then a slow, *evil* smile spread over her face, and when she finally spoke, her voice was steady, unwavering. Determined. "I want you to grovel."

I reared away from her. My gut reaction was to tell her to go fuck herself and then walk back out of her life. Me, Nico Emanuel Trocci, *grovel*? I was the one who made demands, made the rules. Who the fuck did she think she was talking to?

This is Lauren, you asshole, I reminded myself.

Still, it took me far too long to claw my way back from the brink. Goddamn this fucking temper of mine. Goddamn this pride. I was too used to getting my way. Too used to bouncing whenever something started to feel serious or the women I slept with tried to make demands. All my life, I'd kept things surface level. For good reason. I hadn't been lying to Alec earlier; I didn't want to do to anyone what my father had done to our mom. Didn't want to put them at risk from my enemies or make them constantly fear for my life.

But the plan was to get away from my father. Somehow. And that would nullify all of my reasons for avoiding commitment. If I was going to do this with Lauren, *really* do it, I needed to start making changes. None of this half-in, half-out bullshit. I had to be fully committed her. Take my asshole younger brother's advice and be willing to do whatever was necessary to get back in her good graces.

Because Lauren wasn't just anyone. She was the first—and probably the only—girl I'd ever loved. And how had I treated her? Like she meant nothing to me, like she was no one. Sure, I'd done it to protect her, and I would never be sorry for that, but I'd also never forgive myself for how much I'd been forced to hurt her by doing so, and if this queen was seriously considering letting me back into her life, then groveling was probably the lightest punishment I deserved.

Taking a deep breath, I turned her back around to face the wall, whispering into her ear, "Only for you, Lo."

And then I dropped to my knees.

11

LAUREN

I GASPED AS JUNIOR'S FACE pressed against my lower back. His hands gripped my thighs, fingers digging in. I'd told him to grovel, looking for an easy way out of this situation, expecting him to bolt, but instead, he'd fallen to the ground behind me.

I was half tempted to turn around just to see such a thing—I doubted Junior had *ever* supplicated himself for someone like this before—but it would put his face far too close to my pussy for my current state of mind. No, it was better to stay flattened against the cement wall, the chilly surface cooling my feverish skin, anchoring my last shred of sanity. And it had to be my *last* shred after the way I'd led him on a merry (more like horny) little chase to this back stairway.

What the hell was I thinking tonight? I was lucky my choices had ended with him on his knees behind me and not me cut up into pieces in a dumpster out back. Okay, maybe my more hysterical brain cells had formed that last thought, but my decision-making thus far had been *questionable* at best. Still, all wasn't lost. There was time to turn this bus around and start making smart choices, and that was exactly what I planned to do as soon as I gathered the willpower. And by gathered the willpower, I meant muzzled my lust. I was so turned on right now that if I turned to leave, I'd probably end up humping his face instead.

It would be so easy; he was *right there* behind me.

"I'm sorry," he said again, sounding like he actually meant it. "I'm so fucking sorry, Lauren, and I'll do anything to make it up to you. Please, let me make it up to you."

Oh, god. Why was the sound of a man debasing himself so fucking hot? It didn't help that his voice had gone low and gravelly, his accent thickening, tone deliciously rough.

He rubbed his face against my dress and dragged his fingers down my thighs. My knees trembled. I was too turned on for this, didn't trust myself to be the strong, independent woman I knew I was. There was a gorgeous man on the ground behind me, literally *begging* to make me feel good, and I could feel the feminism leaving my body as the urge to give in to him rose.

I must have been losing it. He had *just* confessed to ruining Kelly's life and breaking nearly every bone in our principal's body, and yet I was a split second away from rubbing my ass into him and telling him he could make it up to me by getting me off right here on this landing, where anyone could find us.

That thought sent my heart into a full gallop. I did like it when people watched . . .

"Please," Junior repeated, his hands shifting direction, moving higher. "Please, Lo. I'll do anything."

His voice was raw, *rough*, like he might break if I told him no. I hadn't felt this powerful in years, like I held his fate in my hands and all it would take was one word to either ruin or redeem him.

My breathing hitched as his hands slid beneath the hem of my dress, stroking up, up, all the way to my hips.

"Fuck," he ground out. "Are you bare beneath this dress right now?"

"Yes," I whispered into the concrete.

His forehead hit my low back, and he let out a pained sound. "That whole time you were sitting beside me with only this flimsy fabric covering you?"

I didn't respond. The answer was obvious.

"Let me touch you, Lo," he said, fingers sliding back down my waist. "Please let me touch you. I promise I'll make you feel good."

It felt like time slowed as I went to war with myself. This man had nearly ruined my life, had probably stalked me, definitely hurt people on my behalf, and done god knew what else to others. It would feel so *good* to say no. To ruin him like he had ruined me. But I was too soft-hearted for it, too fair. I couldn't bring myself to hurt Junior right now, not after the way he'd groveled. That couldn't have been easy for a man like him, with so much pride and ego. And yet he'd done it.

For me.

Because I'd asked him to.

Praying I wasn't about to make a huge mistake, I spread my legs. "Touch me."

He groaned and sent both hands straight to my pussy. One set of fingers landed on my clit while two more from the other slipped just inside my entrance, and *oh, fuck*, who had taught him how to do this? Gone were the searching, experimental touches I remembered from my youth. Junior was a man now, with a man's desires and a man's knowledge, and I didn't know if he was just *that good* at what he was doing or if the taboo nature of this encounter was what was pushing me toward the edge so quickly.

He shifted the angle of his hand, and a burst of heady pleasure rushed through my core. Oh, god. Oh, fuck. I was already clenching around him. *Junior Trocci* had his fingers knuckle-deep inside me, and I was about three seconds away from coming all over them.

My thighs trembled. I squeezed my eyes closed as a shudder wracked my body. The fingers stimulating my clit moved faster, the ones inside me pumped deeper, and before I knew what was happening, I was gasping, shaking, coming with such intensity that the noises I made were borderline feral.

Oh, god, *oh, god,* it felt good. Better than anything in recent memory, and I'd come *a lot* in that time. I almost felt betrayed by my own body, that Junior was the one to trigger such a strong reaction. It was unexpected, *overwhelming*, and it didn't help that I'd never come so fast in my goddamn life.

My knees turned to liquid beneath me.

Junior guided me down into his lap with one hand, the fingers of his other one still buried in my pussy. "I want to feel every last quiver," he said, doing *something* inside me that triggered a small aftershock of bliss.

I squirmed on him, grinding against his palm to drag the pleasure out. Holy shit.

"I still don't forgive you," I said, sounding far more breathy than I intended.

His lips dropped to my shoulder, and the bastard had the indecency to chuckle. "Then I guess I'll have to keep apologizing." The fingers inside me hooked forward, and his thumb went to my clit. "I'm sorry," he whispered. His other hand lifted to my breasts, spread wide so he could rub both nipples simultaneously. "I'm sorry."

I managed to hold still for all of two seconds before I arched into him, and . . . uh-oh. Why was I already spinning out again? Usually I needed a breather before I came a second time, but if Junior kept this up, I was going to—

The stairwell door flew open with a *bang!* I had just enough time to catch sight of two figures before Junior spun us away, pulling me close and blocking me from sight with his much larger body.

"Oh, uh . . . sorry?"

I recognized Ryan's voice immediately.

"Guess she didn't need rescuing after all," Taylor chimed in, sounding smug.

"You good, Lauren?" Ryan asked.

"I'm good," I told them.

"What about you, man-I'm-assuming-is-Junior?" Taylor asked. "You don't need rescuing, do you?"

"I'm good," he bit out.

"See?" Taylor said. "They're *fine*. Just having a good ole consensual fingerbang."

Oh, for the love of god.

Junior's breath warmed my neck. "Want me to get rid of them?"

"They're my roommates," I said.

"That's not a no."

I made a low, contemplative sound. "Maybe just Taylor."

"Hey!" she said, her outrage echoing through the stairwell.

Junior huffed a breath. It wasn't a laugh, but it was close.

"Sylvia called a meeting," Ryan said. "We came to find you."

"Be there in a few," I told them.

"Okay," they said. "But don't take too long. She looked stressed out."

"Yeah," Taylor chimed in. "About as stressed as you looked before you landed on stranger danger's fingers."

"Ryan," I groaned.

"I got her," they said.

The sound of a brief scuffle broke out.

"Ouch."

"Fuck."

"Goddamn it."

"I swear to Christ, Taylor."

The groaning of hinges announced the door opening.

"I told you she could take care of herself," Taylor said, her voice retreating.

"It's not *her* I was worried about," Ryan argued before the door clicked shut behind them, stifling Taylor's rebuttal.

My shoulders shook as I laughed. Leave it to them to both ruin a moment and somehow make it even better.

"Your roommates, huh?" Junior said as we untangled ourselves from each other and stood.

"Yup," I said. "Best friends and protectors a girl could ask for."

I turned to him to say more, warn him not to fuck with me or he'd have them to answer to, but his mask was pushed on top of his head, giving me an unobstructed view of his face. The words died on my tongue. Damn him for being so good-looking. It softened me to him even as I tried to resist, made me think of serial killers like Bundy and the Ken Doll Killer, men who'd gotten away with their crimes for so long because "No one that good-looking could do such terrible things." Not that Junior was as bad as them. Or at least I hoped he wasn't.

His eyes snared mine as he lifted the fingers that had just been inside me and slipped them into his mouth. I shivered at the look of hunger that swept over his face as he licked them clean. He'd openly confessed to framing a young woman and attacking a man. I should be pissed, terrified, but all I could think about was getting those fingers back inside my body as soon as possible.

"Here," he said, undoing his shirt. "The front of your dress got dirty from the wall."

I glanced down to see dark streaks smeared across the fabric over my breasts. "Tonight won't be the first time I walk out of Velvet a little worse for wear."

Junior's expression darkened. "I want their names and addresses."

"Ha ha," I said.

His face remained stone-cold, and his stupid dry sense of humor made it impossible to tell if he was joking or truly the psycho I'd accused him of being.

I opened my mouth to tell him to relax, but of course that's when he decided to shrug out of his shirt. Instead of a snarky remark, my mouth immediately turned drier than the Atacama, and all that came out of it was a dehydrated wheeze. Beneath the button-down, Junior wore a muscle top, and *goddamn*, he looked good in it. The white fabric made the dark tattoos sleeving his arms pop, and the way it was pulled taut across his broad chest had me wondering how much ink was hid—

"Are you *bleeding*?" I asked, staring at the red spot staining his side.

"It's nothing," he said.

I highly doubted that, but I held my response in check because I didn't want to seem like I cared by pressing the issue, nor did I really want to know what had happened to him, because I worried it might implicate me after the fact in one of his crimes.

He lifted a hand, offering his shirt to me. Part of me wanted to say no, to put some much-needed space back between us. Another part of me wanted to wrap myself up in his scent and live out my high school fantasies of Junior publicly claiming me with clothing like a quarter-back giving out his letterman jacket. Yet another, larger part of me was fricking freezing, so I took the damn shirt and tried to tell myself I was just being practical.

"Thank you," I said, sliding my arms into the sleeves.

He settled it around my shoulders, and yup, this was a mistake. Because it was warm from his body heat and smelled divine, like his sinful cologne and a hint of masculine musk I'd always found oddly alluring.

I lifted the collar to my nose and took a deep breath. "Is that brim-stone I detect?"

Instead of looking amused or firing something back at me, Junior hooked a finger beneath my chin and tilted my face up. Our gazes caught and held while a long, silent moment passed between us. I could see the thoughts swirling behind his eyes, but when he spoke, it was only to say, "Enjoy the rest of your night, Lo."

■　■　■

"What do you mean, he's raising the rent again?" Taylor asked.

She, Ryan, and I stood together amongst six other people in Sylvia's third-floor office. Antique sconces lit the room, casting the space in warm light. A plush rug was spread beneath our feet, and while the velvet couches and chairs dotting it were soft and inviting, none of us were sitting.

"Just what I said," Sylvia replied, the black fabric of her bodycon dress pulling tight as she paced on the other side of her desk. "The bastard knows we have nowhere else to go and is trying to milk us for all we're worth."

Behind her, the curtains were tied open to reveal the lights of the city. Their glow backlit her, casting her Brown skin in neon blues and fluorescent whites. I knew she was truly stressed, because she lifted a hand and rubbed it over her buzzed hair, a habit she'd picked up when she first cut her curls off and was still trying to break.

"How much does he want this time?" someone else asked.

Sylvia stopped pacing and turned to face us, bracing her knuckles on the desk. "He wants fifty dollars per square foot per year."

I did some quick math in my head.

"We can't afford that," Ryan said. "Can we?"

Sylvia shook her head.

"I can cover us the first month at least," I said.

"I'll cover the next," Taylor added.

"No," Sylvia said. "I appreciate the offer, but if we capitulate too easily, he'll try to milk us for even more. I think it's smarter to make it look like we're scrambling. Besides, if we end up staying, we need to find a way to make the rent sustainable in the long-term."

We spent the next fifteen minutes brainstorming ways to come up with the extra cash, not just to cover rent for the next few months, but so we'd have some savings on hand if we were able to move and needed to make serious renovations. Expanding ownership was mentioned, as well as creating a Kickstarter, limiting how many floors we rented, and threatening our landlord with death and dismemberment (Taylor's suggestion, though I was tempted to second it).

The trouble was, we were limited in our options. This city still had a handful of vice laws on the books, meant to govern the moral behavior of its citizens. Because of them, we were only allowed to operate by being a private, members-only club. We could never own property, and were instead forced to rent out buildings like the one currently housing Velvet. That way, we weren't facilitating sex and therefore couldn't be accused of prostitution; we were only facilitating the space for sex to maybe or maybe not take place in. We couldn't even sell liquor. Instead, we had bartenders who were available to mix and pour whatever drinks our patrons brought in themselves.

Our asshole landlord, a shady, aging man named Patrick McKinney, knew all this and used it against us. This was the third rent spike we'd faced in less than a year, and it was so steep that I worried Sylvia was right, and it would only get worse. Fifty dollars per square foot was an astronomical price. It was as much as what the big buildings charged downtown, and way too costly for a space this size, especially given its location.

Was this McKinney's way of forcing us out? It didn't make sense from a business perspective. We were the only people willing to pay the *current* rent on this place, let alone what he was threatening to raise it to. This wasn't exactly a nice part of town, and the only reason the interior looked as good as it did was because of our renovations. Once we were gone, the building would likely sit empty for god knew how long before McKinney finally came to his senses and dropped the rent back to a reasonable price.

Or was he just such a greedy bastard that he didn't realize he'd finally pushed us far enough that we were ready to look elsewhere? I'd only met him once, but that had been enough to get a good read on the man: slimy, misogynistic, bigoted, and stingy. Those types of people didn't tend to look at the big picture. They just took and took until there was nothing left or the people you preyed upon finally had enough and snapped (I really should have seconded Taylor's suggestion).

We ended the meeting with a game plan going forward, each of us taking on our own tasks. Ryan, Taylor, and I had volunteered to scope out other venues, research current rental standards for large spaces, and see if there were other, more progressive landlords in the city willing to take a look at our books and realize there was cash to be made from play clubs like ours.

I'd stop at nothing until I found a new home for Velvet. I loved this place with my whole heart, and not just because I had a stake in it. Velvet was the *only* play club in the city, a place for people to safely explore their kinks, own their sexuality, and discover their true selves. And that meant almost as much to me as my advocacy work.

I'd do anything to save it, and no one—not even gross old Patrick McKinney—was going to take it away from us.

12

LAUREN

"So did he *actually* grovel?" Taylor asked.

I nodded. "Got on his knees and everything."

She clutched my arm and gave a dramatic, full-body shudder.

"Did you just come?" I asked.

"I think I might have."

On her other side, Ryan rolled their eyes and tightened their hold on Walter's leash. There was a pigeon on the sidewalk up ahead, and Walter had proved he couldn't be trusted around them. It was an absolutely beautiful midsummer day. The cornflower-blue sky was dotted with fluffy clouds, there was a slight breeze, and it was like everyone in the city was out enjoying the weather, dressed in as little clothing as humanly possible.

Several days had passed since my run-in with Junior at Velvet, and in that time, my roommates and I had been like ships passing in the night, each of us busy with our own schedules, especially with the added stress of trying to book so many building tours for this afternoon. So far, we'd seen one with a central location that needed more renovations than we could afford, and another closer to our own neighborhood with great transportation links that was stunningly appointed but too expensive. Now we were taking a midafternoon break to grab coffee and catch up.

"How hard did you make him beg?" Taylor asked.

"Pretty hard," I said, "and I hate to admit it, but the man gives good grovel."

Ryan shook their head. "It's always the scariest people who have the secret begging kink."

Taylor's eyes met mine. "I'm going to need the whole sequence of events that led to you getting hand-fucked in the stairwell."

A passing gym bro heard her and nearly tripped over his own feet. Taylor had never learned how to moderate her volume in public, and it was one of my favorite things about her.

"It started before the show," I said. "Junior manipulated the guy I'd been sitting next to out of his seat and then apologized to me about church and what happened in high school."

"How'd he even know where to find you?" Ryan asked.

I kept my lingering suspicion about demonic summoning to myself and instead gave them a much more rational answer. "I think he must have followed me home after Mass."

Taylor perked up at that. "And where do we think that falls on the creepy versus hot scale?"

"Creepy," Ryan answered.

She nodded. "Cool, yeah, I was totally going to say that."

"Liar," Ryan said.

Taylor laughed. "Okay, fine, but it's a *little* hot that he went through all that trouble just to apologize."

It was, but . . . "I don't know if I'd give him that much credit," I said. "It felt more calculated than that. I keep thinking of Junior as the kid I grew up with, and I need to stop. He could be much more dangerous now."

Ryan nodded. "Especially if he's spent the past decade in the mob. Who knows what kind of fucked-up shit he's capable of."

They had a point there. "Exactly."

Taylor's expression turned contemplative. "Did you feel unsafe with him at any point?"

I thought back over that night. I'd been surprised and worried when he showed up, and even a little afraid, but the fear was more about

Junior embarrassing me than harming me. And after the show, when he'd told me to run in the hall, all I'd felt was excitement. It was like I was back in high school, racing through a corridor to get to our latest meeting spot before we got caught.

"No," I admitted. "I never felt like I was in danger."

"But what if your instincts are wrong?" Ryan pressed.

"I'll be careful," I said. "We can stick to the buddy system, and if he shows up at Velvet again, I can, I don't know, find some way to avoid him."

"Is that really what you want to do?" Taylor asked. "After he, you know . . ." She formed a circle with her left hand and then proceeded to jam three fingers from her right one in and out of it while making suctioning noises with her mouth.

I slapped her hands out of the air. There were children nearby. "Yes, I'm sure. I was horny, and he was there. It doesn't have to be anything more than that."

Ryan narrowed their eyes at me, seeing right through my bullshit like always. "Yeah, but *is it* more than that?"

We'd reached the coffee shop, and I used the excuse of holding the door open for them to delay answering. Sure, Junior turned me on, and it was fun to banter back and forth with him, but I wasn't looking for anything other than a casual hookup right now, and nothing about our shared history was casual. Nothing about the way he'd *begged me* to forgive him was casual.

"It's nothing more than that," I told Ryan when we got in line. And I meant it. Junior had been my first and worst heartbreak; I wasn't going to give him a chance to do it again.

Taylor rolled her eyes. "Fine, then at least give us all the juicy details about what happened between the two of you."

"When we sit down," I promised. There were too many ears close to us to go into detail in line.

Once we were seated at one of the café tables outside, I filled my roommates in on the rest of what happened, sparing no details, because Taylor threatened me with bodily harm if I did.

"And you're really going to avoid him after he made you come that hard?" Taylor asked when I was done.

I eyed her over the rim of my latte. "Did you already forget about the stalking?"

"Pssh," she said. "Who amongst us hasn't stalked someone?"

"I haven't," I told her.

Ryan coughed, and I swiveled my gaze to them. They lifted a brow at me. "Are you forgetting that time you helped me follow my senior crush home after school so we could see how close her parents' house was to mine?"

I grimaced. "Not our best moment."

Taylor leaned forward in her chair. "Or when Jackson and I became exclusive, and you made that fake Instagram account and slid into his DMs to test his loyalty?"

I pointed at Ryan. "It was as much their idea as it was mine!"

Ryan turned beet red and swiveled toward Taylor. "Only because Brett had hurt you so bad, and we wanted to make sure Jackson wasn't another fuckboy!"

"Also," I said. "Technically, that was catfishing and not stalking."

Taylor grinned. "And that somehow makes it better?"

Well, this conversation was going sideways. Time to bring us back on track. "Regardless of whether or not we condone stalking, no, I don't plan on seeing him again." My mind went back to the other night and what might end up being our final encounter. "To give him credit, his apology did seem sincere."

"I thought you said you didn't need him to apologize?" Taylor said.

I smirked. "I don't. I just wanted to see him beg a little."

Ryan shook their head. "You diabolical little bitch."

I nodded, unrepentant, and took a sip of my latte.

They sobered. "I think you're right about needing to be careful around him, though. Aside from the stalking, that confession about framing your old friend and attacking the principal is next-level."

"I know," I said. "He didn't sound at all remorseful about either one."

Taylor shrugged. "I think it's romantic."

Ryan let out an exasperated breath. "Of course you do."

"No, think about it," Taylor said, and for once, she seemed serious. "This has star-crossed lovers written all over it. By lying about hooking up with Lauren, he thought he was saving her, and then he punished the other people who'd wronged her. Guerrilla justice."

"That's so fucked-up, though," Ryan argued.

"I didn't say it wasn't. But two things can be true simultaneously. It can be both fucked-up and deeply romantic." Taylor turned to me with hearts in her eyes. "Like he was trying to protect his fair maiden from afar."

I glanced behind us, looking for the maiden she was referring to. "Oh, you meant me?"

"Yes, you," Taylor said, leaning forward to grab my arms. Her pastel hair swung into the space between us, dark eyes wild as she started to shake me. "Why won't you let him love you?!"

People around us turned to stare.

"Will you quit it, you lunatic?" I said, pulling out of her grip. "I just . . ." God, how to explain all the things I was feeling? "I can't let him back in, because I know he'll only hurt me again, but I won't deny the attraction is still there." Understatement. The attraction had grown from a spark into a blazing inferno. I could practically *see* the flames creeping closer while I sat and drank my latte, a little text bubble floating above my head declaring that this was fine, everything was fine.

"So don't let him in," Taylor said. "What's wrong with keeping it casual?"

I blew out a breath. "Aside from all the red flags?"

She nodded.

"Maybe I don't want to get sucked back into the past," I said. "I already knew Junior was going through some shit at the time, and I see his reasoning, even if I don't entirely agree with it or understand what he was so worried about. And while I do believe he's sorry, being around him reminds me not only of what happened, but what happened after. It was a really dark time in my life. I felt so lost, so let down by not only the kids my age, but by the adults meant to protect me. And the *shame* . . ."

The shame of everyone thinking I was crazy, of them ripping apart my fan fiction after Kelly told them my pen name, of them demonizing my fantasies, making me feel like I was bad or broken or *disturbed* just for having them.

I shook my head, needing a minute. Walter, sensing my distress, stood from where he'd been sprawled at Ryan's feet and put his head in my lap. He really was the best boy. I reached down and stroked a hand between his ears, ruffling the fur at the back of his neck and scratching beneath his collar, just where he liked it. His eyes slitted in euphoria, tail thumping against the ground.

Taylor scooted her chair closer and slung her arm around my shoulder. "You don't have to say anything else. I get it."

I smiled at her, grateful. Taylor understood shame culture better than most. Like me, she'd been raised with a strict Christian upbringing, only instead of being Catholic, she was Mormon. And adopted. Her white parents had been unable to conceive and desperately wanted children, so they flew to Vietnam and welcomed both Taylor and her older sister, Tasha, into their lives. Tasha was the golden child, the perfect straight-A student turned trad wife with a bundle of kids. Taylor had been the "problem child," though that was a relative term. For all intents and purposes, she was a normal kid, but to her super-strict parents and their borderline cultish faith? She was beyond saving.

We'd both put in a lot of hours with our therapists trying to heal from our experiences, and though we never, ever let anyone make us feel bad about ourselves now, the old scars were still there. Who could blame me for not wanting to reopen mine?

Across from me, Ryan fiddled with their empty coffee cup. "So, what are you going to do if Junior pops up somewhere while you're there?"

"Hide," I declared. "My hormones can't be trusted around him."

"That face of his is a problem," Taylor said.

Relief rolled through me, knowing I wasn't the only one affected by it. "Right?"

"He *is* pretty," Ryan agreed, sounding like they didn't want to.

I nodded. "He's funny, too. Dry, sarcastic, but it works."

Taylor leaned closer. "And the way he shielded you with his body when we busted down that door?" She eyed me. "I'm telling you, girl. The man has a white knight kink."

Ryan tipped their head sideways. "Is that a kink?"

I met their gaze. "Literally everything is a kink if you think about it long enough."

They looked unconvinced. "Is that true?"

"Absolutely," I said.

Their eyes narrowed.

"How about a topic change?" I asked to take the heat off me. "I obviously need more time to process everything that happened."

Taylor swirled the dregs of her coffee. "Well, I did get a kind of weird PPV request from a sub and was hoping to get your perspectives on it."

"Weird how?" Ryan asked, and I was grateful they both let the Junior conversation go so easily. They truly were the best friends a girl could ask for.

"Weird like, they want a video of me naked, covered in olive oil and herbs, with vegetables spread out around me," Taylor said. "They even requested that I put an apple in my mouth and baste myself."

Ryan raised their brows. "Baste, like . . . *baste*?"

Taylor shook her head. "No, not shove a baster up my hoo-hah. They want me to baste myself like a turkey."

"Oh, no," I said, gripping her shoulder.

"So it *is* a weird request?" she asked. "Is it a food fetish or something?"

Ryan reached out to grip her other side. "No, honey. It isn't a food fetish."

Taylor looked between us, clearly confused.

I dropped my voice. "The man wants to eat you. And not in a hot way."

Her expression flashed to shock. "No."

Ryan nodded. "It's a cannibal fetish."

Taylor looked like she was going to be sick. "*No*."

"Is this your first one?" I asked.

"WHAT DO YOU MEAN, IS THIS MY FIRST CANNIBAL?" she screeched.

Walter jumped up and started barking his head off. Ryan scrambled to calm him down. Deciding it was time to go, I hauled Taylor to her feet, and between Ryan and me, we got her moving, fleeing the scene of the crime. We were 100 percent going to get banned from this café if we stuck around any longer.

"Is he really a cannibal?" Taylor asked in a quavering tone.

"He might be," Ryan told her. "Or he might just fetishize it. Either way, it's super against the Me4U terms of service."

"What do I do? Report him?"

"You immediately block him," I said, because unfortunately, I'd been through this rodeo before. "And then, yes, report him. You'll need to take a ton of screenshots to send to Me4U admin, but in my experience, they're pretty swift to ban cannibals. I can help you when we get home."

Sometimes I forgot that Taylor was still relatively new to sex work. I felt terrible for not warning her that this was a possibility, but I honestly thought she already knew about the darker side of what we did. Tonight, I'd sit down and talk to her about the other, lesser-known things to watch out for.

Ryan's phone dinged, and they pulled it out of their clutch to check it. "Oh, whoops," they said. "We're late for our next appointment."

We picked up our pace and hightailed it over to our third viewing for the day, all talk of stalkers and cannibals shelved until we were back in the safety of our own home.

13

JUNIOR

I WONDER WHAT LAUREN'S DOING right now, I thought.

It had been too long since I'd seen her, too long since I'd watched a couple of strangers fuck right in front of me, too long since I'd felt her pussy contracting around my fingers as she came, and I was starving for more. I'd been busy as hell since then, knee-deep in sniffing out a rat in our organization, but thoughts of Lauren and the voyeur room from Velvet kept sneaking in to distract me, and I knew I wouldn't be able to think straight until I got her in my arms again.

Across from me, someone farted.

I yanked my shirt over my nose and kicked out at the middle-aged Italian man who'd done it. Everyone else around us chimed in with their own kicks, punches, and fuck yous. Van etiquette 101 clearly stated there was no ripping it in the back, because it wasn't like we could ventilate this space. It was the middle of the goddamn night, and it'd look suspicious as fuck if the rear door of an unmarked van parked on the side of the road suddenly cracked open and a bunch of green-faced men spilled out.

"Jesus, Vinny," the guy sitting next to him moaned. "Did you eat gluten again?"

Vinny gave us an apologetic shrug. "We went to my Ma's house for dinner. What was I supposed to do? Tell her I couldn't eat her food?"

The van was divided. On the one hand, we were all suffering the consequences of Vinny's actions. On the other, not eating the food an Italian woman set in front of you was an egregious insult.

It took five minutes for the smell to clear—or for us to get used to it (shudder)—and by that time we'd all settled back down. I hated stakeouts. Especially if I spent them stuck in the back with the goons. It was boring as fuck, smelly, and hot, especially in the summer. By the time I got away, I'd be ready to scour my skin off in the shower.

But this was the job. I couldn't trust these idiots to get shit done themselves, and even though most of them were older than me, I still had to babysit them. It made me understand Dad a little better, especially his reason for trusting so few people to carry out his orders.

A shoulder bumped against mine, and Alec, trapped in this hellhole with me, leaned in. "You're quiet tonight."

"I got shit on my mind."

"Lau—"

I elbowed him to keep him from speaking her name in front of everyone else. People loved to claim that women were the worst gossips, but they didn't hold a candle to middle-aged Italian men, who'd turned shit-talking into a fine art.

"Girl related?" Alec corrected, rubbing his ribs.

"No," I lied.

"Did you see her again?"

"No."

"And how did it go?" he pressed. Fuck, he couldn't take a hint.

"It didn't."

"Oooh," Vinny said across from us. "Junior's in trouble with his old lady?"

"What?" someone from the far end of my side asked. "Junior's got himself a new woman?"

The entire van turned my way, and I suddenly found myself the center of their unwanted attention. Goddamn nosy busybodies.

Alec and I spoke at the same time.

"No."

"Yes."

I shot my traitor brother a warning look.

"It's still new," he said.

I was going to kick his ass as soon as I had enough room to swing on him.

"And it's not going well?" someone asked.

"I told you it's not going at all," I bit out. "There's nothing to talk about, so everyone can shut up now."

Vinny sniffed. "You must have really messed up."

Jesus fucking Christ.

Beside him, Jimmy sat forward. "I agree."

Nods all around.

"I'm not discussing this with you assholes," I said.

Vinny and Jimmy shared offended looks. "Why not? Between the two of us, we've been married twice as long as you've been alive."

"To six different women," I pointed out.

"Yeah," Alec said. "But that means they know what *not* to do."

The two men nodded sagely.

"We're not having this discussion," I said.

"You plan to apologize, right?" Jimmy asked, ignoring me.

"It's important to do that, even if you don't think you did anything wrong," Vinny added.

"Fuck apologizing," Enzo, one of the big dudes by the door, said. "Alphas never apologize."

I eyed him. "Alpha, huh? Is that a furry thing?"

Alec choked.

No one else seemed to pick up on the joke, and I sighed, lamenting the fact that most of the people I hung out with were too old to get my humor.

"You could buy her flowers," Jimmy said.

"Or chocolates," someone else chimed in.

How had I lost control of this situation so fast?

"Personally, I'm a fan of the grand gesture," another man added.

Vinny looked impressed. "Good idea. Take her out to her favorite place and propose."

"Propose?" I said. "Are you out of your fucking mind?"

"What? Proposals have gotten me out of all sorts of trouble."

"Yeah," Jimmy chimed in. "They're like the universal get-out-of-jail-free card."

Alec started shaking with silent laughter. Kicking his ass wasn't good enough. I was going to take him out in the woods and bury him alive in our graveyard of oddities for this.

Suddenly, the walkie-talkie in my hand crackled to life. One thing I could say about these idiots: They knew when it was *really* time to shut the fuck up.

My brother Stefan's voice came over the line. "His car is pulling into the neighborhood."

"Get ready," I said.

Around me, everyone began pulling on balaclavas and checking their weapons.

"You know the drill," I told them. "We hit him before he gets to the door. And you better not fucking fire on him unless it's to save your own ass. Lorenzo wants him alive."

The walkie-talkie crackled again. "He's rounding the corner."

Enzo grabbed the door handles, ready to throw them open.

I hit the talk button. "Tell us when."

We all shifted forward on the benches, ready and waiting. Anticipation coursed through my body. Our target didn't know he'd been made, but taking him by surprise like this didn't come without risks. Most men in our line of work carried at least one weapon on them at all times. And rats tended to be more paranoid than most—we'd likely face some resistance. Stefan had been in position for hours, scouting out the rat's house. No one else had come or gone in that time, but it didn't mean the man didn't have allies hiding inside, ready to jump to his defense.

It was so quiet inside the van, you could hear a pin drop.

"Go," Stefan said.

Enzo threw open the doors, and we swarmed into the night.

■ ■ ■

Hours later, Alec and I were back at our parents' house. Stefan had arrived well before us, his part of the operation ending when ours began. Greg was who the fuck knew where. These days, he spent more time around dead bodies than live ones, and Dad had him doing all sorts of weird shit with them I didn't want to know about.

I'd showered, changed, and was heading down to the basement incinerator with my bloodstained clothes from earlier when Dad stopped me at the bottom of the stairs. His nickname growing up was the Crooner because he bore a striking resemblance to Sinatra, minus the baby blues. His eyes were cold, dark, and hostile, and I could tell from the look on his face that he wanted to ream me out for staying away for so long. My shoulders stiffened as I braced for an argument.

"How'd it go?" he asked.

"Cakewalk," I told him. "He didn't even get a shot off. We were in and out of there in less than ten minutes."

Dad's gaze dropped to my bloody clothes in question.

"I said he didn't get a shot off, not that he didn't put up a fight."

Dad scoffed. "And you couldn't get him under control without ending up covered in evidence?" He shook his head. "Just when I think you're ready for the big leagues, you prove you're still an amateur."

A sarcastic response was on the tip of my tongue, but heroically, I kept it in, knowing it would only make this situation worse. Instead, I stood there in silence, fuming, because I didn't trust myself to speak. No matter what I did, it would never be good enough for him. There would always be a criticism or an insult.

"I'm going to bed," he said. "You better still be here for breakfast in the morning. Your mother has overnight French toast in the fridge."

I turned and went to burn my clothes, staring at the flames as I mulled over my options. I couldn't keep doing this. Just being here, in this fucking house, set me on edge. Dad only responded to strength and threats, and I was beginning to think that I might end up having to blackmail him into letting me go. God knew I had more than enough dirt on him. I couldn't threaten to go to the cops or the Feds with it—that would be a death sentence if anyone else found out. But maybe I could threaten to tell one of Dad's rivals about one of the *many* times he had smiled to their face while secretly stabbing them in the back.

I'd need to have everything else lying flat first, though, a way to make my own money, *clean money*. I had some saved up, but if I had any chance of offering Lauren the kind of pampered lifestyle she deserved, I needed more, some steady stream of income so I didn't spend the rest of my life draining my savings and stock accounts.

Back in my room, I locked the door behind me and lifted the edge of the area rug closest to my closet. Beneath it was a section of floorboard that I'd pried loose back in high school, the only hiding spot my nosy brothers still hadn't discovered. I pulled the floorboard up and breathed a sigh of relief to see my stash still there. A small floral-patterned notebook was hidden at the very bottom of the pile, and I lifted it out and brushed the dust off before replacing the floorboard and rug.

It was Lauren's diary from high school. I'd stolen it from Kelly's room the night I planted drugs on her. At the time, I'd been worried that fucking turncoat would post more of Lauren's writing online. Once a traitor, always a traitor.

I hadn't looked at it in years, but Jimmy and Vinny's stupid comments about grand gestures had gotten stuck in my head, and an idea was starting form because of them. This diary contained all the things Lauren and I had done together, all the things she'd still wanted to do with me. They were written just for her and me, her most secret fantasies. And what had I done? Pretended they were lies. Of course a normal apology wasn't enough to soften her to me. But what if I gave her something else?

I flipped the journal open and riffled through it until I landed on the night of the fireworks. Reading the sequence of events from Lauren's perspective had been eye-opening all those years ago, and still brought me up short today. I'd known she had a thing for me before that night, but I had no idea just how deep her crush ran until the first time I'd read these pages.

My eyes skimmed over the next entry. It was from the day after the fair. I felt guilty all over again while reading it, seeing how excited she had been, wondering whether or not I was as into her as she was me. Knowing I'd give her a few weeks of bliss only to turn around and crush her made me feel ten times worse than what I'd just done to that rat.

I flipped ahead to her final "fan fiction" about us, the one we'd never gotten to play out. In Lauren's fantasy, we met at the corner arcade in our old neighborhood and she sucked me off in the photo booth while the camera snapped pictures of us together.

I shook my head. Even back then, she'd had a thing for camwork.

My plan began solidifying as I started reading the entry over from the beginning. Vinny was right; flowers and chocolates weren't going to cut it. I needed a grand gesture if I was going to convince Lauren to forgive me, and this journal was the key to redeeming myself. Her memories about it were probably bad because of what happened afterward, but what if we reclaimed them, turned them into *good* memories instead?

A ping sounded from my pocket. I pulled my phone out to see another Me4U photo message from Lauren. In it, she sat spread eagle on her bed, naked, her hands barely covering herself.

Feeling slutty tonight, her message read.

I tapped the "tip now" option and sent her twenty bucks, and another message came through almost immediately. Her hands were still there, but instead of blocking some of the best parts of her from sight, one was on a breast, her nipple pinched between two fingers, and the other was between her spread legs.

Wish these were your hands on me instead, the new message read.

If I got my way, my hands would soon be all over her.

14

LAUREN

I EMERGED FROM MY BEDROOM dressed in comfy sweats. It was late Wednesday night, and it was only me and Ryan in the apartment, because Taylor was sleeping at Jackson's. Suspiciously, it was her turn to cook, and if she thought staying over there would get her out of feeding me, she was forgetting that I'd memorized her DoorDash login.

I rounded the hallway into the kitchen, Walter right on my heels, and was surprised to find Ryan at the island, eating a bowl of cereal.

"You're still up?" I asked, going to the fridge.

"Yup," they said in between bites. "Maxine sent me her video late, and I decided to get it done tonight."

In addition to helping Taylor and me, Ryan did editing work for several other NSFW content creators, and was growing increasingly popular. For good reason. They were great at their job, knew just when to cut clips together, had an amazing understanding of color theory, and were very professional and discreet.

"You've been burning the candle at both ends all week," I said, pouring myself a glass of chilled water from our carafe. "Have you thought any more about hiring someone else?" I set the water back inside the fridge and turned to find them nodding.

"I think it's getting to the point that I have to. I'm just dreading interviewing people."

"An introvert's worst nightmare. Want me to help?"

Ryan looked relieved. "If you don't mind, yes, please."

I opened our junk drawer and pulled out a notepad and pen. "Number one: Must be hot."

Ryan yanked the paper away from me. A brief scuffle broke out over the pen, and I lost the fight when they pump-faked flicking me in the tit. Once I stopped grumbling about how that was obviously cheating, we got down to business and wrote out an actual list of requirements and interview questions. It was surprisingly extensive, but we both agreed that if Ryan was going to do this, they needed to do it right.

We were just finishing up when my phone buzzed. I pulled it out and nearly dropped it when I saw the notification.

"What's up?" Ryan asked.

In answer, I slid the phone across the island. They caught sight of the video request on my screen and started choking. "*Five grand?*" Another round of coughing. "What the hell do they want you to do, film an entire porno?"

"That's only enough for half of one," I joked, pulling the phone back. My eyes flew over the screen as I read on. The request was from NT95. They'd asked for an hour-long session, and when I went to click on "details" there was just an address.

"Oh, Jesus," I said.

"What's wrong?" Ryan asked.

"They want to meet."

Ryan shook their head. "I swear people don't know how to use their eyes anymore."

"No shit," I said, trying not to feel betrayed.

I spelled it out in several places on my Me4U, including in my custom work rules, that I didn't meet in person, and yet I still got several requests like this every month. Usually people just wanted to meet and fuck for free, because audacity. Until now, I didn't think NT95 would join their ranks. He'd never crossed a line before, was one of the few subs I thought I could trust to be a decent person. It sucked to find out I was wrong about him.

I'm so sorry, I typed, sticking to my professional façade. *But I don't meet in person. Please see my "Dos and Don'ts" list here.* I attached a link and hit send before denying the request.

My phone pinged almost immediately. It was another request from NT95, and he'd raised the offer by two grand. Some people just couldn't take no for an answer.

I pulled up the message to deny it again but froze. There was a picture attached. I zoomed in, frowning, not knowing what I was seeing at first. It looked like a page ripped out of a notebook, on lined paper, with—

The phone fell from my fingers and clattered onto the kitchen island.

Ryan stood. "Are you okay?"

I shook my head so fast the room blurred.

"Lauren? You're scaring me."

They crowded close to one side while Walter pressed in on the other, whining, knowing something was wrong.

"My diary," I managed. "He has my high school diary." How did he have my diary? My gaze darted from the basement door to the couch to the closed curtains, imagining perverts hiding behind every corner of the house. No, that couldn't be. If there was someone else in here, Walter would have sniffed them out by now and tried to convince them that he was starving to death and needed to be fed.

Ryan scooped the phone up, and it immediately beeped with another message. Their eyes flashed wide as they read it.

"What does it say?" I squeaked, cringing down in my seat like if I somehow made myself a small enough target, I wouldn't be hit with whatever was about to come out of Ryan's mouth.

Their gaze lifted to mine. "Please, Lo."

I nearly fell off my barstool.

Holy shit.

NT95 was Junior.

Junior was a sub.

My first sub. My *favorite* sub.

And he had my high school diary.

125

I reached for the phone, my voice eerily steady. "I need to see something."

Ryan handed it over, and I finished reading the journal page Junior had sent and then looked up the address he'd asked me to meet him at. As I'd guessed, it was the location of the arcade. I set the phone back down and turned to Ryan, explaining what I'd pieced together.

They frowned. "And he wants to what? Pay you seven grand to go play out your final request?"

"I can't think of what else he could possibly want for that price. Unless this is all some elaborate ruse and he plans to kill me, skin me, turn me into Lauren jerky and spend the next ten years slowly consuming me piece by hard-to-digest piece." What can I say? Thanks to Taylor, I had cannibals on the mind.

Ryan scrunched their nose. "I doubt that. One bite, and he'd realize how bad you taste and throw the rest away."

That startled a laugh out of me, but it sounded low-key unstable, and I quickly cut myself off. "It was Junior all along."

Ryan slowly dropped onto the stool beside me, their expression wary. "I know."

"He was my first subscriber."

They grimaced. "I know."

I buried my face in my hands. NT95 had spent thousands of dollars on custom PPV. We'd spent hundreds of hours sexting each other. I'd even commiserated with him over what a narcissistic asshole his father was, which, hahahahaha, what an understatement.

My mind reeled. I couldn't reconcile what was happening. I liked NT95. I valued him as a sub, borderline thought of him as a *friend*, and it was fucking Junior Trocci this whole time?

"Sooo," Ryan said, "I think it's safe to say the stalking didn't start recently."

I laughed again, and yup, it was definitely hysterical. I *felt* hysterical. My entire body buzzed like I was standing too close to a downed wire. Emotions flashed through me, one after another, betrayal and confusion and rage and something giddy that felt oddly like . . . glee? No, no, that couldn't be right. I must have been having a stroke.

"What are you going to do?" Ryan asked.

I lifted my head up. "Change my identity and move to Europe. I hear Denmark has pretty strict stalking laws."

"I'm serious," Ryan said.

I shrugged. "I have no idea, but that's so much money. Money that could be put toward more outreach programs or ads talking about the bill."

"Uh-uh," Ryan said. "None of that. Take your advocacy work out of the equation. No one would want you to put yourself in danger over it."

I tore my gaze away from theirs. Was I really in danger? My thoughts spiraled back over the past several years. NT95 had been Junior, all this time, just quietly being my number one supporter, never demanding too much, never crossing a line. He was always the first to congratulate me after a rally or a meeting with a politician, and he always asked how my day was when we chatted, like he actually *cared* about me. He was even the one who told us to switch from a VPN to Tor to keep our location hidden online. And not for nothing, but I'd never *felt* like I was in danger in his presence. Not back in high school, and not even now, knowing that he was probably a dangerous man.

Ryan studied me. "You want to accept it, don't you?"

I glanced down and ruffled the fur behind Walter's neck, mulling it over. "I don't know if I can. You were there afterward. You saw what I was like."

They nodded, looking solemn. "I remember."

"You know what's terrible? I'm trying to think of the last time someone got me this worked up, and I'm drawing a complete blank."

They shrugged. "It makes sense. A man you used to be obsessed with suddenly shows back up in your life, trying to make things right, and now he's the one obsessed with you? Anyone would get worked up about that."

"Maybe, but I don't love the fact that he's essentially been cyber-stalking me."

"Me neither," Ryan said.

"But what if it was all so he could make sure I was safe? Does that somehow make it okay?" I rubbed my face in my hands. What was this guy doing to me? My *brain* felt itchy.

"I don't know, Lauren," Ryan said. "I wish I could be more help than this, but you know him much better than I do."

I sighed. "God, what I wouldn't give to be Taylor for a few days, to just take things in stride and not constantly overanalyze everything."

"Seriously," Ryan said. "And I know she's not here, but I feel safe in speaking for the both of us when I say that we'll support you no matter your choice."

I leaned over and hugged them. "You're the best."

They squeezed me back. "If you *do* decide to go through with it, Taylor and I are coming along and standing right outside the door of the arcade. With weapons. And Walter. Just in case."

I glanced down at our angel baby, still pressed to my side, his elephant stuffy clutched in his mouth, dark eyes innocent and guileless as he stared up at me. "Not sure what help Walter will be," I said, trying to lighten the mood. "Besides a tripping hazard."

Ryan chuckled, then quieted for a moment before saying, "You don't have to make a decision tonight."

"I know," I told them.

I was still so torn. Despite the fact that I'd forgiven Junior for what he'd done to me back in high school, it didn't mean that I would *ever* let him back into my life. He'd shown me that he couldn't be trusted with my heart, and I believed him.

On the other hand . . .

If I was being totally honest with myself, I wanted to fuck him. Hard. Dirty. Rough. I wanted everything his reputation promised. I wanted him ruthless. Wanted him to use me like his plaything. And maybe that was because it would be easier to keep myself from getting attached if there was no gentleness or affection, or maybe that was because it was just how I liked it. Either way, the longer I thought about it, envisioned myself dropping to my knees in that photo booth and choking down Junior's dick, the more I wanted it.

This could be the closure Taylor mentioned when I first told her about my past. One last hookup with the man who'd hurt me, one final, *good* memory to say goodbye forever and move on with my life.

I lifted my gaze back to Ryan. "Will you think I'm stupid if I say yes?"

They shot me a look. "Of course not. I just want you to be safe."

"Me, too. Are you serious about coming with me?"

They grinned. "I mean, not *coming* with you, but yes, I'll be nearby with a bat if he turns out to be an asshole."

That was no idle threat. They'd played baseball all the way through high school and had a killer swing. Maybe literally if Junior pushed his luck.

"Thank you."

They nodded. "And you know Taylor will be there with bells on."

"Probably in full Harley Quinn cosplay ready to fuck shit up."

I would never stop being grateful for having such badass, loyal friends.

My gaze slid from Ryan to my phone. Seven grand. I could look at it as Junior's payment for past sins, keep it rough and transactional to avoid getting attached. That way I could get this lingering need for him out of my system, tell him I accepted his apology after all, and then never see him again.

Before I could get stuck in my head about it, I scooped my phone off the counter and hit accept.

15

JUNIOR

I WAS BACK IN THE old neighborhood again, my feet walking the well-remembered path behind the arcade. This was where I'd smoked my first blunt as a teen, where I'd gotten my ass kicked by some older kids for talking too much shit.

It was darker at night than it used to be, without the carnival lights of the pinball machines shining out of the windows. Trash sat piled in the corners of the alley. It smelled like rotting food and stale piss. A lot had changed since I'd last been here, but I remembered when this was *the* place to meet with friends, flirt with girls. It was silent now. Kids didn't need an arcade when they had easy access to endless games on their tablets and phones.

Still, the owners had kept it going for as long as they could, longer than they probably should have, closing the doors only when the pandemic finally forced them to. It had been up for sale ever since, but so far, there hadn't been any offers.

Gino, the owner's son, was an old friend, and when I'd asked him if I could use the building for the night, he passed me a key with no questions asked. Gino was good people.

I tucked my motorcycle helmet under one arm and got the back door open. Inside was like a mausoleum. All the machines were still in their places, standing sentinel along the walls. A thin layer of dust gathered

131

on them, and the air held the stale note of abandonment. Moving deeper into the building, I saw that the front windows were boarded up, but at least the cracks between them were wide enough to let a little light in. Just enough for me to wonder if I'd made a mistake inviting Lauren here. I thought it'd be nostalgic, fun to sneak around our old stomping grounds, but so far, it was just depressing.

Fuck it. It was too late to turn back now. She'd be here soon, and I might as well spend that time making the place more presentable. The photo booth was still where I remembered, tucked in a corner near the back, and the same layer of dust that coated everything else sat like a film over the buttons and curtain. I found some rags in a storage closet and quickly cleaned the booth off, stepping back to take it in once I was done. It looked better, less like something you'd find in a haunted museum, but the thought of pulling Lauren inside it didn't make me especially excited. We wouldn't be able to see shit in there, even with the curtain open.

Hoping I wasn't about to charbroil myself, I grabbed the cord and plugged it in. The photo booth immediately flared to life, light spilling out of it, buttons flashing electric blue in the darkness.

Overhead, I noticed something sparkling along the seam where the walls met the ceiling. Fairy lights. Jackpot. Only once they were on, bathing the space in a soft glow that made it look more cozy than spooky, did I realize I'd just spent over twenty minutes giving a make-over to a derelict arcade because I wanted to impress a girl. And to think, just last week, I'd burned a man's house to the ground and nearly beaten him to death afterward.

I contained multitudes.

My phone chimed. I pulled it from my pocket to see a message from Lauren.

I'm outside, it read. *And I brought two friends with me who are going to post up near the door. If I scream, they barge inside, and you have a very bad night.*

Threats. I liked it.

The door is unlocked, I wrote back. *You know where to find me.*

This was a test. The last time I saw her, I had to chase her down. I needed to know she wanted this, or at least the cash, bad enough to make the first move on her own. If she couldn't work up the courage to walk in here by herself, then she probably didn't have what it took to put up with me.

The door opened with a loud creak.

"That's not creepy or anything," she muttered.

Another creak, and then the sound of the door closing. I strained my ears, trying to figure out whether she was walking farther into the arcade or if she'd taken one look inside and decided to bail. A soft footfall reached me, and then she was there, rounding the corner into the main room, her face turned up as she took in the fairy lights. Her hair was curled into loose waves, and she wore shorts and a cropped tank top. This was the first time I'd seen her up close without heels, and she looked so small without them. Delicate. Breakable. Right until she lowered her gaze to mine and pulled the taser out from behind her back.

"Am I going to need this?" she asked, electricity arcing between the two probes.

I cocked my head sideways, unable to help myself. "Only if you have a pain kink."

Her grin turned diabolical. "Let's find out."

She took a step forward, and I moved sideways, putting a pool table between us. The thing about weirdos like Lauren was you never knew how far they'd be willing to take the bit, and I'd already risked electrocution once tonight.

Her expression was triumphant as she slipped the weapon into her purse, where it was no doubt primed and ready to go. Smart woman.

"So," she said. "NT95?"

I nodded, bracing myself.

The humor fled from her face. "This whole time, Junior?"

"I needed to know you were okay, Lo."

Her mouth opened, only for her to close it again like she didn't know what to say to that.

"I have your diary with me," I told her. "To give back to you."

"You took it from Kelly, didn't you?" she asked.

"Yes."

"I don't want it. Too many bad memories. You should burn it."

"Are you sure?" I asked.

She nodded, and we fell quiet for a moment. A much larger discussion loomed, but I didn't feel ready for it yet, and I could tell from the way Lauren glanced around us, as if looking for a distraction, that she wasn't either.

"This place is bigger than I remember," she said. "But that's probably because there aren't a hundred screaming Italian kids crammed in here with us."

Thank god.

She turned and headed toward a machine along the back wall. My gaze dropped to her ass and the way her denim shorts clung to it, and then down over her toned legs. Fuck, what I would give to feel those thighs squeezing either side of my head while I tasted her.

She stopped at a bright pink machine labeled "Powder Mountain" and turned to look at me over her shoulder. "This one was my favorite."

"I remember," I said, rounding the pool table.

She frowned. "You do?"

I nodded; I remembered *everything* about Lauren. Stepping past her, I plugged the machine in. "You should play a round."

She smiled, her eyes wide as they fell to the control panel. "I don't have any quarters."

I slipped my fingers into my front pocket and pulled out a handful. I was nothing if not prepared. The game cost fifty cents to play, so I popped two in and hit go, leaning back on the next machine over to watch her have her fun. Oddly enough, as impatient as I'd been earlier, I felt no need to rush things now. Watching her in real life was just as mesmerizing as it was online. Her dark eyes creased at the corners as she concentrated, and she bit her lower lip every time she had to perform a particularly difficult move.

"I swear I used to be better at this," she said when she died a short time later.

"Maybe I can help." I stepped behind her, bracing my hands on either side of the machine, where the paddles were, forming a cage with my body. "You work the attacks. I'll work the defense."

She sucked in a breath and nodded. "Okay."

We died almost immediately.

"Well," I said.

She turned in my arms. "That was your fault."

"How so?"

She waved in my general direction. "The standing."

I leaned closer, grinned. "Are you saying I'm distracting you?"

"No," she said.

"The way you're staring at my mouth says otherwise."

She huffed and turned back around. "Let's go again."

I produced two more quarters, and she restarted the game.

"You can do it, Lo," I said. "Show those aliens who the queen of Powder Mountain is."

She died instantaneously.

"That one had to be intentional," I said. "You jumped right into the raptor's open mouth."

"I was trying to kick it in the head," she whined. "Fine. You're distracting me."

I stepped closer, our bodies flush from my thighs to chest. This time when I spoke, my voice came out lower, the careful hold I had on my control slipping. "I haven't even started trying to distract you."

She turned again, her game forgotten.

I grabbed her by the waist and lifted her onto the edge of the machine, putting us face-to-face. Her hands landed on my shoulders, steadying herself, and I reached down and hooked mine beneath her knees, guiding her legs around me, reveling in the feel of her smooth skin beneath my fingertips.

"You're fucking beautiful, you know that?" I said, watching the neon lights dance in her dark eyes.

"*You're* fucking beautiful," she shot back, sounding disgruntled about it.

I smiled and leaned in, brushing my lips against hers, our gazes locked from an inch away. "We don't have to do this if you don't want to."

"I wouldn't be here if I didn't want to be," she said.

"That's all I needed to hear."

I scooped her off the game and strode toward the photo booth, one arm braced beneath her ass, the other around her back. She clung to my shoulders, face buried in my neck, tongue hot against my skin as she tasted me. Fuck, I wanted her. Wanted to be *buried* in her. With a yank, I got the photo booth curtain open and set Lauren down inside. Her hands immediately dropped to my belt, a hungry look on her face.

Initially, my plan was to play out her fantasy to a T, but as much as I loved the idea of her lips wrapped around my dick, the thought of dragging those shorts off and making her come again was much more appealing. Besides, there was an orgasm imbalance between us. She'd gotten me off more times than I could count, and it was time to level the playing field.

I grabbed her wrists, pushing her backward toward the bench. "Uh-uh. You sit. I kneel."

She looked up at me. "But in my diary—"

I silenced her with a kiss. Those goddamn glossy lips had been calling to me like a siren song, and I couldn't resist them any longer. She opened for me instantly, tasting like mint and watermelon lip gloss and memories of a simpler time.

With a groan, I stepped into her, forcing her back against the wall as I deepened the kiss. She clutched at my shoulders, meeting my tongue stroke for stroke. My hands slid from her face to her breasts, palms cupping the sides, thumbs brushing over her nipples slowly at first, and then faster, matching the pace she set in her videos.

She shivered, tilting her head back to give me greater access. I kissed, licked and bit my way to her earlobe, filing every response away, learning what she liked, what she loved. The way she dug her nails into me when I swirled my tongue a certain way. Her gasp when I gently pinched her nipples. And then the soft, breathy little moan that followed when I dragged my mouth down her neck.

"Nic," she said, sounding out of breath.

My answering grin was triumphant. I'd already been promoted from Junior and we hadn't even gotten started yet. "Mmm?" I mumbled, unwilling to take my lips off her long enough to talk.

"I want to feel your mouth on me," she said.

God bless women who weren't afraid to tell you what they wanted.

I turned us, bumping the back of her knees against the bench hard enough to send her falling to the padded seat. Her ass had barely hit the cushion before I dropped in front of her, crowding between her legs, hands bunching her shirt up and over her head, fingers slipping inside the cups of her bra. I kissed her again, toying with her nipples, teasing her until I tugged the lace down and let her breasts spill free. And then I pulled my mouth from hers and leaned down, swirling my tongue over one nipple while my fingers played with the other.

She made a desperate sound and shifted her hips forward, needing friction between her thighs. I tilted my pelvis up just enough to meet hers, the ridge of my cock pressed tight to her sex, giving her something to grind on.

"*Nic*," she said with more desperation.

I lifted off her just enough to speak. "Not as into teasing in real life as you are in your videos?"

"I'm not teasing in them. It takes time to work myself up when it's just me."

My head swam, all the blood in my body rushing south to my dick. It took her time to work herself up, but I'd just gotten my hands on her, and already she was asking for more.

I went back to worshipping her breasts with my mouth while my fingers traveled lower, unbuttoning her shorts and sliding the zipper down. With a tug, I had them moving, and she shifted her hips just enough for me to pull both her shorts and thong free. I dropped them to the floor beside me and leaned back, taking a moment to drink her in. She was stunning, from her large dark eyes all the way to the little rainbow tattoo on her ankle.

Digging in my pocket, I hauled out more quarters and turned halfway around.

"What are you doing?" Lauren asked.

"Creating a memory," I told her, dropping the quarters into the machine and hitting go.

I swiveled back around, ducked low enough to hook her legs over my shoulders, and dragged her to the edge of the bench. I'd been thinking about doing this to her since the night at Velvet when I realized how turned on she was by the sight of another woman getting head, and without preamble, I dove down and buried my face in her pussy.

She sucked in a breath just as the first flash filled the booth. I grinned even as I ran my tongue through her folds, imagining the resulting picture. Then the taste of her hit me and all other thoughts fled from my mind. There wasn't anything else to compare it to. Words like sweet, bitter, sharp, and musky came to mind, descriptors that most women didn't want to hear, because they didn't *sound* like they should taste good. But they fucking did.

Lauren's slickness suddenly had me ravenous, and I groaned, pressing closer, sliding my tongue as deep as I could reach.

"Oh, fuck," she said, sounding caught off guard. A hand hit my shoulder, bracing herself as she arched her hips. Another camera flash turned my vision white—this photo reel was going to be *obscene*.

I replaced my tongue with my fingers, driving them deep, hooking them forward until her soft cries told me I'd found her G-spot. All the idiot men out there who claimed it was a myth either hadn't spent enough time asking their partners what felt good, or they didn't understand basic anatomy.

I curled my fingers inside her in a *come hither* motion and switched from the flat of my tongue to the tip, running it in a circle around her tight little bundle of nerves before flicking over it several times in quick succession.

"Oh my g—what are y—oh, fuck." Her words ended on a moan.

Another flash.

I repeated the motions again and again, until words failed her entirely and she stopped moving, her muscles clenching up around me like her body was about to seize. A feeling of victory mixed with pride swept through me, and I picked up the pace, driving Lauren harder, faster.

She panted, nails digging through my shirt, thighs squeezing the sides of my face. A shudder ran through her. Her inner muscles clenched on my fingers. "*Nic!*"

It was all the warning I had before she came, her body wracked with shivers, legs clamping around me like a boa constrictor. Warmth flooded my fingers as I continued to pump into her. I shifted my tongue to the sides of her clit, knowing direct stimulation while coming could quickly become too much, and slowed my pace, easing her down from her high.

The camera flashed a final time.

I dropped one last kiss on her folds and glanced up to see Lauren looking absolutely wrecked. Her eyes were wild, chest heaving, lipstick smeared like she'd bitten her own lips to keep from screaming.

"What," she said, "the fuck was that?"

I chuckled and gently thrust my fingers inside her, reveling in how wet she was for me. "Does that mean you forgive me now?"

Her eyes narrowed. "Tell me how you learned to do that, and maybe I'll consider it."

"What? This?" I hooked my fingers forward again and stroked her until she moaned.

As tempting as it was to get her off again, I understood the advantage of leaving her wanting more, so I slowly slid my fingers free. I couldn't resist one more taste of her, though, slipping them through my lips and cleaning every last drop of her off my skin. God, the taste of her was a drug.

She watched me with hungry eyes before her focus dropped below my belt. "Get your dick out."

Her order nearly startled a laugh out of me, but I shook my head. Did I want her hands and tongue and mouth on me? Absolutely, but tonight was about her. Leaning forward, I helped her back into her underwear and shorts, one foot at a time.

"Please?" she said, the open need in her voice like music to my ears.

"Not tonight," I told her, because I didn't think I could stop at her sucking me off. I'd need more of her, *all* of her, and I wanted her to be able to scream in peace when I finally got inside her. "Lift your hips," I told her, sliding her clothes up her legs.

She did as I asked, moving just enough that I was able to get them back in place.

Her eyes narrowed as she tucked her tits inside her bra. "Why are you being so nice? I remember you. Don't try to hide from me, Junior." Oh, so I was Nic when I was getting her off and Junior the rest of the time? "You were a grumpy bastard back then, and, judging by the way you death-glared all the church biddies, you're even worse now."

If she only knew what *else* I'd done to the church biddies. "Maybe I've changed."

She snorted. "Somehow, I doubt that."

I gripped her thighs and started to pull her close again. "What do I need to do to convince you? More groveling?"

She blew out a shaky breath. "No."

The suspicion remained in her gaze, so I ran my hands up her legs, gripping her hips. "What if we erase all of it?"

Her brows drew together. "What do you mean?"

"What if we rewrite those bad memories with good ones? Pick up where we left off?"

Her eyes dropped to my lips. "I'm not looking for something serious right now."

I nodded, ready to lie through my teeth, say whatever it took to see her again. "I can't do anything serious either."

Her gaze lifted back to mine, and I could see the turmoil in her eyes as she decided something. "Look, I'm breaking all my rules here, but what are you doing Friday?"

I fought back a grin. "Whatever you're doing Friday."

"Let me show you what else Velvet has to offer, and if you're still interested after, we can talk about this more."

"I'll be there."

16

LAUREN

I STUMBLED OUT OF THE arcade into the humid night air, nearly knocking Taylor over. My legs didn't want to work, and my clit was overstimulated to the point that every rub of fabric was jarring. I had no idea where Junior had learned to do *that*, but I felt like I should send the person who'd taught him a nice bouquet of flowers.

"Woah," Ryan said, grabbing my shoulders. "You okay? He didn't drug you or anything, did he?"

Walter pressed close, too, and I had to dodge sideways to keep his nose out of my crotch.

"I'm fine," I said, grinning.

Taylor snorted. "Oh, she's been drugged, all right. With sex hormones."

I wrapped my arms around my roommates' waists and turned them away from the arcade. "Come on. Let's go home, and I'll tell you all about it."

Back at our brownstone, we gathered on the couch with a bottle of wine, a *Love Island* rerun playing quietly in the background.

"So," Taylor said. "Did you fuck?"

I shook my head. "He didn't even let me touch him. Just carried me into the photo booth and went down on me."

Taylor's eyes nearly bugged out of her head. "And he paid *you* seven grand to do it?"

"Yeah," I said. "I'd feel guilty, but it's his money. If that's how he wants to spend it, who am I to tell him otherwise?"

Ryan nodded. "That's the spirit."

Taylor tipped her head sideways. "You look different. Something's changed."

I had to give it to her; her intuition was killer. "I may or may not have invited him back to Velvet." Quickly, I caught them up on the conversation we'd had post-hookup and the fact that I was considering giving Junior a chance to redeem himself.

Taylor listened with wide eyes. "Wow, you must really like him if you're breaking your one-strike policy."

I stared into my wine, trying to find the right words. "It's complicated. Yes, he hurt me, but I believe that he thought he was doing the right thing, and, more important, I believe he's sorry. And I can't deny the way I feel around him." I shook my head. "There's this . . . pull between us, this connection. I felt it a decade ago, and it's still there. It's not just physical, either. I want to get to know him more, find out who he is now."

Ryan set their glass down and turned to me. "I'm not trying to be a Debbie Downer about all of this, but Junior's still in the Mafia, doing god knows what. And isn't his father, like, the devil himself? Are you really okay with that?"

I sighed. "I'm not okay with it, but I don't think Junior is either. You should have seen how scared he was as a teen, knowing he was about to graduate and go into the family business. He tried to hide it from me, but I could see it in his eyes, hear it in his voice whenever he talked about his dad. I spent half our time together trying to make him laugh just so he'd have a break from all the doom and gloom. I don't think he would have chosen this life for himself if given the chance. And this might sound kind of fucked, but growing up in the old neighborhood, the mob was just something you accepted as part of life. Nonna and Nonno Bianchi owned the corner deli, and I used to do my homework at the counter while they worked the store. Every other Friday, some big goon would come in, and Nonno would hand him a brown paper envelope full of cash."

"Protection money?" Taylor asked.

I nodded.

"Yeah," Ryan said. "Protection against them breaking their kneecaps if they didn't pay on time."

"That's the cliché," I agreed. "But the reality is more complex. Everyone in the neighborhood knows each other. Their kids go to school together, they sit next to each other at Mass every Sunday. If people can't pay, the mob is good about letting it slide. Within reason. And that protection money is *actually* protection money."

"What do you mean?" Ryan asked.

"The store was broken into once when I was in middle school," I said. "Someone smashed out the glass on the rear door, took all the cash from the register, and trashed the place. Instead of calling the cops or their insurance broker, my grandparents called the man who collected their money. By the next afternoon, the store was cleaned up, all the cash was replaced, and the new back door was practically a bank vault. My grandparents were promised it would never happen again, and even after they retired and my older sister took over the store, it hasn't."

"Shades of gray," Ryan said.

I nodded. "Nothing is ever black and white. Not even the mob. All that to say, no, I'm not okay with what Junior does, but it's not enough to push me away either. And it's not like I plan to marry the man, so in the long run, I won't have to go through an existential crisis about it."

Ryan studied me. "So it's just going to be a casual hookup?"

"This feels more like . . . I don't know. Maybe making up for lost time? Exploring the spark between us that we didn't get to before?"

"I get that," Ryan said. "As long as you're being careful."

Taylor grinned. "Double wrap it if you have to."

Ryan swatted her. "I meant be careful emotionally."

Taylor swatted them back. "I *know that*. I was talking about her heart, not his dick."

Thwack. "Why are you like this?"

Thwack. "Because if I wasn't, you'd never laugh, you goth-ass bitch."

I leaned forward and smacked Taylor's thigh.

"Hey!" she cried. "What was that for?"

"I felt left out."

She hit me back. Ryan hit her. I hit Ryan. Why? No idea. It just felt like the right thing to do. Soon, a slap fight broke out that roused Walter. He got between us and started barking excitedly, because *Yay! Playtime!*

"Oh, great," I said. "You woke the baby."

"Us?" Taylor and Ryan chorused.

Eventually, everyone settled down, and we retook our seats. Walter elected to lie half in my lap, his eyes open and shifting among us in case more fun sprang up. I started petting him, hoping he'd relax, and looked over at Taylor.

"I noticed you haven't posted anything in a few days. You okay?"

She drew her knees to her chest and shook her head. "I haven't really felt like posting. That cannibal really freaked me out, and I've been getting more shitty comments than normal."

My heart ached for her. I'd been there before, so, so many times. We faced a constant barrage of comments with words like slut, whore, and every other derogatory word under the sun, and most of the time, we just had to accept it as part of the territory. We'd even done a decent job reclaiming the words for our own, to the point that I didn't even bat an eye when I saw them anymore. Instead, I found a way to use someone's misogyny against them, firing back responses like, *My sexting channel is open if you want to see what a whore I'll be for you*, and then I watched the dollars stack up when they entered the paid-for chat.

But not a day went by that I didn't get at least one absolutely disgusting comment either from a sub or social media troll that totally crossed the line—the block button was my best friend in those circumstances. I'd had random upticks like Taylor's plenty of times over the past several years, where it seemed like every other person thought that just because I was a camgirl, the basic laws of human decency no longer applied to me. This line of work definitely wasn't for the faint of heart, and a lot of the friends I'd made early on in my career had long since given it up to pursue other lines of work or settle down and start families. I was beginning to wonder if Taylor was next.

"Take as much time as you need," I told her. "Your mental health has to come first."

She sent me a sad smile. "Thanks. I'm still good to pay my share of rent and everything."

Ryan waved her off. "Even if you weren't, we'd cover you."

Taylor rested her head on Ryan's shoulder, our earlier "altercation" forgotten. "Did you see Ghost Girl's message?"

We'd spent several hours over the past two days looking into possible hires for Ryan, and there were a couple of great candidates.

"I did," Ryan said. "She's like the third person to recommend Ben."

"Have you seen his work?" I asked.

Ryan nodded. "I did some scrolling earlier, and he's really good, despite being less experienced than I am. I spoke to several people he's worked with, and they all said he's super professional. His style is even similar to mine, so I don't think it would take much training to bring him up to my standards."

Taylor prodded their shoulder. "You gonna offer him the job?"

"He hasn't applied for it," Ryan said.

"So?" I said. "Why not reach out to him first?"

Ryan grumbled, but together, Taylor and I convinced them it couldn't hurt to send an email. The worst that could happen was Ben said no.

We figured it would be a few days before they heard back, but Ryan's phone chimed not five minutes later, and they lifted their head from it, grinning. "He's in."

Taylor shrieked.

Walter started barking.

I gave up on trying to calm him down and let him have his fun.

■ ■ ■

Friday night found me at Velvet, seated in the back corner of the bondage room. Junior and I hadn't spoken much since our encounter at the arcade, just enough to exchange phone numbers so I could text him what time to be here instead of having to do everything through the Me4U app.

I was nervous to see him. And excited. My body was keyed up, ready for more, desperate to get his hands on me again, and vice versa. Maybe I'd get *really* lucky, and he'd finally let me suck his dick. A girl could hope.

My phone buzzed. I dug around in my purse trying to find the device. Cool metal met my fingers, and I pulled out what looked like a quarter, rubbed smooth from age, only twice the thickness of the normal currency. I could have sworn I'd never seen it before, but I had so much random shit floating loose in my purse that it was probably some token from a club or bar that I'd stashed in there and completely forgotten about.

I dropped it back inside and pulled my phone free. Junior had texted. *Running late. Something came up.*

A wave of disappointment rolled through me as I texted him back. *How late? The show is about to start.*

I'm not sure, he said. *I gotta deal with this.*

I didn't bother texting him back. The vagueness told me everything I needed to know.

He was standing me up.

Because of course he fucking was. God, I was an idiot for not seeing this coming.

Anger churned in my belly, more directed at myself than Junior. This was what I got for going against my better judgment. He'd already proved he couldn't be trusted, and I'd stupidly given him another chance to hurt me. At least this time it was only disappointment and not heartache. And honestly? Maybe I should be thanking him for doing this so quickly, for not dragging it out and stringing me along like he had all those years ago, for reminding me exactly why I had a one-strike policy. A sub crossed the line? Blocked. Someone I was dating gave off a creepy vibe? Ghosted. It kept me safe, kept me from getting hurt, and I shouldn't have broken that rule, especially for someone as undeserving as Junior Trocci.

I switched my phone off and dropped it back inside my purse, resolving to forget about him again.

A moment later, a soft chime had me lifting my gaze to the bondage room stage. Sylvia walked out of a side door, her lean frame clad in a black bodysuit and knee-high leather boots, a rope clutched in her fist. She paused, spun on her heel, and tugged, and a few seconds later, Moriah crawled out of the door after her, the rope attached to a collar on her neck.

Oh, god.

Her stunning body was on full display, the white lingerie leaving nothing to the imagination. Watching this alone was going to be torture.

17

JUNIOR

OF ALL THE FRIDAYS FOR my father to call an impromptu family dinner, it had to be *this one*. The night I was supposed to meet Lauren at Velvet.

My parents usually hosted these dinners once a month as a way to sit down with the whole family: Dad, Mom, me, my brothers, and more recently, my cousin Aly and her boyfriend Josh. It was Dad's way of pretending we were like any other family, crowded around the dining table and catching up on one another's lives. In some twisted, narcissistic way, I sometimes thought that was how he truly saw it. That he'd deluded himself into thinking we all gathered willingly, happily, and not because if we refused he'd make our lives a living hell.

Everyone else knew what these dinners really were—just another way for Dad to exert his control over us, remind us who we owed our loyalty to.

I was especially pissed about dinner tonight because he had a habit of dragging them out for as long as possible, and it was a twenty-minute drive from my parents' place in the suburbs to Velvet, without traffic. I'd have to keep my eye on the clock to make sure I got out of here in time to meet Lauren.

My parents' house perched on top of a slight rise, just high enough to see the city spread out in the distance. It was a Tuscan-style villa, clad in light stone, with green shutters and a terra-cotta roof. Towering arborvitae lined the driveway, clipped tight to mimic the Italian cypress trees that couldn't survive our winters. With the sun setting behind it and the outside lights kicking on, the house looked ancient and proud, like it had stood here for hundreds of years instead of being custom-built a decade ago.

I'd never hated the sight of it more.

I parked in my usual spot and was just pulling off my helmet when lights flashed over me. A luxury car rounded the circular drive, and I let out a relieved breath. Aly and Josh had made it. They'd had to skip the last dinner, thanks to their vacation, and Dad had been unbearable because of it. With them here, he'd (hopefully) be in a slightly better mood, and there'd also be more people for him to focus on besides me.

The car pulled to a stop next to my bike, and out popped Josh, grinning ear to ear. He was a big sonofabitch, not just tall, but broad, with the kind of flashy gym muscles women loved. Add in his dark hair, nearly black eyes, deep olive skin, and blindingly white smile, and he looked a little like a superhero. Right until you noticed the hellscape of ink crawling up his arms, each full sleeve filled with demons and ghouls and other dark ephemera.

He held a finger up while racing around to the passenger side. "One sec," he said. "I need to get the door for my *fiancée*."

I rolled my eyes. Josh had always taken great pride in calling Aly his *girlfriend*, and I'd had a feeling it was going to become unbearable once he finally popped the question. Looked like I was right.

Aly, not to be upstaged by him, shot her hand into the air as soon as her door was open. At first, I assumed she was flipping me off—she and I had a somewhat antagonistic relationship—but then I realized she was just showing off the giant rock on her hand. Josh offered his arm, and the rest of her appeared, dark hair pulled back off her face, skin a healthy tan after finally spending some time outside instead of stuck beneath the fluorescent lights of the ER she worked at.

"Oh, hi," she said, still holding her hand up for inspection.

"He sent me a picture of it last week," I told her.

She turned to Josh. "Hey!"

He ducked, looking sheepish. "What?"

"We said we were going to wait until tonight to tell my family."

Josh waved in my direction. "Junior doesn't count."

I arched a brow. "Rude."

He sent me a sideways grin. "Because you're my friend. Aly said I could tell my friends."

I huffed out a breath, feeling awkward. Sometime over the past six months, this giant weirdo who never took *anything* seriously had wheedled his way into my life, and, yeah, fine, I guess we were friends. I was still coming to terms with it, would never admit that I'd missed his dumb ass while he and Aly were away getting engaged and doing whatever else it was in the woods that had left them covered in head-to-toe scratches.

My gaze traced over their exposed skin. It looked like they'd fallen down a mountain. Through pricker bushes. The fuck had they been doing out there? Actually, never mind. I didn't want to know.

Aly swiveled back to me, frowning. "You didn't tell everyone, did you?"

"Fuck, no. You think I want to be the one to tell my old man that *this guy* is about to become part of the family?" I asked, thumbing toward Josh.

"Aww," he said. "I missed you, too, buddy."

He tried to boop me on the nose.

I slapped his hand out of the air and moved out of his freakishly long reach.

"Why is it," my mom called from the doorway, "that I always find you three loitering outside?" She stepped onto the front stoop and motioned us in. "The booze is in there, ya daft fecks. And it's humid as a—"

"Mom, please," I interrupted. "No more nun jokes." She had a godawful habit of comparing the weather to nuns' unmentionable places. Some of the worst I'd heard recently were, "Dry as a nun's fanny," "Cold as a nun's teats," and "Windy as a nun's arsehole." I didn't know how many more I could take, especially if she made good on her threat to drag me back to church again soon.

Aly and Josh started toward her, both grinning. They might have hated my dad, but Mom had wormed her way into their hearts with her dark Irish humor, and they looked genuinely happy to see her.

"Sorry, Moira," Josh said. "My *fiancée* just wanted to show off her ring."

Mom made a noise I'd never heard before, halfway between a sob and a shriek, and launched herself at Aly. The sight rocked me back on my heels. I couldn't remember the last time I'd seen her so happy, grinning and laughing like she didn't have a care in the world. It made me feel like a bastard for staying away, for not spending more time with her. My brothers and I could escape our father; Mom was stuck with him.

Fuck, I hoped I was able to get free of Dad without risking my relationship with her.

As if I'd summoned him, Dad came racing out of the doorway, gun drawn, my brothers hot on his heels. "What is it? I heard you—" He caught sight of Mom pulling back from Aly and lowered the gun. "Why'd you scream, Moira? Jesus, you almost gave me a heart attack."

"They're engaged," Mom said, holding up Aly's hand.

My gaze lasered in on Dad, watching his eyes pinch and his mouth pucker as the news set in.

Be nice for once in your fucking life, I thought.

"I guess I should go get the good champagne," he muttered, stalking away.

Mom let out a sigh of relief. For Dad, that was as nice as it got.

■ ■ ■ ■

The longest hour of my life later, we finally sat down to dinner. I was supposed to meet Lauren at nine thirty, and I kept checking my phone for the time. At this rate, I'd have to run out of here as soon as we were done eating.

"You know the rule," Dad griped. "No phones at the dinner table."

I set it face down next to my plate. "I'm waiting on something from Vinny." It wasn't exactly a lie.

Dad eyed me, most likely wondering what the fuck I could be waiting on, but I held his gaze with unflinching focus, silently daring him to say something else. Mom chose that moment to clear her throat, a subtle reminder that first and foremost, we never discussed business during dinner.

Reluctantly, Dad turned to Aly. "June works best."

She paused, plate held aloft while Josh spooned some salad onto it for her. "For what?"

"Your wedding," Dad said. "The garden is at its peak then, and that'll give us plenty of time to send out invitations." His gaze slid to Josh. "Or for you to change your mind."

Mom narrowed her eyes at Dad.

Aly's glare was just as steely. "First off, we literally just got engaged. We haven't even started planning yet, and second—"

"Good," Dad interrupted, reaching for the stuffed shells Greg passed his way. "That means you're not in any rush." His focus dropped to where the table hid Aly's stomach from sight. "I didn't know if you'd just put on a couple of pounds, or if you were expecting."

Shock rippled through the room. Shit, he'd gone there.

"*Nico*," Mom hissed.

The table rattled as Josh pushed back from it, his expression darkening in a way that didn't bode well for my father. I was half tempted to say something, but out of everyone here, Josh and Aly needed the least help defending themselves, and I wasn't trying to make myself a target tonight.

"Everyone, relax," Dad said, grinning in a way that made my hackles rise. "It was a joke. She's, like, two percent body fat."

Across from me, Alec shoved a forkful of cheesy pasta into his mouth and spoke around it. "Women don't like it when you joke about their weight."

"Don't talk with your mouth full," Dad sniped, gaze shifting to Aly. "Sorry for thinking you were less sensitive than other women."

Mom threw back her glass of wine like it was a shot, muttering darkly.

"Secondly," Aly continued like she'd never been interrupted, "I'm not going to change my mind about marrying Josh."

Dad's expression turned calculating. "Lot of time before now and next June."

Aly shook her head. "Who said anything about us waiting that long?"

"I told you," Dad said. "The garden—"

Aly finally snapped. "Fuck the garden!" Josh put a hand on her shoulder, and she took a calming breath. "Sorry, Moira."

Mom waved her off and reached for the bottle of wine, upending it over her glass.

This was going well.

"We're not having the wedding here," Aly said, her gaze back on my father. "We can barely get through five minutes of dinner without you pissing everyone off."

Dad shrugged, unbothered. "Lot of time for news to get out about your boyfriend's father, too."

Suddenly, everyone's focus swiveled to Josh, questioning. Mom and my brothers didn't know about Josh's dark past, only me and Dad.

And Aly, who looked ready to spit nails. "I warned you not to bring that up again."

A memory flashed through my mind of Aly, Josh, Dad, and me all locked in Dad's study, Aly just as angry as she was now, vowing to never speak to my father again if he outed Josh's secrets.

Dad's eyes glittered with dark light. "Have the wedding here, and I won't."

"I'm not doing this with you," Aly said. "We're leaving. Sorry, Moira."

"Don't be," Mom said.

Josh and Aly said their brief goodbyes to the rest of us, and the only thing that kept my old man quiet throughout their departure was Mom glaring daggers at him.

"I'm done, too," she said when they were gone, grabbing her wine-glass. She paused at the door and shot Dad one last hostile look. "And don't bother coming to bed later."

"Ooh," Alec said after she stormed out. "Someone's sleeping on the couch."

Dad turned to him, silent, his eyes begging Alec to say *one more word* so he had someone to vent his anger on. Alec wisely shut up and stared down at his plate.

And then it was my turn to bear the brunt of Dad's focus. "What are you waiting on Vinny for?"

I cocked an eyebrow. "I thought there wasn't any shoptalk at dinner?"

Dad planted his elbows on the table and leaned forward, dark eyes sparking with menace. "Why are you avoiding the question, Junior?"

Thank fuck I had an actual excuse to have my phone out and didn't need to lie. Lies never lasted long with my father, because he was paranoid enough to double-check every word said to him, even from his own sons. The last thing I needed was for him to catch me in one right now. I wouldn't put it past him to have someone tail me, and I couldn't risk him finding out about Lauren before I was ready.

"Vinny's down at the docks making sure that customs agent's palms are greased," I said.

Dad frowned. "He trying to demand more money?"

I nodded.

Greg blew out a breath. "Why? The boat's full of olive oil, not coke."

"Fake-ass olive oil," I reminded him.

Greg frowned. "So? Get rid of him and find an easier agent to work with."

I shook my head. "There's too much heat in this city right now. We don't need to add another dead body to the pile. Especially because it would lead to an investigation, and if the Feds start digging, the trail might lead back to us. Plus, there's no time. The next shipment comes in later tonight."

Dad tipped his chin in my direction. "What Junior said." He wiped his face with his dinner napkin and set it aside. "Actually, I've been

157

wanting to talk to you about something. We've been thinking about expanding imports. I've spoken to Lorenzo, and we'd like to see you take the lead on this."

Alec nearly choked on his pasta. Beside him, Stefan went still.

Greg let out a low whistle and patted me on the back. "Looks like you're getting promoted."

I shut my expression down, my mind working on overdrive. This wasn't Dad being some gracious benefactor. This was his response to me pulling away. It was his last-ditch effort to tie me closer to him in a setting where I couldn't refuse. Because there was no logical reason for me to decline the offer.

And while I wanted to break free more than anything, as of right now, I wasn't ready, didn't have something to fall back on, had no plan in place for how to deal with the fallout of severing ties with my old man. Which meant I had to say yes.

By heading our oil operation for Lorenzo, I'd be taking on more responsibility than ever, more risk. My head would be on the chopping block if we got caught, and I'd be the one spending my life behind bars.

Heat crawled up the back of my neck as my temper reared its ugly head. I wanted to scream. I wanted to rage. I wanted to flip this fucking table over and beat my father to within an inch of his life. But I had to keep myself in check, had to keep him from growing even more suspicious of me than he already was.

Dad tipped his head sideways, gaze narrowing, a grin spreading over his face that looked more like a baring of teeth. "I can trust you with this, right, son?"

I had no choice but to agree, so I forced myself to return his smile. "Of course." The lie tasted like ash in my mouth, like the ruined embers of my dreams. "I won't let you down."

18

JUNIOR

I REVVED MY MOTORCYCLE, MERGING in and out of lanes as I raced across the city. Lauren had been brave enough to give me a second chance, and I was already fucking it up by running late.

This was why I'd never pursued a serious relationship before; I knew I'd end up disappointing someone. The fact that it was Lo I was disappointing felt unacceptable, made me even more convinced that if I had any chance of gaining some sort of normalcy, I needed to get the fuck out before Dad dug his claws any deeper than they already were.

Up ahead, the light turned yellow. I gunned it, racing through the intersection just as it changed to red.

The wind buffeted me. I kept my head on a swivel to avoid the cars and pedestrians in my path. If Lauren didn't forgive me for standing her up, there'd be hell to pay, fuck the consequences. I was pissed at Dad before, but now that I'd put a little space between us, that anger had morphed into rage. I felt trapped, cornered, like some wild animal with no chance of escape.

I shook my head, trying to dislodge thoughts of my father, trying to unsee the look of triumph on his face when I told him he could trust me. This anger of mine was a problem, and I didn't need it infecting my time spent with Lauren. She was too important, too special.

I parked right outside the club this time and headed toward the front door, handing my helmet and jacket over to the coat check while the hostess scanned my member card. As soon as her handheld device flashed green, I snagged a mask off her desk and strode into the lobby.

Lauren sat front and center at the bar, a gorgeous woman on one side of her and a familiar man on the other. My mood plummeted right back into rage. It was the same collegiate-looking motherfucker I'd seen sniffing around her before.

I stalked toward the trio, feeling eyes on me. People at the bar started to turn like they'd felt the vibes in the room shift, Lauren turning with them, the smile on her face faltering when she caught sight of my expression.

"Oh," she said, "you actually ca—"

I cut her off with a kiss, going into it hard, shoving my way between her legs, hands on her face so I could hold her at the right angle. She tasted like champagne and strawberries, and I was pissed I hadn't been here to watch her consume them.

The mask dug into my face, but I ignored it, too focused on how stiff Lauren was in my grip, her body radiating tension. I slanted my mouth over hers and stroked my tongue across her lips, begging her to let me back in, telling her with my touch how sorry I was. Her palms hit my chest, and I had just enough time to brace myself against getting shoved away before her fingers curled into my shirt and she pulled me closer instead, her mouth falling open on a jagged inhale, the first stroke of her tongue like heaven against mine.

"Woah, hey," the guy beside us said.

I broke the kiss just long enough to tell him to get fucked and went back to claiming Lauren like some sort of goddamn caveman. Sure, I'd been late, but that didn't mean I'd forfeited. It didn't mean the vultures circling Lo could descend in my absence.

Was it my best moment? No. But it also wasn't my worst, and from the way Lauren kissed me back, she didn't seem to mind all that much. I kept going, dropping a hand to pull her leg around my waist, fitting my hips against hers so she could feel how fucked-up I was for her, how hard she made me.

"Where?" I demanded.

"Upstairs," she said.

I scooped her off the barstool and carried her toward the stairs. She clung to me, our chests pressed together, her arms at my neck, legs around my waist. Her dress was short, so I hooked my forearm beneath her ass, tucking the hem of it in place to keep her from flashing the room.

If people had been surreptitiously watching us before, they openly gawked now. Let them. Everyone inside this building needed to know who they'd have to deal with if they went after Lauren. Dropping all pretenses, I let the menace and aggression I felt creep into my expression, my eyes daggers, my sneer a promise of violence, even as I cradled Lo against me like she was the most precious thing in the world. People tore their gazes away when I met them, and it should have been a warning sign that I needed to check my fucking temper, but all I felt was dark triumph, my blood humming, soul baying like a wolf claiming its kill.

Mine.

I carried Lauren upstairs, so distracted by how she felt in my arms that I was blind to where we were going.

She tugged on my sleeve as we were passing a door. "In here."

I turned right, and she released me with one arm to press her card against the lock. The second it clicked open, we were in. I was desperate to taste her again, to drop her onto the nearest flat surface and—wait, where the fuck had all these people come from?

My body jerked to a stop as I took in the room around us. The voyeur room, to be exact. Or at least a carbon copy of it with the same bed and pillows and chair.

"You made it after all," someone said.

I pivoted, still holding Lauren, to see one of her roommates, the tall, androgynous blond who'd turned absolutely scarlet when they'd caught us in the stairwell. They wore a black mid-length skirt and matching tank top, their hair piled in a messy bun atop their head, light blue eyes rimmed in dark liner.

I set Lauren down, keeping her in front of me to hide my obvious arousal. This was . . . not what I'd expected. I'd thought she was leading us to a room where we could be alone, not surrounded by more people.

"Junior, this is Ryan," she said. "They're one of my roommates."

Politeness didn't come easy to me at the best of times, let alone now when all I wanted to do was get Lauren naked, but it was clear that Ryan was important to her, so I shoved my frustration aside and tried to make a better second impression than my first.

I stuck my hand past Lauren toward them. "We've . . ." I cocked my head sideways and grinned, one eyebrow rising in question. "Met?"

Ryan let out an awkward laugh and slipped their hand into mine. "That's one way to put it."

"Sorry for being a dick that night," I said as we shook.

They released me and stepped back. "Understandable, given the circumstances."

"Right," Lauren said. "The staircase."

"Great documentary," Lauren's other roommate chimed in. "He totally fucking did it."

I shook my head and held her gaze with monumental effort, trying not to think about the fact that I'd watched her riding someone's cock the last time I was in this room. "I don't know. There might be something to the owl theory."

She smiled and glanced at Lauren. "I like him. He can stay." With that, she turned and flounced back into the crowd.

Lauren shook her head, looking amused. "That was Taylor."

"I'm going to take my seat," Ryan said. "Nice to officially meet you, Junior."

I tipped my head up. "You, too."

They turned, and Lauren dragged me away from the door to a pair of unoccupied seats in the far corner. I took the one closest to the wall, and when Lauren made to sit next to me, I wrapped my arms around her waist and tugged her onto my lap instead, happy for the shadows on this side of the room.

"I'm sorry I was late," I said.

She might have kissed me downstairs, but I could tell from the stiffness in her shoulders and the guarded look on her face that she was still wary. "I thought you stood me up."

I tugged her close, brushing our cheeks together, barely managing to hold my lower body still against the urge to grind against her. "I would never willingly do that."

"Then where were you?" she asked.

"At an absolute trainwreck of a family dinner."

She pulled back, looking surprised. "Seriously?"

I nodded, holding her gaze, letting her eyes drink me in as she studied my expression, no doubt looking for lies.

"We have them once a month," I told her. "My dad called this one last minute."

"Oh." A little line formed between her brows. "Why didn't you tell me that?"

"I *did*, which you would have seen if you hadn't been so quick to turn your goddamn phone off."

She glanced away, cheeks pinking. "I was in another room and the show was about to start."

I gripped her chin and turned her back to me. "Bullshit." She tried to pull away, but I held her firm. "Why'd you really do it, Lo? The truth this time."

Her response was so quiet I barely caught it. "I thought you were doing the same thing to me now that you did back then."

I swore, low and angry, and tugged her back into my chest. My hand smoothed over her shoulders, and I took a second to choose my words, hoping to get through to her. "I'm not that scared kid anymore. I'm not going to ghost you again. Anything that happens from here on out, I'll talk to you about it first. But you should know, because of what I do, making plans is hard."

"So, what?" She mumbled against my shirt. "I'm just supposed to wait around for you?"

"No. I'm only asking for a little more patience if this happens again."
I dropped my lips to the top of her head, willing her to understand.
"And I promise I'll make it up to you afterward."

"How?"

"However you want me to," I told her.

She leaned back and gifted me a smile, and maybe it was because
of the shadows, but it looked a little scary. "Dangerous words. I'm not
that shy girl anymore."

"What shy girl? The one I remember wrote me an explicit, two-sided
note telling me all the things she wanted to do to my dick."

"She was tame in comparison."

I sent her a flat look. "And you don't think I know that after how
long I've been a sub?"

She shook her head. "Most of what I post, and what you've
requested, has been pretty standard. But I like other things, too, want
other things."

My gaze tripped past her toward the unoccupied stage. "Things like
this?"

"And more."

Our gazes locked. "Things like being chased down a hallway?"

She bit her lip and nodded, shifting a little in my lap, just enough for
me to realize my dick was about to get stuck down a pant leg again.
Sneaking a surreptitious look at our closest neighbors, I slipped my
hand beneath Lauren and adjusted myself. Her gaze followed the movement, the same hungry expression from the arcade taking over her face.

I leaned in again, kissing her cheek, moving back until I caught her
earlobe between my teeth. "Whatever you want, whenever you want it."

She shifted closer, hands gripping my shoulders. "I want—"

The overhead lights dimmed, the warning sign that the show was
about to start.

Lauren let out a frustrated sound and slid off my lap.

I fought to get control of myself while everyone around us took their
seats. What I wanted to do to Lauren right now wasn't fit for public
consumption. Or maybe it was, and I was just too selfish a bastard

to let anyone else in. I wanted her just for myself, couldn't stand the thought of sharing her sighs or moans.

It struck me then, that I was *already* sharing her with thousands of subscribers, and yet, I didn't feel the same possessive need to keep her from them. Maybe because their relationships were transactional and online. Or maybe because it was her livelihood, and even I wasn't a big enough bastard to want to take that from her. Or—

A low chime sounded from the speakers, cutting off my thoughts and triggering an unexpected flood of anticipation through my veins. Yup, I definitely shared Lauren's voyeur kink, because the thought of doing this again—watching two people fuck in person—had me rock hard.

Instead of Morgan and Steph, a Black couple walked onstage, both already dressed in robes.

Lauren leaned close. "Ray and Ella. You're in for a surprise."

My gaze shifted from the lean man with braids to the woman holding his hand. Her hair floated around her face in tight, corkscrew curls. The robe she wore hid most of her from sight, all but her toned calves and bare feet, toenails painted a bright pink.

They stopped in front of the bed, where Ray pulled Ella close.

"Hi," he said, leaning down to bump his forehead against hers.

"Hi," she responded.

"You look beautiful tonight."

"You're not so bad yourself," Ella said.

Well, they seemed like a sweet couple. Hopefully this wasn't about to be boring and sentimental. It would be a letdown after the first performance I'd watched, and with so many charged emotions still swirling through me, I wasn't in the mood for anything soft.

Lauren let out a small sigh, and I glanced over to see her watching the pair with a longing expression. Right now, she looked like someone who wanted what Ray and Ella had, what Morgan and Steph had, too. Had she only *said* she didn't want something serious? Or was it me, specifically, she didn't want to get serious with?

I turned back to the stage to find Ray and Ella making out. The kiss was slow and gentle and exploratory. Unrushed. I was forced to watch it in between other people's heads, having to shift a little to keep the pair in sight. Each row was made up of six chairs, and there were four rows separating us from the stage, which meant I had a clearer view of the crowd than of the performers. It was distracting, especially because no one seemed like they were able to sit still.

Only when the two women right in front of us started kissing did I begin to understand the appeal. Instead of watching just one couple, we had the pick of the room. I could shift my focus to whoever piqued my interest, and no one would be the wiser.

I glanced over at Lauren, wondering if this was her plan all along, and found her unabashedly staring at the women. I'd guessed she wasn't straight given her rainbow tattoo, but watching the intensity on her face now confirmed it. Maybe I should have been worried, or jealous, but all I felt was smug that out of all the people available to her, she was choosing to spend her time with me. It made me even more determined not to fuck it up.

A noise drew my attention to the front of the room. Ray was pushing Ella's robe from her shoulders, slowly, taking time to kiss every inch of skin as he exposed it. He spoke to her, but whatever he said was so low it didn't carry, for her ears only. She lifted onto her toes and arched into him in response, and the robe fell free, revealing her in all her glory.

My gaze ran over her. She was tall, with long, elegant muscles covered in more ink than I was, her sleeve sweeping up her shoulder and then down her ribs before whorling all the way over her thigh. Her breasts were small and pert, nipples pierced, a delicate chain running through both hoops and then dipping between her legs in a way that had me sitting up straighter in my seat. Where the fuck did it go? All it would take was a gentle tug to lead her around by her tits—and pussy?—and I found the idea oddly alluring.

She reached up and pushed Ray's robe off next, and the audience drew in a collective gasp. The entire underside of Ray's fully erect dick was pierced with barbells, like a goddamn Jacob's ladder running up his shaft.

I glanced over at Lauren, knowing I must have looked horrified, because holy shit, that had to hurt. Her mischievous expression was back, and now I was wondering what, *exactly*, we were about to watch.

"Down," Ray said, reaching out to tug Ella to her knees. *By the chain.*

My own nipples felt like they were trying to retreat back into my body, but Ella let out a moan as she hit the floor. Okay, as long as she was into it. Nonconsensual shit was a hard no for me.

"Open," Ray said, and Ella's lips parted at the command.

Lauren moved closer, our arms brushing, but I couldn't take my eyes off the stage, where Ella leaned forward, mouth stretching around the head of Ray's dick, tongue laving the underside. The first barbell slipped past Ella's lips, tugging at them as it went. Jesus, did that even feel good? My eyes traveled up to Ray. He watched Ella working to take him, but nothing in his expression spoke of pain, only pleasure.

Lauren's hand landed on my leg, and finally, I glanced over at her. Her black dress was cut low enough that I had a line of sight straight into her cleavage, where her breasts pressed against the fabric with each breath. Something must have happened onstage while I was distracted by the sight of her, because her nails dug into my leg a little. I lifted my gaze to her face, watching her watch Ray and Ella, enraptured, eyes wide and lips parted like she was imagining trying to take a dick that large herself. Well, if she wanted one, all she had to do was ask.

A nearby gasp had me turning forward again. Ella had worked her way down several more barbells, tears streaming from her eyes. The sight would have made my skin crawl if not for the constant, low moans of encouragement she was making and the way one hand slid down Ray's shaft to cup his balls.

"You're doing so good, baby," Ray said, his fingers sinking into her curls. "Take another."

Goddamn, I thought, watching Ella's heroic effort to fit one more inch down her throat. Yup, porn was ruined.

As soon as that final barbell slid inside, Ella eased back, giving herself a breather, working the head of Ray's cock with her mouth, and his balls with her hands.

Lauren's fingers relaxed their death grip and slid up my leg.

I glanced toward the couple to Lauren's right, but they weren't paying attention to us. No one was. Who in their right mind would look away from the stage right now? Aside from me, because Lauren's hand was creeping higher and higher up my thigh, and I couldn't seem to pull my gaze away from it. Was she really about to touch my dick in a room full of people? More important, was I about to let her?

A round of murmurs had me jerking my head up just in time to watch a curvy, naked white woman with bright red hair walk out of the side door. She went straight to Ella, who was now bobbing on Ray's dick, the barbells slipping in and out of her mouth with audible clicks against her teeth.

"Bri," Lauren whispered.

I couldn't respond, too consumed by the sight of Bri sinking to her knees behind Ella, one hand slipping to Ella's breast, the other between her thighs. Ella reached back and drew Bri's face to her neck, where Bri kissed and sucked her way up to Ella's ear. A threesome. The surprise was a threesome, and Jesus fucking *Christ* did this confirm that I wanted to take part in one before I died.

People shifted in front of us, arms moving as they touched each other. In between their swaying forms, I watched Bri tug Ella's chain, making Ella moan and squirm on Ray's cock, and oh, fuck, that shouldn't have been as hot as it was.

Lauren's fingers brushed over my dick, and I hissed in a surprised breath, glancing at the couple next to us again to see if they noticed. The man's hand was up the woman's skirt as they watched the scene onstage, and between their distraction, the shadows in this corner of the room, and the way Lauren was turned toward me, I doubted they could have seen anything even if they looked.

Lauren flattened her hand and rubbed it all the way up my length. "Whatever I want, whenever I want it," she whispered into my ear, throwing my words back at me.

A promise was a promise.

Our eyes caught, and I nodded. "Whatever you want."

She undid my pants and pulled my dick out right there in a room full of strangers.

19

LAUREN

I NEARLY MOANED AT THE feel of Junior's hard, hot length in my hand, even as I marveled at the events of the past half hour. I'd completely given up on him before he branded me with that kiss in front of half the club, was ready to move on with someone else—or so I'd tried to tell myself—but then he'd shown up and set my blood on fire, reminding me that the pull between us wouldn't be so easily forgotten.

It wasn't fair, what he did to me, the way he scrambled my brain, the way my body responded to him. My mind screamed, *Bad idea!* but my hormones were like, *Step aside, bitch*.

I'd been half tempted to lead him to a third-floor bedroom instead of in here, but if he was serious about sticking around, and if I was seriously about to bend my rules for him again, I needed Junior to understand that hooking up with me meant stepping into my world. One-on-one time was great, but I wanted more than that, *needed* more than that, and I refused to deny or diminish myself. This club was a huge part of my life. Kink play was, too, and I wasn't willing to settle for someone who couldn't or didn't want to take part in it.

Don't get ahead of yourself, I thought, centering myself back in the moment, my gaze going to the stage, where Ray, Ella, and Bri were moving, caressing, *sucking*. Junior's dick was rock hard in my grasp, hot and insistent, telling me how much he liked what he saw.

I stroked my hand up his length. I'd been dreaming about touching him for days, ever since he denied me at the arcade. My bratty side was strong enough that I didn't like being told no. It immediately made me want to act out, and if Junior had been anyone else, I already would have pushed his buttons. But while I'd had plenty of time to explore each and every one of my kinks, it was clear that he hadn't, and I understood the responsibility I had to ease him into things, to not push him too far before he was ready.

I leaned in close and kissed the side of his neck, wrapping my fingers around his straining cock. "Are you sure?"

He was staring straight down, his gaze locked onto where I touched him. "I'm sure," he said, pumping his hips slightly as if trying to get me to move. Always so impatient, this one.

I gave him what he wanted, stroking my hand over his shaft, slowly, taking my time to trace every inch of him, remembering what it had felt like to stretch my lips around his girth, remembering how gentle he'd tried to be when he took my virginity. How much it had still hurt. Until it didn't. We'd only had that one night together before everything went to shit, and I wondered what it would be like now. Certainly easier to take him, if I was good and worked up first. If not . . . god, that would be deliciously rough, borderline painful, but who didn't like a little pain now and then to heighten their pleasure?

I continued to toy with him as I glanced back at the stage. Ray and Ella always put on an incredible show, sometimes sweet, sometimes rough, but always hot as sin, *especially* when Bri joined them.

"Enough," Ray said, and Ella's lips immediately popped open. "Bed. Now."

With a gentle tug on Ella's chain, Bri had her rising to her feet. Junior stiffened beside me, and I smiled, wanting to tell him that Ella was fine, that both Ray and Bri knew exactly how much force to use to keep from hurting her, but I didn't want to distract from the show, so I kept my lips sealed.

Ella got onto the bed first, turning to face the audience, legs spread, revealing the piercing on the hood of her clit and the chain running through its hoop, connected to her nipples. Bri climbed onto the bed after Ella, situated herself between her spread legs, and kissed her way up Ella's thighs while Ray joined them.

I squeezed Junior, gaze dropping to his lap, saliva pooling in my mouth at the thought of licking away the bead of precum on his tip.

Moans swept through the crowd, and I glanced back to the stage to see Bri bury her face between Ella's legs. Ray positioned himself behind Bri, yanking her hips up and fitting his cock to her pussy. Things were about to get *really* interesting, but my gaze slid back to Junior, my thoughts consumed with the desire to go down on him while he watched the scene.

I leaned in, stroking him from base to tip, inhaling the smell of his spiced cologne. "Can I put my mouth on you?"

He turned toward me, nose brushing mine, and our eyes met. I could tell he wanted it, but I didn't press him, letting him make up his mind on his own.

"I don't have to," I whispered. "We can wait until after."

Ray let out a low groan, and Junior's eyes slid away from mine, his face turning back to the stage. Then he glanced at the crowd around us, at all the writhing bodies as everyone else lost themselves to pleasure. Finally, he looked back at me and nodded, legs spreading wide to make room for me between them. "Do it."

I immediately slid from my seat, dropping to my knees on the cold hardwood. Junior shifted his hips forward, and I wrapped my hand around the bottom of his shaft and then my lips around his head. The salty taste of precum hit my tongue, and I moaned, swirling it around, lapping up as much as I could.

I bobbed my head down, just a little, testing the width of him in my mouth. Junior was big enough that I had to go slow at first, coating him in saliva to ease my way. My thoughts went to Ella and how much harder this would be with an added row of barbells to contend with. That woman was a goddamn icon for making it look so flawless.

My hand worked Junior's shaft while I sucked, relearning the feel of him. I wasn't taking him deep, wasn't squeezing him that hard.

Instead, I paced myself, taking my cues from Junior and the audience. Any second now, there would be some sort of mass reaction, indicating penetration, and that's when I would really pick up my pace.

I could tell when it was about to happen, because Junior's dick swelled with a fresh wave of arousal. A heartbeat later, gasps and murmurs filled the crowd. *Showtime.* I tightened my hold on Junior and started working him faster, even as I hollowed my cheeks and took him as deep as I could. His hands slid up my arms, raising goose bumps in their wake, before he slipped his fingers into my hair.

I hummed in approval and leaned in to his grip, the air stirred up by the movement cool against my damp panties. The bondage show had wound me up earlier, but it was nothing compared to how turned on I was now, feeling the hard heat of a man in my mouth, listening to a room full of moans and other, *hotter* sounds. Needing friction, I slipped my free hand between my legs and began rubbing the pad of my finger over myself. I kept my eyes open because the couple beside us was having their own fun, and watching the woman jerk her partner off out of the corner of my eye spun me even higher. At this rate, I might come before Junior did.

His fingers curled, pressing against the back of my head and then releasing, setting a pace for the rhythm he wanted me to keep. I matched it, working him deeper, relaxing my jaw and opening my throat so he could slide into it. A groan told me he liked that. I wished I could look up and see him, watch him shift his gaze between me and the stage, but the angle was off.

His control slipped the longer I worked him, fingers tangling in my hair, hips thrusting with more force. *Yes, fuck my mouth*, I thought, lust tightening my core. I shoved my lacey thong aside and slipped my middle finger into my pussy. My muscles clenched down immediately, and I pressed my palm to my clit, rubbing over it with every stroke.

God, it felt amazing. This was the *more* I needed. This was what I loved: the thrill of being watched by those around us while I got myself off; the exhilaration of watching others chase their own pleasure; the absolute joy of hearing the trio onstage get closer and closer to climax, bringing the whole damn room along for the ride.

"Lo," Junior ground out, fisting my hair.

I pulled off him just long enough to say, "Pour it down my throat," before swallowing him as deep as I could.

With a groan, he started tugging me into every thrust. Yes, this was what I wanted, to feel his control snap, to get a glimpse of the vicious man hiding beneath the careful façade he'd constructed for me. He'd done a good job taming himself, smoothing out his rough edges so he didn't scare me off, but every now and then, the real Junior broke through, like when he'd shut me up with that kiss earlier, and that was the man I craved, that was the man I *needed* to get me off.

His thrusts picked up speed, shaft stiffening, hands gripping so tight it hurt. Tears pricked my eyes. This was perfect, *he* was perfect, giving me everything I wanted and more.

My pussy fluttered around my finger. I was close, but I was too focused on making Junior come to get myself off, and I didn't want the distraction. All I wanted to feel was him unload inside my mouth.

He gave it to me a heartbeat later, barely making a sound. His body told me all I needed to know as he shook and shuddered through it, salty heat exploding over my tongue, branding the back of my throat. I nearly choked, but I managed to swallow it all and keep my pace through his orgasm, slowing only when his fingers slackened.

Before I knew what was happening, he wrenched me off the floor and onto his lap. With a growl, he reached under my dress and yanked at my thong hard enough to rip it off, and suddenly we were skin to skin.

"Move," he said, tugging my hips.

Oh, fuck.

I grabbed the back of the chair to steady myself, barely having to do any work because of how easily he dragged me up and down over the top of his still semi-erect dick. My arousal coated him, turning it into a hot, wet mess that felt amazing rubbing against me. It would be so easy to slip him fully inside, but I didn't know if public, penetrative sex would be too much for him right now, so I let him take the lead.

He leaned forward and tongued my nipple through the dress, and, oh, god, I was going to come so hard.

The room seemed to fall away, leaving only me and Junior and what was happening between us. My fingernails dug into the chair. Spots danced at the edge of my vision. I'd been too aroused for too long, and now my body was punishing me for it, holding me in a state of blissful torture, just shy of where I needed to be.

And then Junior bit my nipple, shoving me over the edge. I slammed my eyes shut, stars bursting behind my lids as my pussy clamped down on nothing and I shattered, writhing, moaning, Junior thrusting against me when my hips lost the rhythm.

I came back to myself with his arm wrapped around me, my head on his chest, his heart pounding out an erratic beat beneath my ear. Slowly, other noises filtered in, louder groans and supplications as the people around us tipped over the edge and the energy in the room rose to a fever pitch. The buzz in the air was palpable. The scent of sex filled my nose. It was like being drunk, when the height of a scene struck, and maybe there was something to that, maybe so many pheromones in such a closed space could have that effect on people. I'd been in crowds that had turned into full-blown orgies before, the doors staying locked long past the end of the scene.

As much as I wanted to turn and look at everyone else, I didn't think I had the energy for it, and from how tightly Junior held me, I wasn't going anywhere anyway.

Not for a long while.

20

JUNIOR

WE WERE AMONG THE LAST to leave the voyeur room. Mostly because we needed that time to get our shit together. Getting swept up in the heat of the moment was all fun and games until the lights came back on and you realized you'd made a mess and ruined another one of your girl's outfits. By the time we reemerged into the hall, the night was winding down, but I wasn't ready to leave Lauren yet.

"Drink?" I asked, threading my fingers through hers.

She nodded, grinning. "Yeah, I could use one."

Downstairs, the foyer was packed, but we managed to find an unoccupied alcove with two cushy leather chairs in a back corner, away from prying eyes. Lauren explained how ordering alcohol worked in the club, offering me some of the champagne she kept stocked in the back. I opted for coffee instead, knowing my night wasn't over yet. I still had places to be after I left Velvet, unfortunately. Our latest shipment was due to come in at 3 a.m. and my ass had to be there.

"So," Lauren said, turning toward me after our drinks were delivered. "Regrets?"

I shook my head and took a sip of coffee. "No, I . . . didn't hate that."

Understatement, but I was still trying to wrap my head around the fact that I'd just watched a threesome while Lauren sucked me off in the middle of a crowded room. It was deviant, depraved. The hottest fucking thing I'd ever done. I wanted more and didn't know how to feel about it.

My gaze traveled over Lauren as I set my drink aside. Her hair was still a little wild, and I didn't like how far away she was. "Come here."

She slid from her seat without protest, just like she had earlier when I'd ordered her between my knees. The word "submissive" floated through my mind, but it was abject, something I'd seen online or in porn. Nowhere on Lauren's Me4U did she mention wanting to be dominated, but maybe she kept her real desires private to leave some space between her and her subs.

I dragged her into my lap, settling her sideways so I could fix the snarls I'd created. She relaxed into my hold, sipping her champagne and idly kicking her feet in a way that was both cute and petulant at the same time. Like this was her due. And maybe it was, maybe I should be the one responsible for setting her straight after I'd been the one to fuck her up.

"There," I said, wrapping my hand around her hip when I was done. I lifted my coffee with the other and relaxed back into the chair, and Lauren came with me, tucking her head beneath my chin. "How's your throat?" I asked. I hadn't exactly gone easy on her.

"That depends."

"On what?"

"How smug you'll be if I tell you it's sore, but it was worth it."

"The smuggest," I said.

She flicked my chest, and I fought back a grin. I shouldn't be happy my dick was big enough to bruise her, but I couldn't deny the fact that I liked that the soreness would remind her of what we'd done.

Her fingers trailed lower, over my abdomen, and I hissed in a breath.

"Oh, god, I'm sorry," she said, starting to lift off me. "I forgot about your wound."

I yanked her back down. "I'm fine. Just watch that side."

A pastel blur passed in front of the alcove and then backtracked. "Oh, hiii," Taylor said, sticking her head in. "Sorry to interrupt the aftercare, but Sylvia wants to see us in fifteen."

Lauren saluted her. "I'll be there."

Taylor returned the salute and spun on her heel, disappearing.

Aftercare? Was that what this was? I thought that was limited to BDSM relationships. This just felt like spending time together after getting each other off.

Lauren tucked her head into the crook of my neck, and I tightened my arm around her. "Who's Sylvia?" I asked, curious.

"Velvet's founder and primary stakeholder," Lauren said. "Me, my roommates, and a few others have bought shares as well."

"Do you meet every night you're here?"

She shook her head, hair rubbing against the bottom of my chin. "No, Sylvia and her partner, Martin, handle all of the day-to-day business. We're mostly financial backers and are only called in when big decisions need to be made."

"Is something like that happening now?" I asked.

She sighed. "Yes. The man who owns the building is raising our rent again, and we're scrambling to come up with an alternative location. Ryan, Taylor, and I have spent all our free time looking at other buildings and putting out feelers to see if someone else would be willing to work with us."

"Any luck?"

"Unfortunately, no. Everything is either too expensive, or people don't want to take on the risk of having us as renters."

"You're not breaking any laws, are you?"

"We do absolutely everything by the books," Lauren said, explaining the city's zoning and vice laws to me. When she was finished, she added, "We've never even had to pay a fine—that's how careful we are."

Interesting. "Are you profitable?"

She blew out a breath. "We would be if our landlord wasn't such a leech."

"How much is he charging you?" I asked, taking a sip of coffee. Her answer almost made me do a spit take. "That's bullshit."

"I know," she said. "But we might end up having to pay it."

"Who's your landlord?" Maybe I knew him and could pull some strings.

"A decrepit asshole named Patrick McKinney." The name was unfamiliar. "I think he's trying to force us out with the hikes."

"Seems like it." I couldn't think of any other reason to drive someone's rent so high. A profitable business was a profitable business, and if they were willing to pay what was already too much money, it didn't make financial sense to risk losing them. Unless you were a fucking prude and wanted them out. Or you were forced to raise rent for some other reason . . .

The wheels started turning in my head. I'd look into it for her. It might be nothing, but I knew a lot about who owned this city and what made them tick. Something didn't seem to add up here.

My phone rang in my pocket, and I jostled Lauren a little to get to it.

I nearly swore when I saw "Dad" on the caller ID.

"Yeah?" I asked, picking up.

"Now," he said.

God-*fucking*-damnit. Couldn't I get just a few hours to myself?

Lauren started to sit up, probably feeling how quickly I'd gone from relaxed to pissed. I tugged her back down, deciding now was as good a time as any to start pushing back.

"I'm tied up," I said. "And I've got to be at the docks soon. Get Alec to handle it."

Dad hung up on me.

I tossed my phone onto the table with more force than necessary and suddenly wished I'd ordered something stronger than coffee.

"Everything okay?" Lauren asked.

I shook my head.

"Do you need to go?"

"We'll see," I said. "I have a few more minutes at least."

"How's everything going," she said, and I could feel her wincing, "with that?"

"With the mob, you mean?" I asked, unable to keep from teasing her.

She flicked my chest again. "With your *dad*, mostly."

I was quiet for a beat. Between our sexting sessions and teenage discussions, she'd probably pieced together how unhappy I was about being forced into the family business. Even back in high school, I'd had to cancel on her more than once, or I'd shown up late covered in dirt, exhausted and needing a distraction to keep from losing my mind. She'd sensed my inner turmoil and asked questions, but most of them revolved around if I was okay, more worried about my well-being than what I had done.

Fuck, I didn't deserve her.

"Things with my dad are . . . tense," I said. "Especially since I'm about to get forced into a position of more responsibility."

"What do you mean?" she asked.

I sighed. "In Italy, the mob has infiltrated the olive oil market. They package and sell what they claim is extra-virgin olive oil, but it isn't really. It's a shitty mix of other vegetable oils they advertise as the real thing and make a killing exporting to other countries. We've brought some of that over here, but our shipments are still small because we're new to it. Tonight, my dad asked me to head the operation's expansion. He wants to build an empire. This scheme has already made the Italian mob billions overseas, and he's hoping to get a slice of that pie."

Lauren jerked upright. "Did you just say *billions*?"

I nodded. "Look up the Agromafia sometime when you get a chance."

"One sec, I'm making a note to." She tipped forward to grab her purse from the table, the front of her dress gaping open, and I lost a couple of seconds staring at her cleavage.

She put her phone down next to mine when she was done and settled back into place. "Is it as lucrative here as it is overseas?"

"Yes," I said. "Unfortunately, my dad still wants to cut as many corners as possible, so there's just as much illegal shit involved in the operation as anything else he has his hand in."

Lauren went still, and I could practically see her mind spinning. "Which means that if you're heading it and something goes wrong, you'll be the one to go down for everything, not him."

"Bingo," I said.

"Let me know if you need a character witness. I would *love* to lie to a judge."

"I'll hold you to that," I told her.

"I'm really sorry," she said, sobering. "That's a terrible position for a parent to put their child in, and I hate that he's doing it to you."

I held her close, something in my chest tightening. No one had ever said something like that to me before. "Yeah, well, it's just another reason for me to get out while I can."

She lifted her head up enough to look me in the eye. "You want out?"

I held her gaze and nodded. "I've been thinking about it for years."

"What are you going to do instead?" she asked.

"I'm considering joining the priesthood."

She grinned. "Does that mean I'll get to call you Daddy?"

I nearly choked. "Isn't it Father?"

"Tomato, tomahto."

I huffed out a breath and took a moment to seriously contemplate her question. "I'd settle for doing literally anything else, but I'd like to run some kind of business. Fuck knows I have the experience for it. And after years managing Dad's cronies, regular employees will feel like a cakewalk in comparison."

She leaned in and kissed me, just a peck on the cheek. "I'm really proud of you."

My heart stuttered, and I had to look away. Hearing those words coming from Lauren, of all people, meant more than I could have anticipated. It made me want to be a better man for her, *continue* making her proud, but suddenly all I could think of was how disappointed she'd be if she ever found out about all the unforgivable things I'd done in my life.

Her father—

Nope. Not going there tonight, I told myself. We needed a subject change. Now.

"What about you?" I asked.

She dropped her head back to my shoulder. "What about me?"

"What do you want to do?" I asked, gesturing past us to the club. "When this is all over?"

I knew the second the words were out of my mouth that I'd misstepped, because she stiffened.

"What do you mean?" she asked, her tone losing its warmth. "'When this is all over'?"

I ran my hand up her back, trying to soothe her. "I just meant whenever you decide to move on from camwork."

She pulled out of my arms, sitting up. Fuck, I'd made it worse. "I don't plan to move on from it."

"I mean like when you're fifty," I clarified.

She stood. Goddamn it, this was *not* coming out the way I'd intended.

"There are plenty of camworkers in their fifties," she said. "And I plan to be one of them. This isn't something I just fell into because I couldn't hack it doing something else."

Shit, I'd definitely hit a vein. "I just meant you used to talk about wanting to be a psychologist, having a family."

She jerked back like I'd slapped her. "I *have* my psychology degree. It's done wonders to help me connect with my subs. And being a sex worker doesn't mean I can't also have a family, if I choose to, but what I *won't* do is have some man try to dictate how I live my life, keep me pregnant and barefoot in his kitchen cooking pasta while he's off doing god knows what."

"Jesus, come on—"

Lauren's eyes sparked with anger. "I *love* what I do, Junior. My subs are my community." She pointed toward the foyer, her voice gaining volume. "These people are like family. They are the most kind, welcoming, nonjudgmental humans I have ever met, and I don't ever plan on leaving them."

"I didn't say you had to," I barked, my voice rising to match hers.

She took a step back, eyes wide. Shit, what had I just done? This *goddamn* temper.

"I think you should go," she said.

My chest heaved as I fought to get myself under control. "Just like that? I say one wrong thing, and it's over?"

She crossed her arms and broke eye contact.

Fuck, I was losing her. I could *feel* it.

"I'm sorry, Lauren. Look, none of what I said came out right, and I—"

Noises hit my ears. Shouting, a scuffle.

I was out of the alcove in a heartbeat, yelling at Lauren to stay where she was. At the front door, three men were trying to gain entry, and the bouncers were having a hard time containing them, obviously trying to keep from using force or escalating the situation.

One broke past them into the lobby and kept on coming. He was large, white, and obviously shit-faced. "Who wants to fuck?!"

The nerdy professor Lauren had been speaking to earlier approached him. "Hey, you shouldn't—"

"Not you," the man said, shoving him so hard that he bounced off the floor. "I want a woman."

The sudden outburst of violence and obvious threat of more panicked the crowd, everyone moving away.

I stepped into the space they cleared and squared off against the drunk guy. "Out. Now."

"Fuck you," he spat.

Couldn't say I didn't warn him.

Adrenaline rushed through my veins as I moved forward. I was already wound up because of my father's manipulation and the misunderstanding with Lauren, and here was my chance to vent some of my pent-up rage. This motherfucker picked the wrong night.

He threw a sloppy punch. I shifted out of the way, grabbed his wrist, and pulled, hard, tugging him off-balance. It was like child's play, stepping behind him, taking his wrist with me, kicking out his knee, and dropping him to the ground. I put my boot on his spine, yanked his arm up, and with a *pop!* his shoulder slid out of socket. The room filled with the sound of his pained bellow. I spun him onto his back and leaned down, punching him twice in quick succession, feeling his nose burst beneath my knuckles on the second blow. Blood sprayed, and he went limp on the floor, dazed.

The whole altercation took less than ten seconds.

My pulse roared in my ears as I lifted my eyes to his two friends and smiled, showing all of my teeth. They put their hands up and wisely let the bouncers escort them out, and I tried not to be disappointed that they'd given up so easily.

"*Junior.*"

A glance toward the alcove revealed Lauren standing in its doorway, Ryan and Taylor at her side, all three of them looking a little green. What? It was only a dislocated shoulder and a broken nose. In six to eight weeks, he'd be fine. It wasn't like I'd permanently disfigured him or anything.

"You need to leave," Lauren said.

I released the man and faced her. "Be reasonable."

Taylor grimaced, shaking her head. Great, I'd said the wrong thing again.

"We don't allow violence in here," Lauren said. "You broke the rules. You have to go."

Fucking hell. "No exceptions for protecting everyone else?"

The crowd watching our little drama play out murmured in what sounded like support, but Lauren remained steadfast in her decision.

"Fine," I bit out. "Just let me grab my phone."

She stepped back as I approached, like she didn't want me near her now.

I snagged the phone from the table and spun on her. "What did you expect, Lo? That after hearing you say how much this place means to you, I'd let some drunken assholes fuck it up?"

"That's not your job."

My anger spiked. "Yes. It is. I've spent the past *decade* protecting you, and it's not like your bouncers were handling it."

Her eyes flashed wide. "What did you just say?"

Shit. This was why I always kept a cage on my temper. I slipped up when it broke free, caused arguments, said too much. "Nothing," I ground out, striding past her toward the door.

"Junior, wait a second," she said, but I ignored her, grabbing my gear from the coat check and striding out into the waiting night.

21

LAUREN

I RUSHED AFTER JUNIOR, WATCHING him shrug into a leather jacket and then pull a motorcycle helmet on. He swung his leg over a street bike, slapped his visor down, and revved the engine, taking off like a shot into the night.

I stared after him, feeling my world shift on its axis, because I recognized that gear and that bike. I'd seen them on my block too many times to count. Did Junior *live* in my neighborhood? Had he been nearby this whole time? Or had he just been . . . watching me?

Ryan and Taylor appeared at my side.

"I knew he'd be a biker," Taylor said. "Maybe if you ask him nicely, he'll fuck you on it after you make up."

I remained quiet, mind racing, and my friends turned to me.

"Hey, are you all right?" Ryan asked.

I shook my head and reached down, digging around in my purse until I pulled out that coin thing I'd found earlier. "Do you recognize this from anywhere? Another club we've been to or something?"

"Nope," Taylor said, looking it over.

Ryan took it from me and gave it a closer inspection, turning it toward the nearby streetlight. "There's writing on it. I think it says SecPro. Don't they make spy gear?"

Cool. Cool, cool. No need to freak out. It definitely wasn't a tracking device or anything. That would be crossing a line that not even Junior would . . . I let the thought go, recognizing it for the bullshit it was. Junior absolutely would, and he'd had plenty of opportunities to plant it on me thanks to the fact that whenever I got close to him, the rational part of my brain fucked off to the moon.

What was it he'd said? He'd spent the past decade protecting me? My mind spun back to his confession about Kelly and Principal Michaels, the way he'd gone after them on my behalf. Who was to say it had stopped there?

I thought of Nonna's frantic phone call after church to make sure I got home okay. If I called her back and asked whose tires had been slashed, would she rattle off a list of all the church ladies who'd been talking shit about me before Mass? And the week before that, when Councilwoman Blackwell had suddenly decided to take a meeting with me after months of politely telling me to go fuck myself, was that Junior? And the week before that, when the parking tickets I went to pay mysteriously weren't on file, and the week before that, when . . .

No. He couldn't have been behind everything. That would have been insane. Junior was a lot of things, but he wasn't crazy.

Suddenly, the smile he'd worn while almost ripping that man's arm off his body bubbled up, and I wondered if maybe he was a little batshit after all.

"It's a tracker," Ryan said, showing me the webpage they'd pulled up on their phone. "But it's not supposed to be available to the public, so I don't know how one would end up in your . . . oh."

"Junior?" Taylor asked.

I nodded.

Angry male voices rose from behind us. The drunk man was being escorted out, his busted arm cradled in front of his chest, blood streaming down his face. It was time to get back inside where it was safe.

I beelined straight to the bar once we were in. "Give me a whole bottle."

Scott, tonight's bartender, didn't even bat an eye, handing it over like the professional he was. We took it back to the alcove I'd been in with Junior, and that's when I spotted his phone still sitting on the table, the phone I clearly remembered him—oh, no. I wrenched open my purse, looking for mine, but it wasn't inside; he'd accidentally taken it instead of his. Unease crept up my spine. *Was* it accidental, or had he done this on purpose just to have an excuse to see me again?

"What?" Taylor asked. "You look like you've had another *oh shit* moment."

I filled my roommates in on the phone swap.

"Here," Ryan said, offering theirs to me, my contact already open. "You can use mine to ask him to bring it back."

I took it from them and tapped the call button.

It rang so long that I didn't think Junior would answer. When he finally did, I heard his motorcycle idling in the background. "Fuck, I have your phone."

"Yeah, I noticed. Can I have it back?"

"No. I'm already on the other side of town, and I got shit to do. I'll bring it to church tomorrow. Whatever you do, don't answer mine if anyone calls." And then he hung up on me.

I handed Ryan's phone back to them with shaking fingers. Where did he get the nerve to be mad at *me*? I wasn't the one who'd stalked him. I wasn't the one who'd hurt people on his account and done god only knew what else. And I definitely wasn't the one who'd denigrated *his* line of work.

With a twist, I popped the champagne cork. And then I refilled my empty glass and slugged half of it back in one gulp, nose burning from the bubbles.

"Sooo," Taylor said, twirling a strand of her hair. "How you doiiing?"

I laughed, humorlessly, and took another swig.

■　■　■

The next morning, I still had no idea how to feel. Besides slightly hung-over. The night before seemed like a fever dream. And the fight with Junior . . . ugh.

I'd had previous partners say they were fine with my job, only to turn controlling, wanting to approve every sext I sent or limit how active I was on my page. One even went so far as to tell me I needed to stop camwork altogether if I wanted to continue dating them. I'd immediately broken things off and then signed them up for every newsletter I could find, turning their inbox into a hellscape of spam. Fuck you very much, *Marcus*.

In the heat of the argument, I'd been worried Junior was like that, that he didn't see my work as valid or worthwhile enough to do for the long haul. And then he'd brought up me wanting a family, and all I could think of were my parents and the parallels between us and them. Before they'd gotten married, my mother had been gainfully employed and living on her own. Then my mobster father came along, knocked her up, and convinced her to quit her job to be a stay-at-home mom, because no woman of his should work (whether they wanted to or not). The control hadn't stopped there, turning from coercion to mental abuse, wearing my mother down until Nonna Bianchi said she hardly even recognized her own daughter. And then one day, Mom had finally had enough, packing her bags and leaving Kristen and me behind, my father coming home late that night to find us dirty and hungry.

I'd been so young that I had few memories of my mother, but every one was of an exhausted shell of a woman who winced at loud noises, never smiled, and had a haunted look in her eyes that I still saw in my nightmares.

I would never *ever* let anyone do that to me. It was one of my greatest fears, and that fear reared its ugly head last night when Junior started insinuating I would one day quit my job and settle down to take care of a family like a Good Italian Woman.

My fear had only swelled when I found the tracker. Junior clearly had zero fucking boundaries if he'd been stalking me. Stalking spoke of control on steroids. The need to always know where I was, always have access to me . . . it wasn't okay. Made me feel like a caged animal.

And then there was the fight. He'd moved so fast, with zero hesitation, like violence was so normal to him that he didn't even have to think about it. The way he'd smiled the whole time . . . I shuddered just remembering the look on his face.

Fuck, I shouldn't have been turned on by it. But there was no denying that I had been. That my underwear was slightly damp from the memory alone.

I shook my head, reminding myself that I didn't want someone prone to violence. I didn't want a toxic partner. Life was complicated enough without adding a high-maintenance man to it.

On the other hand, I *did* want someone that willing to explore their sexuality with me, I *did* want someone who spoke so openly about what they wanted from life, and I especially wanted someone who was quick to apologize and make amends when they fucked up. These things spoke of a person with depth, like-minded openness, curiosity, and self-awareness. Someone with drive.

Those were the traits I wanted in a partner, without question.

It left me wondering: Which version of Junior was the *real* one? Who would he be in a relationship?

My head was clearly scrambled, but one thing I did need was my phone back, so I called Nonna from Ryan's and told her I'd be joining her at Mass. We met outside of her building, only a few blocks from the church, a little earlier than normal because she wanted to stop in at the local bakery.

"I want a good cup of coffee," she said as we waited in line, "before I'm forced to drink that pig shit they brew at church."

The woman waiting in front of us turned with wide eyes.

Nonna met her gaze with a challenging expression. "What? I'm not saying anything that everyone isn't already thinking."

The woman turned back around, looking scandalized.

I shuffled closer to my grandmother and dropped my voice. "Do you know her?"

Nonna shook her head and sent me a sly smile. She'd stopped giving a fuck five years ago, when Nonno died, and now spent her time living for the shock and discomfort of others. *Age disgracefully* was her motto. I wanted to be her when I grew up.

"I need to talk to you about something," she said after we'd gathered our coffees and sat at a small table in the corner of the shop.

"What's up?" I asked.

She reached over and gripped my wrist. "Your father is missing."

I went still in my seat. Was this how it started? With one forgotten conversation, and a year from now, Kristen and I would have to move her into a cognitive care facility? "Um . . . I know, Nonna."

"Don't look at me like that," she scolded. "I haven't gone organic." She leaned in and dropped her voice. "He's *really* missing, Lauren."

I frowned. "What do you mean?"

"Apparently, he has a girlfriend." She rolled her eyes and released me. "Can you believe that cunt tricked another woman into putting up with him?"

A startled gasp sounded from nearby. It wasn't every day you heard an octogenarian drop the c-bomb, but I didn't so much as bat an eye. This type of talk was par for the course with Nonna.

"Poor woman," I said, taking my first tentative sip of coffee.

Nonna nodded. "Yes, well, she went into the deli, panicking, and told Kristen that Tommy hadn't been home in weeks, so Kristen went to the cops and filed a missing person report. The cops spent a few days looking into it, and it turns out your asshole father hasn't used his cell phone or credit cards since he first disappeared."

I blinked. "So wait, he's, like, *really* missing?"

She nodded and sat back.

"Why didn't Kristen tell me any of this?" I asked, confused and a little hurt.

Nonna waved a hand in the air. "You know your sister, always wanting to shield you from Tommy's bullshit."

That was *not* what Kristen did, but I let Nonna go on believing the comforting lie. Kristen loved being the one who knew everything, loved doling out information in tiny pieces, forcing people to ask her question after question while she slowly revealed the rest. And when it came to me? Half the time she wouldn't even answer, just because she liked lording her knowledge over me and watching me get increasingly frustrated. She might have looked just like Mom, but her personality had mostly come from our father.

"What else did the cops have to say?" I asked.

Nonna shrugged. "Just that they're looking into it. If you ask me, my friend Barb is right, and that selfish prick probably has a second family somewhere and is out West visiting them. It would explain all his other disappearances, too."

I nodded. That thought had crossed my mind before. But knowing he wasn't using his phone or credit cards . . .

"Anyway," Nonna said, "I just wanted you to hear it from me instead of anyone else. You know how people at church gossip."

"I do, and thank you." My sister was going to get an earful from me soon. I should have heard it from *her*, the second our father's girlfriend showed up, not weeks later.

Nonna took a sip of coffee, her gaze turning shrewd as she set the cup back down. "Now tell me, who are you sleeping with these days?"

"Would you look at that," I said, glancing at the nonexistent watch on my wrist. "We better go before we're late."

Nonna grinned. "Shut up, we have plenty of time."

"I am *not* discussing my sex life with my grandmother." That was a step too far, even for me.

"Fine," she said. "Just tell me that you're having lots of it. I loved your grandfather more than anything, but my biggest regret in life is that I wasn't a complete skank before I met him."

Someone nearby choked, and I decided it was time to switch topics. And get some answers to a question that had been bothering me since last night. "Did you ever figure out what happened to everyone's tires?"

Nonna eyed me for a second like she wasn't going to let me get away with the subject change, but finally she shook her head. "No. Someone cut the wire to the camera that faced the side lot they were parked in."

"Whose cars were targeted?" I asked, trying to sound casual.

She frowned. "I think just Maria's, Angelina's, and Nina's."

The three women who happened to be sitting directly behind us that morning, whispering amongst themselves. Fucking Junior. He'd totally done it, hadn't he?

Nonna's expression turned serious. "Back to what I was saying."

Oh no.

"I hope you're sowing your oats now." Her eyes fluttered shut, and a look of grief washed over her face. "One penis. For fifty years, Lauren." She blinked and met my gaze. "Learn from my mistakes. Be a slut while you still can."

22

LAUREN

NONNA AND HER FRIENDS HAD moved on from talking about their ailments—thank god—and were now deep into a discussion about some big drama that happened before I was even born. I listened with half an ear, trying not to tap my fingers against the table. We were midway through coffee hour, and Junior was still nowhere to be seen. The prick. I was angry at him and impatient to get out of here, get my phone back, and call my sister to ask her why she felt the need to act like such a controlling bitch.

If Junior was blowing me off, so help me god . . .

An unfamiliar ringing rose from somewhere near the floor, pulling me from my thoughts. I glanced down and realized the sound was coming from my purse. Great, someone was calling him. I was half tempted to pick it up and ask if they knew where he was, but his tone when he told me not to answer it had held serious menace, like something bad could happen if I disobeyed him, and my brat streak didn't run deep enough to put my safety in jeopardy.

Planning to silence it, I lifted it out only to see my own number on the caller ID. I froze. How the fuck had he unlocked my phone?

"Sorry," I told the ladies around me. "I need to answer this."

Nonna's sharp gaze landed on me as I stood, and I turned before she could read too much into my expression.

"Where are you?" I asked by way of answering.

"Here," Junior said, his voice low. "Come find me."

And then he hung up on me. Again.

I curled my hand around the phone and pulled it away from my ear, and the only thing that kept me from turning it into an overpriced frisbee was the crowd of onlookers. The man had the audacity to make me wait an hour and a half for him, and then tell *me* to put in all the effort to meet up? Oh, hell no. I was going to do so much worse to him than fill his inbox with spam.

Taking a deep breath, I strode from the reception room into the hallway where I'd first run into him. He wasn't there. I peeked into the ladies' room just in case he'd gone full-blown creeper, but there was no sign of him inside. Stepping back out, I glanced toward the men's room. Nope. Not even the temptation of regaining my phone was strong enough to lure me in there. With my luck, I'd catch sight of some old man's saggy skin biscuits and need to have my eyeballs removed.

I left the hall and swept through the connecting door into the nave. It looked empty.

"This isn't funny," I said, stalking toward the front entrance, checking between each row of pews as I went, hoping that Junior wasn't about to jump out at me like a fucked-up jack-in-the-box.

I was passing the confessionals when one of the doors popped open and I got yanked inside, a hand covering my mouth before I could scream. There was just enough light to see Junior's face as he pulled the door shut again.

"Let me go!" I said, the words muffled.

He chuckled, the sound diabolical in the closed space.

I tried to stomp on his foot, but my heel clanged off something rock-hard and I almost twisted my ankle. Was he wearing steel-toed boots?

He wrapped an arm around my waist and dragged my back against his chest, his mouth pressed to the side of my head. "Did you miss me?"

"No," I said, but his palm muffled it. I slammed my hands onto his forearm, trying to push him off, but it was like a steel vise around my middle.

"I'm sorry for losing my temper," he said.

I tried to yank free, starting to panic a little. I could feel the heat rolling off his body, smell his heady cologne. The dark of the confessional was too close to our shadowy corner in the voyeur room, and my mind was already starting to torment me with memories of what we'd done there last night.

"And I'm sorry for how my questions came off," he said, easily restraining me. "I think what you do is valid work, and I wasn't trying to imply otherwise. I would never, *ever* try to trap you, Lauren. If you believe nothing else I've said, believe that."

My pulse thundered in my ears as his words sank in. Goddamn it. He sounded sincere. And if anyone understood what it felt like to be trapped, it was Junior. The hunted look in his eyes last night when he told me about his father's plans for him had made that crystal clear.

"I'm *not* sorry for putting down that drunk guy, though," he growled. "If I hadn't stepped in, he might have hurt someone else or tried to assault one of the women."

Honestly, I wasn't sorry he'd done it either, but there was no way to tell him that with his hand clamped over my mouth.

I was just gearing up to bite him so we could have a normal adult conversation when he slowly pulled his hand away.

"I'm sorry, too," I said, and I meant it. I didn't like losing my temper, didn't like snapping at people, no matter *how* they treated me.

He tightened his hold on my waist. "Don't be sorry. No one could blame you for being sensitive about your work, especially not me. I know how much it means to you."

Oof. How was I supposed to resist him when he said things like that? Oh, right, the *other* thing I'd learned last night.

"How long have you been stalking me?" I asked.

He tensed. "What do you mean?"

"I found the tracker you put in my purse," I said. "And I need you to explain *exactly* what you meant when you said you've been protecting me for the past ten years."

His forehead hit my shoulder. "I will. I promise. Just . . . not here."

"But soon," I said. "You'll tell me everything."

He was silent for so long I didn't think he'd answer me. I was just gathering the courage to yank free from his hold and walk out of there when he said, "I'll tell you everything."

"No more lies," I said.

He kissed my shoulder. "No more lies."

A creaking sound announced someone else entering the nave.

Oh, shit.

Junior clamped his hand over my mouth again. "Don't scream."

No threat of that. These people were judgy enough without me getting caught in a compromising position inside one of the most sacred parts of the church.

Voices echoed over the marble. I recognized the low, melodic tone of the priest. Another man spoke, and then another. Were they talking about baseball?

My ears strained as I tried to determine how many people were in the nave. All the fucking marble out there wasn't helping, making their voices echo in a way that made it seem like they were coming from all directions. Was someone right outside the confessional? Were we about to get caught?

Junior, apparently unconcerned with the men's proximity to our hiding spot, nuzzled my cheek. His unshaven face was rough against my skin. Warmth swept over my neck when he exhaled, and suddenly I became aware of every hard inch of him pressed against me. The way his thighs framed mine, the heat radiating off his much larger body. His arm shifted higher around my waist, jacket creaking, the smell of leather and cologne mixing with the faint traces of incense left in the booth. The hand on my mouth loosened, slid lower, gripping my jaw, fingers digging in as he tilted my head sideways and exposed my neck.

Uh-oh . . .

CAUGHT UP

My body instantly betrayed me as the submissive I was, going loose and languid in his hold. Even my brain started to fizzle out with that blissful relaxation that came from handing your control over to someone else. Was I furious about the tracker and the possible decade-long stalking? Abso-fucking-lutely, but all the righteous anger in the world couldn't mask the fact that I still *wanted* Junior. My body responded to him almost against my will, like it had imprinted on the sonofabitch.

What wasn't helping was the adrenaline starting to pump through my veins. I'd *always* had a thing for public sex, for quick, dirty hookups where anyone could catch me in the act. All it would take was one sound to betray us, one sigh or moan, and the taboo thrill of being discovered like this, *in a church*, sent desire racing through my veins.

Junior, feeling my response to him, dropped his hand to my throat and let out a low, masculine hum of approval. He brushed his lips over my jaw and then trailed a line of kisses downward, and I stopped trying to push his arm away and pulled it closer instead, grinding my ass against him, feeling his hard length framed between my cheeks.

What the fuck was I doing?

Probably making a huge mistake, but for the life of me, I couldn't stop myself. Outside the booth, more voices joined the conversation, and a lively debate started over whether the new head coach of our local team would bring the city its next championship title.

I'd never been so turned on listening to a bunch of old men discuss sports before.

Junior must have felt it, too, because his hand dropped from my waist to the hem of my skirt. I immediately widened my legs, telling him with my body that, yes, I wanted this, whatever he was offering.

He yanked the back of my skirt up, pinning it between us as his hand fell away, down to his pants. The sound of his zipper sliding open was loud in the booth, and we froze, spending a breathless minute straining our ears, but the conversation outside kept on going like they hadn't heard a thing. Slowly, Junior's hand moved between us. I felt the tip of his cock press the soaked fabric of my underwear against my pussy, and I had to clench my jaw to keep from whimpering.

As if sensing my near slip, he tightened his hand around my throat in warning. I nodded, squirming in his hold, so fucking turned on I felt like I would die if he didn't touch me. He made another low sound, this one a mix of impatience and lust as he thrust against me. No, this wasn't good enough.

"More," I pleaded, voice so low I barely heard myself speak.

He ripped my underwear to the side and then the head of his cock was *there*, pushing against my entrance. I grabbed the wrist at my neck with both hands, hanging on for dear life, desperate to feel him pushing into me.

We could get caught like this, fucking in a church.

Lust roared through me at the thought. I was so turned on I could already feel myself coating the head of Junior's cock in slickness.

The ghost of a groan slipped out of him, barely audible even though his lips were right at my ear. "Don't move," he whispered.

I held still, clinging to him, shaking with need. He pushed just inside, and, *oh, god*, the stretch was so delicious that it seemed impossible to hold still. I wanted more of him, *all* of him, until he was shoved so deep that I felt him hit the back of my teeth.

But he didn't give it to me. Instead, he held himself there, both of us breathing through our noses to try to stay quiet. A shiver wracked his body, and I knew he was just as close as I was, balanced on a precipice of near violence and trying not to pound into me, giving us away.

His other hand slid around my hip and then between my thighs. My eyes widened at the first brush of his fingertips. I was in a confessional booth, near a packed banquet hall, a group of people just outside, speared on the head of a cock, with a man's hand stroking my clit. It was the most life-altering religious experience of my life. I'd never felt closer to God. And maybe that was blasphemous, but if it was, then I would happily claim the title of heretic, because nothing would ever make me regret doing this, not even if I found out he'd stalked me every single day for the past ten years. Heaven help me, but the slight fear that he might have done just that only drove my desire higher, adding a dangerous thrill that made my heart skip a beat before thundering on.

His fingers rolled over my clit again and again, and I kept waiting for him to push deeper, but he held himself perfectly still inside me, frustratingly shallow. I clenched around him, trying to coax him into moving even as I obeyed his order to stay still, and between the frustration of being denied, the threat of discovery, and the sensation of his fingers playing me like I was his favorite instrument, I quickly climbed higher and higher.

My inner muscles spasmed, desperate for more. I'd never been so aware of the first inch of my pussy in my life. I swore I felt every nerve ending lighting up where we touched, felt the entire outline of his cock head stretching me wide.

Move, I wanted to beg him, but I didn't trust myself to open my mouth without moaning.

My legs shook, threatening to buckle.

Junior's hand tightened on my throat, and I felt his silent command of *Don't you fucking dare fall.*

His fingers picked up speed on my clit, and this time, I couldn't stop a low whimper from slipping out. Lips parted beneath my ear. The sharp pinch of teeth warned me to shut up. Oh, no. I was going to come. Here. In the back of a cavernous church, and if any of the sounds I made were louder than a whisper, they would echo over the marble, and we'd be caught.

I didn't know if I could obey Junior's command. I'd never had to be completely silent before. But it was too late to slow down, too late to talk myself back from the edge, because my fear was amplifying my pleasure, and I could feel a monster of an orgasm building.

Fuck, this was going to be torture.

Heat bloomed low in my belly. My muscles clenched down on Junior's dick and held. I slammed my eyes shut, trying to focus on staying mute, praying like I'd never prayed in my life. A full-body shudder rolled from the top of my spine to the tip of my toes. Only Junior's grip on my neck kept me upright.

I clenched my thighs together, shaking, shivering, my entire being spiraling down to the bundle of nerves between my legs before it exploded outward again, tearing through me, pleasure and euphoria and joy lighting up every single cell in my body as I came harder than I had in years, holding my breath the entire time because I didn't know how else to keep from crying out.

Junior stepped back, slipping out of me, and I felt hot liquid spurt across my inner thighs as his orgasm chased mine. The fingers around my neck clenched, bowing my spine, nearly pulling me off-balance before he came back to himself and steadied us.

"Did you hear something?"

We froze.

"No?" someone answered.

"I could have sworn I heard . . ." The man trailed off, and I stopped breathing again. "Yup, thought so. Sorry, fellas, I think my wife is looking for me."

I nearly collapsed in relief. Behind me, Junior let out a shaky breath. And then his hand found my shoulder and he was turning me, kissing me, his hands everywhere, my own slipping into his hair and tugging him down, almost viciously. I didn't know if I wanted to fight or fuck, and it was confusing as hell.

More voices entered the room, but we were too busy quietly bruising each other's mouths to register them until it was almost too late. "I'm telling you, he's here," an unmistakable, feminine, *Irish* voice said.

Junior tore himself away from me, eyes wide.

"Look," Moira said. "The little GPS dot says he's right here somewhere."

"Junior?" Nico Senior called out.

Oh, no. We'd pissed off God with our antics, and now He was going to punish us.

In record time, Junior had his dick back in his pants and his shirt tucked in.

"Can I help you both?" the priest asked, his shoes echoing over the marble floor as he headed our way.

I ducked down and scooped Junior's phone from my purse, shoving it at him. He had to get out of here. Now, before they caught us together. Jesus Christ, his cum was dripping down my legs.

He pulled my phone from his jacket pocket, and we swapped.

"Oh, hello, Father," Moira said. "You haven't seen our oldest anywhere, have you?"

Junior grabbed the front of my shirt and hauled me toward him, kissing me one last time. And then he let me go, sent me an unreadable look, and slipped out of the booth, careful not to open the door too wide.

"Sorry," he said, sounding more put together than he had any right to be. "I was out late last night and decided to take a quick nap."

"In the confessional?" Moira asked, scandalized. "Please forgive him, Father."

A low chuckle. "No need. I was young once, too."

Lead them away, I silently begged as I slid out of my underwear and used them to wipe myself off. I had a travel pack of tissues on me, but I wasn't touching them. The crinkling of plastic would give me away if I tried, and I needed to get clean, fast, just in case someone decided to come check on what (or more like who) Junior had *really* been doing in here.

"You ready to head to breakfast?" he asked, and the sound of retreating footsteps was like music to my ears.

It took the baseball bros another ten minutes to break apart, and then I spent five more inside the booth after they left, my heart pounding and my ears straining for any hint of noise. Nothing. I cracked the door.

Nonna sat in the pew right outside, grinning like the cheshire cat, and I about had a heart attack. How the hell had she snuck up on me?

"I see you took my advice," she said.

My face flushed with warmth, but as I stepped out of the booth, I decided to feign ignorance. There was no way she could have known what I'd done. She hadn't even seen Junior. "I have no idea what you're talking about."

She crowed with laughter. "Tell that to the handprint on your neck."

23

JUNIOR

"Hey, thanks again for unlocking that phone for me the other night," I said. I sat on my cousin's couch in her small two-bedroom cottage, her huge-ass boyfriend, strike that, fiancé, taking up most of the cushion space beside me.

"No problem," Josh said. "Were you able to track Lauren down and switch them out?"

"Yeah, at church."

He sat forward, eyes narrowed, a sly grin tugging at his mouth. "*Aaand?*" he prodded. "How'd it go?"

"Fine," I said, trying not to think about how Lauren felt milking the head of my cock or the way she silently shuddered through an orgasm while a group of old men held a lively discussion just outside the confessional. I'd never think about baseball the same way again.

There was a game on now, but Josh had the volume so low I could barely hear the announcers. It was just an excuse anyway, a reason for the two of us to get together.

A pathetic mewl sounded from right behind me, all the warning I had before a gray blur streaked over my shoulder and a fuzzy kitten landed in my lap.

"Maud," I said, "I see you still haven't learned any manners."

In response, she jumped sideways at me, swatted my hand, and then dove off the couch. Fred, their other cat, streaked toward her out of nowhere, and together they went racing into the kitchen.

"Fine?" Josh said, not knowing when to let the conversation drop. "Really? That's all you're going to give me after I slaved away for you for *hours*—"

"Minutes," I corrected.

"Cracking open her phone and then *illegally*—"

"Which you seemed fine with."

"Uploading a tracker to run in the background, while you told me absolutely *nothing*—"

"Because you suck at keeping secrets from Aly."

"About who Lauren is and why she's so important to you."

I feigned nonchalance. "Who said anything about her being important?"

Josh scoffed. "Come on, man. This is the first time you've even mentioned a woman's name around me. And I *can too* keep secrets from Aly."

"Like what?" I asked.

The taunting grin slipped off Josh's face, a cold creeping into his eyes that I'd only seen a handful of times before. This look, this look right here was why we were friends. Because beneath the laughter and bullshit was another side to Josh, something vicious and dangerous that made even hardened criminals tread lightly in his presence. It was the same darkness I battled daily, and being around him, seeing him so happy and clearly in love with my cousin made me feel like there was hope for me still, like I might win the fight against my own demons.

He sat back. "Like what I said to your dad to get him to leave me the fuck alone."

I perked up, wondering if I was finally going to learn what happened between the two of them. "And that was?"

"Trust me, you don't want to know." He frowned. "Hey, what happened after we left dinner? You've seemed off since."

I eyed him, thinking about pressing the subject, but if Josh wasn't ready to tell me yet, I didn't want to strain our friendship by pushing him. "Dad wants me to head a new operation."

Josh swore. "I thought you wanted out."

"I *do* want out," I told him, watching Maud and Fred go racing past us again. "If anything, him handing more control over to me only upped my timeline. I'm already toying with the idea of taking on a business venture, but I might need some help with it."

His expression turned hopeful. "*Illegal* help?"

"Is there any other kind?"

"Not in my field of expertise. What did you have in mind?"

"Nothing that you'll need your Porno Joe alter ego for," I said, recalling the stupid mustache and glasses he'd worn the first time I met him.

He barked a laugh. "Just digital work then?"

I nodded. "I need you to find out everything you can about a man named Patrick McKinney who owns a building over on the West Side."

"One sec." Josh set his beer down and vaulted the back of the couch, because he couldn't just walk around it like a normal person. The house shook as he ran toward the bedroom, and a blur of color had me turning my head to watch both cats go streaking after him.

"Oh, you think you're gonna get me?" he yelled, before dropping his voice a whole octave, sounding like a Batman wannabe. "I'm gonna get *youuu*!"

Fred sprinted back into the living room and turned, fluffing up sideways as Josh came running after him. Josh slid to a stop. They eyed each other. Fred let out a loud chirrup and charged Josh, who turned and ran back out of sight.

I'd said it before, and I'd say it again: Cat people were fucking weird.

A loud scuffle broke out in the bedroom, confirming my belief.

"Hey, no," Josh said. "She's just a baby, Fred. You have to be gentle. Ow, Maud. What was *that* for? I didn't do it, *he did*."

God help Aly if they ever had kids.

Eventually, Josh reemerged carrying his laptop. He set it on the coffee table, and an hour later, I had all the dirt on McKinney I could ever want. He was sixty-eight, had been married twice, was a diabetic, owned not one but *four* buildings in Velvet's neighborhood, and was deeply in debt. Not with lenders or credit card companies. It turned out McKinney had a bit of a gambling problem, which was a weakness that would be all too easy to exploit.

My entire life was spent in the shadows of this city, and I knew almost every key player in it, including the people who ran the illegal gambling dens. A couple of phone calls was all it would take to find out who McKinney's bookie was or who he owed the most money to, and then I could start applying pressure. Debts could be bought, usually at a steep discount, since my money was a guarantee and people who racked up astronomical tabs had a habit of not paying them, at least not without a little *prompting*. Most modern bookies tended to get squeamish about breaking kneecaps. If there was a way for them to recoup most of their money without having to spill blood, they would take it, leaving the ugly work to someone else. Someone like me.

"Sooo," Josh said, closing his laptop and leaning back. "Do I get to know what this is all about?"

"No," I said. "You know Aly's rule about keeping you out of mob shit."

His expression became the picture of innocence. "But I thought this *wasn't* mob shit? I thought this was about you going legit?"

I eyed him for a moment, debating. This thing with Lauren was all-consuming, and I was so stuck in my head about everything that it would be a relief to bounce some of it off someone else, get their take on how bad I was fucking up. I'd meant to apologize to Lauren yesterday and then have a real conversation, not desecrate a holy space with her.

I felt stuck, alone, not even able to talk to my own brothers about my life, because I couldn't trust them not to turn around and tell our father everything I said. Which wasn't a dig on them so much as a condemnation of him. Our old man had turned coercion into a fine art, and I wouldn't put it past him to resort to threatening my brothers just to get the dirt on me. I especially didn't trust him with any information about Lauren. His dislike of her seemed personal, and I was betting it had a lot to do with what he saw as her "negative" effect on me ten years ago. He'd felt his influence over me slipping, something that was anathema to a control freak like him, and he'd decided she was the one to blame.

So, no. I couldn't talk to my family, but Josh had proved that he could hold his own.

I turned back to the TV, eyes unfocused, my decision made. "Lauren and I grew up together in the old neighborhood."

While the baseball game moved into the sixth inning, I laid out everything, my childhood crush, the night of the fireworks, Tommy's threats, my abandonment of Lauren, how I tried to make up for it with Kelly and our principal, and almost everything else I'd done to keep her safe and help her achieve her goals. I skipped my involvement in Tommy's "disappearance," because that really *was* mob shit, and while I told Josh about my interest in Velvet for Lauren's sake, I kept my own growing personal interest in the club to myself. Yes, I was finally opening up, but I doubted I'd ever discuss my sex life with another man, especially one—*gag*—sleeping with my cousin.

Josh let out a low whistle when I was done and drained the rest of his beer. "Have you told Lauren how long you've been looking out for her?"

"I slipped up and mentioned something, but I haven't gone into detail. Women tend to frown at being stalked."

"Mhmm, mhmm," Josh said, nodding rapidly.

"What?" I asked.

"Nothing." He broke eye contact, looking anywhere except at me. "Do you plan on stopping now that Lauren knows?"

I shook my head. "I'm not decent enough to do that, especially because I know how dangerous this city is. The thought of her just walking around out there is giving me an ulcer."

"Love will do that to you," Josh said.

Fuck. Was that what this was? Love? Had I *loved* Lauren this whole time? I mean, I knew I had as a teen, but in a puppy-love kind of way that didn't seem too serious. Grown-up love was something else entirely, and I'd never loved anyone else romantically, so I had nothing to compare my feelings to.

"It doesn't matter," I said, talking more to myself than Josh. "I don't think Lauren wants anything serious with a man like me."

"But you're trying to get out," Josh said. "Wouldn't that clear the way for you two?"

I shook my head. "I'm trying. Doesn't mean Dad will let me go that easily. And anyway, I'm pretty sure I might have already ruined it."

I filled him in on the last few days since I'd seen Lauren. She and I hadn't talked much after church, only enough for her to tell me that she needed some space before we spoke again and that just because she'd hooked up with me didn't mean she forgave me for stalking her. She'd also confessed to wondering if I was ashamed of her. So far, I'd always worn a mask in the club, and anytime we met outside of it was in secret. She hadn't missed the way that I'd snuck into church so my parents wouldn't see us together, and I couldn't blame her for misinterpreting why.

"*Are* you ashamed of her?" Josh asked.

"Fuck, no," I told him.

He eyed me. "It's not easy for a lot of people, dating someone who gets others off for a living."

Something about the way he said it made it feel like he was speaking from experience, but he was a hacker, so what the hell would he know about it?

"I don't care that she gets other people off," I said.

"Are you sure?" he pressed. "Like, *really* sure? I can only imagine what Lauren's inbox looks like. If you do manage to free yourself from your dad, you need to figure out how you feel about Lauren continuing with her work even while you're dating. Most of us were raised to expect sexual monogamy from our partners, and some of those ingrained beliefs are hard to overcome."

I shook my head. "Trust me, I'm sure. I've had *years* to come to terms with Lauren's work. I don't give a fuck what she does online as long as it's just me and her offline."

"So you *do* want to be with her," Josh said.

I blew out a frustrated breath. "Have you not been listening this whole time?"

"I have, and I've been hearing a lot of mixed messages. It sounds like as much as you like or maybe even love this woman, you're still finding excuses to not tell her you want something serious."

I rubbed my hands over my face. I'd agreed to keep it casual because I didn't want to get either of our hopes up for something long-term only to have to bail if my dad found some way to force me to keep working for him. Or threatened Lauren's safety. But I couldn't keep my distance anymore either. If the only way to be with her was by keeping things casual, then I would keep them casual. Also . . .

"I hurt her once already," I told Josh. "I don't want to do it again."

"What makes you so sure you will?" Josh asked.

I dropped my hands and faced him, letting my own monster shine through. "Because all I do is hurt people."

That shut him up.

I looked back to the TV, my mind working through the quagmire I'd created for myself with Lauren. "How do I prove that I don't have a problem with her work or that I'm not ashamed of her?"

"Bring her to our engagement party," Josh said.

I pulled my eyes from the baseball game to look at him. "What?"

"We're having it this weekend. Just our closest friends. It'll be small, and you're the only Trocci we're inviting. No one there will know you besides me and Aly, and you can trust us to keep our mouths shut about Lauren."

"Isn't meeting the family kind of a big deal?"

Josh shrugged. "Tell her it's more like a casual barbecue and you don't want to go alone."

I mulled it over. As far as ideas went, it wasn't the worst one I'd heard. I just had to find a way to convince Lauren to go with me.

24

LAUREN

NT95 HAS SENT YOU A custom request.

I stared down at the message in disbelief. I'd asked for space, and Junior's response was to try to pay for more of my time.

"Open it," Taylor said, looking over my shoulder.

"I don't want to."

"What happened?" Ryan asked, perking up from where they'd been half asleep on my other side. It was after midnight, and we were binge-watching more reality TV to unwind from a long day of filming and editing, Walter asleep in his doggie bed nearby.

"Junior sent me another request," I said.

"I'm with Taylor on this one," Ryan said. "You should open it, at least to see what he wants."

My thumb hesitated over the screen. Asking for space hadn't been easy, especially because I couldn't stop thinking about the way Junior and I had defiled that confessional booth. I'd spent the rest of the day turned on, and batch-filming content when I'd gotten home hadn't diminished my desire. Even now, over a week later, the memory of him barely pushing into me had every drop of moisture in my body moving south for the winter. The sound of his breaths near my ear. The feel of his lips on my neck and his hand at my throat. Fuck, I wanted it again.

Which was why I knew that opening his message was a Bad Idea. I didn't trust myself to tell him no. I'd either use the cash he offered or the opportunity to finally get answers out of him as an excuse to meet up again. And then we'd probably have full-blown, p-in-the-v sex and my mind would be so blissed out from dick that I'd forget all about the tracker and stalking and everything else he might have done that I didn't know about.

"Oops," Taylor said, tapping my screen and taking the decision out of my hands.

The first thing listed in PPV requests was always the price, and my eyes bugged out at the sight of it.

"Ten grand?" Taylor hissed, scooting closer.

Ryan pressed against my other side. "To do what? Kill someone?"

"Come to my cousin's barbecue," Taylor read. She looked up at me in confusion. "Is that a euphemism?"

"I have no idea," I said.

Ryan pulled up their phone and started searching. "I don't see anything about it being one."

"Wait," Taylor said. "Scroll down." She slid her finger over my screen and then read Junior's message aloud. "I'm not ashamed of you, Lo. Give me a chance to prove it."

Uh-oh. I could already feel myself starting to cave, willing to hear him out.

I shoved the phone at Ryan like it was a bomb. "Hit deny. I can't do it myself."

They took it, eyeing me. "Are you sure?"

I nodded. "I asked for time, and instead of honoring that, he's pushing for more access to me. That makes red flag number . . . eight? Nine? He needs to start learning how to respect my boundaries."

Ryan hit deny.

A knock sounded on our front door.

Walter leapt out of his bed and ran for it, barking his head off.

No. Fucking. Way.

"Weapons," Ryan said, our standard response to anyone at our door after midnight.

They went scrambling off the couch while I beelined toward Walter. He was barking so loud that even with the insulation, I was worried he would wake our neighbors.

I grabbed the baseball bat we kept propped by the coat rack and ducked, trying to soothe him into silence. "It's okay, bud."

It took a minute, but eventually his barks dropped into a low, steady growling. Standing, I carefully looked through the peephole. Junior was right on the other side of it, wearing his riding gear, helmet dangling from his fingers, hair mussed from wearing it. His jacket was unzipped, revealing a black T-shirt pulled tight across his pecs. My nipples hardened at the sight of him, and warmth bloomed in my core. This was what I got for spending so much time on BikeTok.

Junior suddenly made it worse by running his hand through his hair, his shirt creeping up just enough to reveal a tantalizing glimpse of lower abs. I nearly walked through the closed door trying to get to him, but the sound of my roommates rushing toward me stopped me just in time. I turned to see Ryan holding a can of mace and a taser. Beside them, Taylor clutched the largest, floppiest of her dildos.

Ryan looked over at it agape. "What are you planning to do with that?"

"Dick-whip him," Taylor said.

"That's not going to do anything but make him laugh."

"Oh, really?" She flicked her wrist, slapping Ryan across the thigh with it.

Ryan howled and clutched their leg, dancing away.

Junior pounded on the door. "Lauren? Are you okay?"

"I'm fine," I called over Walter's renewed barking. "What do you want?"

"To talk," he yelled.

"Shut up!" someone shouted from outside, likely one of our neighbors hanging out a door or window. Great.

"Ryan," I said. "Come hold Walter."

They limped over, shooting a glare at Taylor on the way, and grabbed Walter's collar.

I cracked the door. "You have serious boundary issues."

Junior smiled, devilishly handsome in the dim light. "Let me in and I'll show you just how bad they are."

I fought a shiver, refusing to be turned on by that comment. "My roommates are both holding weapons." Sort of. "And Walter doesn't like strange men."

"Good boy," he said.

"Walter is a girl!" Taylor yelled past me for some fucking reason.

Junior's smile widened, eyes boring into mine, and I realized what she'd done. *Oh, no.* He parted his lips and dropped his voice into a bass growl. "Good girl."

Behind me, Taylor let out a sound like a dying whale, clearly overwhelmed by her praise kink.

"You're still not coming in," I said, hating how breathless I sounded.

Junior stepped back on our stoop. "Then why don't you come out here, and your friends can keep an eye on you from inside."

I studied him for a moment. Maybe this was a good thing. Maybe I could get my answers and, if I didn't like them, tell him to get lost, and this would be the end of it between us. For good, this time.

I turned toward my roommates. "If I suddenly crawl into his lap, please come grab me before I get charged with indecent exposure."

Taylor grinned. "No promises. Rap sheets are hot."

Ryan shook their head. "Ignore her. We'll obviously stop you."

I handed the baseball bat to them, gave Walter a grateful pat, and slipped outside.

Junior was leaning against the stoop railing with his legs crossed at the ankle, the streetlights casting his face in sharp angles. God, that jawline was next level. And his cheekbones. There were models who would kill for them. It was like he'd gotten all of his parents' best features. Mom's eyes, father's full lips and strong brows. The way they were put together was devastating, always drew my gaze, always had me hoping he'd gift me with a rare smile because of how it transformed his expression from cold and unapproachable to warm and intimate, just for me.

There were no smiles tonight. Instead, he watched me with a heat in his eyes that had me stopping just outside the door because I didn't trust myself to get any closer. *I've been inside you*, that look said. *I've felt you come around the head of my cock. And if you think that was the last time I'll ever wrap my fingers around your throat, you're out of your goddamn mind.*

He pushed off the railing. "Keep looking at me like that and see if I don't fuck you right here on these steps."

A muffled whimper came from behind me that sounded more like Taylor than Walter, followed by a shushing noise. I loved my roommates, but did they need to hear every word that was about to come out of our mouths? Probably not.

"Let's sit," I said, careful to keep my distance as I walked past Junior. The man had a way of grabbing me that had turned me skittish.

We took the steps down to the sidewalk and sat on the bottom one. Thankfully, they were wide enough that we weren't touching. The smell of leather and cologne brought me right back to the confessional, and the last thing I needed was to feel the heat rolling off Junior's body.

Even looking at him was a problem, so I fixed my gaze across the street, where his bike was parked. "Do you live in the neighborhood?"

"No," he said, voice low and rough, and, god, I was so fucked if even the sound of it was enough to make me shiver. "I just come here sometimes to check up on you."

"How did you even know where I live?"

"I've kept tabs on you over the years," he said.

Part of me relaxed a little at the confession. I'd been expecting an argument, was ready to pry information out of him bit by bit, because he'd always been such a closed book, but him offering it up so freely was a nice surprise. "And the tracker? How long has it been in my purse?"

"Only since our first run-in at church."

I nodded. That made sense. I'd been so distracted when he pinned me to the wall that he would've had plenty of time to plant it on me.

"Don't do that again," I told him.

"I won't put any more trackers on you," he said.

Well, this was going better than I'd hoped. Time to rip off the Band-Aid. "Did you slash a bunch of old women's tires just because they were mean to me?"

He smirked. "I heard the tires slashed themselves."

"Oh my god, you did, didn't you?"

He looked unrepentant. "Let it be their only warning."

I reared back. "What are you going to do if they're mean to me again? Burn their houses down?"

"I would never," he said, the world's most untrustworthy smile spreading over his face.

"Really? Because your grin is psychotic."

He smoothed it out, letting the façade of the reformed mobster slide back into place like a second skin. "I don't think it'll come to that."

No, it definitely wouldn't, because I was never going back to that church again. I couldn't imagine trying to sit through an hour of Mass with the confessional booth at my back, knowing what I'd done in there. In my mind, Jesus Christ himself popped out of it in the middle of the priest's sermon, finger pointed as he accused me of blasphemy.

"What else have you done over the past decade?" I asked Junior, because it was clear his interference hadn't ended with Kelly and our principal.

His eyes were so dark in the shadows that they almost looked black. "How long are your friends willing to wait while I answer that question? We might be here a while."

I blinked at him. "My parking tickets?"

He nodded.

"The smashed side mirror on my car that got magically replaced overnight?"

Another nod.

My mind raced, thinking back to every problem that had mysteriously righted itself. I thought of our last apartment, and our landlord's refusal to fix anything for six months straight before suddenly showing up at our door with a crew of three men and getting it all done in a day. After that, not a week went by that he didn't ask if we needed anything else.

I narrowed my eyes. "Our landlord at the old place?"

A nod.

My heart sank. "Councilwoman Blackwell?"

His expression turned grim, and he nodded again.

I dropped my head into my hands. "Oh, god. I'm going to end up in jail."

He rubbed my back. "No one can connect you to any of it. I made sure of that. And Blackwell had it coming after how long she led you on."

I wrenched my head back up. "What did you do to her?"

"Relax," he said. "Everyone still has all their fingers and toes. Let's just say I got ahold of an interesting video of her son."

I felt like crying. "I've been working my ass off to get these politicians to come around, and if you're telling me they all had to be threatened or bribed, I'm going to lose what little faith I have left in humanity."

He tucked a loose strand of hair behind my ear. "Don't. You did all of the hard work yourself. I only gave one or two of them a nudge."

Oh, no. Patrick McKinney. I'd spilled my guts to Junior about him at Velvet. Was he about to be next?

Do you really care if he is? a small voice asked. The man was a complete bastard and we had nowhere else to go. *Yet.* But we were working on it. My roommates and I were looking at two more buildings tomorrow, and one of the owners seemed really promising. And in the meantime, we had found the money to make rent and buy ourselves another month.

We were going to do this the legal way. The *right* way. Junior was trying to get out of the criminal world, and the last thing I wanted was for him to dig himself deeper on my behalf.

"Please stop interfering in my life," I said.

His one-word response was clipped. "No."

I blew out an exasperated breath. "I'm serious. I hate the fact that my achievements aren't my own. That any of them could have come from coercion or blackmail or violence."

"Look at this place," he said, thumbing behind us. "You did this on your own. You're building your empire brick by brick with your own two hands. It's not like I held a gun to every one of your subs and forced them to follow you. They chose to do it because you're damn good at your job. You make people feel seen and accepted, no matter who they are or what kind of hell they're stuck in."

My heart softened. Was he talking about himself?

"So what if I tried to make your life easier where I could?" he said. "So what if I pushed a couple of politicians into doing the right thing? You shouldn't feel bad for those snakes. Not after the way they lied to your face and the public about supporting your cause."

I shook my head. "I don't feel bad for them. It's not them I care about in this situation."

His laugh was humorless. "Don't feel bad for me, Lo. You don't know what I've done in my life."

"So?" I said. "Just because you've done bad things doesn't mean you're not worthy of my empathy."

He reached over and dragged me into his lap, and I let him, something in his expression telling me he needed this.

Behind us, the door cracked open, Taylor waving the dildo over her head like she was getting ready to lead Ryan and Walter into battle.

I quickly shook my head to stop her.

You sure? she mouthed.

I nodded, and she closed the door again, giving one last shake of the sex toy to remind me to behave.

Junior buried his face against my neck, breathing deeply. This was the problem with us. He could stalk me, interfere with my life, and put up more red flags than an entire circus, and I would still look at him and remember the boy I'd grown up with. The fear, the vulnerability. I knew they were still there, buried deep. I knew he was hurting, that he didn't want to do the things he did. The fact that he was trying to get out was proof enough of that.

It made me want to pull him close and protect him from the world. Which was ridiculous. Despite my lingering memories, he wasn't a boy anymore; he was a grown man, a criminal. I'd seen his temper, how prone he was to violence. And yet, I still felt like there was hope for him. That he wasn't too far gone yet. That I could save him.

Taylor was wrong. Junior didn't have the white knight kink. I did.

"I'm not ashamed of you," he spoke into my skin. "And your work doesn't bother me. You can post whatever you like, and I'll never try to tell you otherwise. I don't want to clip your wings, Lo. I want to see you fly."

Warmth bloomed in my belly that had nothing to do with lust. That was the most affirming, romantic thing anyone had ever said to me, and as his hands stroked up my back and he pulled me closer, I felt the last of my resistance to him melting away. Yes, he'd stalked me, and yes, he'd done other terrible things, but if he was being honest, and I believed he was, then none of it was about control. He'd done it all to protect me, to make my life easier, better, and I wasn't in danger of falling into the same trap my mother had.

"Come to my cousin's barbecue with me," he said. "I'll pay you whatever you want."

I shook my head. "I don't want your money."

"Then what'll it take?" He pulled back enough to look me in the eye. "I won't know anyone there besides her and her fiancé, and making small talk with strangers makes me want to gouge my fuck-ing eyes out. I don't know how to talk to normal people anymore. I don't give a shit about how long the wait list for day care is or what everyone is watching on TV. And one day, the intrusive thoughts will win and the next time someone asks what I do for work, I'll just start talking and see how long it takes before they run screaming away from me." He tugged me close, butting his forehead against mine. "Don't let Saturday be that day. Don't let me ruin my cousin's engagement party."

Despite myself, I grinned. The mobster and the camgirl, out together at a nice family cookout. What was the worst that could happen?

"I'll come."

25

JUNIOR

"YOU'RE SURE I LOOK OKAY?" Lauren asked.

I glanced at her in the passenger seat, sitting demurely in her cute little sundress. Was she serious? "If we weren't already running late, I would pull this fucking car over and have you bouncing on my lap within half a second."

She shook her head. "Don't start. I'm trying to be good."

I raked my gaze over her. "I mean, we're already late. What's a few more minutes?"

"Minutes?" Her tone gained a teasing edge. "Oh, who could *ever* turn down such a promise of pleasure?"

I reached out and gripped her thigh. "I think I've proved that minutes is all the time I need to get you off."

That shut her up.

I grinned and stroked my hand upward. "What are you wearing under this dress? Give me something to look forward to, so I can get through the next few hours."

Despite her telling me not to start, she sure was quick to widen her legs. "Why don't you find out for yourself?"

Up ahead, the light turned green. I swore, removing my hand because I needed it to shift. I should have asked to borrow Stefan's Range Rover instead of taking my own car, but it had been a while since I'd driven

223

this beast, and I thought Lauren would appreciate its throaty engine and the way it sent constant low vibrations through the vehicle.

"Maybe later," she said, grinning like the Cheshire Cat and closing her legs.

What the hell did she have going on under there to make her smile like that?

"Remind me of your cousin and her fiancé's names again?" she said.

"Aly and Josh. Their two cats are Maud and Fred, and I think Josh's old roommate will be there. I don't know who else will be. Probably Aly's work friends."

"You said she's an ER nurse?"

"Yup. We cut 'em up, and she stitches them back together."

Lauren was quiet so long that I snuck another look at her.

Her eyes were narrowed, studying me. "I don't know if you're joking or not."

I winked. "Me neither." She shook her head, expression turning contemplative, and I decided it was time for a distraction. "None of Aly's friends know that she has mob ties, and she wants to keep it that way."

"My lips are sealed," Lauren said.

I glanced at her lap. "Don't break my heart."

She smacked my arm. "I meant my *mouth*."

I grinned and gunned the engine, throwing her back in her seat.

There was a line of cars parked outside Aly's house by the time we arrived. I found a spot as close as I could and went around to open Lauren's door for her while she snagged the gift bag she brought. She seemed perfectly steady on her heels when she got out, but there were cracks in the sidewalk, so I offered her my hand just in case.

"Such a gentleman all of a sudden," she said, wrapping her fingers through mine.

"That's me, a real gentleman. Grab her hand in the streets and her hair in the sheets."

She laughed, a bright, infectious sound that had me turning my head to look at her. It was the first time I'd seen her laugh like this, loud and open, and my ego swelled a little, knowing I'd caused it. Until now, I'd mostly made her frown or moan, and I decided that needed to change. The moaning, we could keep, but the frowning had to go.

A sign on the front door said the party was out back, so we followed the sound of voices around the house. There were maybe thirty people filling Aly's backyard, a grill going on one side, and two sets of cornhole boards set up on the other, with tables and outdoor furniture in between. Josh was easy to pick out because of his height, standing as far away from the grill as humanly possible. Aly was much closer.

"Oh, hey!" she said, turning as we approached. "You made it."

Lauren shifted beside me. I pressed my hand against her lower back and guided her forward. "Aly, this is Lauren. Lauren, Aly."

"Hi," Lauren said, lifting her gift bag. "Congrats on your engagement. Junior said you liked white wine, so I got you a little something."

"Oh, thank you," Aly said, taking the bag and then leaning down to hug Lauren. She pulled back and tugged the wine free, her eyes going wide. "No, really. Thank you."

Huh. Must have been a nice bottle.

Lauren grinned. "You're welcome."

A familiar, pathetic mewl came from nearby, and we turned toward it. Last month, I'd spent a gross, sweaty weekend helping Josh and Aly turn their back porch into what they were calling a catio (See? *Weird*.), framing the space out and then stapling heavy-duty screens in between the wood. All so Fred could sit outside and watch the birds while Josh and Aly drank their coffee. And then they'd adopted Maud, who now had all four paws dug into the screen, crying to be let out. Fred sat on the cat tree behind her, looking unimpressed by her behavior.

"Oh my god," Lauren said. "That is so cute!"

She and Aly headed toward Maud, and I ambled after them.

"Cat people," a low, disgruntled voice said from behind me.

I looked over to see a blond guy almost as big as Josh walking over. "Tyler, right?" I asked as he stopped at my side.

He nodded and took a sip of his beer. "Junior?"

I nodded back.

His gaze went to Lauren. "How'd you manage to bag such a baddie?"

I took a deep breath. Yup, he was still a fucking douche. I'd only met him once before, when we'd helped Josh move in here, but those few hours were enough to get a good read on him and wonder how the fuck Josh had put up with him for so long.

Be nice, I told myself. *You can't go threatening Josh's only other friend in the world just for pointing out how hot Lauren is.*

"I'm good at making her come," I said.

Tyler huffed a low laugh. "Fair enough. She got a sister?"

"Yeah, but she's older and married with two kids."

"Shame." His gaze swung back to me, taking in the tattoos on my neck, the words scrawled across my knuckles. "What is it you said you do again?"

"Imports," I said. "You?"

He grinned. "Finance."

We fell silent, watching the women play with Maud through the screen. At least the two of them seemed to be hitting it off.

A waving motion caught the corner of my eye. I glanced left, over the heads of the crowd, to see Josh motioning to me. I pointed to the women and motioned him our way instead. He shook his head, waving harder.

"He won't come near the grill," Tyler said. "The smell of cooking meat makes him puke."

"Oh, so he's *vegan*, vegan."

Tyler let out a humorless snort. "Yup." And with that, he sauntered off, back into the crowd.

I shook my head at his retreating form and then went to join Aly and Lauren by the catio. "Josh is trying to summon us to his lair."

Aly winced. "I told him we should keep things vegetarian, but he didn't want to put everyone else out."

She headed over to him, and we followed after her. Three feet away from Josh, Lauren stopped dead in her tracks, staring at him. I tried not to let it get to me. I was man enough to admit that Josh was probably the handsomest bastard I'd ever seen outside of a movie, but I didn't love the fact that Lauren seemed to think so, too. Until I realized she wasn't looking at his face, but his arms and the tattoos crawling up them.

She glanced from Josh to Aly and back again. "Aly . . ." Her eyes flared. "Oxen free?"

"Oh, Jesus," Aly said, grabbing Lauren's arm and dragging her away.

I frowned as they brushed past me. "The fuck?"

Josh had a sheepish expression on his face when I turned back around. "Don't look at me. I have no *idea* what that was about."

For some reason, I didn't believe him.

■   ■   ■

Forty-five minutes later, I'd eaten, suffered through small talk with Aly's coworkers, met the older couple who lived next door to her, had another awkward exchange with Tyler, and was ready to get the fuck out of there.

Lauren did much better, befriending everyone she met, kicking ass at cornhole despite the fact that her heels kept digging into the grass, and doing an excellent job of making me seem like less of an asshole.

Josh and I now stood in the corner, him drinking a beer, me a macchiato from the fancy new espresso machine my father sent Aly as a birthday gift. I didn't miss the fact that Josh had spent most of the party half turned away from the others when he wasn't forced into conversation with them. My father was bad, but *his* father was an infamous serial killer, and Josh looked a lot like the guy, something he was still self-conscious about. He'd come a long way in the past six months, but I could tell being around a crowd this size still made him uncomfortable.

"Were you able to find out who owns McKinney's debts?" he asked.

"Jesus, keep your voice down," I said, pulling him farther away from where Aly, Lauren, and a handful of other women sat nearby, sharing the bottle of wine Lauren brought.

Josh winced, glancing over his shoulder like a little kid worried about being overheard. The man was not cut out for stealth work.

"Yes, I found out," I told him once we'd retreated all the way to the fence line.

"Aaand?" he said, excitement in his eyes. This was probably why Aly wanted to keep him away from illegal shit; he seemed far too tempted by it.

I shook my head. "It's some newer bookie. He stepped onto the scene a year ago and has been slowly moving up the ranks, running bigger and bigger card nights, slipping his guys into the horse tracks and the stadiums and pissing everyone off."

"How so?" Josh asked.

"By not doing things the old way. He's crossing into people's turf without asking and then leaving it before they can track him down. Finding him is going to be a pain in the ass, and no," I said, when he opened his mouth, "you can't help. None of this requires a computer."

Josh eyed me. "Everyone has a digital trail."

"Not this guy," I said. "Apparently, he's a paranoid bastard. And cutthroat. I have my brother Stefan on it. He can find anyone in the city." And out of all of my brothers, was most unlikely to rat on me since he was Dad's least-favorite kid (which the asshole made no secret of) and was generally left alone because of it.

"Cutthroat, how?" Josh asked. "You're not putting yourself in danger, are you?"

The concern in his voice made me want to squirm. Having friends was going to take a while to get used to. "I'm fine," I lied—I was always in danger. "He's not any worse than the other people I deal with. I meant cutthroat with money. If I have any hope of getting a fair deal, I need to catch him off guard. If he has time to look into the debt or McKinney's holdings, he'll try to milk me for every penny I'm worth."

Josh frowned. "Let me know if you need extra cash. We have some lying around."

I waved him off. "Save it for your wedding and honeymoon. I'll be fine. Crime is lucrative, and besides my bike and my piece of shit apartment, I don't spend money on anything but investments."

Josh perked up. "I didn't know you were into the stock market. How's that going?"

"Pretty decent," I said. "It's a good nest egg." It was better than a nest egg. I could retire tomorrow and live off the dividends for the rest of my life if I was frugal. Not that my dad would let me.

"No shit?" Josh said, eyebrows rising. "I've wanted to start investing more myself. I have a decent portfolio, but it's managed by some douche on Wall Street. You know, Tyler's a financial analyst. We could invite him over too and make a whole night of it."

I had no idea how to answer diplomatically, so I went with being direct. "No offense, but I'd rather rip my own fingernails off than hang out with *that* guy."

I gestured with my coffee cup behind Josh's back, and he turned to see what I'd been watching this whole time: Tyler, about to start a fight over cornhole. He'd lost and wasn't happy about it.

"Because you kept stepping over the fucking line," he said, loud enough for his voice to carry.

Josh turned back to me, wincing. "He has a thing about rules."

I just looked at him.

"And he doesn't exactly make the best first impression," he tacked on.

"Or second," I said, sipping my coffee.

Josh nodded. "I think he's just not good in new situations or with new people so he ends up acting like more of a douche than normal. But once you get past that hurdle, you'll never find a more loyal friend."

Behind him, Tyler flipped a cornhole board and stalked away from the party.

"I'll have to take your word for it."

Josh turned just in time to catch Tyler disappearing around the corner of the house. With a sigh, Josh swung back my way, eyes snagging on Aly and Lauren and the other women shaking their heads at Tyler's outburst.

"Lauren's nice," he said.

"Too nice for me?"

"Oh, without a doubt."

I shot him an unimpressed look.

He elbowed me. "You guys are good together. Complement each other."

I peered up at him. "Is that what you've been doing over here in your Creep Corner all afternoon? Studying the rest of us?"

"Yeah," he said, and I could hear the unspoken *duh* in his tone. "The fuck else was I supposed to do for entertainment?"

"I don't know, this is *your* engagement party."

"No, it's not. It's hers," he said, tone softening as he glanced toward Aly.

I followed his gaze and caught her admiring the rock on her finger, a smile on her face that told anyone who saw it just how happy she was, how content. She glanced up, saw Josh, and smiled even wider, and he let out a low whuff of breath that made it sound like someone had gut-punched him. I decided in that moment that if my father ever tried to tear them apart, it would be open war between us.

My gaze drifted to Lauren. She was talking animatedly with one of Aly's colleagues, but I wasn't worried about what she was saying. I'd asked her not to bring up certain subjects, and I trusted her to keep quiet. Hell, I trusted her, period. Spending the afternoon in her company, out in the light of day together, had been . . . interesting. Easy. It was a glimpse of normalcy, what life could be like if I was able to break free.

Lauren laughed at something Aly said, and they clinked their wineglasses together before drinking. My chest warmed at the sight of them getting on so well, and I had to remind myself not to get ahead of myself, that we still hadn't discussed what the hell we were doing.

And then Lauren's gaze caught mine and held, heat sparking between us.

I sent her a smile, winked, and turned away, not wanting her to see the rage taking hold of me. My fucking father. His threats, his slyness, his control, they were the reasons I held myself back with Lauren. Because I was afraid of what he would do, how far he would go to retain his hold on me. The mob had rules against hurting women, but

I didn't trust him to honor them, and I knew all too well that you didn't have to use physical force to harm someone. Psychological weapons could be just as devastating.

I just needed to find a weakness I could exploit. Planning a move into legitimate business was all well and good, but it wouldn't free me from my dad's claws, wouldn't keep him from threatening or coercing me into doing whatever he wanted.

Think, I told myself. What did Dad value more than anything? What could I threaten to take away from him that would finally get him to back down?

"You all right?" Josh asked.

I shook my head, trying to pull myself back from the brink. I didn't trust my temper when I got like this.

"Come on," Josh said, shoving my shoulder to get me moving. "Inside."

I stalked into their house, glad for the silence. It was too loud outside to think straight.

"What'd you do to get free of my old man?" I said, finally asking Josh outright.

He looked toward the back door and the party just beyond, checking to see if we were really alone. "Threatened to rip his entire life apart, including your family. No offense."

I blinked. That was it. Family. The one thing Dad cared about more than anything else in the world. It was why he'd blackmailed Aly and Josh into coming to monthly dinners, why he tried to exert so much control over me and my brothers. His own parents had disowned him when he joined the mob, and his greatest fear in life was that everyone else he loved would one day abandon him, too.

"Can you actually follow through on your threats?" I asked Josh.

He crossed his arms over his chest and nodded, his other side entering the conversation. "Yes."

"I've got a plan brewing in my head, but I don't know if it will work or blow up in my face." I laid it out for him from start to finish, watching his eyes widen and his brows climb up his forehead.

When I was done, he smiled. "That sounds like a complete shit show."

"You in?"

"Fuck, yeah," he said.

26

LAUREN

"THAT WAS NICE," I SAID.

I was two glasses of wine deep, warm from spending the day out-doors, and tired from all the talk and laughter. Junior and I were on the way back to my place, and the sun was setting over the cityscape in the distance, painting the sky orange and pink. I yawned and leaned back in my seat. A nap sounded so nice.

"I'm glad you had a good time," Junior said, forearm flexing as he downshifted.

Or maybe some slow, lazy sex, I thought, eyeing him. His hair was mussed from the wind rushing through his open window, and the short-sleeved shirt he wore was pulled tight across his chest and stomach.

I'd never been so attracted to him before. And not just in a sexual way. Earlier, when Aly asked what I do for a living, I faltered, not knowing how to respond. In any other situation, I would have told her with pride, but I hadn't known if that was the right call. It was one thing for Junior to *say* he accepted what I did, but I knew firsthand how complicated family dynamics could be. Even though Aly seemed equally accepting—especially given who she was engaged to—I didn't know how she'd feel about her cousin dating a camgirl. Junior had surprised me by placing his hand on my low back and nodding, telling me without words that I should be honest.

I knew right then that he was serious about not being ashamed of me. In the past, I'd had to skirt around my work on more than one occasion because of a partner's discomfort. That I could be open now filled me with a euphoric feeling of relief, one that fizzed through my body like champagne bubbles, leaving me energized and excited. And when Aly and the other nurses we'd been talking to didn't bat an eye? A weight lifted off my shoulders I wasn't even aware of.

Things were changing. People were kinder and more accepting than ever before. At least in our generation. It gave me hope that someday in the future, sex workers would be able to speak openly about their lives without any fear of judgment or reprisal. And maybe that made me naïve, or overly optimistic, but so much had changed for the better just in the years I'd been camgirling that it didn't seem like a fantasy; it felt not only possible, but inevitable.

Junior shifted gears, picking up speed as we raced down the highway. Had I been too quick to judge him? Too quick to discount what this was between us? We'd agreed to keep it casual, a way to finally explore the spark between us, but this afternoon had me questioning myself, had me questioning him.

The man had spent *ten years* looking out for me. That didn't speak of a passing attraction or idle interest. It spoke of determination. Commitment. And sure, maybe he could have been protecting me out of guilt for not being there when I'd needed him most, but if it was only guilt, wouldn't he have stopped when he realized I was okay? That what happened hadn't actually ruined my life?

This clearly wasn't casual. Not for Junior, and I was beginning to realize not for me either. I cared what happened to him, wanted to see him succeed in going legit, was even willing to help in whatever capacity I could, though I doubted he would let me. And I liked the way he made me feel when we were together: cherished, special. I liked the little glimpses of his humor that were starting to peek through more and more. I liked that he shared my voyeurism kink. I was excited to explore more with him. God help me, part of me even liked the darker aspects of his personality. My line of work didn't come without risks, and knowing there was a scary motherfucker with a skewed moral compass looking out for me made me feel safe and protected. I had no doubt that if a sub ever crossed the line and tried to find me, Junior would take care of it before I was even aware of the danger.

And who knew, maybe we weren't compatible in the long run and our time together was only fleeting, but after today the thought of something *more* with him didn't seem as frightening as before. So, when he pulled onto my street, I turned toward him. "Do you want to come in?"

He sent me a sideways look. "Not if you're planning to feed me to your big scary dog."

"Walter can make up his own mind. It's not for me to say who he should or shouldn't eat."

Junior grinned. "You seem worth the risk."

"Yeah?"

"Yeah. I'll come in."

He dropped me off in front of the brownstone and went to find a parking space while I went to let my roommates know we were about to have company.

Ryan met me at the door. Behind them, Walter was whining his head off.

They stuck their leg out to keep him from escaping. "How'd it go?"

"I asked Junior to come in," I told them.

Surprise flashed across their face. "I take it that means it went well?"

I nodded. "I'll catch you up on everything later. Where's Taylor?"

"Out with Jackson," Ryan said, swinging the door wide and grabbing the leash off the rack just inside. "And I need to go get dinner, because it's her turn to cook, *of course*. I'll bring Walter with me so you and Junior can have some alone time."

Walter rushed me as soon as he had clearance, wiggle-butting so fast that his rear end was a blur. I dropped down to pet him. I loved my roommates, but nothing made my heart sing like this animal and how happy he always was to see me when I came home, or woke up, or walked into whichever room he happened to be in.

"Hi," I said, trying to pet him as he squirmed. "Oh, goodness. Yes, that's your nose." He turned, his tail slapping my arm, my back, my shoulder, and came around for a second pass.

Ryan managed to clip his leash on in the middle of the frenzy, and I thanked them as they led him down the stairs and then in the opposite direction from Junior as he strode up the sidewalk, waving hi before they turned.

"Change your mind about me and Walter meeting?" Junior asked as he took the stairs up.

I shook my head. "Ryan offered to give us some alone time."

The grin that bloomed over his face was wicked. "Oh, really?"

Need crashed through me, my earlier sleepiness forgotten. I'd been holding my desire back all day, trying not to look at him too much, spending time with Aly while he was with Josh so I could put some space between us. Every whiff of his cologne, every touch, reminded me of our past interactions, him getting me off in the stairwell at Velvet, then the photo booth, the way I rode him in the voyeur room, the way he'd managed to hold so still when he was inside me at church. Every time we'd hooked up, we'd either been in cramped quarters or a heartbeat away from getting caught, and while that had been exciting, I couldn't wait to get him alone in my room, where there was a large, comfortable mattress waiting for us and every toy under the sun.

"Come on," I said, grabbing his hand and leading him inside.

His fingers tightened on mine as we took the stairs up to the third floor. I swung open my bedroom door, and he stopped short, tugging me to a halt. My eyes went to his face, a question on the tip of my tongue, but then I saw his expression, the way his gaze danced from one spot to the next: my bed, the oversized armchair, the blank corner opposite the door—all the places I regularly filmed.

"Fuck, Lauren," he said, his eyes smoldering as they finally slid back to mine.

I released his hand and stepped into my room, loving the way he stalked after me, loving the feeling of being pursued, even over such a short distance. He paused just long enough to shut the door and take one last lingering look at our surroundings, and then he was on me, reaching me in a final stride, bracing his hands against the wall on either side of my head.

"I can't believe I'm in your room," he said, his voice gaining a rough edge. "You have no idea the things I've fantasized about doing to you in here."

"Tell me," I said, heat gathering in my core. How many times had I gotten him off without even knowing?

He shook his head. "I don't know how long we have alone, and I'm not wasting another minute of it talking. Now turn around. As much as I like you in this dress, I'd like you out of it even more."

I spun, tugging my hair over my shoulder so he had easier access to my zipper. Instead of undoing it, his hand snaked around my neck, and the memory of the last time we'd been alone together like this surged into my mind.

"That fucking confessional booth," he growled.

I released a breathy exhale. "I know."

His fingers tightened on me. "I will remember the feel of you coming on the head of my dick until the day I die." I nearly moaned as he dragged me backward. "And your pulse," he whispered into my ear. "I'll never forget the way it fluttered against my fingers. Just." He tapped my neck. "Like." Another tap. "This."

My knees trembled at the memory, warmth coiling in my belly. I gripped his wrist. "Junior."

His hold on me eased. "I need to fuck you. No holding back, no being quiet." The fingers of his free hand fell to my side, bunching the hem of my dress up. "You never did tell me what you have on under here."

I widened my legs and grinned, waiting for it.

His fingers kept on going, all the way up, finding me completely bare because I'd liked his reaction so much that first night at Velvet that I'd wanted to see if it drove him just as wild a second time. I knew right when he figured it out, because his progress froze, forehead dropping to my shoulder, hand falling away from my neck.

"All day?" he croaked.

I giggled. He sounded like he was in pain. "Yup."

He made a low, tortured sound and spun me around, and then we were kissing. I tugged at his shirt, wanting it up, off, but he ignored the obvious request, and it made me wonder how bad the wound on his side really was. Our feet tangled, the back of my knees hit the mattress, and down we went, Junior managing to control the fall so we landed sideways.

He rolled us into a more central position with me on top and then pushed at my shoulders until I was straddling him. His hands landed on my hips, biceps flexing. With a tug, he dragged me over his body. "Get up here," he said, voice rough with impatience.

"What do you—"

Another yank, and I was on his chest.

"Grab the headboard, Lauren."

I did as he said, and he scooted lower, clearly intending for me to ride his face.

"What if I suffocate you?" I asked.

"You don't have to look so excited by the idea," he shot back.

I grinned. "It'd be the perfect murder."

He laughed. "Then I guess that makes me your willing victim." With a final shove, he disappeared from sight beneath the skirt of my dress.

My answering chuckle turned into a gasp as he tugged me down. Straight onto his face. One thing I was learning about Junior was that he didn't fuck around; instead, he got right down to business. His tongue tasted my entrance and then pushed inside, curling, twisting. *Oh, fuck*. My fingernails dug into the headboard, and I held perfectly still, kneeling there, unable to bring myself to put any more weight on him, despite his *If I die, I die* attitude.

A low growl vibrated through me, and I shivered, despite his obvious displeasure. He tugged again, harder this time, hard enough that I was finally pressing down. My eyes fluttered shut as he continued to devour me, that magic tongue of his making me want to grind on him despite my lingering hesitation. One hand left my hip and slipped beneath my dress. His thumb brushed against my clit. I moaned for him, loud, making up for how quiet I'd had to be the last time he touched me.

He pulled his mouth away. "Move, Lauren. I won't say it again."

And then his tongue was back and his thumb kept working me, and I swear I was going to do what he said but it just felt so *good* to stay right where I was that—

He spanked me.

I yelped, caught off guard, my eyes flashing wide.

Another slap, not hard enough to really hurt, but with enough force that it was obvious he was trying to get me to move. This was probably a good time to mention that I actually *enjoyed* a nice, firm spanking.

His hand left my ass again, and I glanced right to see it hovering behind me in idle threat. I shifted forward over his face, still thinking this was risky, but the act of squeezing all my inner muscles as I rolled my hips felt so good that I decided to it again. And again. And, *oh, fuck*, now that I'd started, I didn't want to stop, because every fall had me pressing into his tongue and every rise had me thrusting into his stroking finger, and based on the encouraging noises Junior was making, he didn't want me to stop either, so I kept going, my hands gripping the headboard and my hips picking up speed. I really hoped he knew his own limits and had the strength to push me off him if this was too much, because now I couldn't seem to control myself.

His tongue stroked deeper, thumb worked faster, the hand on my ass shoving me forward like he was more than into this, and soon my back was arching and my head fell forward, lips open on a strangled scream as my pleasure peaked and I came all over his face. It was rough, messy, the first time I'd come in this bedroom in a long time without having to worry about lighting or camera angles or if what I was doing looked good. For once, all that mattered was how I felt, how he'd *made me feel*.

I tumbled off him, boneless. "Oh my god, Nic."

He crawled up my body, slowly, dropping kisses every few inches, shoving my dress up as he went. "Mmm," he said. "I like hearing you call me that."

I lifted my head to meet his eyes. "Nic?"

He nodded. "Say it again."

"Nic," I breathed.

"That's the name I want on your tongue," he told me. "Not Junior. And yes, I know you've been using it intentionally to keep some space between us, but I don't want you to anymore, so cut it the fuck out, Lo."

My pussy spasmed at the authority in his tone. "Don't boss me around or I'll come."

He dropped his forehead to my belly, shoulders shaking with laughter. I wound my fingers into his hair, just because I could, just because I wanted to, and relaxed deeper into the mattress, loving the weight of him pressing me down, loving the fact that I had actually made him laugh.

A sharp ring cut through the room. His phone, always ruining the mood.

I let my arms fall away, forcing myself to keep quiet instead of telling him to ignore it. He'd promised to never interfere in my work, and the least I could do was return the favor. If he had to take the call, he had to take it, and I had to accept that this would be part of our dynamic if we continued spending time together.

With a groan, he rolled off me, tugging the device from his pocket and bringing it to his ear. "What?" He shot upright. "Where?" He swore. "I'll be there in twenty." He hung up, and the expression on his face as he turned toward me was tortured. "I'm sorry."

I sat up. "Don't be. It's okay."

"I'll come back," he said.

"No worries." I shrugged. "Casual, remember?"

His eyes darkened, and in a blink, he'd flattened me back to the mattress, elbows braced beside my head, hips pinning mine. He rolled into me, his jean-covered erection rough against my sensitive skin, sending an aftershock of bliss rocketing through my core. "What if I said I want something more than casual?"

I stilled beneath the weight of his gaze, digging deep and trying to find courage, trying to ignore the memories of how badly he'd once hurt me. "I'm scared," I confessed.

He tipped forward, pressing our foreheads together. "I know. We can take it as slow as you need."

I searched his eyes, wondering if I was making a huge mistake. Slowly, I nodded. "Okay."

He surged forward, kissing me, tongue merciless and demanding, working my mouth like he'd just worked my pussy. I wrapped my legs around him and drew him closer. With a shallow thrust, he ground his erection against me, making me squirm, making me wish we had more time. I wanted his dick inside me. His *entire* dick this time, hard and fast and brutal, but I doubted we had the time.

With a groan, he broke away. "God, I want to fuck you." His eyes were wild in the dying light. "And I want to talk about what's going on between us, but I have to go, and I hate that I'm leaving you like this."

I grinned. "Like what? Wrung out from how good you tongue-fucked me?"

He shook his head. "You know what I mean." His brows drew together. "I don't know how long this will take."

I leaned forward, pressing one last kiss to his lips. "It's all right if you can't make it back. Just let me know you're safe."

Several minutes later, we crept downstairs. I didn't hear any sounds in the apartment, so I figured Ryan was still out.

"Incoming!" they yelled as we hit the first floor, making me jump.

Walter came tearing around the corner toward us, and I had just enough time to get *really* nervous, because this wasn't how I wanted him and Juni—no, *Nic*—to meet, but Nic held a hand up and said "stop" in the most commanding tone I'd ever heard, and Walter scooted to a halt and sat without having to be told.

The two eyed each other for a long moment.

"We good?" Nic asked.

Walter ducked his head, tail thumping, and I knew everything would be fine.

"All right," Nic huffed, squatting down to Walter's level. "Come on, then."

Walter went bananas, sprinting the final few feet to Nic, sniffing every part he could reach and whacking him with his tail more times than I could count.

"I've never seen him so instantly obsessed with someone before," I said.

Nic shot me a smug look. "Takes after his mother."

Ryan guffawed from nearby. Taylor let out an answering snort, and I yanked my gaze up to see my roommates and Jackson all spread out on the couch. Huh. We must have been in my room longer than I realized. It felt like the face riding had lasted all of a minute, but now I was starting to wonder if sex with Nic was so good that I'd ended up in a time warp or something.

"All right. I know," he said, straightening. He gave Walter one last pet before raising his gaze to mine. "I've got to go."

"Drive safe?" I said.

He nodded and turned to wave at our onlookers. "Enjoy the rest of your night."

Taylor waved back. "You, too, you dirty little slut."

Nic shook his head, dropped a parting kiss on my forehead, and left.

27

JUNIOR

"HERE?" I ASKED STEFAN.

He nodded.

I pulled my gaze from him and looked around. We stood in the shadows of the old port, massive, industrial buildings rising like mountains around us in the darkness. Our elected officials liked to call this part of town a scar on the city. It was run-down, abandoned, a playground for criminals, the unhoused, and urban explorers. Huge silos crumbled into the water. Thousand-gallon diesel tanks bore the tags of a hundred graffiti artists. The concrete was buckled and broken, making driving all but impossible. We'd had to leave our cars at a nearby shipping warehouse and hoof it in on foot.

According to Stefan, somewhere amongst all this rot and decay, a nosebleed poker game was taking place, ultra-high-stakes, invite only.

I had no idea where, since the lights meant to keep this place illuminated constantly got shot out, and the city had finally given up on replacing them, effectively handing this part of the port over to the underworld. I kept looking for the outline of a doorway, or a lit-up window, anything to indicate there was life in this place besides us, but I saw nothing.

The sound of a slap had me turning my head to the five figures standing nearby, dressed in dark fatigues, enough weapons on them to take down an entire squad of soldiers. I'd worked with them before, most notably when covering up for Aly and Josh's crimes. They weren't associated with the mob, or anyone else in the city; they were hired muscle, glorified mercenaries, known for bouncing between one client and another depending on who was footing the bill. The reason they were so in demand was because they kept their mouths shut. That was why I'd called in a favor to get them down here with us. Out of everyone operating in the city, they were the only ones I trusted not to go running to my father afterward.

Their point man, David, a squat bald guy in his mid-forties, held his hand to his neck. "Fucking mosquitoes."

I nodded, hearing the low whine of more bugs descending upon us. We needed to get moving or we'd be eaten alive.

"Where?" I asked Stefan.

He waved me forward and walked to the side of the building we hid behind. Together, we peered around the corner.

"There," he said, pointing.

I followed the line of his finger. Instead of a building, I was looking at a four-hundred-foot derelict freight ship that had been rotting here since the late '80s. It rose from the night-black water like a ghost, its once-crisp white paint weathered to a muddled gray, rust spots crawling upward from the hull all the way to the deck. The massive chains mooring it to the steel cleats on the dock flashed silver in the moonlight, groaning as the boat bobbed on the tide.

It looked like the least-inviting place for a poker game I could have imagined.

My gaze swung back to my brother. He'd never given me a reason to distrust him, at least not any more than I distrusted everyone in general, but I couldn't have imagined a more perfect setup for an ambush if I tried.

"You trying to get me killed?" I asked.

In answer, he flipped me off and walked away, disappearing into the darkness like the phantom he was becoming.

David stepped up next to me and glanced around the side of the building, eyeing the ship. "I don't like this."

"Me neither," I said, retreating into the shadows.

His four other guys ambled over, quiet, letting the boss do all the talking, their eyes constantly shifting as they looked for threats. Every single one of them came from spec ops military units, and it showed. The only time I'd seen them slip up was when Josh tagged along with them, and I blamed that on the fact that he never shut the fuck up and had driven them to distraction. Every other time I'd worked with them, they'd been flawless.

David glanced around the side of the building at the ship again and then turned back to us. "One, north silo," he said, and a man peeled off into the darkness. "Two, south silo. Three, diesel tanks. Four, grain barge."

The men disappeared one by one, leaving David and me behind.

He turned my way. "You good here on your own?"

I nodded. "I'll probably find some way into the building and see if there are any windows or cracks that face the ship."

"Good," he said. "I'm going to take point and get as close as possible. Radios only from this point out."

With that, he turned and melted into the night.

I adjusted the battery pack hooked to my holster and fastened the attached throat mic around my neck. A thin but ultra-strong braided fiber line led to the earbud, which I fit into place before flicking it on.

"Testing," I said, keeping my voice at a whisper because I knew firsthand how sensitive this gear was.

The rest of the men checked in, and we went quiet as they got into position. I turned and inspected the building at my back. It was squat, constructed from concrete and metal, its bunker-like structure making me think it used to house flammable materials before it was decommissioned. The moon hung low over the harbor, out of sight on the other side of the building, casting my immediate surroundings in dense shadow. It made seeing anything difficult, and I was forced to pick my way around the perimeter slowly.

Close to the front, I found a door, its black outline the only distinguishable marker. It was wide open, a gaping maw of darkness, whatever wood or metal that had once stood sentinel in its frame lost to the elements or vandals. I paused at the sight of it. Anyone or any*thing* could be inside—a murderer, a cannibal, thousands of tiny spiders waiting to crawl all over me. I don't know what it said about me that the last possibility was the only one that freaked me out.

Another bonus of working with David was that he always kitted me out in their gear: mic set, night vision goggles, even a soft red flashlight that was hard to detect from more than a few feet away. I unhooked it from my holster and clicked it on, crossing over the threshold into a large, open room filled with the signs of its industrial past. Broken tables lay in pieces on the dirt-covered concrete. A row of metal cabinets lined the far wall, either too big or too heavy to be carried away by looters. Overhead, busted-out fluorescent lights hung from the ceiling.

No signs of a murderer, but I didn't let my guard down. The spiders could be anywhere.

A narrow set of open stairs climbed the wall opposite the cabinets. I beelined toward them, watching my step, skirting all the trash on the floor. The stairs looked rickety as fuck when I got to them, but I didn't see any other options. Moonlight filtered in from above, meaning whatever window or hole was up there faced the ship.

I ascended carefully, testing each step to see if it would hold before putting my full weight on it, and even then I was ready to leap backward at the first sign of collapse. The second floor seemed more stable than the stairs, made of poured concrete like the one below. I paced across it to the hole in the roof, a narrow gash too thin to fit through. Didn't matter. All I needed was a line of sight to the freighter.

I slipped on my night vision goggles and peered out into the darkness. One look at the boat deck was enough to tell me we were fucked. I noted five men standing guard in the shadows, and it looked like they had—

I ducked before getting spotted. "They have goggles, too," I warned the others.

"Roger that," David said. Everyone else remained quiet.

The silence held for what felt like an hour but was probably no longer than twenty minutes. Finally, David's voice came over the line. "They have half a dozen men waiting on the deck alone, and there's no way to know how many more are below. I don't see a way to approach the ship without getting spotted. Confirm?"

Four confirmations followed, one after another.

"I have to give it to the guy," David said. "This is a genius location for a black-market poker game."

Despite my annoyance, I was impressed, too. No wonder the other bookies had a hard time tracking him down and were always a step behind and a day late. The fact that Stefan had been able to do what they hadn't was impressive as hell, and it made me wonder if maybe I'd been underestimating my quietest brother.

"Do you recognize the crew on deck?" I asked. David made it his business to know every other merc operation within the tristate area.

"Yeah, it's Oscar's," he said. "They might be thugs, but they know enough to be dangerous."

Impatience clawed at me. I wanted to get this over with and get back to Lauren. "What are you thinking?"

"We wait them out," David said. "Eventually, they'll have to leave, I'm guessing before dawn. By that point, they'll have been up all night, and I'm hoping their fatigue will make them less alert. We can grab him then."

Given the circumstances, it was probably our best option. Which meant we had a long night of waiting ahead of us. God, I loathed stakeouts, especially when I was unprepared.

Fitting the goggles to my eyes, I rose up just enough to peer out of the roof again and confirm everything David had said. The men on deck seemed mostly focused on their immediate surroundings, few looking up. As I watched, a new figure crawled out of the deck hatch. I almost discarded him as more hired muscle—he was big enough for it—but he was dressed in a suit. One of the gamblers? This could be promising. If tonight didn't work out, maybe I could ID this guy and exploit his connection with the bookie.

He stood side-on to me, speaking to one of the guards, looking like he was issuing orders. My heartbeat picked up. What if he wasn't a player, but the bookie himself? I rose to my feet, trying to get a better fix on him, when suddenly he turned, and recognition tore through me like a bullet.

What the *fuck*?

I was looking at Josh's former roommate, Tyler. Maybe if I hadn't just seen him a few hours ago, I wouldn't have been so sure, but there was no mistaking his douchey face or his smarmy grin. Finance, my ass. No wonder he'd looked so smug when I told him I ran imports. The motherfucker probably knew who I was.

"Change of plan," I told David. "I'm going to walk right up to the ship."

"Do not recommend," he said, as brusque as ever.

"Yeah, well, turns out I know this asshole."

"Wait for us to get to high ground, then," he said. "We'll cover you from up there."

"Roger."

I checked my weapons while I waited: the guns in my holster, the one on my right ankle, the knife sheath tucked into my left boot. No doubt the guns would get taken the second I stepped on board, but I was hoping they'd miss the knife and I'd have something to fall back on in an emergency.

One after another, the men checked in from their new positions.

"Whatever you do," David said as I walked back into the night, "don't leave the deck."

"I'll try not to," I told him. "I'm taking the radio off so they don't realize I have backup until I'm on board. I'll leave it outside the door here."

"Roger," David said.

I disentangled myself from the thing and set it on an overturned plastic bucket before striding around the side of the building. Instead of taking a stealthier route, I walked right into the open with my hands in the air so the men on board would see my approach and know I wasn't a threat. Moonlight turned my surroundings into a world of grays. Gravel crunched beneath my shoes. The sound of the creaking ship echoed off the nearby buildings, almost loud enough to drown out my pulse beating in my ears.

This was probably the dumbest thing I'd done in months, but poker games like this one were prided for their discretion, and nothing would draw the cops like gunfire ringing out through the night. I was banking on that to keep them from shooting me.

As I got closer to the ship, I noticed something that had been hidden by my vantage point: a ladder strung from the deck to the pier. It was made of rope and wood, and from the way it swayed in the breeze, I knew it couldn't have been easy to traverse. Beneath it, black water waited to swallow up anyone who fell. The people playing poker in the belly of this beast must have been deadly serious about the game.

"Stop right there," someone called.

I did as they said, craning my head back to see three men looming over the side of the railings high above.

"Tell the blond guy up there with you that Junior Trocci is here to see him," I yelled, withholding Tyler's name because I wasn't sure if he was using an alias and I didn't want to immediately get on his bad side by doxing him.

A fourth head popped into view. "What the fuck are you doing here?" Tyler demanded.

I hated putting my business out in the open, but I doubted they'd let me up unless I gave them something. "I want to talk to you about buying a man's debt."

"And you couldn't have done it earlier?" Tyler asked in a pissy tone that had me clenching my jaw.

Be nice, I told myself for the second time today. I needed something from him, and there were weapons trained on me.

"I didn't know you were the guy I was looking for," I said with a shrug.

"How'd you find me?" he asked, a note of suspicion joining the pissiness.

"A contact," I called, getting impatient. "You gonna let me up, or what?"

"Fine." He disappeared from sight.

I dropped my arms and paced over to the ladder. It looked worse than the stairs I'd taken earlier, but I didn't see any alternatives, so I grabbed the ropes, put my foot on the bottom rung, and started up. It immediately swung right, and I had to stop and steady myself before it dumped me into the water.

Goddamn pain in the ass jungle gym fucking bullshit.

Carefully, keeping my weight centered on the rungs, I ascended. Two goons waited to search me at the top. They found all three guns and the knife.

Tyler stood several feet away, arms crossed, watching. "Lot of fucking weapons for a talk."

"Relax," I told him. "I didn't know what I was walking into."

He glanced at the surrounding darkness. "Anyone else here with you?"

"Yup," I said, letting him know it wouldn't be smart to try and get rid of me. "They'll be fine as long as we stay up here."

He gave me a discontented look and turned on his heel, waving me after him like he was calling a dog to heel. I balled my hands into fists and followed in his wake. *Be nice, be nice.* We strode to the back of the boat, passing shipping containers and old storage drums. A cry rose from down below, and then cheering. The game sounded like it was in full swing. How the fuck had Tyler wormed his way into this world without anyone finding out who he was? And how had he clawed his way up to this level so fast?

"Get lost," he told the men guarding the stern.

They lumbered away without comment, but I could tell from the looks on their faces that they liked him about as much as I did.

"You should be more careful," I said when they were gone. "Men who make enemies in this city don't live very long."

He waved me off. "Why should I worry about being nice when I'm paying them more than they're worth?"

I shook my head. "I never said to be nice. But a little respect goes a long way."

He snorted. "Sure."

I could tell from the dismissal that there was no point in arguing, so I let it drop.

He leaned against the taffrail and eyed me. "Whose debt are you after?"

"Patrick McKinney's," I said.

"Why?"

"Because he pissed me off."

"You're not going to kill him, are you?" he asked. "Dead clients don't bring in any more money."

So he *did* know what I really did for work. "No," I said. Not that I would tell him if I *was* planning to off the guy.

Tyler pulled his phone from his pocket and looked to be checking over something. "He owes me two million."

"Bullshit," I spat.

Tyler's douchey expression disappeared, replaced by something far more ruthless. Great. He and Josh were more alike than I'd realized. "He's a drunk old fuck who thinks he's more important than he is, so he weasels his way into high roller games and then loses his ass because he's also a goddamn idiot."

I let my own crazy shine through, taking a step closer. Tyler might have been bigger than me, but I doubted he'd ever been in a *real* fight before. "If I find out you're lying about the amount," I said, "not even your friendship with Josh will keep you safe. I'll tear this entire enterprise down around you and then scatter your body parts all over the city."

"I'm not lying," he bit out, wariness creeping into his expression for the first time since I'd met him. "McKinney owns a bunch of buildings over on the West Side. He thinks he can keep piling on the debt, because he just turns around and squeezes more out of his tenants to cover the monthly payments."

My mind went to work. So that explained the constant upticks. How many more people besides Lauren and the other owners of Velvet was McKinney fucking over?

"That's what you're after, isn't it?" Tyler said. "One of his properties."

Goddamn it. I really wished he was as stupid as he looked. It would make dealing with him so much easier. "None of your business."

"Are you trying to expand mob territory? Is that it?"

This nosy motherfucker was getting on my last damn nerve, and it was time to turn the tables. "Josh know about your little business venture?"

Tyler's expression shut down, all the answer I needed.

"Tell you what, give me McKinney's debt for a million, and I won't say anything." I grinned. "To Josh, *or* all the other bookies who are after you."

Tyler took a menacing step toward me.

"Careful," I said, pointing at the little red dot that suddenly bloomed on his chest.

He glanced down, saw the laser, and swore, stepping back. A calculating gleam entered his eyes as he studied me. "Your father know what you're up to?"

"Yup," I lied.

"Somehow I doubt that, or you would have come here with a bunch of mob thugs instead of whichever mercs you hired."

I shrugged, feigning nonchalance.

"So, if I show up at Nico Senior's house tomorrow to hand over McKinney's slips, he'll be fine?" Tyler asked.

Shit. We were at a stalemate, and I could tell from his expression that he knew it.

"I can't let it go for a million," he said, eyeing me. "Not unless you take me on as a partner."

Was he serious? "Fuck, no. We don't even get along. Why would I want to work with you?"

"Because it makes fiscal sense," he said, like that answered everything. And maybe for him, it did, but the thought of having to deal with this asshole all the time gave me an instant headache.

"I'll stay silent," he went on. "Let you handle all the daily bullshit as long as I get my cut."

"Careful," I said. "Verbal agreements are binding in my line of work."

"I'm serious, bro."

I almost said no just for him calling me bro, but my curiosity won out. "What's in it for you?"

"I'm empire building." He gestured toward our feet and the hoots and hollers echoing through the hull. "I recognize that this might be temporary and want as many valid businesses as possible to balance it out. Plus," he said, grinning, "I'll always welcome another way to launder money."

I shook my head. "It has to be legit. I'm not after McKinney's building just to turn it criminal."

He frowned. "So it's really not a mob thing?"

"It's really not."

He eyed me, considering. "Fine. You in or not?"

The full two million would clear me out. All my savings and both stock portfolios. It was too much risk. I didn't know much about Tyler, but it was obvious he had a brain underneath all that blond hair and understood how to be discreet. The fact that no one but Stefan could find him proved that. He also seemed to value the importance of diversification, something I couldn't say for my father or his compatriots. As far as silent partners went, I could have done worse. Most important, I couldn't afford to do it without him, so it wasn't like I had much of a choice.

Praying I wasn't making the biggest mistake of my life, I offered my hand to Tyler.

He grinned as we shook. "This is going to be fun."

Somehow, I highly doubted that.

28

LAUREN

"So, you're, like, together now?" Ryan asked.

It was late the next morning, and my roommates and I were gathered in the kitchen, Taylor and Ryan seated at the island while I cooked pancakes and caught them up on everything they'd missed.

"I don't know that I'd go that far," I said. "We more agreed that it wasn't as casual as we first thought."

"No labels," Taylor said. "Very cool. Very modern."

I chucked a blueberry at her head.

She dodged out of the way, and Walter went skittering over the hardwood after it.

I turned back to the stove and poured a few more pancakes. Nic had texted me late, apologizing for not being able to make it back. Afterward, I'd tried to go to sleep, but I'd been too wired, too worried about what he was up to, if he was okay. I hadn't missed the way he flinched every time I touched his side. Whatever wound was there was still healing, and it made me wonder how often he got hurt, how dangerous his line of work really was.

I'd gotten another text early this morning from him saying that he'd made it back to his apartment safely, and finally, I'd been able to pass out. We'd agreed to try for something less casual, but I hadn't really stopped to consider what a relationship with Nic would look like. How many nights would I spend sleepless and worried about his safety? How often would he have to race off to follow his dad's orders? I could imagine countless scenarios in which it happened. Post-sex again. While running errands. In the middle of date night at a restaurant, him leaving me to awkwardly finish my meal alone.

Whatever Nic was working on to go legit, I hoped it would happen soon; I didn't think I had it in me to be a long-term mob moll. Almost as bad as the thought of him getting hurt was the thought of him hurting other people, possibly *innocent* people. There was already too much darkness in Nic's eyes. I couldn't stand the thought of having to watch the last spark of light fade entirely.

I flipped the pancakes, thinking back over the past few days, wondering if I'd been too quick to overlook certain things. Nic had agreed that there would be no more secrets between us, but I couldn't shake the thought that there was more he was keeping from me. Like the oh-so-careful way he said he wouldn't put *more* trackers on me . . .

It made me wonder what other lies Nic was telling, by omission or otherwise. Maybe I was just being paranoid, but there was an uneasy feeling in my gut that wouldn't go away, and I'd learned to trust it over the years. It had rarely led me astray.

I scooped three pancakes onto a plate and turned toward Taylor, setting them in front of her.

She picked up her fork and stuffed one in her mouth, mumbling "thank you" around it.

"You're welcome," I said, turning back to the stove, distracted.

I felt unsettled, like I had unfinished business. Not just with Nic, but with my sister, too, and even though I'd planned to spend the day filming, I decided to go see Kristen first to try to have an adult conversation with her for once instead of falling back into our usual childhood bickering.

By the time I sat down to eat, Taylor and Ryan were done with their food, and Ryan was filling us in on Ben accepting Ryan's offer to work together.

"He's bringing over his own client list," they said. "It's smaller than mine, but that's good, because I'm trying to do less work, not more, so I can hand some of mine over to him."

"Was that who you were FaceTiming earlier?" I asked.

Ryan's cheeks pinked, and they dropped their gaze. "Yup."

I zeroed in on it. "You think he's cute."

Their eyes flashed wide. "What? No." Ryan was a horrible liar.

Taylor set her coffee down. "Oh my god, you do!"

I poked Ryan's side with my fork. "You can't hit on your employee, you ho bag. It's unethical."

"He's not even my employee yet!" Ryan argued, squirming away.

Taylor and I spent the next five minutes teasing them until they finally caved and showed us Ben's social media.

"Oh, he's pretty," I said.

Taylor agreed, grabbing the phone out of Ryan's hand and punching the screen with her finger. "Oops! Just followed."

The blood drained from Ryan's face. "I'll kill you this time."

With a shriek, Taylor went sprinting toward the stairs, Ryan hot on her heels, Walter hot on *their* heels.

I sighed as I watched them disappear up the stairs, praying the insulation was thick enough to smother the noise they were making.

■ ■ ■

My grandparents' store occupied the first floor of a hundred-year-old building in the heart of Little Italy. They were both first-generation Americans, their parents fleeing Mussolini and the rise of the fascists in the 1920s.

This country loved shitting on immigrants, despite the fact that almost everyone here was descended from them, and back then, the Italians had been the chosen group to bear the brunt of that hatred, with laws enacted to limit their immigration and prejudice against them running amok. They were often ostracized and segregated to certain areas, forced to band together to keep safe and preserve their culture while surrounded by people who wanted to tear it apart. That was part of why there was a "Little Italy" in almost every large city in North America.

My grandparents had been determined to claw their way out of the poverty that ran rampant through the old neighborhood back in the day, and, seeing a need for a deli, they scraped and saved until they were able to open one. It started small, operating out of the front room of their tiny apartment, before slowly becoming profitable enough that they were able to rent out a storefront. Now, over fifty years later, Nonna owned the building outright, the ground floor housing a large deli-cum-general store, and the second floor outfitted with a decent-sized three-bedroom apartment that my sister and her family had moved into when they'd taken over the store after Nonno died.

The bell above the door chimed when I walked in, announcing my arrival. It was midday Sunday, and all the churches in the neighborhood had just let out. The place was packed. I wove my way through the familiar aisles, memories of running up and down them as a toddler, and then later, stocking shelves as a teenager, flooding my mind. Everyone knew everyone here, and I stopped several times to exchange pleasantries with my middle school history teacher, a girl I'd played soccer with, and, awkwardly, the first boy I'd ever kissed. Neither of us made eye contact. I was sure we were both remembering the way he'd come in his pants and then panicked and said he'd pissed himself like that was somehow better.

Hugo, my brother-in-law, saw me approaching and flipped up the section of counter next to the register so I could slip through. He was a big man, tall, husky, with broad shoulders and a barrel chest. If this were a Scorsese movie, he'd be cast as Goon #2, wearing a full tracksuit and smoking a cigar in the background of a scene while the A-listers discussed offing someone in the foreground. Most of the time, he put his size to use working guard detail at the estate of Lorenzo Brusomini, the current head of the mob, but on Sundays, Kristen had the day off, and Hugo took over the register.

"Hey, good to see you," he said, leaning down to give me a one-armed hug.

"You, too," I said, squeezing him back. "Is Kristen upstairs?"

"Yeah," he said, releasing me. "Go easy on her, eh? This kid's giving her a harder time than the other two did. One second, Joe," he told the man waiting to check out. He turned back to me. "Capiche?"

I nodded, keeping my mouth shut instead of pointing out that of the two of us, I wasn't the one who started shit. Hugo was Kristen's husband; it was his job to take her side.

"Hey," he called as I headed toward the storeroom door. "Be quiet going up. She just put the kids down."

"I will," I said, slipping into the back.

I paused when the door clicked shut behind me, taking a deep, calming breath filled with the familiar scents of my childhood: coffee and parmesan and fresh basil and the sweet hint of anise-flavored biscotti, all paired with the gym-sock smell of sliced salami, soppressata, and prosciutto. It sounded disgusting when listed out, but to me, it was heaven. I felt safe in here, protected, reminded of my grandparents taking me and my sister in and giving us the best childhoods they could.

With one last inhale, I passed through the door in the back corner and took the stairs up.

"Kristen?" I whisper-hissed after using my key.

"In here," she hissed back.

I followed the sound of her voice into the living room, where she was sprawled out on the couch, a book in her hand. She lay on her side, her other hand around her burgeoning belly, where my third niece or nephew was incubating, or growing, or whatever the term was. Her dark hair was piled on top of her head in a messy bun, and she wore sweats and one of her husband's old shirts. There were dark circles under her eyes that made me wonder if she hadn't been sleeping, and suddenly, I was less concerned about how she treated me than I had been before coming over. My sister was clearly having a hard time, and even though we didn't get along that well, I still cared about her.

"How you doing?" I asked, weaving around discarded toys as I made my way closer.

She set her book down and lifted the plastic tub just beside her on the floor. "Well, I'm six months into this pregnancy and still have to cart an emergency puke bucket everywhere I go, so you tell me."

Her tone was harsh, but I tried not to take it personally. I'd be pissy, too, if I was constantly upchucking. "I'm sorry," I said. "Can I get you anything?"

At this, she perked up. "Peppermint tea?"

I nodded and went to the kitchen, trying to be as quiet as possible. I pulled their tea kettle out of a cupboard and set about boiling water. Our conversation about her behavior could wait. Clearly, she wasn't in any state to have it. Instead, I'd leave it at asking if she'd heard anything new about our allegedly missing father. And then I'd offer to help clean up a little and play with the boys when they woke from their naps so she could have more time to herself.

"Thank you," she said, sitting up to take her tea when I reentered the living room.

"Careful, it's hot."

She nodded, bringing it close to her face and breathing deeply. "I know, but the smell alone can help with the nausea."

"Do you have that thing Kate Middleton did?"

She shook her head. "It's called hyperemesis gravidarum, and no. Some women just randomly puke for all nine months."

"That sounds . . ."

"Horrible?" she asked, looking up. "Unfair? Like complete fucking bullshit since we're already dealing with stretch marks and incontinence and nonstop farting and insomnia and mental fog and about nine million other discomforts?"

"Yes. That."

Every time I got around pregnant women and they started talking about what they were going through, it made me question whether or not I wanted to have kids, or at least whether or not I wanted to bear them myself. Surrogacy or adoption were looking real tempting right now.

"You've had help with the boys, right?" I asked.

She set her tea on the side table. "Yeah. Thank god for Hugo's family. I'd be losing my mind without them. Between his sisters swinging by and his parents offering to have the boys over for sleepovers so I can actually rest, we've had a decent amount of help."

"I'm sorry I haven't been around more," I said, feeling guilty.

She shook her head. "Don't worry about it. I know you have a whole life downtown, and kids don't belong in it."

Ouch.

That was the trouble with Kristen, just when I started to feel like maybe we'd finally go an entire conversation without her bringing up what I did, she'd slip in a subtle insult or cutting remark. I'd learned to bite my tongue because fighting had never made it better, but it sucked to always have to be the bigger person.

"I'm just so mad at Mom and Dad, you know?" she continued. "Between Mom taking off when we were little and Dad being absent all our lives, I feel like we were robbed of the kind of childhood Hugo had, and I don't think I'll ever forgive them for that. I would kill to have two loving, supportive parents who are still around to help out with their grandkids."

"Yeah, but we had Nonna and Nonno," I said.

Kristen shook her head. "It's not the same. You're not a parent, so you don't understand how fucked it is that ours just up and abandoned us."

Annoyance flared through me again, and it was on the tip of my tongue to argue with her, to say that I didn't need to be a parent to understand that, but I held my response back, reminding myself that she was six months pregnant and exhausted. I loved my sister, I really did, but sometimes, I didn't like her all that much.

"Have you heard anything else about our father?" I asked, switching gears.

"No, but Hugo thinks someone got rid of him."

A shiver slid down my spine. She said it with almost no tone to her voice, like the news of his potential death meant nothing to her. Like it was just an offhand comment to be made. To me. His other daughter. And look, I liked him a hell of a lot less than I did her, but Jesus Christ, she could be coldhearted sometimes.

I inspected her face, looking for any trace of worry or empathy, but she only looked tired and bored with this conversation, her eyes drifting toward her discarded book like she couldn't wait for me to leave so she could go back to reading.

"And you didn't think to tell me before now?" I said, unable to help myself this time.

She rolled her eyes. "Oh my god, don't start this shit again."

"What shit?" I asked.

"Being so dramatic," she said. "Like everything I do or don't say is some sort of personal attack against you."

My anger flared. "Well, I did have to find out about our father's disappearance from someone else, and in the less than ten minutes that I've been here, you've insulted me, belittled me, and then revealed that you've been holding on to another pretty important piece of information for god knows how long, so excuse me if it feels that way sometimes."

"What was there to even tell you?" she asked, her voice rising. "Hugo has no idea what actually happened, he just thinks someone finally offed Tommy, because the last time anyone saw him, he was with Nico Trocci."

I sat back in my chair, stunned. "What?"

"Nico? Trocci?" Kristen said, like I was stupid. "Dad of that asshole you fucked in high school?"

"I heard the name," I said. "Why is it important?"

She shrugged. "Because according to Hugo, his guys are Lorenzo's cleanup crew."

"Cleanup crew," I repeated. My ears were ringing, and I could barely hear anything over the sound of my own pulse.

"Jesus Christ, you're slow today," she said, twisting her voice into something ugly and mocking. "He takes the people and makes them go buh-bye."

"I have to leave," I said, struggling to my feet.

"Great visit," Kristen sniped. "Thanks *so* much for coming."

I turned on her. "You know what? I don't care that you're pregnant, and I know that by saying this, I'll probably lose all visitation rights with your kids, because that's the kind of bitch you are, but go fuck yourself, Kristen."

"Auntie Lawen?" a sleepy little voice asked.

I wheeled around to see my four-year-old nephew, Enzo, standing in the living room doorway, one hand rubbing his eye, the other clutching his favorite blankie. Shit. We'd probably woken him up with our arguing.

There was no coming back from this, was there?

"*Get out*," Kristen said, pushing up from the couch, fury replacing exhaustion.

"Sorry, bud," I told Enzo, and then I left, stumbling down the stairs and out of the store.

The sun bore down on me, hot and oppressive, but despite its rays, my skin felt clammy and my head spun. Was I about to pass out?

I leaned against a light pole, trying to catch my breath. I'd convinced myself that I needed to hash things out with Kristen, that *that* was why I'd come over here, but deep down, I'd also been hoping to get some answers about Nic. Thanks to Hugo, my sister knew more about the mob than anyone else in my life, and part of me had been planning to find some way to bring Nic up, mention that I'd been seeing him again. But then Kristen had dropped that bomb, and now I wished I hadn't come to see her at all. I felt like the last bride of Bluebeard discovering the forbidden closet, only instead of finding Nic's other wives inside, I was staring down at the corpse of my father.

Tommy went missing, and suddenly, after ten years, Nic came waltzing back into my life. I felt like a fucking idiot for not seeing the connection sooner, but up until today, I'd honestly thought Tommy was just lying low for some reason. That he would show up again when he was ready to. Because that's what happened every time he'd gone "missing" before.

Oh, god, was any of it even real, between Nic and I, or was I some sort of pawn? Did Nic and his family think I had information on Tommy that they planned to trick me into giving them? Or were they just trying to keep a close eye on me because I was an easy mark and the best shot they had at learning about the inevitable investigation into my father's disappearance?

Anger replaced my terror. If it was all an act, and Nic planned to abandon me again as soon as he got what he wanted, or worse, do to me what they'd done to my father, I would spend the rest of my life, or afterlife, depending on the outcome, making him regret it.

Starting now.

29

JUNIOR

ACCORDING TO TYLER, MCKINNEY LIKED to tell people he lived in the penthouse apartment of his nicest building, which sounded extravagant but in reality was much more mundane. His nicest building was only six stories tall, narrow, and sandwiched between a parking garage and a row of new-build apartments that were still undergoing construction.

The security was abysmal. It had one of those older-model buzzer systems, and I didn't even see a speaker on the panel. I lifted a hand and pressed it against the top row of apartment buttons, slowly dragging downward over them, ringing every single one because there *had* to be someone waiting for a delivery or a friend or—

The door chimed. I turned and pulled it open. Inside, the foyer was surprisingly decent, the terrazzo tile in good condition, considering its age. A wall of mailboxes stood to my right, the art deco–style bronze detailing on them harkening back to a time gone by.

The elevator was dead ahead, but I decided to take the stairs to get a better look at the place. I kept my eyes peeled, but I didn't see a single security camera. McKinney was either too cheap for them, or too lazy. He was also stupid, because a lot of insurance companies required them these days and wouldn't pay out unless you had video proof to show that you weren't personally responsible for the damage. Too many slumlords had fucked up their own property hoping to cash in, and the adjusters in the city had cracked down on everyone else as a result.

I reached the sixth floor and stopped on the landing, looking left and right. There wasn't one door up here, but three, so either McKinney had been lying about having the penthouse, or these doors all led to the same apartment. The numbers on them were different, though, and Tyler told me McKinney's was 600. Guess that meant 601 and 602 belonged to other people.

I rapped my knuckles on the door with the 600.

It swung open a few seconds later, no "who are you?" or "what are you doing here?" to precede it. In front of me stood a short, balding white man dressed in slacks and a button-down. He looked clean and put together, but I could smell the alcohol on him even before he opened his mouth.

"Can I help you?" he asked, looking me over.

I had worn my best suit, the starched white collar of my shirt hiding my neck tattoos, hands shoved in my pockets for the same reason. Like this, with my hair slicked back, I could have passed as Tyler's fellow finance bro. "Are you Patrick McKinney?"

He frowned. "Yeah, who's asking?"

In answer, I surged forward, shoving him into the apartment and slamming the door behind us. A punch to his gut aborted his shout of surprise. I kicked his knee out, stepped behind him, and twisted his arm behind his back, much like I had that drunk man at Velvet, only this time, there was no one to stop me as I dug a pair of pliers out of my pocket and fit them to McKinney's pinkie.

"Scream, and I'll take it off," I told him.

He wheezed, cheek pressed to the carpet, trying to regain his breath. "What do you want?"

"You owe Mr. Strickland two million dollars and you're late with your monthly payment again." Why Tyler had chosen that name for a cover, I hadn't asked, nor did I really care. As far as aliases went, I'd heard much worse.

"I can pay," McKinney hissed, trying to squirm away from me.

I squeezed the pliers hard enough to pinch. "Stop moving. Mr. Strickland has given you more than enough chances."

"Wait!" he said. "I *can* pay! I'm just waiting for a check to clear from a bunch of dirty perverts who rent one of my units."

That almost made me laugh, thinking back to the other night and Taylor calling me a dirty little slut as I said goodbye to Lauren.

"It's too late," I said, dropping my voice to cover my amusement. "I own your debt now."

McKinney's breath wheezed out of him as he tried to get a better look at me. "Who are you?"

"People call me Junior, but all you need to know is that instead of owing a bookie, you now owe the mob."

He made a distressed sound that made me think he'd finally realized just how fucked he was. "What do you want?"

"That building full of dirty perverts."

"What?" he said, still trying to crane his head up.

I put my boot on his cheek and held him in place, twisting his arm a little harder, squeezing the pliers a little tighter. "The deed."

McKinney started to struggle. "You can't be serious!"

"Keep your voice down," I said, my own deadly calm. "I won't tell you again."

A well of blood bubbled up around the plier jaws.

Beneath me, McKinney whimpered. "That building's worth three million dollars, not two."

"So?" I said. "Would you rather lose a million dollars and live? Or die? The choice is up to you."

He went still. "You won't do it. You won't kill me. If I die, you don't get anything."

He sounded so sure, so *smug*.

Some people just had to be taught the hard way.

I clipped his finger off.

Before he could register the pain, I had an arm around his face, muffling the delayed screaming, the spurting hand held out wide to keep from getting blood on my suit.

"No," I said, close enough for him to hear the menace in my voice, "I won't get anything if you're dead, but there are a lot of body parts to carve off in the meantime. You're going to sign the building over to me, and you're going to drop the rent on all your other tenants, or you and I are going to be seeing a lot more of each other."

Eventually, his shouts turned to a pathetic mewling, and I fought back an unwelcome wave of guilt. This was my chance to go legit, and I wasn't going to lose it because my conscience was trying to make a reappearance after lying dormant for a decade. If everything went to plan, McKinney might be the last person I had to hurt. The last ugly memory I might ever make. And if he wasn't stopped now, it would only get worse. He'd keep targeting Lauren and Velvet and all his other tenants who were slowly being squeezed to death because of his addictions.

What little remorse I had evaporated at the thought. I'd take every fucking one of his fingers if I had to and then start in on his toes before making good on my threat and working my way up the rest of his body, inch by bloody inch. I had to get free, would help as many other people in the process as I could. And while I knew that it didn't make up for all the pain and heartache I'd caused in my life, it was as good a place to start as any.

"There's still time to get the finger reattached," I told McKinney. "If you make the right decision. Otherwise, I'm putting it in my pocket and leaving with it, and tomorrow, I'll be back for another one."

He nodded, and I slowly pulled my arm away.

■ ■ ■

It was late by the time I finally headed back to my apartment. McKinney might have seen reason pretty quickly, but the way he'd dragged his feet afterward, begging and pleading for mercy I didn't have, took up so much time that day had bled into night, and I was fucking exhausted from being around that emotional leech for so long. In the end, the only thing that had gotten him to sign on the dotted line was shaking the baggie of ice I'd put his finger in and reminding him that if he waited too long, it'd be too late to get it reattached.

At one point, I'd gotten so sick of his complaining that I ended up lecturing him like he was a child instead of a man old enough to be my father, telling him to look at the bright side: His debts were cleared, and he still had income properties that he *was* going to drop the rents on back to city standards. If he stopped losing his ass in gambling dens, he could comfortably live out the rest of his days in peace.

I could tell from the way he'd bitched and moaned about how it wasn't *his* fault he'd lost so much that there was no way he'd get his shit together and do what I said, so I would definitely be paying him another visit. But for now, I had what I wanted: freedom, or at least the means to achieve it. Tomorrow, I would start the arduous process of assessing the building I'd acquired, going over the income history with a fine-tooth comb, and figuring out just how many repairs and renovations were needed to turn Velvet into the safest, most profitable play club in the country, because if I was going to do this, I was going to *fucking* do it. Full send.

I called Tyler on the way back to my apartment, his voice loud in my helmet as I raced across the city's most iconic bridge.

"How'd it go?" he asked.

"I got us the building."

He was quiet for so long that I wondered if we had a bad connection. "Already? Just like that?"

"Just like that." He didn't need to know the gruesome details. "Tell me we're not going to lose our asses on it."

"We won't," he said. "I looked into McKinney's financials months ago. I do it with every high roller to make sure I can recoup their losses if they can't pay their debts."

Thank fuck for that. "I got him to drop the rents on all his other tenants, too."

"How the fuck did you do that?" Tyler asked.

"You really want to know?"

He fell silent again, so I filled the gap by telling him a watered-down version of my visit with McKinney.

"What a fucking pain in the ass," he said when I was done. "I'm glad to be rid of him."

"Oh, he'll be back. He's too stupid or sick to stay away."

"He's not coming back to *my* games. I banned him for not paying his debts."

"Good," I said. When word of the ban got out, other bookies would be less likely to spot McKinney money, slowing down his debt accrual. "I'm going to start digging into everything tomorrow, and I'll let you know if anything major crops up."

"In that case, I hope I don't hear from you," he said.

Despite myself, I grinned.

We said goodbye and got off the phone, and I spent the rest of the ride trying to think about all the shit I needed to do, but my brain kept chucking thoughts of Lauren at me. How she'd felt riding my face. The evil little grin that took over her expression whenever she had a particularly diabolical thought. How happy she'd be when she found out Velvet was no longer at risk.

I was entering my neighborhood when I hit a red light. Did I even need to go home, or could I go see what Lauren was up to? I'd been careful not to get blood on me, so it wasn't like I needed to change. But she'd mentioned that her filming schedule was all over the place in a previous sexting session, so I didn't want to just drop in unannounced. Plus, she might not even be home.

The light was still red, so I tugged off a glove and unlocked my phone, where it sat in its holder. I went straight to the tracking software Josh had installed on her cell for me and frowned when the map popped up. Lauren wasn't at her apartment across town. She was at mine. How? She'd never been there before, but she was smart enough that I wasn't all that surprised she'd figured out where I lived.

Was she planning to surprise me or something? Oh, I liked that thought.

I tugged my glove back on, slapped my visor down, and took a sharp left, gunning it down a side street because I was suddenly too impatient to sit in traffic. My heart pounded as I wove through cars, lane splitting, tailgating, even swerving over the line into oncoming traffic because I had *just* enough room to pass the idiot slowing me down.

I cut the engine as I approached my apartment, not wanting to alert Lauren of my arrival. As excited as she probably was to surprise me, I was much more excited to get the drop on her instead. The thought of sneaking up on her and pouncing before she knew I was there was far too appealing to pass up, and after what she'd revealed about wanting to get hunted down, I thought she'd appreciate the turn of events just as much as I would.

Instead of parking out front, I rolled into a spot half a block away and hoofed it back on foot, careful to stay close to the buildings so she wouldn't see me coming. I looked for her on the sidewalk and didn't see her, so I pulled up the map again. Oh, shit. She was *in* my apartment. That sly little vixen. How the hell had she pulled this off without a key?

I took the stairs up to my place, careful to avoid those that creaked. I even kept my keys cradled in my hand so they wouldn't jiggle as I slid the one to my door into the lock. A heartbeat late, I was turning the knob, slowly pushing the door open, stepping inside, and—

Searing pain stabbed into my lower back. I spun on instinct, knocking the weapon away, grabbing my assailant by the throat and slamming them against the wall beside the door. My fist was two inches from Lauren's face before I realized it was her, and I barely swung wide in time to keep from knocking her out. Instead, I punched through the drywall half an inch away, my knuckles screaming in pain.

"Fuck!" I roared, pulling free and releasing my hold on her.

She sank to the ground, gasping, hands clutching her throat.

I kicked the door shut and dropped to my knees. "Lauren, shit, are you okay?"

I reached for her, but she lashed out at me and half fell trying to get away.

"What are you doing?" I said, following after her. "Let me see your neck. You could be hurt." Goddamn it, I'd grabbed her so *hard*.

"Don't," she wheezed, scrambling backward, one hand holding her throat. "I'll scream."

I went still. "What? It was an accident, Lo. I didn't know it was you who'd . . ." I trailed off, belatedly realizing that she'd *attacked me*.

My gaze dropped to the discarded taser on my floor. That she'd just shoved into my back.

What the fuck?

I lifted my eyes to see her sandwiched in the corner as far away from me as she could get. "Listen, I know this is still new and we haven't really dug into all our shared fantasies, but I feel like I should tell you, getting jolted with electricity? Not one of my turn-ons."

"Are you cracking jokes right now?" she rasped, eyes flashing.

"No?" I said, growing increasingly confused about what was going on here.

"My dad," she said, and it felt like she'd dumped a bucket of ice over my head.

Oh, she'd attacked me *for real*.

I schooled my face, wondering how much she knew. "What about him?"

"He goes missing, and suddenly you show back up?"

"I wanted to see how you were doing," I said, which was the truth. Or at least part of it.

"So it's just a coincidence then?" she demanded. "You had nothing to do with his disappearance?"

No more lies, she'd said, and I'd stupidly agreed. Fuck.

"Lauren . . ."

"I knew it," she said, drawing her knees to her chest like she was trying to protect herself from me. Like she was scared. I shuffled forward, and she put her hands up to ward me off. "Don't come any closer."

Her voice was coming back, gaining volume, and despite the fear on her face, I was relieved. Maybe I hadn't hurt her too badly after all. I wasn't about to take any chances, though.

I whipped my phone out. "I'm calling Aly to come look at you."

She lunged forward and slapped it out of my hand.

"I'm trying to help you, Lauren."

"Bullshit. You were going to call your father for backup, weren't you?"

I opened my mouth to tell her that wasn't something I would *ever* do, but she tried to scramble past me toward the taser, and nope, not getting jolted again, thank you very much. I reached out and grabbed her, pulling her off-balance, and with a twist, I had her seated on my lap. She flailed, trying to get away, but I wrapped my arms around her and held on tight, letting her tire herself out. As soon as she calmed down and we got this Tommy discussion out of the way, we were going to talk about how easy it was to restrain her. Aly took self-defense classes somewhere downtown. Maybe I could ask her about bringing Lauren along to teach her the basics.

Better yet, I'd just never let Lauren out of my sight again, would follow her around the city like her own private security detail.

"Are you done?" I asked.

Instead of cursing me or screaming, she burst into tears.

Oh, shit.

I loosened my arms, and suddenly the woman I'd been holding morphed into a wildcat, all tooth and claw. There was a slap to my face, nails dragging down my arm, a foot in my gut, and then she was standing several feet away again, her expression contorted with anger even as tears streaked down her face.

Maybe she didn't need self-defense lessons after all.

"You killed him, didn't you?" she said.

I slowly got to my feet. "Lauren, wait. I—"

"My sister said that's what you do! That you and your family are Lorenzo's cleanup crew!"

I fought back a snarl. Fucking Kristen Marchetti. She'd been an asshole in high school, the epitome of a mean girl, and from everything I'd heard, she was still an asshole today. Her goddamn husband must have been saying shit to her that he shouldn't have, and somehow, she'd passed it on to Lauren. I hadn't seen this coming, couldn't have anticipated it. The sisters weren't even close. How the hell had this happened?

"Go ahead," Lauren snapped. "Break your word to me. Lie to my face, *Junior*."

Hearing her use that name again felt like another slap, and my temper flared. "Is that how little you think of me? That I would kill a man and then go after his daughter?"

She crossed her arms over her chest. "You said it yourself. I have no idea what you've done in your life, what you're capable of. You've already stalked me. You've already hurt people who made my life difficult."

"Which is why it's stupid of you to think that I'd suddenly become the one to make your life difficult!"

"The only stupid thing I've done lately is believe I could trust you!" she spat.

"You *can* trust me!"

"Then prove it," she said, voice shaking. "Tell me you had nothing to do with my father's disappearance."

I clamped my jaw shut, chest heaving, realizing I'd walked right into this one and had no way out. Tears continued to stream down her face while she waited for me to answer, and the sight *wrecked me*. I hated that she was in pain, hated that I was the one hurting her. I wanted nothing more than to pull her into my arms and beg for forgiveness, but I could tell she wouldn't let me. Hell, she *shouldn't* let me. She was right; I'd been lying to her all this time.

"You can't say it, can you?" Her voice broke on the last word.

"Lauren, you don't understand. Let me just explain."

She stumbled back, hand rising to cover her mouth. "Oh my god. You killed him."

"Yes!" I roared, losing the battle with my temper. "Is that what you want to hear? I killed that old bastard and then decided to spit on his grave by fucking his daughter."

A sob wracked her body, horror filling her eyes.

My stomach dropped. What had I just done? All these weeks I'd been worried the explosion was coming, and now it was happening at the worst possible time, with the worst possible person.

"Lauren, wait," I said, stepping toward her.

She leaped sideways. "Stay away from me!"

I stopped dead in my tracks. "I'm sorry, I shouldn't have said that. I didn't mean—"

"I don't want to hear it," she cried. "Why would you think I'd ever believe you after that?"

I took a step back, and then another, putting space between us, trying to make it clear I wasn't a threat. She was right. How could I ask her to hear me out now?

Because you love her, I realized. *And if you don't say something, you might lose her forever.*

"I didn't kill him," I said.

She took a step toward the door, snatching her purse from the floor and clutching it to her chest like a shield. "You just told me you did."

I dragged in a breath, cursing myself for potentially ruining the only good thing in my life. "I know, and I'm sorry. I was angry that you thought I could have done something like that."

She took another step, bending to scoop up her taser, immediately flicking it back on. "How do I know that's the truth? How do I know you're not just lying to me again to get me to drop my guard?"

I held my hands up to show I was unarmed and retreated even farther. "Because I'm about to let you walk out of that door without trying to stop you."

She brandished the taser at me. "Don't try to follow me."

"I won't," I told her. "I know you don't want to trust me right now, and I don't blame you for that, Lo, but I would never hurt you. *Never.*"

She pointed to her neck. "You *just* hurt me. You're hurting me even more, right now." She dashed the tears away from her cheeks, but they continued to fall.

Fuck, she was right. "Lo, I need you to keep what you learned today to yourself. My father might do worse if he finds out you know what we do for Lorenzo."

The blood drained from her face, turning her tan skin ashen as she reached for the door.

Panic swirled in my gut. She was leaving, and after how I'd handled this situation, she'd probably never want to see me again. "I'm sorry, Lauren," I repeated. "Just . . ." I raked my hands through my hair, fighting back the urge to grab her, trap her here until she agreed to hear me out. But I'd already done one unforgivable thing today, and I didn't know if she and I could survive another.

"Don't," she interrupted, gripping the doorknob. "I don't want to hear anything else you have to say. *Ever.*"

"Lauren, please. Give me another chance."

She laughed, an ugly, humorless sound. "I've already given you more chances than you deserve. I'm not letting the man who killed my father feed me any more lies."

With a tug, she had the door open.

And then she walked out of my life.

30

LAUREN

I LAY CURLED IN MY bed, curtains drawn, a cold towel over my eyes to reduce the swelling. Three days had passed since I'd confronted Nic, and I'd spent most of that time locked in my room, crying. Everything hurt. Not just my heart, but my throat from where he'd grabbed me, and my shoulders and back from getting slammed against the wall. Add to it the pain of betrayal, and I couldn't gather the strength to get out of bed for anything besides going to the bathroom and showering.

My roommates had brought me food, but most of it remained untouched, carried away by them later. They'd been hovering, concerned, because they'd seen the marks on my neck and thought I'd been mugged or something. I couldn't bring myself to tell them the truth, that I'd trusted the wrong man, *again*, and this time, he'd done the impossible: hurt me even worse than he had when we were kids.

I'd also kept my mouth shut because I didn't want to endanger Ryan and Taylor. The one thing Nic had said that I wholeheartedly believed was that if word got out that I knew about his family, I might be the next one to go missing. So I held it all inside and suffered in silence. And, yes, I was scaring my roommates, but I'd rather have them scared than dead.

I rolled over, curling into Walter, who'd been glued to my side this whole time. He let out a low whine and wriggled closer, and I threw my arm over him and burrowed my face against his neck.

How had I not seen this coming? My instincts had tried to warn me, tried to get me to break things off with Nic every time he let me down, but I'd ignored them, because whenever I got around the man, my brain abandoned ship, and my hormones took over the helm.

I felt like a fool now. Nic had killed my father. Or, at the very least, had something to do with his disappearance. Hid his body, maybe. Cleaned up the scene where he was murdered. I'd imagined countless scenarios over the past several days, couldn't stop picturing all the horrible, gruesome things Nic might have done. And, no, I didn't *like* my father, had barely spoken to him over the past decade, but that didn't mean I wanted the man dead. That I'd be okay with my . . . whatever Nic was, having something to do with it.

He'd been lying to me, the *whole time*. Hiding so much. And I'd just blindly walked right into his clutches like the horny little idiot I was. I'd gone against all my better judgment and given him a second chance, and then a third. I'd begged him not to betray me, and he'd promised he wouldn't. I'd started to trust him, started to feel hope that there might be something *more* between us, that maybe I wasn't as unlucky in love as I'd always believed.

I'd handed him my battered, bruised heart and told him to be careful with it, and instead, he'd crushed it in his fist.

God, he must have thought I was so stupid, so gullible, so *easy*. Had he been secretly laughing at me? Toying with me? Having the time of his life while he strung me along?

I squeezed my eyes shut and rolled onto my back, trying to turn my mind off, trying to force it out of the constant loop of self-doubt and recrimination it had been stuck in, trying to forget the fury in Nic's face when he screamed at me that he'd done it, that he'd killed my father and then fucked me just to spite him.

As much as that image was burned into my brain, the one that followed was equally unforgettable. The way Nic's expression had crumpled, shoulders slumping, regret replacing rage. I couldn't stop replaying it in my mind. It was the one thing tripping me up. Because if he'd really done everything I'd accused him of, if he was really as big of a bastard as I feared, then why had he looked so distraught?

A noise came from downstairs. It sounded like the front door closing.

Walter bounded from the bed to go check it out. No doubt it was Taylor coming home from Jackson's, or Ryan getting back after meeting with Ben.

Walter let out his usual whines of *hello*, followed by a series of squeaks that told me he'd grabbed his elephant. I heard a murmur and assumed it was Ryan even though the pitch was lower than their normal register. My senses were all fucked up from crying so much. I couldn't smell anything, and food had become tasteless, so of course sounds would be the next thing to go.

Footsteps thudded up the stairs. I rolled toward my door, straining my ears. They sounded heavier than Ryan's, too.

"Hello?" I called, my voice hoarse.

No answer.

"Hello?" I said again, louder.

Still no answer. My roommates would *never* ignore me like this.

Fuck. Someone else was in our apartment, and since Walter wasn't barking his head off, I assumed that meant he'd met that someone before.

Nic?

I scrambled out of bed, looking for a weapon. My purse with the taser in it was downstairs, hanging from its usual hook on the entryway wall, and the bat was still propped by the front door. I had nothing in my room to defend myself. Nothing except sex toys, that was.

Taking a page out of Taylor's book, I wrenched open my closet and grabbed my favorite whip, the same one Walter had chewed on all those weeks ago.

My door creaked. I turned toward it just in time to see Nic slip inside and close it behind him, shutting Walter out. He looked terrible, face drawn, expression grim. In his usual head-to-toe black, he could

279

have been the grim reaper come to collect me. My eyes dropped to his gloved hands, gloves that would prevent any fingerprints from being left behind. Oh, god.

"Please," I said. "I haven't told anyone. You don't have to do this."

He shook his head and reached into his jacket, where I assumed a gun was strapped to his side. I'd love to say that's when I snapped the whip at him and fought my way free, but I'd never faced such a threat of violence before, and I froze, staring in horror, unable to move a single muscle despite everything in my being urging me to scream, to run. I think maybe I was in shock that the boy I'd loved as a teen was about to end my life.

Nic pulled out an envelope instead of a gun, stepping forward to set it on the edge of my bed.

"W . . . what is that?" I rasped. It looked too small to be a bomb, but I couldn't rule out the threat of anthrax. He *was* wearing gloves to handle it . . .

"It's the deed to Velvet's building," Nic said, his voice as raw as mine.

My hands started to shake, the whip falling from my numb fingers and clattering across the hardwood. He wasn't here to kill me?

"I bought the building from McKinney," he said. "That's why I had to leave the other night, that's what I was doing the day you snuck into my apartment. I'd planned to use it to help me get free. I wanted to lower the rent back down, expand Velvet, help it grow." His eyes slid away from mine, looking bleak. "Show you how serious I was about building a life with you. I realize that's probably impossible now, so I want you to have it."

My head swam, and I had to sit down before I fell down, lowering myself to the floor.

Concern swept over Nic's face. He took a step forward, but something in my expression must have given him pause, because he stopped several feet away, breathing hard, his gaze running over me.

"I didn't kill your father," he told me. "But I understand if you don't believe me, especially after what I said to you. I was hurt and scared of losing you and my *fucking temper*." He balled his fists and took a deep breath, visibly trying to get ahold of himself. "I'm sorry," he said. "I know that's not enough to make up for what I put you through, but I have to say it anyway."

My eyes shifted from him to the edge of the bed. Quickly, because I was still afraid he was feeding me more lies, I leaned forward and snatched the envelope off my duvet. It was heavy in my hand, stuffed full of paper, and when I opened it, the deed tumbled out, or at least a convincing copy of one.

I brushed my fingers over the notarized seal at the bottom, my thoughts churning. It certainly didn't *look* fake, and why would Nic go through all this trouble to set me at ease if he was planning on hurting me? The dates next to the signatures confirmed his timeline, official-looking stamps beneath them with the city seal in stark relief.

I lifted my gaze, searching his face, looking for any sign of duplicity or malice, but instead, I might as well have been staring into a mirror. He looked just as exhausted as I felt, just as wrung out, just as depressed. Like our fight had hurt him as much as it had me. I set the deed back on the bed, frowning. Even if he hadn't killed my father, he'd been lying to me, and I wasn't about to let him get away with it.

"Tell me what happened to Tommy."

Nic's shoulders dropped, some of the tension leaching from his body when I didn't immediately order him out. "Can I?" he asked, motioning toward the bed.

I nodded, and he sat, facing me, elbows braced on his knees. His green eyes met mine before slipping down to my rumpled T-shirt and sweats. I looked like hell, but from the way he drank me in, you'd never know it.

His gaze returned to mine. "Tommy *was* last seen with my father."

"So he's dead?" I asked, my heart breaking all over again. Some stupid, small part of me had been holding out hope that one day, my father would change, become a better person, or that I'd at least get closure on our relationship. With his life cut short, the chances of either of those things happening disappeared.

Nic shook his head. "We don't just disappear dead bodies. We hide live ones, too."

I blinked at him, fighting back a wave of disbelief, trying to determine if I had heard him correctly. "What do you mean?"

"Your dad cooked the books for a couple of the higher-ups, including Lorenzo," he said. "The feds were moving in on him, hoping he was a weak link they could exploit. Tommy went straight to Lorenzo with the news, which is probably why he's still alive. Instead of Lorenzo putting a hit on him, he decided to get him out of here. He's back in the old country working for one of Lorenzo's cousins."

"Can you prove that?"

He nodded and pulled his phone from his jacket, turning the screen to face me.

It took a second for what I was seeing to sink in: my father, sitting at a table drinking wine, the rolling hills of Tuscany spread out behind him. As far as I knew, he'd never been to Italy before, and he looked decrepit in the photo, even worse than the last time I'd seen him, so it couldn't have been an old picture.

"I have more proof, if you need it," Nic said. He tapped the screen a few more times and turned his phone back to me.

This time, a video played, Tommy smiling, his arm around the waist of a much younger woman. "Thank you, Lorenzo!" he said, looking like he was having the time of his life.

The video ended, and Nic slipped the phone back inside his pocket. "We use videos like these to blackmail the people we help, remind them who they owe their lives to and what will happen if they don't fulfill their end of the agreement."

"He's alive," I said.

"He's alive," Nic confirmed.

I shook my head, *pissed*. Forget it. I no longer needed closure. Tommy Marchetti might have been alive, but he was officially dead to me. "That motherfucker. He didn't even think to tell us so we didn't worry?"

Nic tipped his head sideways. "No offense, but *were* you worried?"

"Well, no, not at first. But when I thought he might be dead? Yeah, obviously."

"I'm sorry for how everything unfolded. At first, I thought this thing between us was only temporary, and it wouldn't matter in the long run, and then I was distracted with other shit, but that's not an excuse. I should have been the one to tell you about Tommy."

"Yes," I ground out. "You should have."

He glanced away, looking mollified, and I didn't know what to believe anymore.

"Tell me now," I said. "Walk me through everything that happened. I just . . ." I paused, fighting against a wave of exhaustion and hurt. "I need to know."

His eyes came back to mine. "It has to stay between us."

"It will."

"I mean it," he said. "Even if you never speak to me after this."

I clenched my jaw and nodded, bracing myself.

Haltingly, he recounted the night that he and his brothers disappeared my "father" down at the docks, Greg stealing a corpse from the morgue he worked in, and them cutting its head and hands off to keep it from being easily identified if Tommy's car was ever found.

"But the DNA . . ." I said.

Nic shook his head. "The DNA backlog in this city is one of the worst in the country, and without dental or fingerprints, it would take forever for the cops to get a positive ID, if they even pursued it. The police don't really prioritize solving the murders of criminals."

I frowned, snagging on something he'd mentioned. "And that's how you spent your birthday?"

His expression hardened. "That's not even the worst one I've had."

Damn it, I was *not* going to feel bad for him.

"Is there a tracker on my phone?" I asked.

He winced. "Yes."

"Any others?"

He shook his head.

"What happened with McKinney?"

"He's a gambler," Nic said, filling me in on all the work he'd put in after the night I told him about Velvet's financial woes.

I sat there, stunned, listening to how he'd gotten Josh to do some hacking for him and then hired a whole ass merc team to hunt McKinney's bookie down. My jaw dropped when he told me the bookie was Josh's douchey friend Tyler, of all people.

"And then I went to McKinney's place and convinced him to sell to me," Nic finished.

I eyed him. It couldn't have been that easy. I'd met McKinney, and he was as selfish and greedy as they came. "How, exactly, did you convince him?"

His eyes slid away from mine.

"The truth, Nic," I said. "It's the least you owe me."

With a sigh, he nodded. "I may or may not have used force."

Unease wormed its way through my stomach. "How much force?"

He winced. "I took his finger off."

"You *what*?"

His tone turned placating. "He got it reattached."

I gaped at him. "That doesn't make it any better!"

"Look," he said. "It was the last awful thing I ever plan on doing, but I would have done much worse to get free from my father, because taking a finger off is a fucking cakewalk compared to most of the shit I get told to do. I can't keep this up anymore, Lauren." He tapped his temple. "I can fucking *feel* myself dying, feel pieces of my soul withering up every time I get a phone call. At this rate, I'll either be dead or incarcerated or beyond all hope within a year or two, and I don't want that to happen. I don't want to become my father."

My heart stuttered in my chest. "You're not your father."

The fact that he was so tortured over the possibility of turning into him proved that. And while I might not be ready to forgive Nic yet for everything he'd done, there was no way in hell I was letting him sacrifice his freedom for me.

I picked the deed up and held it out to him. "I can't take this from you."

He made no move to accept it. "Why not?"

"Because as mad as I am, I won't steal your chance to get out."

"You're not stealing it. I'm giving it to you."

I shook the papers. "I don't want it."

He pushed them back at me. "Your happiness means more to me than my freedom. And don't worry about me. I'm sure I'll find some other way to get out."

Yeah, but will it be too late by then? I wondered.

"You have to take it back," I said, trying to stand. My head swam again, exhaustion and hunger and dehydration winning out as I started to tip sideways.

Nic caught me before I fell. The world tilted, and suddenly, I was flat on my back on the bed, with him rising above me. His hands stroked my hair from my face, so gentle, like he would never hurt me. "Lauren? Are you okay?"

He looked so worried, so helpless, that I finally let myself accept the fact that he hadn't come here to harm me; he was only trying to make things right.

"Please," I implored him. "Take the deed. If you don't, I'll just find some way to give it back to you."

His hands stilled, cupping my face. "I don't want to ruin your feelings about the club by being the building's owner."

I shook my head. "Nothing could ever ruin my feelings about Velvet. This is your chance, Nic. You have to take it." He frowned, but I could see the hope building in his eyes, so I pressed on. "If you're really trying to make me happy, then keep the building. I could never live with myself if I knew my gain led to your continued misery."

He bumped his forehead against mine. "Why are you so good to me? I don't deserve it."

"Because even after everything, I care about you." More than I was willing to admit. "I don't want you to turn into your father. I don't want you to have to hurt anyone else ever again." I gripped his biceps, squeezing, trying to make him see reason. "It's not worth losing more of yourself, not now that you have a chance to escape."

His expression shifted into remorse. "I'm sorry for keeping so much from you."

I nodded, unable to speak, my head and my heart and my body all warring with each other.

"I don't want to lose you again, Lo."

A tear slipped down my face.

He saw it and swore, gathering me up in his arms and turning us sideways on the bed.

"You really hurt me," I said.

His arms tightened, face pressed to my neck. "I know."

He was so big, so warm against me, felt so good that I couldn't help but snuggle closer. His hand rubbed over my back. Whispered apologies fell from his lips.

"I hurt you, too," I said.

"I deserved it."

"No, you didn't." I finally gave into the need to touch him back and wrapped my arms around his shoulders. "I should have known better than to take my sister's word as gospel. I should have at least heard you out before accusing you of killing my father."

"Lauren, stop," he said. "No one could blame you for how you reacted."

"I blame me," I said, more tears wetting my cheeks.

I'd spent my whole life waiting for people to hurt me. And not just because of what Nic had done. Because of what my parents had. Because of what Principal Michaels had. Kelly. All our classmates. My sister. Every one of those betrayals was another brick in the barrier I'd built around my heart, walling it off from the world. I'd convinced myself that if someone hurt you once, they'd do it again and again. So I'd stopped letting them, looking for any excuse to push people away the second things started to get real or messy or hard. Now, seeing how hurt Nic was, I looked back and wondered how many other people I might have harmed with my behavior.

I held Nic tighter, willing myself to let my baggage go, to stop making assumptions and instead let Nic's actions speak for him. No, he wasn't perfect—he'd lied and made mistakes, and his methods of protecting me were questionable at best—but here he was, showing up for me, fighting for me, ready to sacrifice himself for me.

"I'm sorry," I said again. "For how much I tried to push you away."

"You were only protecting yourself," he said. "And I went about this the worst way possible. I should have just approached you after Tommy fled and laid all my cards on the table, told you that he'd threatened to kill me and that's why I lied about us being together back in high school."

I went completely still against him. "He . . . what?"

Understanding washed over me, the puzzle pieces finally clicking into place. All this hurt, all this heartache, a *decade's* worth of baggage, and somehow, it all came back around to my fucking father.

31

JUNIOR

SHIT. I'D DONE IT AGAIN, put my whole-ass foot in my mouth.

Lauren's arms loosened around me, and I pulled back enough to look at her. "I didn't mean to keep that from you, I swear. I just had all this other shit filling up my mind."

"Okay," she said, and I could tell from the look on her face that this time, she was finally willing to give me the benefit of the doubt, thank god. "Can you please tell me what happened?"

"There's not much to tell. He found out about the diary somehow and beat the shit out of me. Then he told me if I ever so much as looked at you again, he'd kill me."

Understanding dawned on her face. "That's why you weren't there the Monday I went back to school."

I nodded. "My face was so swollen I could barely see, so my mom let me stay home most of that week."

"I'm sorry he did that to you," Lauren said. "Even at my angriest, I never would have wanted you hurt."

Too good. She was too good. I couldn't believe she was even talking to me after the way I'd yelled at her, after the things I'd said.

I took a deep breath. "That's not the worst part."

"What else did he do?"

"Not him. *My* dad."

Her expression turned wary. "Do I even want to know?"

"No more lies," I said. "Not even by omission."

She nodded. "Tell me, then."

"My dad threatened you, too."

"What'd he say?"

I shook my head. "It wasn't said so much as implied that it was good things ended the way they did before you *really* got hurt."

"Because he would be the one to hurt me?"

"That's the way I took it."

She blew out a breath. "What a pair of fathers we have."

I snorted. "At least yours is out of the picture."

Her fingers dug into the back of my shirt. "When do you plan on telling Senior about going legit?"

"At our next family dinner."

She bit her lower lip, eyeing me. "Can I come?"

Holy shit, was she serious?

Her smile was a small, *evil* thing. "I want to see the look on his face when you tell him to go fuck himself."

I groaned and rolled her onto her back, trying desperately not to get my hopes up. "Does this mean that you forgive me?"

"Not for everything," she said. "Not yet."

"That's fair." This was more than I'd hoped for on my way over here. I'd expected her to take one look at me and call the cops.

"I do forgive you for the other day, though," she said, wincing. "Especially since I opened that conversation by tasing you."

I grinned. "You should see the burn on my back."

She slapped a hand over her eyes. "Oh, god. I'm so sorry."

I chuckled. "Don't be. The knife wound on my side has entered the itchy phase, and it was driving me crazy to keep from scratching it. The pain of the burn is a welcome distraction."

She let out a tortured sound.

I sat up enough to yank my shirt off, turning so she could see. "Look. It's really not that bad."

She was so quiet that I turned back around, and fuck, I wasn't in the right state of mind to see her like this, sprawled beneath me, legs akimbo, heat in her gaze as it raked over me. I started to reach for my discarded shirt, but she stalled me with a touch.

"Don't," she said. "I want to look at you."

"Lauren." My voice was low, guttural. I had *just* gotten her to relax around me again. The last thing I needed was to scare her off by getting ahead of myself, and yet there went my dick, reminding me that I still hadn't gotten fully inside her.

She dropped her gaze to my crotch, but instead of looking freaked out, she looked turned on. I held myself perfectly still, worried that I was misinterpreting her expression, not wanting to say or do anything to ruin the tenuous peace between us.

She reached out and stroked her fingers down my lower abs.

I leaped off the bed, putting as much space between us as possible. Less than five minutes ago, she'd almost keeled over right in front of me. Less than ten minutes ago, she'd been convinced I killed her father. No way was she in the right headspace for something physical.

She swung her legs over the edge of the bed and stood, stalking forward. "What was it you said the last time you were in my room?" she asked, her voice low, sultry. "I need to fuck you?"

Jesus Christ.

"Lauren, I don't think this is a good idea. We still haven't talked everything through, and I don't want to put my hands on you only for you to turn around and regret it."

She shook her head, pulling off her T-shirt, and, *goddamn it*, she wasn't wearing a bra. "I won't regret it. Physical touch is healing for me. I need it to feel close to you, especially after a fight."

"But nothing's settled between us," I argued, telling myself to lift my gaze up from her tits and failing spectacularly. In my defense, they were perfect tits.

"It doesn't need to be settled for me to want you." She stopped a foot away, her tongue peeking out to trace her bottom lip. "In fact, I like that it's not. I'm still mad at you, and I know you're still a little mad at me."

I started to shake my head, but she pressed her finger to my mouth.

"You are. Don't lie." She ran her finger down my lip, lower, between my pecs, over my stomach, stopping to hook it into the top of my pants. Her eyes bored into mine, lust and anger turning them bottomless. "Taking it out on my body will make you feel better." She shoved her sweatpants down, and then she was nude in front of me.

Fuuuck.

With a groan, I reached for her, but she was already moving, crashing into my chest. My back slammed against the wall, picture frames rattling. A yank on my neck had me jerking forward so she could kiss me, her hands everywhere, needy, impatient sounds crawling up her throat. The cut on my side burned with fresh pain—at this rate, it was never going to heal—and the chair rail dug into my taser burn, but I ignored them both, infected by her sudden desperation.

A gust of air at my crotch alerted me to the fact that my dick was free from my boxers. I hadn't even felt her undoing my pants. Lauren scrambled up my body, and I caught her, cupping her ass as her legs wrapped around me and her tongue continued to ply my mouth. Her hand slipped between us and—*oh, fuck*—I was inside her.

I groaned, lost to the feeling of her working me, working to *take me* without enough foreplay. She pulled her lips from mine and bit her way along my jaw, teeth pinching hard enough to hurt, ass bouncing in my grip as she sank deeper and deeper onto my cock.

Was this what it felt like to get fucked against a wall? No wonder women were so into it.

Her mouth parted on my neck, and then she was sucking at me in a way that would absolutely leave a hickey. I used my grip to help her fuck me, shoving with every rise, tugging with every drop, gaining inch by precious inch until she was fully seated on my cock and I couldn't just stand there anymore.

She'd made her point. Now it was my turn.

Wrapping an arm around her waist, I took us to the ground, plowing into her, pushing her thighs wide so I could get as deep inside her as possible.

She cried out, hands scrabbling at my back, begging, "Harder, harder."

I grabbed her hair and wrenched her head to the side, marking her neck like she'd marked mine, thrusting into her with so much force that she was going to end up with rug burn from the way she was sliding across the carpet. I'd been waiting to fuck her for ten years, had imagined every scenario under the sun, dreamed of getting her off over and over before I let myself come, but now that it was finally happening, all I could think about was unloading inside her wet, welcoming cunt.

With difficulty, I pulled myself back from the brink. "Do I need to put a condom on?"

"No," she said, her spine bowing, hips slamming up to meet mine. "I need you, Nic."

"You have me," I told her. "All of me."

Not just my cock, but my protection, my loyalty, my trust, and even my heart. I loved this woman. I'd always loved her. Always *would* love her, no matter what other crazy-ass shit happened in the future. She was who I was breaking free for, she was who I wanted to build a life with, a *real* life, lived out in the open and not in the shadows, where I'd spent every moment up until now. I wanted to explore my kinks with her, go to brunch with her and her friends, watch TV together, do all the other cute couple shit that I never thought I would get to experience.

She made me feel alive. She made me want to fight to keep living, to not let the monsters and the darkness win, because it was so much better being surrounded by her light. And if her penchant for taser play had taught me anything, she could more than put me in my place if necessary. She was my match, my queen, and I would spend the rest of my life worshipping her like one if she let me.

"Nic," she moaned, hips rolling, head falling back, pussy clenching and, oh, god, she was coming.

My balls tightened, dick stiffened, and then I was coming, too, unloading into her, feeling her tight little pussy milk every last drop out of me.

Afterward, we lay there panting, her legs dropping away and her arms splayed wide as she went boneless. I rolled us, holding her close to my chest, her head tucked under my chin and her heart beating erratically against mine.

"You bought the building," she said in disbelief.

"I'd buy the whole goddamn block if you asked me to."

She snuggled closer. "I don't think that will be necessary, but I'll let you know." We were quiet for a minute, relearning how to breathe, before she spoke again. "I'm still mad at you."

"I know. I'm mad at you, too. But I don't want to be."

She said nothing.

I tightened my arms around her. "Do you want to be mad at me?"

"No," she finally huffed. "I think it'll take a couple more hate fucks for me to get over it though."

"I could never hate you, Lo," I said.

She sighed. "I could never hate you either. But this has to be the end of it, Nic. I can forgive you for everything you've already done, but I can't be with you if you continue to do bad things."

"I'm done," I promised.

She relaxed back into me. "When is the next family dinner?"

Hope flared in my chest. "You're serious about wanting to come?"

"Are you kidding?" She sat up enough to look at me. "I might try to find some way to film it."

"It'll be a few weeks," I said, relaying the plan Josh and I had come up with, watching the smile spread over her face and wondering if maybe Lauren had a little more darkness inside her than I'd realized.

"I wouldn't miss that for the world," she said.

"So we're doing this?" I asked. "Really trying to see if we can make this work?"

She bit her lip, looking scared, but finally nodded. "Slowly. Because trust takes time to rebuild."

"I'm sorry I hurt you," I said.

"I'm sorry I hurt you, too," she told me. "I just got so mad and so scared that you were breaking my heart again."

I pulled her to me, my pulse picking up. "Does that mean I have your heart?"

She nodded, cheek rubbing over my chest. "Be careful with it this time."

"I'll guard it with my fucking life."

32

LAUREN

"ARE YOU NERVOUS?" I ASKED Nic as we drove up his parents' driveway.

He nodded, downshifting. "Of course."

Two weeks had passed since that night in my apartment. We'd spent almost every day together since, rebuilding the trust between us, talking through all the things we'd left unsaid, splitting our time between my place and setting up his new one just a block away from Velvet. Almost no one knew about his acquisition, because he'd threatened McKinney to keep his mouth shut and everyone else in on it knew not to talk. Secrecy was the bedrock of Nic's plan tonight. If his father had time with the news, he'd have time to scheme, time to figure out some way to trap Nic into staying.

"Are *you* nervous?" Nic asked.

I laughed, stiffly, a *ha ha ha* that sounded as off as I felt. "Not nervous. Terrified."

"You'll be okay," he said.

Yeah, but would *he*?

We rounded the circular drive in front of his parents' house—more like mansion—and parked next to Aly's car. She and Josh got out as Nic cut the engine. Clearly, they'd been waiting for us. I was grateful for that, that we'd walk in together. Nic seemed unflappable, but I knew there were deeper emotions brewing beneath the surface. His father had manipulated, controlled, and emotionally abused him his entire life, and breaking away from that was a big deal.

Josh and Nic greeted each other as I rounded the trunk of the car. Aly was coming around hers, too, and she smiled when she caught sight of me, pulling me in for a hug.

"How you doing?" she asked as we released each other.

"Full panic," I said.

She nodded. "We'll sit you in between Josh and Nic. They'll keep you safe."

Josh step-slid next to her, both of his arms raised as he flexed. "I'm very intimidating."

Nic backhanded him in the stomach, and Josh wheezed and dropped his arms. I shook my head, wondering why no one else looked as worried as I was.

"Is the party out here tonight?" a lilting voice asked.

I jumped, so on edge I'd turned skittish, and turned to see Moira standing right behind us. I hadn't even heard her walk up. From the way she smiled at our surprise, I had a feeling that was intentional.

"Just saying hi to my favorite cousin," Nic said.

Aly rolled her eyes. "*Only* cousin."

Josh put his arm around her. "Which means you win by default, baby. Soak it up."

"Lauren," Moira said, and I braced myself and turned back to her. Her smile was warm, welcoming. "It's nice to see you."

"You, too," I said, grateful that Nic chose that moment to slide his arm around my waist and pull me close.

Moira's gaze shifted between us, smile widening, like she was actually *happy* about this development. "It took you two fecking long enough."

I blinked, caught off guard, but Nic only shrugged.

"Yeah, well," he said. "Better late than never."

Moira's smile slipped as she took in our little group. "Are we ready to go face him down?"

Nods all around, and I realized then that I wasn't the only one who was nervous, just the only one doing a shitty job of hiding it.

"Then I think we're going to need something stronger than the wine I uncorked," she said, turning.

Nic snagged her wrist.

She paused and turned back to him.

"I love you," Nic said. "And no matter what happens tonight, I don't want to lose you."

Her expression softened, eyes creasing at the corners as she lifted a hand to cup his cheek. "You'll never lose me."

Nic let her go, and she headed back toward the house.

I glanced up at him. "Did you tell her your plan?"

He shook his head. "No, but she's the real brains of this family. I'm sure she took one look at you and realized a confrontation was coming. And I told her about Dad threatening you, back then."

"He threatened Lauren?" Josh asked, his voice eerily calm.

Aly put a steadying hand on his arm. "Babe."

"I just want to know," he said, but the grin spreading over his face was unholy. "A grown man, making threats against a teenage girl? I feel like that's something we should discuss."

Aly grabbed his hand and dragged him away from us, calling, "One second," over her shoulder.

I turned to Nic, brows raised.

"He has a thing about men targeting women," Nic said.

"Shouldn't everyone?"

He nodded, glancing past me at the couple. "Yeah, but he's kind of next-level about it. I'll explain later."

I followed his gaze and saw Aly tug Josh down so their foreheads touched. She said something to him, too low to hear, hands running up and down his arms like she was trying to soothe him. If this was how the night was starting, I could only imagine how much worse it might get.

"Sorry," Aly said a minute later, towing Josh behind her as she made her way back to us. "We're ready to go play nice." She threw a glance at her fiancé. "*Right?*"

"Right," Josh grumbled, looking mutinous.

Nic used his grip on my waist to turn us toward the front door. "Let's get this over with, then."

Moira greeted us just inside, a martini in hand. "Greg's making a whole tray of them, if anyone wants one." Her eyes went to Nic. "I told your father Lauren was with you."

"Thank you," Nic said.

Moira nodded, expression grim, and I wondered how bad it had been. That she'd broken the news and dealt with the fallout herself, and was obviously on Nic's side through whatever was about to come, made me look at her with newfound respect.

"Hey, you made it," Nico said, sweeping into the entryway. His arms were spread wide and his smile was charming, and if I hadn't known better, I might have bought the welcoming host act.

"Dad," Nic said, "you remember Lauren."

His gaze swung to me, and suddenly, I'd never felt more like a bug under a microscope. "Of course." His smile fell. "Shame about Tommy going missing. Any updates on his whereabouts?"

"No," I told him. "The reigning theory is that he has a secret family out West somewhere." My tone was casual, dismissive, filled with the very real disdain I had for my father.

Nic had warned me how manipulative his dad was, how he never did or said anything without having some sort of ulterior motive, and we'd suspected he might try to find out how much his son had told me. He would already have enough reason (real or imagined) to want to get rid of me by the end of the night; I didn't need to add more fuel to the fire by telling the truth.

Nico eyed me for a moment, dark eyes boring into mine, as if looking for any tell that I was lying. I held perfectly still, refusing to give him any more ammo to use against his son.

"The cops are on it," Nic said with a shrug. "They'll figure it out."

Nico looked at him before turning toward Aly, the smile spreading back over his face. I let out a shaky breath as soon as the coast was clear. It felt like I'd dodged a bullet.

"There she is," Nico said, arms rising as he stepped toward his niece.

She lifted a hand in a halting gesture. "Still a no from me. Especially after how you behaved last month."

He chuckled. "One of these days, you'll come around."

Her smile was strained. "Unlikely."

Oof. Awkward. But good for her for standing her ground.

Nico just shook his head, unperturbed, like this was a game they played, and stepped back. "The rest of the boys are in the sitting room. Drinks and apps are in there, too."

Moira, who'd been silently watching the whole exchange, motioned us forward, and Nic and I preceded everyone down the hallway. I could tell from how tightly he held my hand that he was uneasy, and I tried not to let it spike my own runaway anxiety. Between the immediate barbed question, that terse exchange with Aly, and the fact that Nico hadn't even acknowledged Josh's presence, the undercurrents of dysfunction were strong enough to carry us out to sea. Were all their family dinners this uncomfortable?

"Lauren?!" Alec said when we walked into the sitting room. He glared at his older brother, tone mocking. "Ohhhhh, I see how it is. 'It's not anything serious.' 'Don't worry about it.' 'Mind your business, you nosy asshole.'"

Greg, whom I hadn't seen in years, snorted. "You *are* a nosy asshole."

Beside him, Stefan nodded in agreement.

Alec glared at them. "Fuck you both."

Josh brushed past me, voice low. "Booze?"

I nodded emphatically. I was going to need *all* the alcohol to get through this.

The Trocci brothers continued to rib one another for a few minutes before their parents finally joined us. I tried to tamp down my curiosity about what had held them back. I didn't take it as a good sign that Moira's martini glass was empty and the first thing she did was beeline toward the drink cart.

"How's work been?" Nico asked Aly.

"Fine," she said.

"Any standouts?" Alec asked.

"I got to assist in a finger reattachment a few weeks ago. Those are always fun."

Nic went completely still at my side, and I nearly fumbled the drink Josh handed me.

Alec grimaced. "How does something like that even happen?"

His cousin shrugged. "Saw blades, kitchen accidents. This one happened to a semipro basketball player during practice. He went up to dunk, and his wedding ring caught on the net. The weight of his body falling just, *shwoop*, popped the finger right off."

Gross, but I still exhaled in relief. For a second there, I was worried she'd treated McKinney, but I should have known better. This city was huge, with several ERs, and while Nic had told me he had shitty luck, I knew no one's could be *that* bad.

"What about you, Lauren?" Nico Senior said. "How was *your* work week?"

"Good," I told him. If he was hoping to shame me or put me in my place by bringing up my job, he was sorely mistaken. Everyone here knew what I did, and I wasn't about to tiptoe around it. "I gained twenty new subs, got ahead of my filming schedule so Nic and I could spend the rest of the weekend together, and heard back from another city councilmember willing to back the Expanded Safeties for Sex Workers Act. How was your week, Mr. Trocci?" I smiled and took a sip of my martini, and I swore I heard a low *ooh* from Josh.

"It was fine," Nico said, sliding one hand inside his pocket. "Would have gone a lot easier if someone wasn't slacking off." A pointed look at his eldest told us exactly whom he was speaking about.

Moira shook her head. "No shoptalk until after dinner."

Nico's expression shifted into remorse, and he tipped his head toward his wife. "Apologies." Somehow, he looked like he actually meant it, eyes soft, smile just for her.

The sight was unsettling. I wanted him to just *be* an asshole, all the time, like my father was. This turning on and off the charm was confusing as hell, kept lulling me into a false sense of calm before my brain kicked back on and reminded me that this was the same man who had threatened my safety as a teenager and was hell-bent on turning his sons into soulless mobsters.

"Mrs. Trocci?" a heavily accented voice said.

I turned to see a middle-aged woman standing in the doorway.

"Are we ready?" Moira asked.

"*Sì*," she said, before continuing in Italian. I only caught every other word. I spoke what I liked to call restaurant Italian, meaning I could order off a menu and hold the most basic of conversations. Anything deeper than that, and I was lost, and lord help me if someone started speaking fast.

I caught just enough to figure out that dinner had been served, and thinking ahead, I downed the rest of my martini and scooped one of the last two off the drink cart. Aly grabbed the other one, and we shared a conspiratorial glance before turning and following our significant others into the dining room, where the real show began.

33

JUNIOR

AS FAR AS DINNERS WITH my family went, this one didn't even rank in the top three worst. Yet. But the night was young, and from the way Dad kept glancing between me and Lauren, there was still plenty of time for it to go off the rails. Everyone else seemed to understand that, too, taking longer to eat than usual, dragging the meal out with idle chatter.

Despite the forced levity, the tension just kept building, brewing out of sight like a storm on the horizon. Dad's answers became increasingly terse. A deep groove formed between his brows as he frowned down at his plate.

"Maria!" he finally snapped, and in swept my family's housekeeper and cook.

"*Sí?*" she said, wiping her hands on her apron.

"We're done." He waved at the table. "You can clear the plates."

Silence descended as she gathered our dishes. Beside me, I could feel Lauren tensing up, and I reached out beneath the tablecloth and put my hand on her thigh. Her skin was smooth and warm beneath my touch, and I couldn't help but stroke my thumb over it, squeezing once to let her know that everything would be okay. Because it would. One way or another.

Calm descended upon me as we waited. My entire family was here, blood and found, and I knew that I wasn't about to face my dad alone.

"So," he said when the last plate was cleared, and Maria shut the kitchen door behind herself. His gaze rose to mine, and I could already see the anger building in his eyes. "What is it you wanted to talk to me about? Lauren?" His focus shifted from her to me and back again. "Is she who I would have chosen for you? No."

I waited a beat, giving him a chance to say more, maybe add a *But I won't stand in your way*, or even a *But I realize my mistake now that I see you two together*. The words didn't come, and I decided that this was the last family dinner I would attend until he came to terms with my relationship and apologized to Lauren. No way in hell was I subjecting her to his censure again, and I wouldn't go anywhere she wasn't welcome with open arms.

Lauren's hand landed on top of mine, squeezing, reassuring, like she was more worried about how I felt than anything else, reminding me what a lucky bastard I was that she'd chosen to be with me.

"Nico," Mom said, low and warning.

Dad ignored her, eyes still locked on me, and from the way Mom stared daggers into the side of his head, he was going to regret it. "What is this all about?" he demanded.

Lauren squeezed my hand again, and I braced myself for whatever was about to happen.

"I bought a building," I said.

Surprise rippled through my brothers, but I kept my gaze on my father.

"From who?" Dad said, expression inscrutable.

"Patrick McKinney."

He frowned. "I don't know the name."

"He's no one important."

"Is that so?" Dad asked, eyeing me, and I knew that the second I left this house, he'd have every single one of his cronies looking into McKinney. He tipped his head sideways. "A whole building."

It wasn't a question, but I answered anyway. "Yes."

"Where is it?"

"Downtown. West Side."

"Where'd you get the money?" he asked, tone deadly calm.

My hackles rose, but I kept my anger out of my voice. "I didn't steal it from you, if that's what you're implying."

"Then where, Junior?"

"From my savings and investments."

"Bullshit," he spat. "You don't have downtown money."

"I don't need to because I bought out his debt from a bookie and then blackmailed him with it."

Mom's eyes flashed wide, straying toward Aly and Josh. "No shop-talk at the din—"

Dad shushed her.

Mom turned back to him, slowly, à la *The Exorcist*. He was going to need to hide in their panic room at this point.

"What kind of building is it?" Dad asked.

Here we fucking go.

"It's commercial," I said. "Rented out by a members-only club."

His gaze shifted to Lauren. "You plan on running girls out of it? Is that what this is? You're a wannabe pimp now?"

Lauren's fingernails dug into the back of my hand.

Across from us, Aly made a low, angry sound, and I could see my brothers shifting in their seats out of my periphery. "No. It's a legal club, and I plan to let them keep operating out of the building for as long as they like."

"You want to use them to help launder money?" Dad asked.

I shook my head.

"Move drugs?"

Another head shake.

"Then what, Junior? What's the con?" he demanded, because to him, there always was one.

"There's no con. They are a legitimate business. This is me striking out on my own. I don't want to do this anymore," I said, gesturing between us. "I don't want to run oil or any of the other shit you want me to."

He shot forward in his chair. "*Are you fucking*—" His gaze slid past me, to Lauren, and then over to Aly and Josh, reminded of our audience, silenced by their presence. Dad's number one rule was that we never discussed mob shit in front of people who weren't in the know.

"Get out," he spat at Aly.

She lifted her glass and took a sip of her wine, unperturbed. "Nah, I think I'll stay right where I am."

"You were so quick to run out of here the last time things got tense," Dad said. "*Now* you want to stay?"

Aly settled back in her seat. "Yeah, I do."

Josh wrapped an arm around her shoulders, smiling ear to ear, and I'd never been more grateful to have these two assholes in my life.

Dad shifted his focus to Lauren.

"Don't," I said. "She stays."

Fury crawled over his face, and he jabbed a finger toward her. "I fucking *knew* this little whore would be trouble."

Aly swore. Greg drained his drink and set his glass down hard enough to rattle the table. And Mom . . . God help Dad after we all left and she had him alone to herself. Josh was the only one as still as I was, likely gone to that empty place in his head that he'd tried to explain to me a few months ago. My own quiet was much calmer. This wasn't anything I hadn't anticipated. My father wasn't stupid. Like Mom, he probably sensed that this was the "big one," and I knew that meant he would be at his worst.

"Are you okay?" I asked Lauren.

She surprised me by laughing. "I'm fine. That is the least creative way to insult me he could have chosen." She leaned past me, looking at my father. "If you were a sub, I would respond by inviting you to a private chat so you could find out just how big a whore I am." She added a wink for good measure, and my love for her swelled.

My father's expression shifted into disgust. "This is who you choose to be with? Someone who says shit like that at the dinner table? Think of your future. How will you ever be able to bring her around your friends? Your family?"

Aly leaned forward. "You literally just called her a whore at the dinner table, you fucking hypocrite."

A glance at Lauren revealed her looking unconcerned, but I'd felt her tense up, knew that Dad's words had struck deep, hit some lingering vulnerability. I squeezed her leg, telling her that I was here, that I had her, that I wasn't about to let my father get away with speaking to her this way. I'd warned her how bad his temper was, how cruel he could be, and that he might turn his fury on her. She'd remained determined to come tonight, assuring me that there was nothing he could say that she hadn't heard before, which led to me asking her for names, which led to her telling me to stop acting so crazy.

I lifted my gaze back to my father's. "Don't ever speak about my girlfriend like that again."

"Or what, Junior?" Dad bit out "What are you going to do?"

This was the moment I needed to stand my ground. My father only seemed to understand downside, only responded to strength. And it had taken me nearly ten years to realize I held the trump card all along.

"Never speak to you again," I told him. "Carve you out like a cancer and never look back." As far as threats went, this was the worst one I could make. I'd considered blackmail. Lord knew I had enough of it. But after my talk with Josh, I'd realized that threatening to break up our family like this was the biggest weapon in my arsenal.

Dad didn't say anything in response, but his fingers tightened around his wineglass, and I could tell from the look in his eyes that if we had been alone, we'd be having a much different conversation. This was why Josh and I had come up with the plan to do this out in the open for everyone to see. To not let Dad hide his abuse and vitriol behind a closed door anymore. To have witnesses to this exchange so *everyone* knew I wanted out, making it harder for Dad to force me back in without drawing suspicion and pissing off the whole family, risking all his relationships.

"So that's it?" he said, cocking his head sideways. "This is how you tell me you're done?"

"Yes," I said.

He threw his glass at my head.

I barely ducked in time to keep from getting hit, but there was no stopping the ruby red liquid from soaking me and Lauren.

She gasped, pushing back from the table, and then everything was happening at once. Aly, on her feet, yelling; Josh holding her back; Mom shoving Dad so hard he went tipping over sideways in his chair; Stefan slipping out of the room; Greg and Alec exchanging looks like they didn't know whether or not they should follow after him.

Dad popped back to his feet surprisingly fast for a man of his age. "After everything I've fucking done for you?" he roared.

I positioned myself in front of Lauren. "Everything you've done for me?" I yelled back. "Like steal my entire goddamn childhood, groom me to become a thug, constantly put me in danger? You want me to keep going? Because I can."

He stepped sideways, trying to look past me at Lauren. "This is your fucking fault, isn't it?"

Josh materialized at my side. "Take another step toward her, Nico. I dare you." He held something dark in his hand, and my stomach dropped, thinking he was about to shoot my father, before I realized it was just a cell phone.

Josh tapped its screen, and all the lights in the house flickered. "One. More. Step."

Dad stopped moving, jaw clenched in fury. A foot away, Mom was staring at him with her hands balled into fists. We needed to end this before a full-on brawl broke out.

"You know," Dad said, "Italy is just a phone call away. It wouldn't be that hard to make Tommy disappear for real."

"Woah," Aly said. "Did you just threaten to have Lauren's father killed?"

Dad jerked, unused to an audience to his outbursts, forgetting we were all pretending that Tommy was just missing. "No," he ground out, but his mutinous expression said otherwise.

"I'm done," I told him. "And nothing you say or do will ever change my mind."

He laughed, the sound ugly. "You won't last a fucking week without me."

"Yes, I will," I told him. "And I know that's got to hurt, but you brought this on yourself."

He lunged. It happened so fast and was so unexpected that I didn't get my arms up in time to block him. For all the awful shit he'd said and done over the course of my lifetime, he'd never hit me, and it took me a moment to realize that his hands were around my neck, and he was *squeezing*, his expression a rictus of rage, black eyes burning with fury.

Time seemed to slow. I tried to drag in a breath and couldn't, staring at him in disbelief, feeling like I was having an out-of-body experience. My own fucking father was strangling me in front of my girlfriend and entire family. I thought I'd known the worst of what he was capable of, but I'd never expected *this*.

With the last of my breath, I wheezed, "Dad."

The word seemed to ricochet through him like a bullet. His fingers slackened on my neck. The fury bled from his eyes. I watched his lips part and horror creep into his expression like he finally realized what he was doing.

It was then that time righted itself. I saw several people rushing toward us, but Lauren got there first, electric blue flaring in my periphery. Dad jerked and let me go, and I dragged in a breath full of the smell of his searing flesh as Lauren ground the taser into his neck, following him to the floor when he went down.

Nearby, Josh retched and spun away, Aly racing after him.

"Lauren," I said, wrapping my hands around her shoulders and gently pulling her back. From the look on her face, she wouldn't have stopped otherwise. My very own white knight in a sundress.

"*Nic,*" Mom said, and I turned to see her openly weeping for the first time in memory. Her eyes met mine, voice hoarse like she'd been the one who was choked. "I'm so sorry."

I shook my head. "None of this is your fault."

Alec stepped into view and spat at Dad's still twitching form. "Fucking bastard." He turned to Mom. "You're coming to stay with me. Enough is enough."

Mom shook her head. "I'm staying here. Someone has to make sure he's all right."

"So call an ambulance after you leave," Greg said, joining us. "He did this to himself. You don't have to keep trying to fix everything for him."

Determination crept into Mom's expression. "You don't understand. He wasn't always like this."

"But he's like this now," Greg said. "He's *been* like this for years. And he isn't going to get any better if nothing changes."

Mom darted her glance among me, Alec, and Greg.

"He was about to release me," I said. Not because I was defending my father but because I couldn't bear to see the look of abject misery on my mother's face, like the last of her hope was fading away. "When I said 'Dad' he seemed to come back to himself and realize what he was doing."

"You should still go to teach him a lesson," a low voice said. We turned to see Stefan standing nearby, a bag slung over his shoulder. "We all should."

With that, he left, and for some reason, I had a feeling that none of us were going to see him for a long, long time.

Mom met my eyes. "You go first. He could wake up, and if you're still here, he might find a way to make everything worse than it already is."

"Are you sure?" I said.

"Yes. I'll be fine." She wiped the tears from her cheeks and shook her head. "I've dealt with worse shite than this before."

"Go," Alec said.

Not needing to be told again, I grabbed Lauren's hand and led her out of the room, feeling her fingers tremble in my grip. Or maybe it was mine that were shaking.

"Are you okay?" Lauren asked as we neared the front door.

I paused just long enough to pull her into a hug. "Yeah, you?"

"I think so?"

A grin tugged at my lips. "Thanks for saving my ass. It was hot. Maybe I *am* into taser play."

She shook her head, tugging me down for a quick, hard kiss. "What can I say? My savior kink took over."

We walked outside and found Josh and Aly near the far bushes, Josh bent over at the waist, Aly rubbing his back.

"He okay?" I called.

"Yeah," she said, heading our way. "He's just dry-heaving now."

I eyed Josh's back, wondering what in the fuck had happened to him that the smell of burning flesh made him puke. And then I recalled who his father was and immediately decided I didn't want to know.

"I can't fucking believe that piece of shit," Aly said, glaring back toward the house. She turned, clutching Lauren's face, taking in her ruined dress. "Are you okay?"

"I'm fine," Lauren said.

Aly released her and rounded on me. "Come here."

I opened my mouth to tell her I was fine, too—his hands had only been on me for a few seconds—but she was already moving, tipping my head back so she could check me over, suddenly all business.

"Does this hurt?" she asked.

"No."

"How about this?"

"No."

She poked and prodded until I finally pulled away. "He didn't really hurt me, I was just . . ."

Lauren threaded her fingers through mine. "Shocked?"

I looked down at her and nodded.

Aly gripped my shoulder. "I'm really sorry."

"Don't be. If I'd done that alone, it would have been much worse."

I filled her in on how Dad had been about to let me go, but her gaze drifted back to the house while I spoke, and she still looked mad enough that I was worried she might storm back inside. Josh finally joined us then, popping a piece of gum into his mouth and then wrapping a preemptive arm around his fiancée's waist.

Aly sighed, realizing her chance had passed. "Please tell me Moira isn't staying."

"She's probably staying," I said.

"Why has she put up with him for so long?" Aly asked.

I sighed. "He's not always like this. You've seen that. He can be funny and charming, and most of that is reserved for Mom. She gets the best of him. Hell, I think she might be the only person he truly loves."

Lauren made a small sound of distress and slipped her arms around me. "That's so sad."

I hugged her back. "And it's true that he wasn't always this bad. He's gotten much worse over the years. I think a lot of it comes down to fear and perception. Me breaking away from him shows the people in our world that there's weakness in his house, and there are plenty of others just like my dad looking to exploit that to their own advantage. He's terrified of being usurped, of becoming expendable, because he knows better than anyone what happens when you are."

Aly frowned. "Do you think he's going to come after you?"

I shook my head. "No. Mom's staying for more than herself. She's staying for all of us. She's Dad's last tether to his humanity, and I'm sure she'll spend the next several days reminding him that if he does anything to *really* hurt me, this family will be broken beyond repair and he'll be the architect of his own demise, left completely alone in the world."

Lauren frowned. "So, what? You think he'll come back around? Try to make amends?"

I nodded. "Eventually. That split second before you tased him, I felt like I was looking at the old Dad. The one who taught me how to throw a baseball, the one who used to put Greg on his shoulders during parades so he could see over the crowd."

Aly looked unconvinced. "Well, no matter what happens, I think we can all agree that we're done with these dinners."

"Oh, fuck, yeah," I said.

Josh made a contemplative sound. "Maybe we start having our own family dinners instead."

Aly beamed, looking to Lauren and me. "What do you think?"

"I like it," Lauren said. "Nic?"

I grinned. "I'm in."

34

LAUREN

"How are you?" Nic asked, rubbing a hand over my back.

"A little nervous," I admitted. "It's one thing to do this in the comfort of my own bedroom, another in front of a live audience."

He nodded and stepped closer. "We don't have to go through with it if you don't want to."

I shook my head. "No. I want to."

Two months had passed since Nic took ownership of Velvet's building, and a lot had changed in that time. Renovations were in full swing on the third floor. We'd opened our doors on Thursday and Sunday nights as well, and were already doing enough business that they'd become profitable. Hoping to capitalize on our earlier brainstorming, we were even subletting to boudoir photographers and camworkers during the day. Velvet was pulling in more money than ever before, and not just because Nic had kept good on his word and lowered our rent.

Things had changed between us as well. Nic had barely let me out of his sight that first month, concerned that he'd miscalculated and his father might actually do something to hurt us. But Moira had stayed when everyone else left, and she spent that time pulling Nico Senior back from the brink inch by bloody inch. Now they were in couples therapy, and the thought of reconciliation didn't seem as impossible as it had in the days right after that disastrous family dinner.

Nic was slowly starting to relax, starting to believe that he was really, truly free, and the change coming over him was incredible to witness. He'd stopped wearing his mask in the club. We'd spent every weekend visiting the various rooms together, learning what we liked as a couple. Voyeurism remained our most deeply shared kink, but Nic had other tastes that he was still exploring, and it turned out exhibitionism and bondage were two of his favorites. Hence us standing in the narrow back hallway that ran behind all the private rooms, me dressed in lingerie and a silk robe, him, a pair of low-slung jeans.

My eyes kept catching on his naked torso, the tattered wings tattooed on his chest, the guns on his ribs, and then his abs, unmarred by ink but dotted with scars. Nic's muscles weren't showy. They were dense, compact. He didn't have a gym rat body; he had the physique of someone who had gained his muscles the hard way, and I was addicted to the sight of it. Especially because half the time we fucked, I was in such a rush to get him inside me that he rarely had time to do anything except unzip his pants. I kept telling myself to slow down, to take my time, but even several months since the first time I'd laid eyes on him again in the church hallway, I still lost my head around him, and honestly? I hoped that never changed.

"Are you sure you don't want to know what you're in for?" he asked.

I shook my head. "Not knowing is half the thrill."

His lips pulled up in a devilish grin. "Suit yourself then."

My gaze dropped to his favorite red rope in his hands. The sound of it creaking in the narrow hall sent my pulse racing. I'd seen him practicing knots with it almost nonstop over the past month—while we were on the couch watching TV, just beyond my camera whenever he sat in on one of my filming sessions, even at the dinner table after he'd finished eating. He was like one of those grannies who carried around her latest crochet project everywhere she went, only he was learning all the ways to tie me up with it instead of making me a nice pair of gloves.

Not that I was complaining. I loved that he was coming out of his shell. Loved that I was able to share my world so openly with him. He'd stayed true to his word, never getting jealous over my work or trying to restrict me in any way. Just last night, he'd gone down on me while I was sexting with a sub, and I swear it resulted in the most inspired sexts of my life.

"Hey," he said, slipping a finger through the tie of my robe and using it to drag me forward.

I gazed up at him, my nerves and desire competing for dominance. "Yeah?"

"You know I love you, right?" he said.

I smiled. "I know. And I love you, too."

He nodded. "Good. Keep that in mind, because you might start thinking you hate me halfway through this."

What the—

The chime rang out that indicated the start of the show, and Nic threaded his fingers into mine and led me through the door. Each room in Velvet was different, decorated to capture the mood of what went on inside them, kink-specific props on every stage. In the bondage room, the lighting was soft and warm, the hardwood lacquered to allow for easy cleaning. My heels clicked over the floorboards as we passed a Saint Andrews cross, a flogging horse, and a queening chair.

I kept my eyes straight ahead, focused on Nic's broad back, because I knew that if I looked out at the crowd, my anxiety would spike. I wanted to do this so badly, had dreamed about it for years, but this was our first time performing. No matter how turned on I was by thoughts of what was to come, of being *watched* so closely, I was still nervous.

Nic stopped us next to a simple padded leather tantra chaise that had been conveniently moved to the center of the stage—at least I'd be somewhat comfortable through whatever was to come. He tossed his rope onto it and turned toward me, cupping my face, tilting me up until our gazes locked. His eyes were darker than usual, a deep emerald because of how wide his pupils were, and knowing that the promise of tying me up and getting me off in front of everyone had him so turned on only served to spin me higher.

"Thank you for doing this with me," he said, pressing his forehead to mine.

I let out a shaky breath, willing the last of my nerves to disappear. "You're welcome."

"I love you, Lo."

"I love you, too."

With a tug, he had me rising onto my tiptoes so he could seal his mouth over mine. I opened for him immediately, loving the way his tongue slid against mine, how he stepped closer, as if even the slightest gap of air between us was unacceptable. He didn't just kiss me; he claimed me, marked me, telling everyone else in the room that while they were allowed to watch, only he was allowed to touch.

His hands dropped from my face, and a tug at my waist told me he was undoing the sash on my robe. Cool air raced over my skin when it fell open, making me shiver, and then he was pushing it off, down over my arms, so everyone could see the barely there lace I wore beneath it.

A whistle cut through the crowd, and then Taylor's familiar voice. "Yas, bitch!"

Everyone laughed, including me and Nic, and I was going to give her the biggest hug after this for keeping her promise to immediately break the tension. Perhaps most people wouldn't have wanted their friends watching them with their partner, but Taylor and Ryan had already seen every part of me, had helped me nitpick my videos. To me, this wasn't much different, and the thought of them out there gave me heart, reminded me that everyone in this room was here with good intentions.

Music filtered down from overhead, dark and melodic. The lights dimmed, and suddenly it felt like it was just Nic and me in the room. He guided me to the chaise and bid me to lie back on it. And then he was on me, hands braced by my ribs, lips trailing down my neck. He moved lower, tonguing and biting at my nipples through the lace until I was panting, digging my fingers in his hair to keep him there. But he had other destinations in mind and kept moving, gently pulling out of my grip to make his way down my stomach. He placed a single chaste kiss on the fabric covering my pussy, and then hooked his hands beneath my knees and pushed them up, so it looked like I was sitting on an invisible chair while lying down.

"Keep them there," he said, voice rough.

I nodded, watching, waiting with bated breath to see what he would do next. He lifted the rope and uncoiled it, revealing that it was actually three separate pieces. Two, he dropped onto my stomach, and the third, he folded in half, creating a bend—more often referred to as a "bite" in bondage terms. He wrapped the rope around my left thigh, just above the knee, once, twice, three times, and then tied two simple square knots to secure it, leaving the bite sticking out. With a tug, he tested it to make sure it would hold, and then straightened that leg so he could kiss the inside of my calf.

His eyes, dark and smoldering with desire, met mine. "Not too tight?"

I shook my head, anticipation rising.

He grinned and slid his hand down my leg, smacking the side of my ass hard enough to sting. "That's my girl."

Several low sounds from the audience told me I wasn't the only one who appreciated the praise and the reminder that we were being watched left me breathless, in a good way. This wasn't much different than what I already did, but instead of getting my feedback through messages and tips, I got to hear it live, and knowing that we were about to get a room full of people off sent my desire into the stratosphere.

Nic dragged one of the spare ropes from my stomach, taking his sweet time trailing it between my legs, and tied it around my other leg in exactly the same manner as the first. I had no idea what he was doing. This wasn't one of the bonds we'd practiced before, but I trusted him not to hurt me, to know my limits. And if things got out of hand, I could always use my safe word: taser.

He stepped between my legs when he was done, grabbing the end of the first rope. Then he leaned forward, hand around my neck, helping me to sit up just enough to wrap the rope behind it. He looped it beneath my armpit and pulled it to the front again, where he slipped one end through the bite on my opposite leg. Then he tied another simple square knot and tugged, tightening the bond, drawing my knee close to my chest.

Oh my god, he was going to bind me up like *this*? I wouldn't be able to wrap my legs around him. I wouldn't be able to grind against him. I'd be almost completely motionless from the waist down. No wonder he worried I would hate him; he knew how much I loved to move when we fucked.

But then I realized it also meant that he would have complete control over me, and my submissive little soul lit up with pleasure. If I'd been wet before, I was about to be completely soaked for him now.

He leaned down, kissing me, pressing my leg even closer to my chest, tightening the bond still more. His erection, hidden inside his jeans, pressed against my core. I squirmed against it, wanting him, *needing* him, but he chuckled and pulled back, and it left me wondering when our roles had reversed and *I* had become the impatient one.

"How's that?" he asked, tying the rope off.

"It'd be a lot better if you were already inside me," I grumbled, unable to stop myself.

Someone snorted in the audience, and while a few low chuckles rolled through the crowd, Nic got to work binding my other leg, jerking that one a little harder than the first. I gasped, and he grinned, securing it in place, and then his hands fell away, and I settled into the bond, finding it surprisingly comfortable. The ropes held the weight of my legs, so I wouldn't have to strain to keep them aloft, and I could already imagine how good it would feel pressing against them as I moved. Plus, my hands were free, so I'd be able to—wait a second, where had *those* come from?

Nic dangled a pair of red wrist cuffs from a finger.

"Lift your arms overhead," he said, moving out from between my legs.

I nearly whimpered at the loss of him, at the delay. I needed him inside me, *now*.

He went to the raised side of the chaise while I followed his order. It was then that I noticed a metal loop at the very top and realized he wanted me completely helpless. My mouth went dry. Him taking full control like this? *Yes, Daddy.*

His fingers were warm against the skin of my wrists as he bound them with the cuffs and then used the last piece of rope to tie them to the hook. Once done, he repositioned himself between my legs, looking down at me, admiring his handiwork his gaze lingering on where the ropes dug into my thighs. I could feel the heat rolling off him, see the need in his eyes. Oh, yeah, this was his favorite kink, all right. The sight of me bound like this was *destroying* him.

"Lo," he said, deep, guttural. He placed his hands on the backs of my thighs, and I could feel them trembling. The man was about three seconds away from losing control, and he needed to know I was right there with him.

"Fuck me," I begged. "Please."

His hands left my legs. I felt a jerk, heard the sound of tearing, and realized he'd ripped the crotch of my panties. Moans and gasps sounded from the audience, but I could barely hear them over my pulse pounding in my ears. Nic spit into his hand, and I had no idea why the sight was so hot—maybe because he was too impatient to reach for the lube on a nearby shelf, or maybe because it wasn't a "nice" thing to do. The longer I was with him, the more I realized that nice was overrated. His other hand went to his pants just long enough to free that big, beautiful dick, and then he was coating himself with his own saliva, fitting the head to my pussy, and shoving just inside.

I sucked in a breath, every muscle in my body tightening. Tied up like this, he felt huge, almost too big to fit, and as much as I wanted it hard and fast, I realized he was going to have to take his time to keep from hurting me.

So I gave up. I let my own wants and needs go, handed him all the power, and settled back against the chaise to enjoy the ride, my inner muscles loosening, making it easier for him to thrust deeper. He must have felt the change come over me, because his eyes lifted from where we were joined, and the look on his face was so raw, so full of need and devotion and possession that I fell in love with him all over again.

His hands landed back on my thighs, pushing down, stretching me even farther as he shunted his hips forward and fucked into me. The ropes tightened. My chest heaved as I sucked in a breath, and his gaze fell to my tits. I felt every glorious inch of him rubbing inside me as he pulled out. Another thrust, deeper this time. His jaw clenched, and I knew he was holding back, being careful, barely restraining himself. I loved it, because it showed how much he cared, how much he wanted this to be good for me, too.

My arousal eased his way, and with one last thrust, he bottomed out, pausing there, fingers digging into my thighs, breathing hard. Around us, the sound of others joining in echoed through the room, and I realized how good the acoustics onstage were, much better than out in the audience, every sigh and moan perfectly audible. It was fucking hot. Sex amplified, playing right into my ears.

Nic must have noticed, too, because he paused, his eyes locked on mine, and canted his head as if listening. A sly glance toward the crowd had his dick stiffening inside me, confirming that he liked being watched just as much as he liked tying me up. He and I were going to have *so* much fun performing together.

His gaze came back to mine, scorching, and I had just enough time to realize what was coming before his hold on me tightened and he thrust forward, hard and fast. All I could do was lie there, shifting my hips up to meet him and clenching my thighs around his waist as he started a steady rhythm. The ropes dug into me, not hard enough to hurt, but hard enough that I couldn't forget that I was bound, restrained, at his mercy.

He leaned forward, bracing a hand on the chaise, his other gripping my hip, and, *oh, god*, that changed everything. Now he was hitting me right where I needed him, stroking a spot deep inside that made my eyes roll back in my head. His pelvic bone rubbed over my clit with every thrust as he tipped his head down just enough to tongue my nipple through the whisper-thin lace of my bra.

I met him stroke for stroke, reveling in every sensation, dragging the pleasure out for as long as possible instead of racing to the finish line. It was incredible, the ass shaking, titties bouncing, thighs clenching, toes curling, lip biting, stomach quivering, breath stealing, kind of fucking Nic did best, and suddenly I was jealous of everyone in the crowd for getting to watch him at work. If I'd thought ahead, I would have set a camera up somewhere so I could relive this moment over and over again for the rest of my life.

My pussy pulsed around him. I arched my back as much as I could, changing our angle so he slid even deeper. He pulled his lips from my breast, and I craned my head up. Looking down my body at him, seeing the ropes pulled taut on my thighs and his stomach flexing as he pistoned into me was so erotic that it made all the other scenes I'd watched pale in comparison. No wonder we had so many repeat performers at Velvet. The adrenaline of doing this was like a drug, and I flew higher and higher, never wanting the moment to end.

A moan hit my ears, and I finally turned my head, looking into the crowd. They were little more than abstract shapes at first, but as my eyes adjusted, I saw arms working, heads bobbing, even a full-on threesome in the back row, and the realization that Nic and I were the ones to put them in this frenzy pushed me over the edge, the orgasm I'd been holding off breaking through my defenses to slam into my body like a tidal surge breaching a dam. I cried out, shaking, shuddering, my muscles clenching as Nic continued to pound into me, drawing it out.

He came with a groan a heartbeat later, dick so rigid inside me that I knew he was riding the same high I was. Afterward, he half collapsed onto me, forehead resting between my breasts, lungs heaving against my bound thighs.

A cheer rose from the crowd, started by Taylor, and the scene ended the way it began: with love and laughter.

EPILOGUE

"THANK GOD THE WEATHER HELD," Aly said as she led the way out her back door.

I followed after her, laden with wineglasses, careful to turn sideways on the way out so I didn't accidentally hit the doorframe and shatter one. "I know," I said. "I was worried yesterday when I saw the possibility for rain. Don't get me wrong, this still would have been nice indoors, but not like this."

Ahead of us, two picnic tables were pushed together on the back deck. White tablecloths covered them, and running down the center was a series of pots and vases filled with white hydrangeas, the last of the season. We'd placed white pillar candles all around them, and each setting had a round wicker placemat with a plate on top of it and a white napkin pulled through a wicker napkin holder. Gold cutlery sat on each side of the plates, and we were just about to deposit the gold-rimmed glasses that would complete the look.

Josh and Nic had strung café lights on tall garden stakes overhead, and Aly and I had moved all her potted plants onto the patio to frame the table. Hurricane lanterns stood among the greenery, lighting the paving stones and casting the whole scene in golden light. It was stunning, a master class in al fresco dining that we'd only pulled off thanks to copious amounts of late-night Pinteresting.

The sound of crickets filled the yard as we put the glasses in place, soft music filtering out from inside. We'd gotten lucky with this late-season heat wave, but I could smell autumn on the air, that distinct mix of fallen leaves, rain, and rich, dark earth. It wouldn't be long until the cold crept in, and it made me cherish these fleeting days all the more.

Ryan walked through the back door carrying two bottles of wine, one red and one white, Walter fresh on their heels.

Walter bounded up to me, the new elephant stuffy Nic had bought him in his mouth. "All done playing with the kitties?" I asked.

Ryan set the wine on the table. "Fred jumped onto his back and tried to ride him like a pony."

I dropped to a squat, smooshing Walter's face. "Oh, no, honey. Did the big mean kitty scare you again?" That cat was fearless, had no concept of his own size or mortality, and Maud was even worse. Thank god Walter was so good with them.

Walter panted, just excited to be the center of attention, his terror already forgotten.

I pulled the stuffy from his mouth and chucked it across the yard, and he took off after it. He nearly collided with Ben, Ryan's employee turned new flame, as he rounded the corner of the house.

"Sorry!" I yelled.

Ben steadied himself, clutching two six-packs in his hands. "It's okay! I saved the beer!"

"Who said beer?" Jackson asked as he and Taylor swept outside, carrying the first dishes of food.

Josh caught the door before it could swing shut behind them and looked imploringly at his fiancée. "Baby, *pleaaase*?"

"No!" Aly yelled back.

"I did!" Ben answered Jackson.

"Oh, thank God," Jackson said. "I'm too uncultured for wine."

"Not even in their little outdoor enclosure?" Josh whined.

"They cannot come outside," Aly said. "They'll just cry the whole time, and you know it."

"What did you bring?" Jackson asked.

Josh stuck out his lower lip. "But they'll be so sad all alone inside."

"An amber ale and a pilsner," Ben answered.

Aly stomped over to Josh. "They'll be fine. Stop making me feel like a bad mother."

"Hey! Are you bitches going to help me carry out the rest, or what?" Taylor asked me and Ryan.

I laughed and followed her inside, reveling in the chaos. This was only our third family dinner, but they all seemed to go this way, everyone talking over each other, three conversations happening at once, half a second away from spilling into full-blown chaos. I loved it, drank in every second and committed these moments to memories I could look back on fondly when I was old and gray, remembering my wild youth.

Wondering where Nic was, I stuck my head into the living room.

"Help me," he said, slumped down in an armchair with Fred in his lap and Maud on his chest. Neither were asleep, neither were curled up. They just . . . sat on him, like they were actively pinning him down and he really did need to be rescued.

I went over and scooped Maud up first, depositing her on the couch. Fred turned in my arms as I lifted him next, presenting me with his big belly. Aly had him so well trained. "I have too much bronzer on for fur therapy," I told him. He purred and started making biscuits on my neck, and I was helpless to resist, very carefully face-diving into his fluff.

Nic got to his feet behind me. "I think they were plotting something."

I set Fred down and turned to him. "What is it with you and cats?"

He pointed past me. "Look at them and tell me I'm wrong."

I turned. Fred and Maud were sitting right next to each other on the couch, staring unblinkingly at Nic. Okay, maybe he had a point.

I grabbed his arm and dragged him from the room. "It's because they know they haven't won you over yet."

"I don't think that's it," Nic said. "After Fred ran my guard dog off, Maud threatened me with a knife."

I snorted. "Sure she did."

We grabbed more food dishes from the kitchen and headed back outside, and the next five minutes passed in a flurry of activity as we all worked together to set the table, pour drinks, and settle down to eat.

"No Moira tonight?" Taylor asked.

Nic shook his head. "Her and my dad are at couples counseling."

The fallout from the last Trocci family dinner was still unfolding. Stefan was nowhere to be found, and Greg and Alec had threatened to move out of their parents' house if things didn't change. Nico Senior wasn't handling it well, to say the least, but I took heart in the fact that he was at least willing to continue therapy, and Moira had said he'd started asking about Nic recently. And not in an information-gathering kind of way, but like he was genuinely curious about Nic's new life.

Who knew, maybe he'd actually make some progress and learn to be a better person. But we weren't holding our breath.

"Where's Tyler?" Aly asked.

Josh took a sip of wine and set his glass down. "He said he's running a few minutes late and to start without him. Oh, and he's bringing a date."

Aly's brows rose. "Do we know who?"

Josh shook his head. "No. It's weird, I used to beg him to stop over-sharing with me when we lived together, but ever since I moved out, I've had no idea what's going on in his life."

That was my cue to turn back to my own wine. Tyler had kept his promise and mostly let Nic handle the day-to-day operations of their new joint business venture, and while I hated keeping secrets from friends, this one wasn't mine to tell—I'd promised Nic I wouldn't repeat it. I just hoped that Aly and Josh understood when it finally came to light. It seemed likely they would, what with how many secrets they kept themselves, but you never knew.

We plated our food and tucked in to eat, talking and laughing as day faded into night. Tyler showed up halfway through the meal, towing a tall, stunning woman behind him. Stella, he told us. The pair looked like an odd couple, at first, him with his blond hair and corn-fed good looks, and her with her raven-dark locks and innumerable tattoos, but something about them *worked*. Maybe it was because they were both impeccably dressed, like they planned to attend some sort of gala or art exhibition after dinner, or the way they eyed each other as they approached, kept finding excuses to touch each other as they sat at the end of the table.

Tyler immediately started piling food onto his plate, but Stella abstained.

"I'm so sorry," she said, her voice lower than I expected, cultured. "I ate before we came. I have food sensitivities and didn't want you to have to worry about it. It's my fault we're late."

Tyler reached out and took her hand in his. It was a gesture of comfort, of kindness, the least douchey thing I had ever seen him do, and it had me looking at Stella in a new light.

Aly waved her off. "Oh, you're fine. We're a sensitivity household, so next time just let us know ahead of time, and we'll make sure you have options. Or you can bring your own food. We won't be insulted."

Stella smiled, and it was like the sun had come back out to shine down on our party. There were a lot of pretty people at this table, but Stella gave even Josh a run for his money. She was obviously way too good for Tyler, but from the way he doted on her during the meal, he seemed to know it and was on his best behavior. I prayed she stuck around. With her here, his presence was 90 percent more tolerable.

"You want another beer?" I asked Nic as dinner was winding down. He'd finally started drinking some, and I found his rock-bottom tolerance for alcohol adorable. He was cute when he was tipsy, cuddlier than normal and more effusive.

"Are you driving us home?" he asked, leaning in to kiss my shoulder.

"Are you actually going to let me drive your precious baby?" I shot back. While the sun was still warm during the day, temps were starting to drop at night, and the bike was almost done for the season, so we'd taken his car.

"Can you drive stick?" he asked.

I slipped my hand beneath the tablecloth and ran my fingers over his crotch, framing his dick. "You know I can."

Aly made a retching noise. "I heard that."

I pulled my hand away and shot her a grin. "Sorry."

"No, you're not," she said, slugging down the rest of her wine.

"She really isn't," Ryan confirmed. "Just yesterday, I caught them—"

"So! Tyler!" Josh interrupted in the most unsubtle topic change ever. "How did you and Stella meet?"

The pair turned toward each other, sharing a look that seemed to encompass an entire conversation. Finally, Stella gave the briefest of nods.

"Well," Tyler said, glancing back up the table, "that's kind of a long story."

ACKNOWLEDGMENTS

It really does take a village to get a book published, and that is *very* true for this one. First and foremost, I need to thank every single sex worker who took the time to speak to me one-on-one or answer my questions in forums while I was researching and writing. You are all so badass and kind and welcoming and patient. I hope I made you proud, and you can see your beautiful, joyous selves in Lauren and her found family.

To my agent, the incomparable Jill Marr, for all your wisdom and guidance throughout my publication journey. I love that I can call you in the middle of a full "menty b" and know we'll end the conversation cackling like a pair of witches standing around a cauldron plotting world domination. And to everyone else at SDLA, especially Andrea, Nick, and Jake, for all your hard work.

To Hayley and Sierra, the best "yes, and" and "ooh, but what if" publishers a girl could ask for. Thank you, *forever*, for taking a chance on me. Thank you for never telling me to tone it down (even my deranged email responses). Thank you for always having the best insights and ideas. And to everyone else on the Slowburn/Zando team: Molly, Anna, TJ, Julia, Natalie, Emily, Nathalie, and Ashley. I'm sure I'm forgetting someone because there have been so many incredible people getting shit done behind the scenes. If I am, I'm sorry and I love youuu!

Thank you so much to all my foreign publishers who are tirelessly translating and bringing the Lights Out series to your markets. There are almost too many of you to list and more are joining the party every week. I cannot wait for all your amazing readers to join us on this wild ride.

To my great-grandparents who fled Italy and came to America in search of better lives. So much of their story inspired this one. And to the rest of my family, who continue to cheer me on and read everything I publish, even if I ban them—I AM LOOKING AT YOU, MOM.

To my three ride-or-die besties, my secret keepers, who have been with me from the very beginning: Ange, Khanh, and Sarah. I haven't forgotten our joint retirement plan to buy a vineyard in New Zealand and age disgracefully and drunkenly on it, and you better not have either!

And lastly, but most importantly, to my IRL leading man, my husband: Hi. You're hot. Let's make out.

ABOUT THE AUTHOR

New York Times and *USA Today* bestselling author NAVESSA ALLEN lives on the shores of Chesapeake Bay with her husband and their spoiled cats. She posts her books in serial format to her website via Patreon. To catch up on her latest work in progress, read exclusive bonus scenes, and feast your eyes on NSFW character art, please visit: patreon.com/navessaallen.

The Into Darkness Trilogy

BEGINS WITH

LIGHTS OUT

Available Now